TALES OF MAGIC LAND 3

THE YELLOW FOG

and

THE MYSTERY OF THE DESERTED CASTLE

by
ALEXANDER
MELENTYEVICH
VOLKOV

Translated from the Russian by
PETER L. BLYSTONE

RED BRANCH PRESS
Staten Island, NY
2007

Published by Red Branch Press
Staten Island, NY 10306

THE YELLOW FOG
First published in Russian 1974
THE MYSTERY OF THE DESERTED CASTLE
First published in Russian 1976

Translations ©2007 by Peter L Blystone

ISBN: 978-0-6151-7459-4

Publisher gratefully acknowledges the aid and support of Marcus Mebes, without whom this publishing project could not have been successfully accomplished.

To my friend (and mentor)

CARLO VIOLA

who has taught me,
among other things,
the value of returning
GOOD for EVIL!

— PLB

TABLE OF CONTENTS

THE YELLOW FOG

INTRODUCTION

Part III
TILLY-WILLY
THE IRON PALADIN

THE MYSTERY OF THE
DESERTED CASTLE

INTRODUCTION

Part I
FIRST DAYS ON EARTH

TABLE OF CONTENTS

THE
YELLOW
FOG

INTRODUCTION

Chapter 1

A FIVE-THOUSAND-YEAR SLEEP

At the end of a long, narrow ravine within the World-Encompassing Mountains there lay a warm, cozy cave with a high ceiling, smooth walls, and a level floor. In the far corner of this cave loomed an enormous bed, and there, on the soft mossy bedding, a woman of colossal size lay immersed in deep slumber.

Her sleep was not of the ordinary variety: it had been going on for tens of centuries. Who could have contended with this giantess? Who had inflicted this magical sleep upon her, and for what misdeeds?

To learn how and why this amazing deed was accomplished, let us turn our thoughts back several thousand years, to that bygone era when the mighty wizard Hurricap first appeared in that country which would later be called Magic Land.[1]

It was Hurricap who partitioned Magic Land off from the rest of the world by means of the Great Desert and the World-Encompassing Mountains. It

---

[1]See the story *The Seven Underground Kings*.

was he who gave the animals and birds that inhabited it the gift of human speech, and who made the hot summer sun shine all year round on its forests and fields.

Hurricap did many good things for Magic Land, and the tribes of little people who dwelt there led lives of happiness and contentment, and of peaceful, untroubled labor.

A thousand, or maybe two thousand years went by — then suddenly, one unexpected calamity after another began to afflict the residents of Magic Land. One time, a tornado descended out of the clear blue sky onto a community of people. It toppled the houses, killing and maiming those who were unable to escape their dwellings in time. Then a flood inundated a village on a riverbank. And after that, a general epidemic attacked the livestock, and cows and sheep died by the dozens.

When Hurricap consulted his magic books, he learned that a witch named Arachna had come to Magic Land from the Outer World. In height, she only came up to Hurricap's waist, but the good wizard's head was on a level with the tops of the tallest trees. Which meant that Arachna, though shorter than him by some thirty cubits, was herself a giantess.

Arachna was an *extremely* wicked witch. If any given day went by and she did not in some way hurt someone, she considered the day wasted. And whenever she did inflict misfortune on anyone, she laughed so loudly that the trees in the nearby thickets shook, and their fruit fell down from them.

There was one tribe of people alone to whom Arachna displayed any leniency, and that was the small tribe of Gnomes, whom she had brought with her to Magic Land from beyond the mountains. The Gnomes served her faithfully and with devotion, for their forefathers had sworn a mighty oath that they would do so. If the enchantress should do anything to harm these subjects of hers, the Gnomes would scatter all over the country, and she would be hard put to find them in the thick forests and in the tall grass of the meadows: they were only about a cubit in height, and they were amazingly clever at concealing themselves.

Teeny-weeny old men with long white beards and neat little old ladies wearing white bonnets, saw to every one of their mistress's needs with the utmost attention. They roasted oxen and rams for her; the Gnomes led them to the lush mountain pastures. They baked splendid rolls from the wheat that they cultivated in the fertile soil of their secluded valley. They shot plump pheasants and partridges with their tiny bows; they wove cloth and dyed it blue, and they sewed it into a new cloak when the enchantress's clothing wore out.

In return for these inestimable services, Arachna granted the Gnomes her protection: Arachna's incantations extended their life-span to 150 years, and their children grew up without ever knowing any illness. Their arrows never missed when they were loosed at game, and the biggest fish always wound up in their nets. But doing good was very much contrary to Arachna's nature, and she made it up to herself by playing every possible dirty trick on the other tribes of people.

So when Hurricap learned about this, he resolved to render the wicked sorceress harmless. But how could he go about it? The simplest way would be to kill the witch by bopping her on the head with his ponderous fist. But the wizard was much too kind, and he never killed anyone. Even when he walked across the meadow, he purposely made a lot of noise and shuffled his feet, and all the frogs, small insects, and water-bugs had plenty of time to get out from under his enormous boots.

There was only one choice left to Hurricap: to put Arachna into a prolonged sleep. He ransacked his Book of Spells and found that the longest stretch of magical sleep into which he could plunge the wicked enchantress was five thousand years.

"Well, that's a perfectly suitable interval," mumbled Hurricap reflectively. "Perhaps after so much time, she'll get out of the habit of doing evil... But it's written here that in order for my magic to succeed, I'll have to muster all my will-power, and most important, I'll have to be standing right next to Arachna when I utter my incantation, or else it won't work. That'll be hardest of all..."

From what all his spies — the animals and birds — told him, it would be impossible to catch the witch Arachna unawares. The Gnomes constantly swarmed about her, and they'd alert their mistress to any danger. Moreover, the enchantress knew how to assume any shape she wanted. She could pretend to be a fox or a great horned owl, an apple blossom or a dried-out tree-stump. It would require the utmost ingenuity to catch her.

Hurricap prepared himself carefully to carry out his design. He learned the long, dreadful incantation by heart, so that he would not be distracted at the crucial moment, groping with his eyes through the lines of his Magic Book. Then he enlisted the aid of all the animals and birds in the forest. The animals and birds responded gladly to the Wizard's call: Arachna had molested every one of them more than sufficiently, and they would all be glad to be rid of the wicked fairy.

The appointed day and hour arrived, and the valley where Arachna's retreat was located was surrounded by unnumbered hordes of animals of all species. There were bisons and aurochs, lions and tigers, hyenas, jackals, wolves, badgers and hares, mice and rats, while opossums, martens, and squirrels leaped from branch to branch in the trees. The air swarmed with flocks of eagles, condors, and hawks.

Magpies chirped, crows cawed, and the air was sliced by the swift wings of swallows...

A dreadful racket and pandemonium filled the vicinity. And this whole uncountable legion advanced relentlessly on Arachna's retreat and encircled it on every side. Heading these forces was the giant, his gray locks streaming loose, his eyes blazing with wrath. In a thunderous voice that drowned out all the noise of his discordant army, Hurricap proclaimed: "Come out, Arachna! The time has come for you to answer for your wickedness!"

The Witch's heart pounded with terror. Her first thought was to hole up in the Cave, but then she realized that it would be easiest of all for them to capture her there. In the twinkling of an eye, an eagle flew out of the Cave and sought to lose itself in the flock of other eagles. No good! The eagles were on the alert, and they treated the uninvited newcomer to such forceful blows of their talons and wings that the false eagle quickly transformed itself into a swallow and plunged into the thick of those agile little birds. But the swallows likewise did not just stand there gaping, and they instantly identified the impostor.

Arachna did not give up. One more mouse now appeared among the swarm of mice that covered the ground in a thick carpet, this new one perhaps the hundred-thousandth in number — but once again they quickly singled her out. A wildcat grasped her firmly in its talons and gave out a meow in a voice positively choked with joy: "Here she is! I'm holding her, master!"

Without losing even a second, Hurricap sank to his knees among the mice, which drew to the side, and quickly, quickly, he uttered his inexorable incantation.

And then, oh wonder! there lay Arachna the witch, stretched out on the ground to her full enormous length. She had been plunged into deep slumber, and now she was doomed to sleep for five thousand years.

The Wizard thanked the animals and birds for their kind assistance, and the latter quickly dispersed throughout the woods and fields. Hurricap stood over the sleeping fairy, lost in thought, and all of a sudden, a feeble voice reached his ears. When he looked down, he saw a Gnome clambering up onto the enchantress's breast. White-bearded Antrero addressed Hurricap: "Mighty leader! You have put our mistress to sleep, and we dare not challenge your will: Arachna truly did commit much evil. But she was good to us, and we don't want the jackals and hyenas to rend her body to pieces. Allow us to transport her into the Cave and to stand guard over her until the moment has come when she's due to reawaken!"

Hurricap smiled. "You are good little people, and I commend you highly for your concern. Do with your mistress as you wish, for I never had any intention of killing her, and was merely acting to prevent her from committing further evil."

Hurricap left to return the castle where he lived, and the Gnomes, under Antrero's leadership, set to work. In spite of their small size, they were accomplished craftsmen. Some of them put together a sort of long chariot, while others made up the stone bedstead that was located in the furthest, warmest, and most secluded corner of the cave, covering it with a thick layer of fresh moss.

Then hundreds of Gnomes swarmed about the body of their sleeping mistress, just like ants, and with the help of pulleys and levers, they loaded her onto the chariot, hauled her into the cave, and with the greatest difficulty, they laid her on the bed.

The Gnomes did not know for how long Arachna was destined to sleep, and for this reason, they arranged things so that everything would be ready if she were to awaken at any moment.

By the head of the bed stood a barrel of water, which was frequently changed so that it would not go bad. Every three days, a pair of bulls was roasted on spits: their ruler was sure to be hungry when she awoke. But since there was no way of preserving meat for long stretches of time, the Gnomes ended up eating it themselves and then quickly roasted a replacement. There were always fresh rolls in the oven.

In short, no matter when the witch awoke, she would have no cause to complain of lackadaisicalness on her servants' part.

But generation of Gnomes succeeded generation, and the wicked enchantress continued to lie there in her magical sleep: Hurricap was not one to stint when it came to spells.

Once every hundred years, when Arachna's blue cloak rotted away, the old women spun yarn, wove it into cloth, and sewed a new cloak, and then the Gnomes went through enormous difficulties to put it onto the enchantress's lifeless body.

And how the tireless guardians looked after the cleanliness of the cave! The floor, the ceiling, and the walls were swept every day, and washed once a week. Any mosquitos, flies, and spiders that slipped into the premises were destroyed without mercy, while mice and rats were driven out in disgrace. A large fan was placed over the head of the sleeping witch, and guards were placed on duty round the clock to keep it in motion, so that the air around Arachna would not grow stale. Was it not through these attentions by the devoted Gnomes that a long string of centuries passed without a trace over Arachna, and she lay there on her soft bed as rosy and fresh as she was at the moment when Hurricap put her to sleep?

As the ages went by, the Gnomes forgot about the circumstances under which the fairy had been put to sleep, and it seemed to them that she would always remain in that magic slumber in her cave, and would continue to sleep until the very end of the world. But caring for her developed into a veritable religious ritual, and was most rigidly observed. The slightest deviation from it was regarded as a sin and was punished mercilessly by the elders.

Time seemed to stand still in the dark cave, but it did not do so in the Outer World beyond the World-Encompassing Mountains. Mankind gave up stone tools in favor of ones of bronze, and then of iron. Boats equipped with sails navigated the seas. The Greco-Persian Wars were fought and won. Roman legions moved freely about a cowed Europe, sweeping away everything in their paths. The epoch of medieval barbarism began and ended. Columbus discovered America, and Magellan's comrades-in-arms became the first navigators to make a voyage around the world. Balloons rose into the air, the first steamboat slapped its wheels against the water, the first clumsy locomotive pulled funny-looking boxcars along steel rails... And the witch kept right on sleeping her magic sleep.

What was happening in Magic Land? Here, too, history moved forward at its leisurely pace. Tribes of little people followed one another in succession, little states rose and fell, each of them proudly thinking of itself as the center of the world, and one royal dynasty succeeded another. And the Gnomes who were the sleeping Arachna's subjects kept watchful eyes on all these things.

They prowled invisibly around the country, observing, listening, and committing everything to memory. And when thoughtful old Hurricap revealed to the residents of Magic Land the secret of writing — which he had invented — long before it became known in the outer world, the Gnomes began to keep a chronicle. As scouts returned to their native cave, they told the news to the appointed Chronicler, who carefully recorded it on parchment scrolls which the tiny people had skillfully manufactured out of calfskin.

Chapter 1: A FIVE-THOUSAND-YEAR SLEEP

These parchment scrolls accumulated and accumulated, presently filling an entire cabinet in the cave, and they made up a true account of all the events that had taken place in Magic Land during the millennia of Arachna's enchanted sleep.

The Gnomes treated the Chronicles as if they were the most sacred objects, and once a completed scroll had been placed on the shelf, no one dared touch it. And so the scrolls lay there in a useless pile throughout tens of centuries.

Part I

ARACHNA
THE WITCH

Chapter 2

THE AWAKENING

It was a remarkable day in the little kingdom of the Gnomes. Everything went as usual in the morning, but at noontime, a strange sound shook the cave. It resembled a combination of a mighty sigh, a booming gust of wind, and the roar of some enormous beast. The air inside the cave became agitated, and some of the lamps went out. Small rocks rained down from the ceiling of the cave, and the echo of the mysterious sound swelled out of the cave and threw everyone in the vicinity into a panic.

The Gnomes who were in the valley dashed toward the cave as fast as their feet would carry them, and they found a terrified guard running forward to meet them. All of them asked each other in amazement: "Did you hear that? What on earth *is* it? Is the end of the world upon us already?!"

Only wise old Castalyo, the eldest of the Gnomes and their Chronicler, guessed what was happening. He raised his finger and proclaimed solemnly: "Our mistress has awakened!"

Castalyo was right. The strange sound had been merely the enchantress's yawn as she woke up. It was followed by others no less turbulent, and these extinguished the remaining lamps and shattered the furniture — the Gnomes' diminutive tables, chairs, and beds — making the walls of the cave crackle in an ominous manner.

Then Arachna was fully awake. The sleeper was unaware of the passage of time, and to the Witch, it seemed as if it were only a few minutes ago that she had escaped the army of beasts that the mighty Hurricap had set upon her. The only thing she could not understand was where the birds and the animals had disappeared to, and why she, Arachna, was lying on a bed in her own cave. "Hey, who's there?" the Enchantress shouted. "Come over here!"

The Gnomes entered the cave timidly, making their way through the debris and lighting their path with torches. Castalyo headed the procession.

"Summon Antrero!" ordered the Witch. "Let him explain what has happened here."

"We have no such person here, mistress," Castalyo ventured to report. "No one in our tribe has borne that name for a long, long time."

"Are you saying that I've been asleep for a very long time?" asked Arachna in disbelief.

"You have been slumbering for many centuries within human memory, mistress," said the aged Gnome. "We don't know when and how you went to sleep, or why your slumber lasted for so long. But we've always remembered our obligations and done a good job of guarding your rest."

"I thank you for your faithful service," said Arachna casually. "Now, I hope you'll give me something to eat: I'm famished."

Arachna's dinner-table was a tall rock with a flat top, located near the entrance to the cave: it had been preserved since the ancient times. The Gnomes climbed on top of it with long ladders, and in order to move the dishes up onto it, one after the other, they made use of an ingenious system of blocks and tackles: the Gnomes had kept all these things safe throughout the centuries.

The Witch ate everything that they had in their stores, and demanded seconds. She put away four roasted oxen and three rams, seventeen pheasants and sixty-four partridges, and she downed two dozen rolls and drank an entire barrel of water. Then, rubbing her belly, she said softly: "After a meal like that, it would be advisable to take a nap." But the Enchantress quickly realized that she had been sleeping far too long, so she decided to get down to business.

"In any case," she rumbled, "it's necessary to find out how long this sleep lasted that Hurricap brought down upon me."

She questioned Castalyo about the mighty wizard. The Witch felt a sort of malicious satisfaction when she learned that no one in these regions had even heard of any necromancer of that name throughout many generations. "So, you miscalculated, buddy-boy," grinned Arachna venomously. "You haven't been around in the world for a long time, but I'm still alive, and now there's no one to prevent me from managing this country the way I see fit."

Chapter 3

THE GNOMES' CHRONICLE

Arachna began her perusal. The parchment scrolls were arranged by numbers, so it was not difficult to decide which one to begin with. The Sorceress was not good at reading and writing, so her progress was very slow.

Arachna took only a cursory look at the accounts of ancient times. But she studied most attentively the chronicler's account of how Hurricap had put her, Arachna, to sleep. She learned that the good wizard had given the Gnomes permission to cart her now-lifeless body to the cave and to care for it, in order to preserve her through the long centuries. When she read about the precautions her subjects had taken to protect her from the harmful ravages of time, something resembling gratitude was stirred even in her heartless breast. "I'll have to reward the Gnomes," said the Witch to herself. "I'll let them hunt as much game as they want in my forests, and catch themselves as many fish as they want in my streams..."

Arachna threw the histories of the ancient kingdoms and empires aside without even bothering to read them. "The kingdom of Theom... The empire of Ballanagar... The mighty conqueror Agranat... Of what use to anyone are these phantoms who have long since departed for the world of shadows?"

She began to feel an interest in the Chronicle only when it took up the account of the kingdom of Bofaro, who lived in the Western region a thousand years ago. Bofaro had conceived the idea of ousting his father from the throne because the latter, in the son's opinion, had been reigning for too long.[2]

Filial ingratitude came as no surprise to the evil woman. She herself, in fact, had robbed her own mother, swiping all her equipment of the craft of sorcery. Moreover, she had brought the Gnomes, her mother's subjects, into Magic Land from the Outer World and left the now-helpless old woman to live out her life in loneliness.

Arachna read with interest about how Bofaro and his supporters, exiled to a perpetual resettlement in gloomy Underground Land, made a life for themselves down there. They began to mine metals, and for this reason, they were nicknamed the Under-

---

[2] See the story *The Seven Underground Kings.*

ground Ore-Diggers. The Sorceress enjoyed reading about how Bofaro, the first king of the Cavern, not being in a position to make a choice of any one of his seven sons, designated all of them as his successors to the throne, and they began to rule in succession, each of them a month at a time. When the Chronicler told of the chaos and confusion that resulted from this, the Witch was transported with delight.

Seven kings! And each of them had his own retinue of courtiers, his own army, his own laws which lasted only for a month, his own taxes that he collected from the people...

Arachna guffawed so loudly that the roof of the cave almost collapsed in on her, and the Witch was obliged to dash outside in a hurry. The Gnomes, scrambling in with ladders, began to cement the roof.

"Good for Bofaro!" screamed the Enchantress, enraptured. "Well done! He established *some life of happiness* for his subjects, I must say!"

The Witch grew calmer when she read in the Chronicle that after several centuries of harsh life, a spring of Soporific Water was discovered, quite by accident, in the labyrinth that surrounded the Cavern. When a person drank this water, he would go to sleep for a long time, and when he awoke, he would be ill adjusted for life, just like a newborn baby. He had to learn everything anew. Of course, his re-education took only a few days to accomplish.

The wise Time Keeper Bellino came up with the idea of putting to sleep the hungry hordes of courtiers, soldiers, and spies, simultaneously with the kings themselves (and their families) who were not actually reigning. The kings' lives turned into an unbroken round of celebration, interrupted by six-month periods of enchanted sleep, which flew by as if they were but a minute.

As she went through the scrolls, the Witch threw them aside, since she found nothing in them of interest to her. But then one later event riveted her attention. Beyond the World-Encompassing Mountains, beyond the Great Desert, in different corners of the vast continent, there lived two good and two wicked witches. The good witches were named Villina and Stella, while the wicked ones were Gingema and Bastinda. Human settlements were encroaching ever closer upon the witches' retreats, and when they looked in their magic books, they all happened to think of Magic Land.

All four fairies set out on their journeys at the same time, and they were not too pleasantly surprised when they bumped into one another face to face in their new place of residence. They exchanged a few angry words, but they were determined not to fight, and they divided up Magic Land. "If only *I'd* been around when those chatterboxes were engaged in this parceling out!" exclaimed Arachna angrily. "I'd really have made them see stars!"

The subjects of the good witches continued to lead happy, peaceful lives, but a bitter lot fell to the Munchkins, who came under the sway of Gingema, and the Winkies, who were now ruled by Bastinda.

Castalyo told the Sorceress that a multitude of manuscripts were stored in the cabinet — the Chronicle of Magic Land. Before undertaking any definite acts against the inhabitants of this forgotten little world, Arachna decided to acquaint herself with its history. After the passing of many centuries, another powerful magic-worker had thus suddenly appeared, one whom it would be necessary to beware of.

Chapter 4

THE EVENTS OF RECENT DAYS

The centuries continued to flow slowly by. Arachna slept her magical sleep, while four witches, both good and wicked, governed their peoples. Then, about forty years before the Witch awakened, some amazing events took place. One day, during a windstorm, an enormous globe drifted groundward from out of the clouds into the central part of Magic Land. A basket was dangling down from the globe, and from it, a man jumped to the ground, a man dressed in a multi-colored suit and wearing a strange hat on his head. This extraordinary newcomer was named James Goodwin, and the inhabitants of that region took him to be a Mighty Wizard: he had come down from the sky, after all, and in his own words, he was a close friend of the Sun.[3]

"Hello, still another magician puts in an appearance," grumbled the fairy in annoyance as she read the Chronicle. "They creep in here just like flies to honey." (Arachna had entirely forgotten that she herself had likewise come to Magic Land uninvited and unbidden.)

Goodwin made himself ruler of the central region. Under his direction, a splendid city was erected, and it was named the Emerald City: it sparkled with emeralds embedded in the City walls, in the roofs of the houses, and even in the slits in the pavement. Goodwin began to style himself the Great and Terrible Wizard of the Emerald City.

The Witch was spending more and more time on her reading: she sat over the Chronicle for days on

---

[3] See the story *The Wizard of the Emerald City.*

end, and sometimes she even forgot to eat, which was quite surprising for someone with her appetite.

Remarkable new events had taken place in Magic Land. A tornado conjured up by the witch Gingema bore from beyond the mountains a house-trailer, and a little girl named Ellie and her dog Totoshka were inside it. The house crashed down on the wicked Gingema and crushed her to death. The dog found some magical Silver Shoes in Gingema's cave, and he gave them to his young mistress.

The good fairy Villina appeared there at the site where the house touched down. She said that if Ellie brought about the granting of the fondest wishes of three beings, then the Mighty Goodwin would send her back home to Kansas. So Ellie, after putting on the Silver Shoes, started bravely for the Emerald City, down the Yellow Brick Road. The sprightly Totoshka accompanied her.

Ellie did not have to wait long to meet three beings who had fondest wishes. In a wheat field, she removed a straw man named Strasheela from a pole. Strasheela declared that his fondest wish was to acquire brains.

Further on, the new friends found the Iron Woodman in a forest: he had been standing there for a whole year, after rusting from rain and bad weather. When they oiled him and he was able to speak, the Woodman confessed that his own fondest wish was to obtain a loving heart.

The third being who had a fondest wish was a Cowardly Lion. He was so timid that he was afraid even of the small animals, and he wanted courage more than anything else in the world.

This strange company, after overcoming many obstacles along the way, reached the Emerald City and told Goodwin about their wishes. The Great and Terrible told the supplicants that their wishes would be fulfilled only when they had defeated the evil Bastinda and deprived her of her magic power.

This was a difficult task, but they were all able to handle it, in spite of everything. Bastinda was fated to die by water, and for five hundred years she had never washed, nor even cleaned her teeth. During an argument, Ellie drenched her with a bucket of water, and the Witch melted away like a lump of sugar in a cup of tea.

After Ellie and her droll, loving friends returned from their victory and demanded that Goodwin fulfill their wishes, the Great and Terrible confessed that he was really not a wizard at all, but just an ordinary humbug who had been deceiving people. He hid in his palace from the real witches, because he was dreadfully afraid of them.

"Right from the start I could feel that something was wrong," observed Arachna with self-satisfaction. "I saw through this self-styled friend of the Sun at once. Well, so much the better — one less adversary to worry about."

However, false wizard though he was, Goodwin was astute enough to give Strasheela wise brains made out of bran mixed with needles and pins. He hung in the Woodman's chest cavity a cloth heart stuffed with sawdust, and he gave the Lion a drink of courage from a golden saucer, where it fizzed and foamed. The three friends became proud and happy, for their fondest wishes had been granted.

Goodwin had had his fill of hiding from people, so he returned to Kansas in the same balloon in which he had flown to Magic Land. In his place, he designated Strasheela the Wise as monarch of the Emerald City. The Iron Woodman returned to the Winkies and became the ruler of Violet Land. The animals chose the Courageous Lion to be their king.

"Look at that, will you, how curiously it all turned out!" said Arachna in surprise when she learned how the adventures of Ellie's friends had concluded. "They all became eminent personages, kings and emperors. But what about the brat? What happened to the brat?"

As the Witch read further, she learned that Ellie had returned home: Gingema's Magic Shoes had transported her to Kansas.

Summoning Castalyo — for he was the one who had written the most recent of the Chronicles — Arachna asked him severely: "Listen, you half-pint, all these things you've written down about Ellie and her friends, are they fact or fiction? It all seems very much like a tall tale!"

"All this is the plain truth, mistress," maintained the Chronicler, "I swear by the lives of my grandsons! But read on, and you'll find things that are even more amazing."

Arachna, after eating three oxen and a couple of rams, took up the Chronicle again with renewed interest. From the next scroll, she learned that before her death, Gingema the Witch had taken into her service a wicked and envious joiner named Urfin Jus. When Ellie's house crushed Gingema to death, Urfin went off into the forest and lived there all alone, not loving anyone and not being loved by anyone in return[4]

One day, a storm brought to his garden the seeds of an amazing plant, one possessed of an extraordinary life force. It sprouted in his beds, and when Urfin pulled it out, chopped it into pieces, and dried it out on iron baking trays, the end product was a Powder of Life.

Urfin built an army of mighty wooden soldiers and called them the Deadwood Oaks. After bringing the Deadwood Oaks to life, Jus, with their help, made himself ruler of the Munchkins and the Winkies and king of Emerald Land.

Though they were now Urfin's prisoners, Strasheela and the Iron Woodman refused to recognize the usurper's authority. They contrived to write a letter

---

[4]See the story *Urfin Jus and his Wooden Soldiers*

to Ellie, and Kaggi-Karr the Crow undertook the long journey to Kansas and sought out the little girl.

When Ellie learned that her friends were in trouble, she hastened to their rescue, but she did not go alone. She was accompanied by her uncle, Charlie Black the one-legged Sailor, a jack-of-all-trades. The Sailor and the girl traversed the Great Desert in a Land Boat on wheels. Then they crossed the World-Encompassing Mountains, and they ended up — in Magic Land.

The struggle with Urfin and his Wooden Soldiers was long and difficult, but it ended in victory for Ellie and her friends. Urfin Jus was condemned to exile, and at Strasheela's suggestion, happy, smiling faces were carved on the heads of the Deadwood Oaks to replace their savage mugs, and the wooden men were transformed into industrious, conscientious workers. And now that they had put an end to Urfin's sway, Ellie and her uncle returned home.

As she learned of the inglorious end of Urfin Jus's brilliant career, Arachna felt sorry for the joiner: the Witch had taken quite a fancy to his wicked and envious disposition. "I'll have to make note of this enterprising individual," said the Witch.

Arachna was interested in the fate of Ruf Bilan, who had been Chief Minister of State under King Urfin the First. Urfin had elevated Ruf Bilan to this exalted position in exchange for his treason: the man had betrayed his City and secretly opened the gates to the enemy. When Urfin's power collapsed, Ruf Bilan had no intention of waiting around to be punished for his crimes — he fled Underground. While escaping his pursuers, Ruf Bilan lost his way in the labyrinth and blundered right into the spring of Soporific Water. Using a pickax that he happened to find there, the traitor began to hack a passage for himself through a little stone wall that surrounded a basin;

he cut off the flow of the streams of water, and the water drained into the ground[5].

For this grievous offense, the king who was on the throne at the time demoted the ex-Minister to lackey, and the loss of the Soporific Water disrupted the system that had prevailed for centuries in Underground Land. Kings who had ended their terms of rulership and were supposed to be put to sleep for half a year, now loitered about the palace with their families, in a regular stupor. Nor could the courtiers, the lackeys, the soldiers, the agents go to sleep either...

It was the working class that had to feed this whole voracious horde, and since there were not enough foodstuffs to go around, a famine seized the land. And then, quite unexpectedly, Ellie appeared in Underground Land.

As Arachna read through all this, she snorted with pleasure. "That brat is pretty dashing at that! To all appearances, she's a fairy. I sense that she's someone I'll have to do battle with if she stands in my way!..."

Ellie and her second cousin, Fred Canning, sailed in a boat down an underground river and into the Cavern of the Seven Kings. Ruf Bilan made a statement (untrue) that Ellie had the power to restore the Spring of the Soporific Water, whose disappearance had occasioned such grievous hardships in Underground Land. The kings decreed that Ellie and her cousin would remain there in captivity until the Sacred Spring began to function once more.

They had to send a messenger to Strasheela, the Woodman, the Lion, and Ellie's other friends. Lestar, the skilled mechanic, brought a squad of Deadwood Oaks down with him, along with pumps, augers, and

---

[5] See the story *The Seven Underground Kings*.

other essential tools. The craftsmen bored a deep slit, let pipes down into it, and reached the stratum to which the water had flowed down into the earth. When the fountain of the Soporific Water began to gush again, they explained to the kings that it was Ellie's magic that had accomplished it.

"Yes, no doubt, that's *just* what it was," muttered Arachna in disbelief.

When the Soporific Water was available once more in Underground Land, the wise Strasheela came up with another clever trick. All seven kings were put to sleep at the same time, with no one left on the throne. And when they reawakened, innocent as newborn babes, it was imparted to them that one of them had formerly been a weaver, a second had been a smith, a third, a plowman… And they settled down to modest working-class lives.

Thus ended the government of the Seven Kings, and the land became free. The Underground Ore-Diggers resettled on the surface, under the blessed sun of Magic Land. They constructed villages near those of the Munchkins and occupied themselves with agriculture and the herding of livestock.

When she had reached this point in her reading, Arachna smiled sarcastically. "So they became free, did they, my fine people? Well and good — but when *I* get my hands on you, you'll wish you had your Seven Kings back!"

In the final days of her sojourn among the Ore-Diggers, Ellie had met with Ramina, Queen of the Field Mice. And the Queen had predicted that the girl would not be returning to Magic Land any more. Strasheela, not to mention all of Ellie's other friends, felt very sad when they heard this prediction, and they promised that they would preserve forever their happy memories of that little girl from the outside world who had accomplished so many good things for the peoples of Magic Land.

Ellie and Fred took their seats in a little house fastened to the back of Oyho the Dragon, and the Dragon flew them back home to Kansas.

The Witch asked the Chronicler: "Tell- me, Castalyo, was Ramina right, and did Ellie really never return to Magic Land?"

"Read on, mistress," replied the Gnome evasively. "Read, and you'll learn everything."

Chapter 5

THE FIERY GOD
OF THE MARRANS

Arachna resumed her perusal. The Chronicle returned to Urfin Jus and began to relate how he spent years of boredom in his secluded house in Munchkin Land.[6]

Urfin rooted in his garden for ten years, and then all of a sudden his fate changed abruptly once more. A giant eagle, Carfax, fell to the ground near his house, after being wounded in a fight with some other eagles. The ex-king nursed Carfax back to health, and a friendship developed between them. The cunning Urfin convinced the good-hearted bird that he had only one thought in mind: to make other people happy. It would be a good thing if he could make himself king over some backward people who were living in poverty and ignorance. This people would then begin a life of glory under Urfin's rule.

---

[6] See the story *The Fiery God of the Marrans*.

The most unprogressive nation in Magic Land were the Leapers, who inhabited a secluded valley up in the mountains. The Leapers, whose name for themselves was 'Marrans,' were so far behind other people that they did not even know the use of fire. The shrewd Jus took advantage of this fact. He flew to Marran Land during the night, on the giant eagle's back, wearing purple clothes and carrying a lighted torch in his hand. Jus proclaimed himself a god of fire who had come down to them from the sky, and the credulous Marrans subordinated themselves to his dominion.

Urfin began by winning the princes and the elders over to his side. Warm, comfortable houses were built for them, to replace the huts that they had been living in before. Jus taught the aristocratic Marrans to cook tasty dishes over a fire, and accustomed them to luxury and banquets, so that they closed ranks behind him: he brought them a life of freedom and ease, at the expense of the commoners.

The common people were on the point of rising in rebellion, but Urfin cleverly redirected their anger against the neighboring tribes. "Your fortune isn't here!" Urfin said to the Marrans. "I'll lead you away from your meager, barren land, to conquer the rich plains, with their fruit orchards and their flocks of fatted sheep. We'll seize the comfortable dwellings of the Winkies and the Munchkins, and we'll capture the riches of the Emerald City itself."

The bellicose Marrans responded with enthusiasm to Urfin's call. A mighty army was assembled. Jus took the Iron Woodman captive, subjugated the Winkies, and then led the soldiers to Emerald Land. By that time, the Emerald City had been converted into an island, as the Deadwood Oaks, under the direction of Strasheela, had surrounded it by a broad artificial lake.

Urfin's soldiers extended a bridge over the lake, and the City's fortifications fell under the onslaught of the enemy. Strasheela, Din Gior (the Long-Bearded Soldier), and Faramant (Guardian of the Gates) once again became the prisoners of the presumptuous invader. And once again, a girl and a boy from the outside world came to their assistance.

When she had reached this point in her reading, Arachna exclaimed triumphantly: "Aha! I *knew* that Ramina was wrong! Ellie did come to Magic Land once again."

But the Witch quickly fell silent. The little girl turned out to be Ellie's younger sister, and her name was Annie. Annie was ten years younger than Ellie. Hearing her fill of Ellie's accounts of her marvelous adventures there, Annie and her friend Tim O'Kelly had dreamed of making a trip to Magic Land — and their dream became a reality. They crossed the Great Desert and the World-Encompassing Mountains on some amazing animals known as mules. As to what sort of beasts these "mules" were, the Gnomes had never been able to find out properly, but they *did* manage to learn that the mules fed on sunlight. Annie and Tim visited the Kingdom of Foxes and did an enormous favor for the Fox King, Keensniffer XVI. The latter, in appreciation, gave the girl a Silver Circlet that made anyone who put it on turn invisible.

This Magic Circlet, not to mention an All-Seeing Magic Box that Strasheela had received as a gift from the Good Fairy Stella, were of great help to Annie and Tim in their struggle against the villainous Urfin. After freeing the Woodman and the other prisoners from their captivity, Annie and Tim proceeded with them to Violet Land, which had already thrown off the dominance of the Marrans.

Urfin led his army on a march against Annie and her friends. It just so happened that as Urfin's army was approaching the Violet Castle, two Winkie teams were engaged in a final game for the all-Country volleyball championship. (Tim O'Kelly had taught the

Winkies how to play volleyball.) The Marrans were in the most warlike spirit possible as they marched against their foes. They were thirsting for revenge: Jus had concocted a story that their friends and relatives who had been left behind in Violet Land to maintain order, had been beaten by the Winkies, that the troops had been cut up into little pieces and fed to the pigs.

And now the Marrans, dashing forward for a fight to the finish, observed their friends and brothers among the players and the spectators, the very ones who, according to Urfin, had been brutally slain. These "dead" men were laughing, kidding around with the Winkies, and gaily throwing the ball back and forth.

The Marrans understood now that they had been deceived, that the Fiery God was nothing but an impostor who set peoples against one another for but a single purpose — to dominate them. Urfin's power crumbled away in an instant, and the overthrown god fled in disgrace. Once again, his grandiose hopes had collapsed.

"Ah, how unlucky that poor man was," sighed Arachna sympathetically. "He had such big plans, but not enough ability…"

The Witch read on about how the warriors of both armies had broken ranks and begun to play volleyball, forming mixed teams. Then Tim and Annie had gone home on their solar-powered mules.

This had happened about a year ago.

Chapter 6

THE TEMPTATION OF URFIN JUS

Her perusal of the vast account of the events in Magic Land during the most recent decades took Arachna several weeks. After that, she was seized by a dreadful longing to take some kind of action. She felt bitter anguish at having been asleep at a time when such amazing events were occurring there.

"Ah," sighed the Witch, "if only I hadn't fumbled like the most abject fool, how I would have shown all those rulers! They would have learned what it's like to deal with Arachna!"

The ambitious Sorceress was haunted by the image of the purple imperial mantle, or, at the very worst, the royal crown. She imagined herself as ruler of Magic Land, and in her daydreams, she was issuing orders not only to her humble deputies Strasheela and the Iron Woodman, but to those haughty fairies Villina and Stella as well.

Several obedient Gnomes, headed by the ancient Castalyo, went out to fetch Urfin Jus, to bring him to Arachna's cave. Would they be able to carry out this mission, and would the ex-king agree to enter the Wicked Witch's service?

To answer this question, let us go back a year and see how the deposed ruler took his latest downfall.

Neither the Marrans nor the Winkies wanted the pretender put to death: they merely drove the former Fiery God away amid whistles, shouts, and jeers. The loyal Topotun had left his master, Eot Ling, the wooden Clown who had been so devoted to Urfin, had been lost in the bustle, and only Guamoko the Great Horned Owl remained with Jus.

The Owl, perched on Urfin's shoulder, whispered in his ear: "It's all right, don't lose hope. Bear up!... Our time will come, and then we'll show those hecklers..."

Urfin realized that these were only empty words, uttered for the sole purpose of cheering him up, but all the same, he was grateful to the Owl for his comforting speech.

Urfin's mind was afire with an unbearable humiliation. He recalled the past. Only a few months before, dressed in a fiery-colored cloak and carrying a burning torch in his hand, he had appeared before the Leapers under extraordinary circumstances, on the back of the giant Eagle, and those simple-minded people had readily acknowledged his godhood and placed their fate in his hands.

And what good had he accomplished for them? He had made their rich richer and their poor poorer, he had instilled greed in their hearts for other people's property and led them into war against their neighbors. And what calamity this had ended in for him...

What was he going to do now? There wasn't a single person in all Magic Land that Urfin could call his friend, and there was no shelter for him anywhere. Even his humble dwelling near the village of Cogida he had burned down when, mounted on Carfax's back, he set out to call on the Marrans. Now, empty-handed, with empty pockets, he faced the unknown. All of his property remained in the Leapers' supply depot: his bed, his warm clothing, his weapons, his tools...

Should he go back and ask for it? The generous Marrans would certainly return his things to him, but could he listen to their ridicule or, even worse, their pity?... No, that was something he couldn't bear! So Urfin, glumly gritting his teeth, frowned as he walked quickly away from Violet Land.

"No one has yet died of hunger in Magic Land," thought Urfin. "The trees have enough fruit, and enough branches to use for building shelters, so I can spend the nights in the woods, and I can break them with my bare hands..."

When he had calmed down a little, Urfin recalled that on his old farmstead in Munchkin Land, there had been a little cellar outside the house, and that he had stored in this cellar a spare set of joiners' tools: an ax, saws, planes, chisels, and drills. Though his house may have burned down, this cellar, of course, must be intact, which meant that the tools must be intact as well. The honest Munchkins would never have disturbed anything — that was something that he could be sure of.

"What's the matter with me?" thought Urfin, smiling crookedly. "Twice in my life I've been a joiner, and twice in my life I've been a king. Now, for the third and last time, I'll have to become a joiner again..."

Jus shared his intentions with the Great Horned Owl, who was now his sole counselor, and they met with Guamoko's approval. "There's no other course left to us, Monarch," said the Owl. "Let's go back to your farmstead, build another house, and settle down there until something else turns up."

"Ah, Guamoko, Guamoko," sighed Urfin, "there's no point in your consoling me with false hopes. I'm no longer young, and I simply don't have the strength to wait ten years for some new miracle. And please don't call me Monarch. How am I a monarch, and who is subordinate to me? Just call me Master!"

"Very well, Master," replied Guamoko obediently.

Urfin directed his steps resolutely toward the west.

Urfin Jus's journey through Blue Land proved to be a difficult one. The traveler spent the nights in the woods, protecting himself from the night chill by burying himself in dry leaves or by building simple shelters. He couldn't even kindle a campfire for himself: his celebrated cigarette-lighter likewise remained in the depot among the Marrans. He fed himself on fruit and on ears of wheat that he picked in the fields. Several times, the Owl brought him partridges that he had caught, but Urfin could not eat them uncooked, and with a sigh he returned them to Guamoko.

The wanderer became very gaunt, his swarthy cheeks became hollow, and his large nose appeared to grow even larger and stuck out like a tower over his sunken mouth. Urfin's face became overgrown with clumpy stubble of beard, but there was nothing for him to shave himself with.

Nagging thoughts about the past continued to crawl through Urfin's head. Had he been happy when he ruled over Magic Land? "No, I wasn't," the ex-king admitted to himself. "I seized power by force and took away the people's freedom, and everyone hated me. Even my courtiers, to whom I gave exalted positions, they were only pretending that they loved me. Flatterers and toadies sang my praises during banquets, but only so that they would receive a decoration or some other favor from me. I ravaged the Emerald City and removed the precious stones from the houses and the towers, and bricks flew down at me when I walked through the streets. For what, then, did I strive for power? For what?..." Urfin could find no answer for this question.

Urfin crossed the Great River on a little raft that he threw together as best he could, and, most inopportunely, the memory returned to him of how his wooden army had ended up in the water during his march on the Emerald City. "It would have been better if the river had carried them away altogether... That confounded Powder of Life! Why did it fall into my hands? Everything started with that..."

It became easier for Urfin when he finally reached the Yellow Brick Road. It shone in front of him in a friendly manner, as if inviting him to continue his journey along it. He approached the regions where he had grown up, and even the air there appeared fresher and more fragrant to Jus than it was abroad. And the soft-hearted Munchkins that he encountered on the road behaved pleasantly enough toward the former monarch.

More than once, the little people dressed in blue, wearing sharp-pointed blue hats with little bells on them, invited the weary traveler into their blue cottages behind their blue fences. At a table covered by a blue tablecloth, on blue plates, they served delicious food, as the smiling farmwife regaled her famished guest liberally. Two or three times, Urfin even spent the night in cozy little blue cottages.

Urfin Jus's dour mind began little by little to soften. "How can this be?!" he thought with remorse that was long overdue. "I committed so much evil against these kind people and dreamed only of subordinating them to my power and oppressing them, and yet they've forgotten about all the bad things I've done to them and are treating me in such a cordial manner... It's obvious that I haven't been living my life the way I should have been..."

Jus decided not to share these new thoughts and feelings with the shifty, malignant Great Horned Owl, for he realized that the wicked bird would not approve of them.

And so, one fine noontime, the wanderer found himself back at the ashes of his home. Of the house, nothing remained but the corners, which the rains had eroded, but Urfin saw with joy that the cellar was intact, and that the lock on the door had not been touched. And when Urfin pulled on the ring and opened the door, he observed that every one of his ample set of tools was still there. Tears flowed down Urfin's overgrown cheeks...

"Munchkins, Munchkins," he whispered, sighing. "Only now do I begin to understand what good people you are... And how guilty I am for what I've done to you!"

While still on the road, Urfin had decided to select a new homesite for himself, somewhere as far as possible from Cogida and as near as possible to the World-Encompassing Mountains. "Let the people forget about my wickedness," thought the former ruler of Magic Land. "That'll happen more quickly if I'm not constantly present among them and if I resettle somewhere as far away as I can..."

Before leaving his home farmstead, Urfin decided to take a walk around every corner of it, to say goodbye to the beds that he had cultivated so long and so carefully. As he was walking along the unused land that was separated from the garden portion by a fence, he gasped and pressed his hand against his heart. In the furthest corner of it rose a thicket of bright green plants with oblong, pulpy leaves, with prickly stalks.

"Oh!!!" exclaimed Urfin numbly.

Yes, that's what they were, the selfsame remarkable plants from which he had derived the Powder of Life so many years ago. Had their seeds reawakened after a long period of dormancy, after being buried deep in the earth? No, the wind had most likely brought them there again. Urfin recalled a violent storm with rain and hail that had occurred two days ago, when he had had to seek shelter from it in a forest thicket, under a spreading tree.

"Yes, of course, it's another prank of the windstorm," said Urfin, and Guamoko the Great Horned Owl began to hoot joyfully.

Urfin Jus was strongly tempted. Here it was, the very miracle that Guamoko had been talking about while they were on their way back home. And there would be no need for him to wait ten years, for here it was, right before his eyes. Urfin reached out for one of the stalks with his hand, and then drew back after pricking himself on a sharp thorn.

Here, then, was the possibility for him to start all over again. And now that he had vast experience, he would not repeat the mistakes of the past. He could prepare five hundred... no, a thousand powerful, obedient Deadwood Oaks. And not only Deadwood Oaks: he could make invulnerable flying creatures, wooden dragons! They would travel quickly through the air and assail the heads of the terrified people like an unexpected thunderstorm! All these ideas flashed instantly through Urfin's mind. He looked gleefully at the Owl. "Well, Guamoko, what do you have to say about this new gift of Fate?"

"What can I say, Monarch? Prepare as much Powder of Life as you can — and it'll be our turn! We'll show them, those mockers!"

But Urfin's lengthy reflections during their journey home had had their effect. Something in his mind had changed. The dazzling vista that had once again opened up before him did not attract him. He sat down on a stump and thought for a long time, eyeing attentively the drop of blood that was running down his finger as a result of being pricked by the thorn.

"Blood..." he whispered. "More blood, people's tears, suffering. No, I've got to be done with such things once and for all!" He fetched a spade from the cellar and dug up all the plants by the roots. "I know you," he muttered angrily. "If I leave you here, you'll soon fill up the entire neighborhood, and then someone will figure out your magic power and do something stupid. Once was enough!..."

The Great Horned Owl was in utter despair at his master's unexpected decision, and for a long time he besought him not to turn away the good fortune that once again had fallen to his share. "Well, at least prepare a handful or so of the Powder, just in case," he droned angrily. "Who knows what might happen?"

Urfin refused this request. Drying the plants out on baking trays was a time-consuming process, so

Jus burned them in a bonfire. When nothing was left of the miraculous stems but ashes, Urfin buried them deep in the ground. Then he fashioned a wheelbarrow, loaded it with the property that had been stored in the cellar, and set out on his journey.

The indignant Guamoko stayed behind at the farm. But after about two hours, Urfin heard the sound of flapping wings: it was the Great Horned Owl, flying to catch up with him. "You know, master," Guamoko admitted in an embarrassed tone, "you may be right! Nothing good will come to us from the Powder of Life, and you did the right thing when you refused to start with that business all over again."

Guamoko, of course, was resorting to guile: he could not possibly change over so easily and so quickly to the right way of thinking. It was simply that in the course of his long life, he had learned to live with people, and it would only be most boring for him to live in the woods all by himself. Urfin understood this perfectly well, yet he was happy all the same: it would be difficult for him, too, to pass all his time in solitude.

For several days the man and the Owl continued their journey toward the mountains. When only a short distance remained between them and the mountains, Urfin happened upon an enchanting glade; a transparent brook flowed through the glade, and on its banks grew trees whose branches were loaded with fruit. "Here's a good place to settle down in," said Urfin, and the Owl agreed with him.

So Urfin built himself a hut here and planted a garden. His days passed in labor and chores, and the harsh memories of the past began to fade from the outcast's memory.

It was here that Arachna's messengers found Urfin Jus a year later. This turned out to be no easy matter. The Gnomes were tiny, their legs were very short, and no matter how fast they hurried, they couldn't make more than two or three miles in one day. And finding Urfin's new homestead was no easier. Castalyo and his companions traveled first to Blue Land, and the Munchkins there told them that Jus had departed from his homeland.

They had to question the birds and the beasts, and after a long and exhausting journey that took an entire month, the delighted Gnomes reached at last the beautiful glade where Urfin's new hut stood.

Jus was extremely surprised to see the white-bearded little men down by his feet. He had been living in Magic Land for forty years, but never had he even heard of the existence of the Gnomes. However, he knew that the wonders of Magic Land are boundless, and for that reason, he greeted his unexpected visitors politely and inquired about what business brought them there.

Castalyo had barely opened his mouth to begin speaking, when all of a sudden he collapsed motionless to the ground. The same thing happened to the other Gnomes. Urfin Jus slapped himself on the forehead.

"What a fool I am!" he said. "You're tired and hungry, yet right away I turn the conversation to business. Please forgive me, but in living here all alone, I've completely forgotten how to be sociable..."

After an ample meal and period of rest, Castalyo informed Urfin of his reason for coming. He told him who Arachna was, and of how the mighty wizard Hurricap had put her to sleep back in time immemorial. Nor did he conceal the fact that the Witch intended to become ruler of Magic Land and was counting on the help of Urfin Jus, who had twice succeeded in conquering the Emerald City. In sending the Gnomes to Urfin, Arachna implied that she would reward her helpers generously, making them overlords and viceroys of the subordinate lands.

Urfin Jus was silent for a long time. Once more was destiny leading him into the greatest of temptations. All he had to do was to enter into the service of the Wicked Witch, and once more he would become ruler of the Emerald City or Marran Land, and could pay them back with interest for all the humiliation that they had inflicted upon him. But the question was — was it worth it? Again he would attain power by force, and again the oppressed people would come to hate him...

The year that he had been living in solitude, turning so many things over in his mind, had not been wasted. Urfin lifted his head and, looking Castalyo in the eye, he said firmly: "No! I will not enter into the service of your mistress!"

Castalyo was not surprised to hear this answer, but he asked him: "Esteemed Urfin, perhaps you could tell this to our sovereign in person?"

"What for?" inquired Jus. "Are you really unable to convey my words to her yourselves?"

"You see, the problem's like this," explained the Gnome. "Our mistress told us that if we don't bring you to her, that means we're poor, lackadaisical servants. And if her mission is unfulfilled, she'll deprive us for a whole month of the right to hunt game in her forests and catch fish in her streams. Oh, well, we'll draw our belts a little tighter and manage somehow with what we have in reserve."

Urfin grinned. "Can't you catch fish and hunt game without your mistress knowing about it? You're so small and agile that she couldn't possibly track you down."

The eyes of Castalyo and the other Gnomes opened wide in horror. "Steal game and fish?!" exclaimed Castalyo in a quivering voice. "Esteemed Urfin, you don't know the tribe of the Gnomes! They've existed for thousands of years, but never has one of them broken his word, once given, and never deceived anyone. We'd sooner starve..."

Urfin, deeply moved, seized Castalyo in a firm embrace, carefully clasping the old man to his breast.

51

"My dear little people!" he said tenderly. "In order to avoid bringing trouble down on your heads, I shall depart with you and personally explain the matter to Arachna. I hope she won't punish you because I decline to become her aide?"

"We are not answerable for your acts," explained Castalyo with dignity.

"We'll set out on our journey tomorrow," said Urfin. "Today you'll have to get a good rest."

To entertain his guests, Urfin brought a pile of toys from the hut and spread them out before the Gnomes. These consisted of wooden dolls, clowns, and animal figurines. The craftsman had painted them in bright shades, the faces of the dolls and the clowns were smiling, the deer and the chamois were so light and airy that it seemed as if they would run away at any minute. How remarkably different these gay, sunny toys were from the bleak, somber ones that he had used to make in order to frighten children.

"I work on these in my spare time," explained Urfin modestly.

"How delightful they are!" exclaimed the Gnomes.

They picked up the dolls and little animals, clasped them affectionately to their breasts, and caressed them. It was clear that they were inordinately happy with these marvelous playthings. One little old man sat on the back of a wooden deer, while another began to dance around with a little toy mouse. The guests' faces radiated bliss, though, it must be confessed, for beings their size, the toys were naturally somewhat too big.

Seeing how happy the Gnomes were, Urfin said generously: "These toys are yours. Take them back to your own country, and let your children have fun with them." The Gnomes' delight was beyond describing, and they didn't know how to thank Urfin.

The next day, the party took to the road. After the first few hundred paces, Urfin could not help feeling that something was wrong with the whole business. The Gnomes were not good at walking even under the best of circumstances, and when they were loaded down with toys almost as large as they were, they panted and wheezed, just barely plodding along — but they had no intention of parting with the toys. The distance that Urfin could cover in two minutes required twenty for them. Urfin burst out laughing as he looked at the puffing, sweating Gnomes. "No, my dear little old men, we can't have it like that! How much time did you spend on your journey to me?"

"A month," answered Castalyo.

"And now it'll take a year."

Urfin returned to his farmstead and rolled a wheelbarrow out of his shed, and he placed little men and toys alike inside it. Then he set out with light, springy steps, pushing the wheelbarrow before him. The Gnomes couldn't have been more delighted.

The journey to Arachna's cave took Jus no more than three days.

While waiting for Urfin Jus — and Ruf Bilan — to report to her, Arachna decided to check out her skills in witchcraft. It was only right to verify that all her magic charms had retained their evil potency, before taking on the peoples of Magic Land in battle.

My readers remember, of course, that Arachna had possessed the magical ability to transform herself into any kind of animal, bird, or tree... This had been her first and foremost means of gaining victory over her foes. And Arachna saw now that she no longer commanded this spell. This was a huge misfortune for her.

How could it have happened? The fact was that the incantation involved was very long and complicated, and so secret that Arachna was afraid to write it down, lest it fall into her enemies' hands. And while she was sleeping, she had forgotten the incantation altogether! But what can one do? Sleeping for five

thousand years straight is not the same thing as doz-
ing off after dinner. In such a circumstance, a person
could forget even his own name!

No, Arachna could no longer transform herself
into a squirrel or a lion, a mighty oak tree or a fleet
swallow during battles with her enemies. The Witch
would henceforth be able to rely only on her gigantic
size and strength.

It turned out that Arachna had lost some of her
other witchly spells as well, but she retained more
than enough of her capability to hurt people. She had
not lost her capacity, for example, to conjure up earth-
quakes, hurricanes, and other natural disasters.

"No matter, we'll still fight," said the relieved
Witch to herself, when, at her command, a cliff came
tumbling down from the top of a mountain and shattered into a thousand pieces.

Yes, the wicked enchantress Arachna was a formidable adversary, and woe to anyone who dared to
oppose her!

It was at that time that Urfin Jus arrived in
Arachna's valley, wheeling the merry little company
of Gnomes in his wheelbarrow. After indicating the
cave entrance to Urfin, the tiny little men dashed at
full speed to their own homes, which were hidden in
bushes and under large rocks, and they summoned
every one of their little wee ones to give them good
Uncle Urfin's gifts...

At this point, the author must lay down his pen,
because there is just no way of describing how delighted the children were. During all the thousands
of years that the Gnome tribe had been in existence,
never yet had their children beheld such splendid
toys...

Urfin Jus walked into Arachna's cave with leisurely steps, and he bowed to the Witch in a digni-
fied manner. "What would my lady like?" asked Jus.

He had promised the Gnomes to pretend that he
had no idea of why Arachna had summoned him.

And he was not the least bit frightened when he saw the evil fairy's gigantic form and her thick eyebrows that frowned in a sinister way.

"Do you know who I am?"

"The esteemed Gnome Castalyo has told me about you."

"That means you know that I was asleep for five thousand years and am now afire with a craving to go into action! My first intention is to seize power over Magic Land, and then I may even extend it beyond the mountains."

Jus shook doubtfully his head, which was now beginning to turn gray. "I tried twice to become monarch of Magic Land," said Urfin quietly, "and you know how that turned out."

"You're only a contemptible worm compared to me!" shouted the Witch arrogantly, and she straightened up in such a way that her head pressed firmly against the ceiling.

"Excuse me, madam," replied Jus resolutely, "I didn't exactly jump into it rashly. The first time, I had a mighty army of obedient wooden soldiers, and the second time, an army of two thousand strong, agile Marrans. I suffered failure both times. Madam, I've been doing a lot of thinking this past year, and I've realized that it's just not that easy to knock free peoples off their feet..."

"What, you still dare preach moral admonitions to me?" sneered Arachna contemptuously. "From your words, it appears to follow that you don't approve of my designs and are refusing to serve me."

"That's right. I don't approve of them, and I do refuse! My life has taught me many things, and I prefer to live by myself until the people whom I've wronged have become reconciled with me."

"Go, you pitiful human," ordered the witch in a fury, "and forget all about our conversation! You'll have cause yet to regret your refusal. I could have raised you to such heights!..."

Urfin retired with a bow. When he was on the threshold, he turned around and said: "I fear that when you set out on the road to war, you'll be going to meet your doom!..."

Arachna smiled scornfully, but she was moved in spite of herself to feel respect for this little man who was not afraid of her, mighty enchantress that she was. "And I would have showered this stubborn person with honors if he had agreed to serve me," thought the Witch. "One can sense that this man can move resolutely toward any goal that he's set for himself."

On the clearing outside the cave, Urfin encountered Ruf Bilan, whom another party of Gnomes had gone to fetch from Underground Land. The former king turned aside with contempt from his former Chief Minister of State. "There's a man who won't refuse Arachna's tempting offers," thought Urfin.

And was he right!

Chapter 7

THE TEMPTATION OF RUF BILAN

After sending Urfin Jus away, the Witch sat there for a long time, lost in thought. Then she shook her enormous head and ordered that Ruf Bilan, whose arrival the Gnomes had reported to her, be brought into the cave.

Ruf Bilan crept into the cave almost on his knees, his ruddy face pallid with terror. He hardly dared raise his eyes to the Witch, and when he did, he lowered them at once in fear.

Chapter 7: THE TEMPTATION OF RUF BILAN

"Are you Ruf Bilan?" asked the Witch.

"Yes, ma'am," replied Bilan in a trembling voice, "that's what an Underground Ore-Digger says is my name. But I remember nothing of what I was and what I did earlier in my life..."

He had indeed forgotten his past. When the Gnomes sought out Bilan in Underground Land, it had been only two days since he had awakened from a long sleep. Up to that moment, he had little by little been relearning how to walk and talk, and his state of development was reminiscent of that of a five-year-old child. The Ore-Digger who was his instructor had not yet been able to impart to Bilan what was good and what was evil.

Taking advantage of a moment when Ruf's instructor was absent, the crafty Gnomes had coaxed this overgrown child out of the Cavern, tempting him with sweets that they had brought along with them. When they were on the road, Bilan's companions declined to answer his questions about where they were taking him and what would happen to him.

The sight of the giantess threw Ruf into consternation, and he gazed with terror at the gigantic fairy.

"So," asked the Sorceress with a sinister sneer, "they've concealed from you the fact that you once occupied a very exalted position in your own land?"

"I know nothing about that, ma'am," said Ruf Bilan meekly, but his eyes were shining with a strange feeling akin to pride.

The astute Arachna noticed the impression that her words were making, and she decided at once on a plan of action. "Castalyo," commanded the Witch, "you're to take this person to your place, teach him to read and write, and then have him read everything in the Chronicle that tells of his life and his deeds. And when Bilan recalls his past, bring him to me again." The chronicler understood very well what his mistress was driving at.

Two weeks later, Castalyo led Bilan once again before the Witch. The facial expression and the bearing of the former Minister of State were altogether different now. He stood straight and tall, and he walked with confidence. Ruf Bilan recalled everything that had ever happened to him, down to the smallest detail. He had decided to start all over again, if the opportunity should present itself. He was no longer the weak, helpless infant that he had been when the Gnomes had led him forth from the Cavern. Before Arachna stood a grown man, a schemer and an ambitious creature capable of any form of treachery. Arachna's sly maneuver had resurrected in Ruf Bilan all of his basest qualities.

Nodding her head slightly in response to Bilan's bow, the Witch said: "You'd like to know, no doubt, why I have summoned you here?"

"That's right, ma'am, but first, may I have permission to ask one question?"

"Speak!"

"Who was that person I ran into in your dominion two weeks ago?"

"That was Urfin Jus, former King of Emerald Land."

"Ah, so *that's* why his face looked so familiar to me! It was under him that I was the Number One Man in the whole kingdom." Bilan stood up tall and proud.

"Yes, and you may rise to great heights again if you enter into service with me! My powers are immeasurably greater than Jus's were — though I do admire his mettle. What a pity that his failures have broken him, and that he's made his peace with destiny!"

Arachna now let Ruf in on her plans, and told him that she was minded to become Empress of Magic Land. "Would you like to become my comrade-in-arms?" asked the Witch.

Chapter 7: THE TEMPTATION OF RUF BILAN

"Most gracious mistress," exclaimed Bilan with delight, "I am prepared to serve you to the utmost of my abilities."

"And do you think that what I desire will become a reality?"

"Of that there isn't the slightest doubt! The peoples of Magic Land will consider themselves fortunate to bow down before such a mighty ruler as you!"

"Are you certain of that?" asked the Witch doubtfully.

"I'll stake my life on it!"

"Your former king thinks otherwise."

"He's mistaken, most gracious of monarchs! He's mistaken, and you'll soon see that fact for yourself."

"Good! Ruf Bilan, I accept you into my service. You shall be my ambassador, to deliver important messages, and if you distinguish yourself in that, then I shall promote you still higher!" Ruf's face lit up with joy, and he began to assure Arachna once again of his devotion.

"Go!" the Witch nodded to him, and Ruf Bilan exited the cave, backing away and bowing continually.

"What a little worm!" said the fairy contemptuously. "A real piece of mold! At the first convenient occasion, he'll betray me just as readily as he agreed to serve me. But unfortunately, I have no other choice…"

Chapter 8

"IF AT FIRST YOU DON'T SUCCEED..."

Among Arachna's magical possessions was a Flying Carpet that she had stolen from her mother when she ran away from her to come to Magic Land. It was a very ancient, threadbare carpet, and only the tireless efforts of the Gnomes had preserved it from dampness and moths. Every month, the diminutive men had cleaned it with brushes, beaten it, dried it out in the sun, and darned it, so that it would be ready for use at a moment's notice when the Witch awoke.

As the first step in the realization of her plans, Arachna decided to fly over all the regions of Magic Land, one after the other, to see how matters stood there, and to demand the acknowledgment of her supreme authority.

Arachna spread the Carpet out in front of the entrance to her cave, and she sat down in the middle of it and seated Ruf Bilan by her side, so that he could carry out negotiations in her name. "Carpet," commanded the Witch, "carry me to Rose Land, to the Sorceress Stella."

The Carpet rose at once into the air and moved swiftly along, with the ground below. Bilan's face turned white with alarm, and he let out loud groans.

"What's the matter?" asked Arachna drily.

"Most gracious mistress, I implore you in the name of all that's sacred, don't take on the Sorceress Stella in battle."

"And why not? Do you think she's stronger than I am?"

"I don't doubt your strength, mistress, but you should be aware that Stella knows the secret of eternal youth."

"And what's that to me," retorted Arachna haughtily, "*me*, who counts more thousands of years than I can remember since the time of my birth?"

"All right, mistress," said Ruf Bilan in agreement, "we won't discuss age. But Lady Stella is on excellent terms with the mighty tribe of Winged Monkeys. They're dreadful beasts, and if the flock of them should attack you, I wouldn't guarantee victory for us, in spite of all your power and might."

The Sorceress became thoughtful; she ordered the Carpet to stop, and it hung there motionless in mid-air. "Yes, I've heard a few things in the old times about the Winged Monkeys," concurred Arachna. "Perhaps it *would* be better not to take on those creatures. What do you say we pay a call on Villina and demand that *she* submit to us?"

"Why are you so obsessed with these fairies?" begged Bilan. "You're a fairy yourself, and, if you'll pardon my frankness, you're well aware that they're an exceedingly troublesome people! Lady Villina may be old, but she has the magical ability to transport herself instantly from place to place. Now she's here, and a second later she's a thousand miles away. How could you possibly defeat such an elusive foe?"

"I guess you're right," admitted Arachna reluctantly. "Let's leave the fairies be. There are plenty of territories and peoples in Magic Land without them. In Castalyo's Chronicle, I read about the Marrans. They're the most ignorant and backward people in these precincts. Why don't we start with the Marrans, Bilan?"

"Yes, let's start with the Marrans, mistress," said Bilan happily, although, having been sleeping in the Cavern through all the past decade, he knew precisely nothing about the events that had been unfolding in their country. He had not had time to finish reading the chapters of the Chronicle that dealt with them.

Arachna commanded the Flying Carpet to take her to Marran Valley. After several hours of flight, the Carpet alighted on one of the mountains that formed a chain around that country.

Great changes had taken place in Marran Valley since its inhabitants had banished Urfin Jus, the Fiery God. After settling their score with the pretender, the Leapers had wrought a true revolution: they had broken the power of the aristocrats and ceased working for them. The earlier pitiful straw huts inhabited by the common people, had been replaced by neat little villages, with straight streets lined with small but warm, cozy little houses. Smoke was coming out of the chimneys, which bore witness to the fact that the Marrans had forgotten their age-old fear of fire and learned how to make good use of it.

The poorly-cultivated wheat fields had given way to splendid orchards, whose trees were laden with ripe fruit. Herds of cattle and sheep were grazing on the mountain slopes, under the watchful eyes of gleeful lads. And beside each village, the obligatory volleyball court was visible — for volleyball, the legacy of Tim O'Kelly, had become the Leapers' national sport.

When Arachna's enormous black form, standing there on the mountain, was seen outlined against the blue background of the sky, the alarm was raised in the Marran villages. The women and the children took shelter in the houses, while the men conferred excitedly with one another.

Before long, the figure of Ruf Bilan appeared on the road leading to the central town of the Leapers; positively strutting with pride, he was coming as the wicked fairy's ambassador. Hart, Boice, and Clem, the Marrans' elected elders, dashed forward to meet him.

They bore heavy clubs in their hands, just in case, and Ruf Bilan lost his nerve. Instead of talking in a loud and imposing manner, he babbled in a trembling voice that he had come from the mighty Witch Arachna with a demand that they, the Marrans, acknowledge her as their empress and pay her a yearly tribute.

The elders looked at one another, and Boice said: "Let him relay it to his mistress that we ask for a half hour in order to consider it, and then we'll report to her with our answer." Bilan perked up at once, and he ambled back in an arrogant manner, confident that the deed was done.

"Needless to say, mistress," he reported to the Witch, "those simpletons were frightened to death when I laid your demand before them. They'll soon be reporting to you with an expression of their submission, and the only thing they'll have to ask, obviously, is that the tribute that you impose on them not be too heavy." The Witch drily thanked Bilan with a nod of her head and began to wait.

A lively movement was evident inside the Leapers' little domiciles. Men scurried from house to house, handing something to one another, while boys dashed from yard to yard, often bending down to the ground.

Then a crowd of several hundred people made its way toward the mountain where Arachna was standing. It appeared strange that no children, no women, no old people were anywhere in evidence — it consisted solely of strong, full-grown men, the flower of the whole tribe. Their postures were equally strange: each of them walked with his right arm behind his back, concealing something from the Witch's sight.

The crowd surrounded the Enchantress in a semicircle as she stood there on the Flying Carpet. She looked haughtily at the people approaching, while

Ruf Bilan huddled at her feet. Elders Clem, Boice, and Hart stepped forward.

"Witch Arachna," Hart addressed her in a sonorous voice, "you want us to submit to you and pay you a tribute. Well, we've had enough of princes, wizards, and gods! Here is our answer! Fire!"

Hart threw his right arm into the air. At his signal, loaded slingshots were instantly lifted above the heads of the crowd and fired, and stones by the hundreds came whistling through the air! Three of the missiles hurtled into the Witch's spacious forehead, two hit her in the chin, while a few dozen stones struck her in the shoulders, the breast, and the stomach; an ordinary cobblestone knocked Ruf Bilan off his feet.

The attack was so well-organized and sudden that Arachna was flustered. But when she saw the Marrans bending down to pick up more stones to fire at her from their slingshots, she cried out in a wild voice: "Carpet, take me away from here!"

The Carpet rose at once into the air. A few missiles, fired by the most skilled of the marksmen, hit the Carpet and put holes in it (which, as it happened, rather diminished the Carpet's lift and its speed).

The Witch was so furious with Bilan that she squeezed him in her fist and was about to crush him to death — for which only the least little bit of her strength would be needed. But, reflecting that she still needed the traitor's services, she let him go and contented herself with hissing wickedly at him: "So that's the kind of submission in which you brought the Marrans to me, you fool!"

Ruf Bilan extricated himself cleverly. "If your wisdom was not able to reveal their shifty designs, then how could you expect me, a mere mortal, to discern them?"

The Witch bit her tongue. Indeed, what could she expect from Bilan when she herself, an enchantress accustomed since childhood to all manner of guile and deceit, had fallen into such a simple trap?

As a means of exacting revenge upon the Marrans, Arachna decided to call up an earthquake. But in the heat of her exasperation, she mixed up the incantation, and the earthquake that she produced was very weak: a few stones came loose from the mountains, and dishes fell off the shelves of houses here and there.

If Arachna and Ruf Bilan had known the proverbs of the far-off northern land beyond the ocean, they would have said, most appropriately: "If at first you don't succeed, try, try again."

Chapter 9

LESTAR'S CANNON

A wise old Jay witnessed Arachna the enchantress's humiliating failure. Reasoning that Violet Land would be next in line to be threatened with attack, the Jay quickly sought out a Swallow. "Fly to the Violet Castle with all speed," she ordered. "Have the first associate you meet transmit to the Iron Woodman via the avian network the news that disaster is moving in the direction of his domain: a giantess-witch thirty cubits high wants to conquer it. Have the Winkies prepare for it!"

This avian network was something that was quite familiar now to those in Magic Land. It had been organized by Kaggi-Karr the Crow, who was Chief of Communications and had performed great services in this capacity.

It is necessary to say at this point that the people of Magic Land live in friendship with the forest animals and the birds. The fertility of nature blessed the people of the country so abundantly with harvests of cereals, vegetables, and fruit, and so many head of livestock grazed in its meadows, that there was absolutely no need to hunt game in the forests.

On the contrary, the people often came to the aid of the denizens of the forest. If there were a drought, and fruit, still unripe, fell from the trees prematurely, the villagers fed the animals and birds out of their own stores. The animals and birds, in their turn, helped people when they were in need. And the avian network was just such an aid.

The swift-winged flyer set out, cleaving the air with a whistling sound. She had no trouble at all in outdistancing Arachna's Flying Carpet, which had been damaged by the Marrans' projectiles. The news was transmitted along the network with such speed that it left Arachna three hours behind.

What consternation ensued! For the past year, after the overthrow of the Fiery God of the Marrans, the Winkies had been living in peace and friendship with all their neighbors. They had heard nothing about any wicked wizards or witches, and nothing had appeared to be threatening the peace of the land.

However, there could be no doubting it. Danger was on the way, and awesome danger at that: only the most important messages were relayed along the avian network, while the wooden couriers, who had once been Urfin Jus's policemen, were entrusted with delivering ordinary dispatches.

The Iron Woodman had just completed his regular health treatment. They had taken him apart once more, cleaned and oiled all his small parts, and stuffed his silk heart with fresh sawdust. He stepped out of the workshop freshly polished, and shining so brightly that it hurt the eyes to look at him.

Chapter 9: LESTAR'S CANNON

When Lestar the mechanic, the little old man who moved about in such a lively manner, informed him of the calamity that was on its way, the Monarch immediately issued a series of orders, which bespoke his intellect and his great experience in military matters.

Messengers ran out in all directions, bearing the order to evacuate the nearest villages: the residents were to leave their farms and seek refuge in the Violet Castle, behind its sturdy walls. Herdsmen drove their flocks into ravines that they alone knew about. Some fighting men armed with bows took up defensive positions in little stone towers, others seated themselves on the roof of the castle, hiding behind the chimneys, while still others concealed themselves in ambush behind huge rocks that lay scattered along the road.

Thus the area around the Violet Castle took on the appearance of an army camp, ready for a siege.

Lestar the mechanic occupied himself with a large wooden cannon, the same one that had once allowed the Winkies to defeat the Deadwood Oaks without a fight by frightening them off with only a single shot. Of course, the cannon had burst when this shot was fired, but Lestar repaired it on the spot, fastening iron hoops around the barrel. The mechanic still had a supply of the gunpowder that Charlie Black the one-legged Sailor had prepared.

Lestar loaded the cannon with powder, and instead of buckshot, he poured bent nails, fragments of horseshoes, and other little scraps of iron into it. The weapon was ready for battle. The bombardier stood by with a burning wick in his hand.

The Flying Carpet now appeared in the air, with the immense black form of Arachna the Witch upon it. This time, she had armed herself with an enormous tree trunk, which she had yanked out of the ground roots and all. The Carpet alighted on the ground at a certain distance from the Castle, and Ruf Bilan, in his capacity as envoy, moved toward the Iron Woodman — only, instead of a flag, he waved a white towel. (He had seized it from the vacated cottage of one of the Winkies.)

The Woodman recognized Ruf Bilan. He said to him contemptuously: "Is that you, you traitor? You mean to say that they didn't wring your neck in Underground Land after all?"

"Why should they want to wring my neck?" retorted Bilan. "But right now the talk is not about me, so let's get down to business. You see, over yonder, the mighty Witch Arachna. I have come here as her ambassador."

"And what message has she ordered you to convey?" inquired the Woodman.

"First of all, she demands your unconditional surrender and acknowledgment of her as your Queen from now through all the centuries to come."

"Yes. Is that all?" asked the Woodman calmly.

"No, of course not. You will pay the Queen an annual tribute of a thousand oxen and two thousand rams, and as many ducks and geese as she requires. To begin with, you will roast three oxen and five rams for your monarch, while I myself will be satisfied with a fat hen: my mistress and I have grown hungry in the course of our travels."

"Why, didn't the Marrans treat you to an ample breakfast?" the Iron Woodman asked Bilan with feigned simple-mindedness.

Ruf Bilan eyes popped wildly: he realized that news of Arachna's débacle with the Leapers had already spread to Violet Land by some means or other, and the arrogance fell away from him at once. "Do you mean to submit to Arachna or not?" he asked, losing every trace of conviction.

"Go back to your mistress," exclaimed the Monarch angrily, "and tell her that we're going to fight to the last man. And don't forget, it was only your flag of truce that saved *you* from death." And he swung his ax so forcefully over the traitor's head that it made the air buzz around him. Bilan's legs gave way from fear, and he hurried back to his mistress, stumbling as he went.

When the Witch heard Bilan's report, she was enraged, and she advanced upon the Winkies, relying on her monstrous club. Arrows whizzed at her from every direction: they flew out from the watchtowers, from the roof of the Castle, from behind the rocks along the road. They pierced the Witch's forehead and cheeks, stuck in her cloak, and struck her bare ankles. Of course, these were no more serious than pinpricks for the giantess, but even pinpricks are not very pleasant.

In spite of all this, Arachna's giant form continued to advance, and her club dug out deep pits as she struck the ground with it. How the Iron Woodman regretted now the fact that, during the first days of his reign, he had ordered the removal of the high wall with the sharp spikes on top of it, which had surrounded the Violet Castle during Bastinda's time. When the wall was up, the Castle had strongly resembled a prison, but now, at least, the wall might have stopped Arachna…

At this moment, Lestar's cannon gave out with a deafening boom. The load of shot, fired at close range right into the Enchantress's breast, had a devastating effect. Arachna even staggered and almost fell down, but she managed to stay on her feet. The wound was not fatal to her, nor even dangerous, but it seemed to the giantess that she had been struck by some giant, one whose strength was on a par with her own, and she took the roar of the cannon as the voice of an enraged monster…

And was Arachna frightened! Yes, she was frightened, and she threw her club aside and ran to seek the safety of her Magic Carpet. Along the way, she crashed blindly into two of the defensive towers and crushed them, but fortunately, the fighting men who had been sitting inside them jumped out in time and landed in the ditch.

In her rush, the Witch lost her leather shoes, and she did not even stop to pick them up. Their fate is extremely curious. The shoes were waterproof: either the shoes were saturated with some special substance, or Arachna had enchanted them. The Iron Woodman knew how to make use of this property of the shoes. He ordered that they by hauled to the Great River. There, the Winkies fitted them up with decks, masts, and sails; they attached rudders to them, and the shoes thus became boats, with the names *Right* and *Left*. They became a part of the Violet Land fleet, and the Winkies used these boats to make long voyages, transporting loads of cargo in their holds. *Right* and *Left* stood out from other boats in their great cargo capacity and their maneuverability.

But the most fascinating of their properties was the way they repelled the crocodiles which were found in abundance in the river. Those monsters often attacked wooden craft, and it was necessary to fight them off with arrows and spears. But the moment the crocodiles saw the leather boats, they scattered in whatever directions they could. They may have been frightened by the unusual appearance of the Shoe-Boats — or else they didn't like the sharp odor that emanated from them. In any event, there was no end of people who wanted to sail on the Shoe-Boats.

The battle between the Winkies and the mighty Arachna did not last more than ten minutes. The Witch's retreat was greeted by triumphant shouts on the part of the victors.

The Sorceress, after raising the Carpet into the air and directing it as far away from that place as possible, thought to herself: "Maybe Urfin Jus was right:

it's just not that easy to subjugate freedom-loving peoples. But we'll still see..."

She commanded the Carpet to carry her to the Emerald City. She did not know that, far ahead of her, reports were being relayed to Strasheela, via the avian network, about all that had happened in Marran Valley and at the Violet Castle.

Chapter 10

A NIGHT ATTACK

Arachna's Carpet trundled through the air with all the speed of a run-down railroad train, and the Witch relived over and over again the humiliation that she had suffered in her encounters with the Marrans and with the Winkies. How could it happen?! Those pitiful little people had forced her to flee in disgrace — her, a powerful Sorceress, who had hitherto never been beaten by anyone except Hurricap! But it had to be admitted that the strength was on their side.

"It's all because there are many of them and only one of me," Arachna reasoned. "I certainly can't count as my helper this miserable coward squirming about at my feet. He can't carry out even the simplest assignment properly. But who else can be induced to join forces with me?..." When she thought about it, the Witch could not but recognize that not one person and not one beast who would aid her could be found in all of Magic Land.

"Well, since that's how it is, I'll just have to act on my own, as I did before," muttered Arachna indignantly. "There's no point in paying any heed to Urfin's

71

drivel." But the mere fact that the Fairy said this meant that the former king's prediction was still very much on her mind.

The Witch's mood was downright abominable, not only because she had lost both battles, but also because her bare feet were chilled to the bone, and she was suffering from hunger. She had had nothing to eat all day, and was ready to devour a whole herd of oxen. But no livestock were to be seen anywhere. The farms that lay in her path were all vacant. The birds, flying on ahead of Arachna, had warned the farmers of the danger, and the latter had managed to put their livestock in a safe place and then take refuge themselves in shelters. Arachna was forced to land in an orchard and avail herself of the fruit there, even though she couldn't stand it!

After getting a bite to eat as best she could, the Witch moved onward. But by that time, the avian network had already reached the Emerald Island with news of the enemy's approach. Strasheela summoned his Staff at once. The first to answer to his call was Field Marshal Din Gior; he had used his golden comb to arrange his luxuriant beard, which came all the way down below his knees. After him came Faramant, manager of military provisions, and Kaggi-Karr, who was in charge of communications. But before they could make any decision, they had to find out just what sort of danger threatened.

On the night-table stood a rose-colored box with frosted glass on one side, a gift from Stella. The staff members took up positions around this television, and Strasheela pronounced the magic words: "*Birelya-turelya, buridakl-furidakl, The edge of the sky turns red, The grass turns green instead. Little box, little box, be obliging, show us the Witch flying on her Magic Carpet!*"

The magic screen flashed at once into light, and they quickly saw, against the background of the sky, the Carpet spread out flat in the air, and the giantess seated on it. The sight of such a spectacle knocked all the members, even Strasheela himself, for a loop. The Witch already presented a most ominous appearance with her long blue cloak, her savage red face, the shock of black hair on her head. A small form cowered at Arachna's feet, and Strasheela and his friends recognized this as Ruf Bilan.

"Look at that," said Faramant in surprise, "that traitor's still around. How did *he* ever manage to get together with the Witch?"

"Cr-r-reeps stick with other cr-r-reeps!" declared the Crow with vexation. "And I wouldn't be the least bit surprised if that tireless megalomaniac Urfin Jus were likewise in the vicinity. He's a bird of the same feather..."

Strasheela was afire with curiosity. "Indeed, now that you mention it, why *don't* we take a look and see just where that bird is. It's always useful to observe the enemy. I'm so at fault because I don't use Stella's gift often enough." He addressed the Television: *"Little box, little box, be obliging, show us Urfin Jus, wherever he might be."*

The screen quickly displayed a beautiful glade with a cozy little house, with a few out-buildings in the background. In the foreground, Urfin was down on his knees among his vegetable patches, weeding the cucumbers. Guamoko the Great Horned Owl was perched beside him, and Strasheela and his friends could hear their conversation.

"...not in any way?" the Owl concluded a sentence that he had obviously already started.

"Not in any way," Urfin agreed. "She spoke to me this way and that, but I said just one thing over and over again: 'You'll get no help from me in this shady affair!'"

"Is that really what you said, Master?"

"That's what I said!"

"And what did she say?"

"She stamped her feet and yelled so loud that the cave shook, and I thought it was going to collapse on us. She screamed, 'I'm a mighty Sorceress!' Then she screamed, 'I'll crush you with one finger, like a fly, if you don't come into my service!'"

"And you said...?"

"I said once more, 'Crush away, but I'm not going to fight my own people. I've already done them enough dirt...'"

"And she said...?"

"She threatened me with a fist as big as my house!..."

Strasheela and his friends looked at one another in both bewilderment and joy. So this was the stand being taken by the same Urfin Jus who had twice seized power over Magic Land? Of course, the listeners had no way of knowing that in reporting about his conversation with Arachna, the former king was exaggerating the wicked fairy's threats — to put it simply, he was bragging a little — but, in the main, what he said was correct, and he was telling the truth! Had he given in to the Witch's blandishments, then he would now be sitting beside Arachna on the Flying Carpet. Instead, he was at home, growing cucumbers on his own distant farmstead...

The conversation between Urfin and the Owl turned now to other matters, but what Strasheela had heard was sufficient. Urfin was not their enemy, but their ally, and it was not impossible that he might even come to the people's aid if they called on him.

Strasheela turned off the Television. Now he and his Staff knew whom they would have to deal with. They felt no great fear. They had had to defend the Emerald City against hundreds of Urfin's Deadwood Oaks and a whole army of Marrans, and here, now, was only a single foe. True, she was enormous and very strong, but still, there was only one of her: Ruf Bilan was not even worth counting.

They had a whole day ahead of them before Arachna would be arriving, and the townspeople set about to prepare for defense. The City's military leaders already knew, thanks to the birds, that the Sorceress had ravaged an entire orchard, and this meant that she had an appetite. They would have to deprive her of any edibles!

All farms in the immediate area were evacuated. Some of the livestock were herded into the City, and the rest were concealed in backwoods in such a way that even the most skilled detective could not have located them. Once again, cauldrons of water, with brushwood burning beneath them, appeared atop the City walls. Archers, holding their bows and arbalests in readiness, concealed themselves behind the stone merlons, while Din Gior, with his beard thrown behind his back, set up catapults, with whose help they would be able to hurl huge stones.

Arachna approached the Emerald Island, not suspecting that those on duty were following her every move on the Magic Box. Even her conversations with Ruf Bilan came across loud and clear on the screen.

"We'll sneak up on them by night," said the Witch trustingly to her companion. "No one in the City knows anything about me, of course, and they'll all be peacefully sleeping. I'll climb over the City wall, make my way into the palace, and capture their monarch, that straw man whom popular talk praises to the skies — though heaven knows why! *Then* we'll see if his subjects will dare oppose me..."

Though Ruf Bilan doubted very much that the people in the Emerald City were unaware of the Enchantress's approach, he discreetly kept his doubts to himself. But Faramant, who was on duty before the Television, writhed with laughter as he pictured to himself the giantess Arachna trying to force her way in through the doors of the palace, thinking that only the usual people were on guard. "All right, braggart, all right," promised Faramant, threatening the screen with his fist, "we'll arrange a reception of honor for you, complete with torches."

By dallying as much as necessary, the wicked Fairy indeed reached the vicinity of the Emerald City that night. But to her utter amazement, she found it to be surrounded by a broad artificial lake; no bridge spanned it, and the ferry was on the opposite shore. This would prevent her from sneaking up to the City unnoticed.

"Why didn't you *tell* me your City was built on an island, you blockhead?" the Witch pounced maliciously on Bilan.

The traitor began to justify himself. "I swear by my life, mistress, it wasn't that way ten years ago! This lake was dug after I left the place."

"*Was* it, you clod?!" said Arachna with contempt. "Well, what of it? I don't think the water's very deep."

Arachna left the Carpet on the shore, with Ruf Bilan watching over it, and flopped into the lake. At first the water came up only to her knees, and then it reached her waist, and higher — it kept getting deeper and deeper... Now nothing was visible in the water except the giantess's shoulders, and her head with its enormous knot of black hair. At that moment, bonfires blazed up on top of the City walls, and bright lanterns began to burn. Hundreds of resinous torches began to glow in the hands of the townspeople, making the area around it as bright as day.

Din Gior and his assistants bustled about the catapults. They released the latches holding back the ropes of twisted ox sinews that took the place of springs. The ends of the long logs sprang at once into the air and began to hurl out enormous blocks of stone.

The water around the Witch began to seethe under the impact of the falling missiles. The giantess cast about this way and that, and then an enormous millstone hit her right on the top of her head. Her mop of hair softened the blow, and the Sorceress's skull was so thick that it was not easy to pierce. Even so, Arachna lost consciousness for a moment and disappeared into the depths of the lake.

The townspeople let out cries of joy, but the Witch quickly recovered and came back to the surface of the water. There was no longer any question now of Arachna stealing unnoticed into the City and grabbing Strasheela, and she took to her heels. She was pursued by arrows, which struck her unprotected neck and shoulders. It was as if this gigantic woman were being stung by a swarm of infuriated wasps.

Beside herself with pain and panic, the Enchantress managed somehow to scramble ashore, and she plopped herself down on the Carpet and commanded it in a slurring voice to betake itself away from this dreadful place. "Ar-r-rachna is a cr-r-reep!" is the last thing the wicked fairy heard as she flew away.

Thus did Kaggi-Karr bid her goodbye, while up on the city walls, the delighted townsmen lifted onto their shoulders Strasheela, Faramant, and Field Marshal Din Gior, who had gotten all tangled up in his luxuriant beard.

"I wish I had an army of such brave fighters," murmured Arachna, just barely conscious. "With them, I'd conquer the whole continent..."

Chapter 11

WHAT HAPPENED TO THE CARPET

The Carpet bore the Enchantress to the Land of the Underground Ore-Diggers, and she thought to herself: "In my first skirmish with the people, I was bruised on the forehead and chin; in the second, some sort of raging monster wounded me in the breast, and I was left barefoot; in the third, my head was almost cracked open, and I might have drowned... The further I go, the worse it gets. What lies ahead of me yet? Suppose death does await me, as that luckless king predicted? I certainly can't simply return to the cave and live out the centuries in peace as ruler over my loyal Gnomes, can I?... No, I must go all the way in seeking my destiny!..."

Thus did her stubbornness and rage drive Arachna on to new, perhaps even more perilous adventures.

After finding herself a suitable clearing in the forest, the Witch wrung out her soaked clothes, dried them over a fire, and tossed and turned all night on the hard ground. Ruf Bilan, though trembling with fear, was still by her side. He was no longer glad that he had allied himself with Arachna: it was clear that serving her would not earn him any wealth or rank. It would sooner, in fact, get him strung up on the gallows. But when Bilan tried to make a run for it at daybreak, Arachna awoke, and she squelched him in such a manner that his arms and legs were paralyzed. "If I observe you doing that one more time," screamed the Fairy, "it'll be death for you!"

At noontime, the town of the Underground Ore-Diggers appeared before them. Of course, the people living there already knew about Arachna's impending attack, and they had prepared a reception for their uninvited guest. The women, the children, and the old people had gone into hiding, while the men armed themselves with swords and daggers. For the giantess, these were no more dangerous than toothpicks, but the Ore-Diggers had other things in readiness as well.

The town was ringed by Sixpaws. Of course, these beasts barely came up to the Sorceress's knees, but if this savage herd of them attacked Arachna from all sides at once, she would get the worst of it from their mighty fangs and their sharp claws.

"Maybe I won't be *too* demanding," said the Fairy to Bilan, "and I'll content myself with just the title of Mistress of the Underground Ore-Diggers, without their even paying me any tribute." As one can see, her claims had grown considerably more modest after the defeats she had suffered.

The Flying Carpet, obeying its mistress's commands, described a circle over the village, and the Witch endeavored to make out what further means the Ore-Diggers had of fighting her. And while she was flying over a grove of palm trees, a scaly head the size of a small barrel suddenly emerged from within it, and it flicked open its tooth-filled mouth and seized the edge of the Carpet. This attack was so unexpected that the Carpet tilted sideways, and Arachna almost lost her balance. The terrified Ruf Bilan rolled down the Carpet, and he would have fallen off it to the ground if the Witch had not managed to grab him in her enormous hand.

The battle began. Arachna, bringing all her will-power to bear, commanded the Carpet to rise higher in the air, but Oyho the Dragon pulled it stubbornly in his own direction. And so great was the winged beast's strength that the Carpet began to descend. The Dragon's huge paw was already stretching out toward it, when all at once the fabric gave way, and a large piece of it tore off with a ripping sound. Oyho's head plunged back into the grove, prize and all, while the Carpet, swaying in an outlandish manner, bore its mistress skyward.

It is necessary to speak here of the fate of that piece of the Magic Carpet that thus fell to the Underground Ore-Diggers. It retained its lifting power in proportion to its size, and was able to carry one person through the air. The Ore-Diggers cleaned the Carpet, darned it, and sewed over the edges, and Rujero, the ruler of the land, began to use it for his official trips around his domain. And once he even flew on it to visit his friend Prem Cocus, ruler of Munchkin Land.

When the skirmish with Oyho was over, Arachna exclaimed in exasperation, "No, I've had enough! I see that Urfin Jus was right! People just don't want to give up their freedom... Back to the Cave, Carpet!"

But Ruf Bilan now spoke up: "Most gracious mistress, we still haven't visited the Munchkins. I'll guarantee with anything you please that they'll submit to you the minute you make an appearance in their country. They're the most timid and peaceable people in the world, and they're dreadfully afraid of weapons of any kind. Even the sight of a kitchen knife is enough to make them tremble. Let's fly to the Munchkins, mistress!"

"All right," the Witch conceded sullenly, "I'll listen to you this one last time. Carpet, take me to the Munchkins!"

Yes, the Munchkins were indeed a timid and peaceable people, and they would never have dared meet the mighty Enchantress in combat. But they had come up with another means of saving themselves from Arachna's onslaught.

Having long since been alerted, by the avian telegraph, to the imminent coming of the Witch, they had taken refuge in thickets and out-of-the-way places, which abounded in their country. A year before, while preparing for the attack by the Marrans, they had excavated roomy underground bunkers in the thick of the forests, and that is where they hid now, along with their families and their domestic animals.

When the Flying Carpet, which could now barely keep its balance and was constantly tilting sideways, brought Arachna to Blue Land, the Enchantress and her underling rummaged in vain through the gay, friendly little Munchkin villages. Everywhere they went, all was completely empty.

The Witch's rage knew no bounds. When she found a cat that had been left behind in one of the huts, she seized the unfortunate animal by the tail and whacked it so hard against a tree that there was nothing left of the cat. "That's what I should do with *you*, you confounded liar!" she hissed, glaring wickedly at Ruf Bilan, who was quite numb with fear. "'The people of Magic Land will gladly subordinate themselves to such a mighty monarch as you!'" she said, imitating the traitor's voice. "Where is all this joy, where is it, tell me! I didn't notice any of it!" Arachna tauntingly questioned the little man as he shook with terror.

The woods and fields, clothed in mist, slipped by slowly beneath them.

Part II

TROUBLED TIMES FOR MAGIC LAND

Chapter 12

THE YELLOW FOG

The damaged Flying Carpet somehow managed to get its mistress back to the cave. No sooner did she see the Gnomes who had run forward to meet her, than Arachna shouted out peremptorily: "Food! Roast me some oxen! On the double! And as many as possible!…"

Oxen were roasted over three fires, and then they vanished, one after the other, into the Giantess's huge maw. The Gnome chefs were already collapsing from weariness when the Witch finally settled back from her table. "Now to sleep…" she mumbled.

Before lying down, however, Arachna ordered the Gnomes to sew together a new pair of shoes for her. Castalyo the Chronicler was very curious to know how his mistress happened to be without shoes, but he did not dare question her about it.

It was Ruf Bilan who satisfied his curiosity. The garrulous traitor was unable to resist the temptation of blabbing to the Chronicler the whole story of Arachna's unfortunate adventures. Castalyo wrote Bilan's account down in the next volume of the Chronicle, and that is how these events have become known to us.

No sooner did the Enchantress reach her bed than she fell into a death-like sleep. She slumbered for three weeks straight, and the Gnomes were already beginning to feel hopeful that a centuries-long sleep had once again taken hold of her. But the little men did not dare disobey her command, so they cobbled a new pair of shoes for their mistress.

This was not an easy task for them! No fewer than a hundred ox-hides were needed to fill this order, and it was fortunate that such a quantity was on hand in the little people's storerooms. After measuring the sleeping Witch's feet, thirty cobblers set about their cutting and sewing, in the clear area before the cave, while ten apprentices prepared the waxed thread. The cobblers handled the soles of the shoes without much difficulty, but they had all the annoyance they could wish for with the sides and the tops: they had to stand ladders up against them.

In the course of fashioning these shoes, the cobblers used up 417 balls of waxed thread and broke 754 awls: the leather was very thick, and the work was awkward. But still and all, a colossal pair of shoes was standing there in the yard by the time Arachna awakened. The Witch put them on, and she was very happy with them — the craftsmen knew what they were doing.

"Now get me something to eat!" she commanded.

After satisfying her hunger, the Fairy stretched out in the sun and began to reflect on ways of getting back at the people.

"Suppose I conjure up a nice little earthquake for them?" Arachna pondered. "But I don't think that would work. I couldn't even make Marran Valley tremble the way it was supposed to, and doing a job on all of Magic Land would be quite beyond my powers. Maybe I could inflict a plague of locusts upon them? That spell worked pretty well for me before my long sleep. The locusts will consume the harvest in the field, the grass on the meadows, the fruit in the orchards... But what then? The farmers' livestock will die of hunger, and then *I* won't have anything to take away from them. No, that won't do!" Arachna herself was the first to admit that. "But what else do I have in store? Aha, a flood! That's how I'll sap them! I'll keep the rain coming down in a cloudburst for three weeks or so, and the rivers will overflow their banks. The people will have to take refuge on their roofs from the rising waters, and then they'll really howl!"

But after a moment of silence, the Witch continued: "They'll howl fit to be tied, but what good will that do *me*? They won't believe that I was the one who did it all, and they'll say, 'It's nature.' Just try to prove otherwise!"

Arachna lay there for a long time, lost in thought, and then all at once she jumped up, delighted. "I just remembered! The Yellow Fog! That's when they'll begin to dance to my tune, those dear friends of mine!... The Yellow Fog! I recall how my mother Carena broke the proud Taureks by visiting the Yellow Fog on their territory. They could take it for only two weeks, and then they came to her with their heads bowed. What's the benefit of the Yellow Fog?" Arachna continued to think it over. "I can call it up and get rid of it at any moment, so everyone will know that it's caused by my witchcraft... But most important of all, it's never occurred before in Magic Land, so it'll be something new and dreadful for man and beast alike."

The Witch went at once into her cave and, after driving the Gnomes out of it so that they would not observe what she did, she reached into a secret niche and drew out a book of incantations. Despite the passage of millennia, the book, which was written on parchment, was in a good state of preservation.

Arachna leafed through it, and she found the page she needed.

"Here it is!" she said as she consulted the book. "Let the following be kept in mind: my command is to be accomplished when I say the words 'one, two, three!' But remember this beforehand: the Yellow Fog must not penetrate to the domains of Villina and Stella. I don't want to get involved with those haughty dames, for I know them, and what kind of witchcraft they have in store and how they could use it to pay me back. Secondly: the Yellow Fog must not extend over the vicinity of my cave, nor above my fields and orchards, nor above the meadows where my flocks graze. And now, listen:

Uburru-kuruburru, tandarra-andabarra,
Faradon-garabadon, shabarra-sharabarra,

Yellow Fog, appear over Magic Land! *One, two, three!*"

No sooner had the last of these words flown out of the Witch's mouth, than all of Magic Land — with the exception of the territories of the three fairies: Villina, Stella, and Arachna — was immediately enveloped in a mysterious Yellow Fog. This fog was not very dense, and the sun was visible through it, but it resembled a large crimson ball, as it might appear at sunset, and one could gaze at it to his heart's content with no fear of being blinded.

So it would seem that the apparition of the Yellow Fog was not such a great disaster for Magic Land after all — but wait: as this story continues its truthful course, you'll be learning all about its harmful properties.

To begin with, the Magic Television in Strasheela's palace ceased to function. The monarch of the Emerald Island and his friends had been following Arachna's misadventures all the while. They saw how the resourceful Dragon had torn an entire corner off the Flying Carpet, and how the Carpet just barely flopped about through the air after that. They laughed as they watched Ruf Bilan rummaging through the villages vacated by the Munchkins, searching for edibles, and returning each time to his mistress with a glum face. The Witch's harsh treatment of the poor cat outraged Strasheela and his friends, while Arachna's monstrous feast made them laugh until their stomachs ached. "What an appetite!" exclaimed the faraway observers as they watched one ox after another being transferred from Arachna's dinner table to her boundless belly.

They observed with curiosity as the Gnomes fashioned Arachna's colossal shoes, and they were captivated by their skill and their industry. Strasheela and the others asked likewise to see what was happening in Marran Valley and among the Winkies. Everything there had been put back in order after the victory over the wicked Enchantress, and everyone was going about his business.

Then suddenly their daily surveillance came to an end: nothing was visible in the magic glass but a murky, swirling veil of mist. They had lost their means of monitoring their enemy's activities, and now there was no way of predicting what Arachna would undertake.

Chapter 13

ARACHNA'S AMBASSADOR

Visibility in the Yellow Fog was reduced in a strange way. Objects located within about fifty paces one could still just barely make out, but everything beyond that disappeared into a murky gloom, and that had a truly depressing effect. Each person's world thus shrank to insignificance. As for events occurring beyond the confines of this miniature world, people could only guess at them by their sounds — but the sounds themselves were distorted in the Fog. A human voice could be confused with the cawing of a crow, while the tap of horse's hooves was transformed into a beating of drums. People found everything that surrounded them strange and unnatural. But they supposed that the Yellow Fog was merely a natural phenomenon, not suspecting that it was one of the tricks of Arachna the Witch, and they hoped that the calamity would soon be over.

The residents of Magic Land did not learn straightaway that breathing the Yellow Fog was harmful. Then after a few days, when the people had become accustomed to the peculiar circumstances in spite of themselves, they suddenly began to experience intermittent bouts of coughing. As it turned out, the minute particles that made up the fog irritated the lungs when they penetrated into them, and this irritation increased with each passing day. The sounds of coughing were heard everywhere in Magic Land. Humans coughed, deer, elk, and bears coughed in the forests, squirrels coughed in the trees, birds coughed when they were at rest — and when they were in flight, their fits of coughing positively choked them.

On one of those calamitous days, a chubby, ruddy-faced individual approached the ferry that transported travelers to the Emerald City. He was in a splendid mood. With a smile, he asked the Deadwood Oak ferry men to take him across the lake. The latter set to work, in their usual manner. As they pulled the ferry forward along the cable, the traveler engaged them in conversation: "Well, brothers, how do you feel today, with the weather so nice?"

Chapter 13: ARACHNA'S AMBASSADOR

"What's that to us?" replied Arum the ferryman. "It's bad for the humans, but doesn't matter to us."

Indeed, the Deadwood Oaks were impassive to the Yellow Fog, since they didn't breathe. Of all the inhabitants of Magic Land, only the Deadwood Oaks and the wooden Couriers — in other words, those beings brought to life by Urfin Jus's miraculous Powder — felt normal. And, of course, the Yellow Fog did no harm to Strasheela or the Iron Woodman, since they likewise lacked lungs.

The ferry was moored to the City-side bank, and the traveler rang three times the bell over the gate. A little window opened, and out peered Faramant. The Guardian of the Gates did not leave his post, regardless of the circumstances!

"Ruf Bilan!" exclaimed Faramant in surprise as he recognized the visitor. "Why have you come to our City?" Faramant's talking was broken off by a choking fit of coughing.

"I have come here on very important business," replied Bilan calmly to the Guardian of the Gates, "and I request that you take me to his Excellency, the monarch of the Emerald Island."

"Very well, let's go," muttered Faramant. "I'll take you to Strasheela the Wise. But first of all, you'll have to put on some green spectacles."

"You mean you still wear green spectacles? Nothing is visible in this pea-soup anyway, whether you have them on or not."

"The law is the law, especially when it was established by the mighty Goodwin!" retorted Faramant sternly.

Overriding Bilan's objection, the Guardian of the Gates put a pair of green spectacles on him and fastened them from behind with a tiny lock. The range of visibility dropped at once to about three or four paces, and it seemed to Bilan that he had just plunged into the darkness of night. He almost had to grope his way along behind his escort, and he was able to maintain his sense of direction only because he had been born and brought up in the Emerald City.

"How should I announce you to Strasheela the Wise?" Faramant asked ungraciously when they had reached the Palace.

Ruf Bilan, his hands on his hips, replied, "I am the ambassador of her Grace, the mighty Enchantress Arachna!"

"Ah, the same individual whose head we pasted a rock to!" Faramant elaborated scornfully.

"Don't worry, you're paying a heavy price for that rock," replied Ruf Bilan.

These words were meaningless to the Guardian of the Gates, but he said nothing in reply, and he went straight in with his announcement. Strasheela received the messenger at once. His Staff, as usual, was assembled in the hall: Din Gior the Long-Bearded Soldier, Faramant the Guardian of the Gates, and Kaggi-Karr the Crow. The now-useless Television was sitting there on a night table.

"With what announcement do you come to us?" asked Strasheela.

"With a very important one," replied the envoy impudently. "Let it be known to you that the Yellow Fog, which I see is making all of you miserable, has been unleashed over Magic Land by my ruler, Arachna, for the purpose of compelling its peoples to submit to her."

Bilan's announcement was met with disbelief. "What proof do you have of this?" Din Gior asked him, coughing all the while.

"Proof? If I give you my word of honor, you'll believe me, won't you?"

The Staff members burst into laughter, mixed with coughing. "Word of honor from a traitor?" exclaimed Faramant. "I swear by the throne of the Mighty Goodwin, this is the most insolent announcement I've ever heard!"

Chapter 13: ARACHNA'S AMBASSADOR

"I knew you'd say that," said Bilan, taking no offense. "But observe my healthy appearance, and note the fact that I'm not coughing. How do you explain that?"

"Most likely you're sitting it out in some shelter where the Yellow Fog can't penetrate," suggested Din Gior as he lovingly smoothed out his beard — an occupation that he would not relinquish even under these trying circumstances.

"This time you've guessed right," said Bilan in agreement. "Only this 'shelter' is large in extent: it's the whole territory of the Fairy Arachna, which is totally free of the fog."

The Staff members, who still did not believe him, remained silent. The envoy remarked condescendingly: "I can understand it if you find even this evidence doubtful. Well, I have something ready that's more weighty, and absolutely convincing." Then he asked, "It appears to me that it is now a few minutes before noon?"

"The sundials aren't working, since the sun doesn't cast any shadow," answered Faramant. "But you're correct — it really will be noon shortly."

"Well and good, your Excellency, and all of you, my lords, who are assembled here." Ruf Bilan said this with an air of triumph. "At exactly twelve noon, the Fairy Arachna will remove the Yellow Fog, and once again you'll see the bright sunlight and the blue sky. This will last exactly five minutes. That will be enough to prove my case, and then I will dictate to you the conditions under which Arachna will rid you of the Yellow Fog for good."

The minutes of tedious waiting ticked slowly by. Then all at once... A blinding light illuminated the Throne Room, and since the people were no longer used to it, it seemed so bright that Din Gior and Kaggi-Karr were forced to squint. Only Strasheela's painted-on eyes were able to tolerate such a sudden

93

change of luminosity without hurt, while Faramant and Ruf Bilan, for their part, were wearing green spectacles.

Everything around them seemed magically transformed. The uncounted emeralds sparkled on the walls and the ceiling and on the back of the throne, and now it was truly difficult to endure this uncommon splendor without green spectacles.

The Staff members had not even had time to get over their surprise, when Strasheela, who had maintained his composure, hurried over to the Television, at the same time making a sign to Faramant. The Guardian of the Gates understood it, and he quickly escorted the envoy to the door: there was no way that they were going to divulge the secret of the Magic Box to the enemy!

Strasheela, after wiping off the misted-over glass of the Television, quickly pronounced the secret words and asked the Box to show him the Enchantress Arachna. And see her he did!

The Witch was standing at the entrance to her cave, with her Magic Book in her hands: it was evident that she had just pronounced the incantation that removed the Fog. She wore a look of triumph, with the Gnomes swarming about her feet, and with the Flying Carpet drying out nearby on the yard.

No, there could no longer be any doubt: the Yellow Fog was indeed the handiwork of the Fairy Arachna. It struck all those present in the room like an unexpected thunderbolt. Then the Witch's voice was heard over the screen: "Castalyo, take a look at the sundial. Have the five minutes passed?"

"The interval has gone by, mistress," was the answer.

Then suddenly, it was as if a dark shroud rose before the eyes of Strasheela, Din Gior, and the others. This had such a depressing effect on them that they were hard put to hold back their cries of sorrow.

Chapter 13: ARACHNA'S AMBASSADOR

"You see now how great my mistress's power is," said Ruf Bilan with self-satisfaction, after being led back into the room. "She can even control the sunlight. I won't bother telling you that the Yellow Fog is lethal, for I must assume that you've already observed that fact for yourselves. A choice is now open to you: either acknowledge yourselves slaves to the mighty Arachna and pay her the tribute that she will deign to impose upon you, or else wither away slowly in the poisonous air until death overtakes you."

Strasheela and his Staff members maintained a gloomy silence. What could they possibly say now? It is a terrible thing to die, but a life of slavery is no easier. The straw man, of course, faced no threat of death by suffocation, but what was he to do when none of his subjects was left except the Deadwood Oaks? No, if that were to happen, he'd find himself a speedy death by fire.

Ruf Bilan began to speak once more. "Mistress Arachna does not require an immediate answer. She is giving you three days to think it over. At the end of that time, you will have to make your decision and report it to me."

Faramant led Ruf Bilan back to the City gate and removed the green spectacles from him. Everything was light again before the ambassador's eyes, and he smiled condescendingly. "What strange people, foisting such a burden upon themselves!"

After crossing the lake, Bilan walked to a nearby grove and began to wait until Arachna flew there to pick him up. The Flying Carpet had been trimmed and sewn in such a way that it once again had its proper rectangular shape. Its area was smaller, but on the other hand, it no longer swayed in the air, and it no longer lost its balance.

Chapter 14

A DISCOVERY BY
DOCTORS BORIL AND ROBIL

The deadline that the Witch Arachna had given to think things over soon passed. Three days had gone by, and Ruf Bilan was due to appear at noontime for the response.

The Yellow Fog hung over the land as before, and fits of coughing, growing more and more severe, afflicted man, beast, and bird. Strasheela's palace was the scene of uninterrupted meetings, which anyone who wished could attend. Among those who took part in the conferences were Prem Cocus and Rujero. A few days after the onset of the Yellow Fog, Rujero, deeply worried, seated himself on the small Flying Carpet and ordered it to fly to the residence of Prem Cocus, ruler of the Munchkins. It was a good thing that the Magic Carpet could find its own way to its designated goal, even in pitch-dark night, because otherwise, Rujero would definitely have strayed from the route in the yellow gloom that covered everything all around him.

After deliberating, the two rulers decided to go and meet with Strasheela the Wise, who was the wisest person in all Magic Land, having received his brains from no less a one than Goodwin the Great and Terrible. The Carpet was not intended for two people, but, though straining itself considerably, it did convey Rujero and Cocus to the Emerald City. They joined all the others in racking their brains to find a way out of this tragic position that Arachna had put them in.

Should they give in to her? And become her slaves through all the cycle of generations? Or should they respond with a proud refusal and thereby condemn the entire nation, in particular the innocent children, who were finding it hardest of all to exist in the poisonous air?

Faramant proposed that they pretend to agree to the Witch's demands and thereby gain a temporary respite, then afterwards seek some means of fighting Arachna. But others felt that the wicked Fairy would not be so easily fooled. She would insist on hostages, and if the people rose in rebellion, then the hostages would perish.

Just as the debate was at its most heated, the door to the Throne Room unexpectedly flew open, and in ran Doctors Boril and Robil. Readers probably remember chubby, jocular Boril and gaunt, lanky Robil, two doctors from the land of the Underground Ore-Diggers. These friendly rivals were continually squabbling, continually making fun of one another, but they could not pass a day without getting together.

Boril and Robil looked strange. Cotton was sticking out of their noses, and their mouths were covered with large leaves held on by pieces of cord. The doctors were rapidly and excitedly mumbling something, but it could not be made out because the leaves prevented them from speaking. Then Boril angrily jerked the cords and removed the leaf from his mouth. "A discovery! A great discovery!" he began to cry out. "We've found..."

"A means of combating the Yellow Fog!" interjected Robil, who had likewise divested himself of his leaf: he could not bear the idea that his friend alone should tell the whole story.

The doctors, in great agitation and constantly interrupting one another, told the following. After the Ore-Diggers and their families had gone back down into Underground Land to escape the Yellow Fog (since Arachna's witchcraft did not extend into the Cavern), and taken the Munchkins down with them as well, Boril and Robil alone had remained behind in the village. This was a real act of heroism on their part, because they were coughing no less than any of the others. But the two doctors thought nothing of undergoing a prolonged exposure to the poisoned air: they were seeking a means of counteracting it.

At first, they observed that if a person breathed through gauze soaked in water, the Yellow Fog would have a less devastating effect on the lungs, and the coughing would be eased. A fine plan, no doubt about it — but where would they be able to obtain enough gauze to equip the entire population of Magic Land, from the youngest to the oldest? Besides, they had to think of the animals and the birds. The doctors decided that Nature would have to provide the help.

"In our forests," thought Robil and Boril, "there must surely be trees whose leaves are porous enough to let fresh air through, yet hold back the harmful particles of fog?"

They made the rounds of forests and woods for dozens of miles around, checking out hundreds of species of trees. Any flat, leathery leaves they discarded at once without even trying them out — it was plain that they would hold back not only the fog, but the air itself.

On the other hand, if the leaves had little tiny holes — pores — the doctors examined them and tested them with particular care. Their patience was finally rewarded. The leaves of the *rafaloo* tree were all that could possibly be desired. Their pores held back the poisonous droplets, but the clean air came through freely. And rafaloo leaves were sturdy enough to be attached with cords. Of course, it would be necessary from time to time to wipe the leaves clear of the droplets of fog that had accumulated on them, but that would not call for much effort.

When they were absolutely certain of the extraordinary value of their discovery, the delirious Robil and Boril raced to the Emerald City. "We've been breathing through rafaloo leaves during our whole trip," reported the doctors, both talking at once, "and our coughing is almost gone."

This announcement was received with delighted applause.

"We must fit up an expedition at once to Blue Land to collect rafaloo leaves," ordered Strasheela.

"Don't worry about that, your Excellency," replied Boril. "In our village there were five Deadwood Oaks at work on the construction of a dam, and in accordance with our dictate, they've brought ten huge sacks of the precious leaves here. That's enough for the whole country!"

The monarch of the Emerald Island walked over to a wall cabinet, opened it, and took out two medals. He silently pinned them to the tunics of the doctors, who blushed with happiness.

"A temporary in-firm-ar-y will now be opened in this hall," said Strasheela. Then he ordered Faramant, "Assemble at once all the City's doctors, nurses, medics, and orderlies. And you, gentlemen, dem-on-strate to them the use of the rafaloo leaves, and they'll instruct the people."

"In-firm-ar-y... Dem-on-strate..." whispered the Crow in a tone of deep respect. "What difficult words! And to think I was the one who first advised Strasheela to procure brains! I can't believe my ears..." Strasheela overheard Kaggi-Karr's words of praise; his head began to swell with pride, and the needles and pins stuck right out.

It was at that moment that Ruf Bilan walked into the room. Faramant's assistant, who was on duty at the gate, had let Bilan into the City without the green spectacles. As he observed the lively activity in the hall, Arachna's ambassador said: "Judging by your happy faces, my lords, I assume that I will be taking a favorable answer back to the Fairy Arachna. You have evidently decided to submit to her?"

Strasheela took his time walking over to the throne, and he sat down pompously on it and pronounced the following words in a stern voice: "Our happy faces indi-cate that we scorn your mistress's threats and cat-e-gor-ic-al-ly reject her authority. I'll have you know, you trai-tor, that we've found…" Strasheela looked now at Rujero, who raised his finger to his mouth as a gesture of cau-tion, and he cleverly equivocated. "We've found a way more befitting our dignity to answer her audacious claims with a refusal! And that is what you can take back to your mistress!"

Ruf Bilan left the palace in a state of bewilderment, and Rujero said to the Monarch: "You almost divulged to the enemy our most important military secret!"

"Yes, I admit it, I almost slipped up because of a fit of temper. Who knows *what* steps the Witch would have taken if I'd blurted out our secret to Ruf Bilan? But as long as the subject is on this traitor, tell me, esteemed Rujero, why didn't your Ore-Diggers re-educate Bilan after he awakened?"

Rujero replied: "From a message sent by the person in charge of the Cavern, I know how the matter turned out. When Ruf Bilan awoke, his re-education followed the usual course. But they were only two days into it, and then Bilan disappeared. In the house where he was living, they found some half-eaten candy from the up-per world, and alongside his footprints in the road, they saw prints of someone's tiny feet…"

"Now it's clear," said Strasheela. "Arachna's emis-saries took him away with them, and the Witch re-edu-cated him her own way. It's a great pity that it had to happen like that, but there's nothing to be done about it now…"

By now, the medical personnel who had been sum-moned to the palace began to assemble in the room: doctors, nurses, and orderlies. The Deadwood Oaks brought in sacks of rafaloo leaves and whole arm loads of cords. Doctors Boril and Robil showed the medics on what side to place the leaves over the mouth, how to attach the cords to them…

While the hustle and bustle of business was going on in the hall, Strasheela beckoned to the Crow. "What do you think, Kaggi-Karr? Do rafaloo trees grow in the vicinity of the Emerald Island?"

"Why do you ask that?"

"As you can see, the doctors have brought many leaves, but there are only enough for the humans. We've also got to take care of the animals and the birds. For that reason, the expedition that I mentioned before should still be made up. But Blue Land is too far away from here. Perhaps rafaloos may be growing somewhere a little closer?"

The Crow lost herself in thought. "Unless my memory serves me wrong, I've feasted on rafaloo fruit in the Saber-Toothed Tiger forest, and that's closer to the Emerald Island by half."

"Then I hereby request that you take charge of it and send the Deadwood Oaks there, and have them take along as many sacks as possible."

The audience in the hall began to thin out as the doctors, nurses, and orderlies left the palace, carrying with them all the essential material for protecting the people from the poisonous fog. Strasheela, in whose head such wise ideas were born, began a conversation with Boril. "Esteemed doctor, we'll be shielding thousands and thousands of people from illness, but what do you say about the animals and birds? Can we really leave them to their fate?"

"Under no circumstances, your Excellency!" replied Boril ardently. "But with them, the problem is very complicated. It'll be necessary to attach leaves to their nostrils. And I doubt if cords will be very helpful…"

"Well, suppose we glue them on?" asked Strasheela uncertainly.

The doctor was electrified. "Your Excellency, you've given me a marvelous idea! That's just what we'll do, we'll glue them on! We'll glue small pieces of leaf over the nostrils of the animals and the birds, and in this connection, I'm telling you, the matter will even be much easier with the birds! Yes, I'll try it out at once! Miss Kaggi-Karr, could you come over here for a minute?"

The Crow, who had still not been able to leave the hall, flew over to the doctor. The latter took a rafaloo leaf and skillfully cut two small round pieces from it with a pair of scissors, and then he took a little bottle of glue from his medical kit, rubbed it on the edges of the circles, and deftly stuck them over the bird's nostrils. Kaggi-Karr couldn't get over the way her beak was adorned on each side by the two green filters, which would now hold back the lethal fog particles. "Well, my friend," said Boril with a smile, "do you like it? In my opinion, those two little pieces of leaf become you. Have a look in the mirror."

Everyone who was present was delighted with the doctor's skill. Kaggi-Karr, for her part, already found herself able to breathe more easily, and she thanked Boril very warmly.

* * *

Several infirmaries opened in the City, where the doctors and nurses would equip the populace with the rafaloo filters, and the first to receive care were the children and the old people. Of course, they would have to remove these filters for eating and drinking, and when carrying on a conversation. But eating and drinking occupied a small portion of the people's time, and the doctors advised them to do as little talking as possible.

This did not suit certain garrulous gossip-mongers, but they made the best of it, like it or not. However, the health of the residents began to improve, and they praised the resourceful doctors Boril and Robil to the skies.

In accordance with Strasheela's command, sacks of rafaloo leaves were sent out to the Winkies and to Marran Valley.

Strasheela did not forget about Urfin Jus either. It was essential that they show their appreciation for the selflessness that he had displayed and save him from death. Urfin, of course, would perish in his solitude, since he knew no way of combating the dreadful fog. So the wooden courier Rellem, who was utterly tireless and had no fear of the poison, ran day and night toward the World-Encompassing Mountains with a sack containing a small packet of rafaloo leaves, with instructions on how to use them, and a small bottle of glue for the Great Horned Owl.

In connection with this, Faramant had written the joiner a letter, at Strasheela's request, inviting him to come to the Emerald City.

> *One can't fight disaster all alone, —* the Guardian of the Gates had written. *— Here, among other people, you'll find help and support. As far as your offenses against the inhabitants of Magic Land are concerned, they've been forgiven and forgotten. We know how nobly you behaved during your meeting with Arachna, we know that you did not go into her service... You may ask how we found out about it. But that's a military secret...*

The first to return were the Deadwood Oaks that had been sent out to Violet Land. The Iron Woodman conveyed his heartfelt thanks for the invaluable antidote against coughing, which had been put into effect at once. Of course, he had no need of this antidote himself, but his iron limbs rusted with amazing speed from the poisonous droplets of Yellow Fog. To prevent his joints from squeaking and to keep his jaws moving, he found it necessary to oil himself twice every day, in the morning and in the evening.

A few days later, the second party of Deadwood Oaks reported back, the ones who had visited Marran Land. They brought a most curious piece of news. The valley was found to be deserted: not a person, not an animal, not a bird was in evidence! At first, the wooden men assumed that the population of the valley had died out. But if that were the case, then where were the bodies? Commander-in-Chief Giton had not been too lazy to move a few miles further to the northeast — and then, emerging from the Fog, he found himself under a warm sun and a clear sky: he had reached the domain of Stella, where the was no Yellow Fog. Giton discovered the entire Leaper tribe there in Rose Land. They had sought refuge with Stella, and the good Fairy had hospitably admitted them, along with their modest belongings and their livestock. (The wild animals and birds, of course, needed no permission to enter!) Many of the Marrans were put up in the houses of the Quadlings (for such were Stella's subjects called), and those for whom there was not enough room set themselves up in huts and tents.

The Marran leaders likewise sent Strasheela their greetings and their heartfelt thanks. They held on to the rafaloo leaves and the instructions for their use, just in case: the wicked Arachna might get around to them yet!

In due time, the nimble Rellem ran back with a letter from Urfin Jus. The deposed monarch was very happy that the people had forgiven his past wickedness, and he hoped sooner or later to show his appreciation for the generosity that they had displayed. He made a very witty joke about the "military secret" that Faramant had written about. Of course, it was Stella's Magic Box, which a boy from the Outer World had once used to bop him on the head — but that secret could remain a secret.

In connection with the hospitality that they had offered him, Urfin admitted that he would still find it hard to look the same people in the eye whom he had formerly so oppressed and persecuted. Let the time pass, and everything would settle down, wrote Urfin.

But he had come up with his own means of combating the Yellow Fog. He had in his garden a small shed with thick walls. He sealed up every crack, covered the door with rabbit skins, and used a method of his own devising to expel the fog that filled the interior space. In an iron brazier, he kindled a small fire of wooden chips and dried grass, striving for as much smoke as possible. The smoke particles, as they settled, attracted the droplets of fog to them. [At this point, the fire was extinguished,] and thus the air inside the structure was cleansed. Then Urfin and Guamoko spent their time there inside the shed, as in a besieged fortress, leaving it only for the shortest intervals. Urfin Jus shyly expressed his hope that the method he had found to combat the Yellow Fog might be of some little help to the residents of the Emerald City and other lands.

When Faramant had read Urfin's letter to the Staff members, Strasheela went into raptures. "I always said that Jus had an unusually good head on his shoulders," exclaimed the monarch of the Emerald City. "The trouble was that before, he was directing it toward evil purposes, but just look at what a clever scheme he's come up with now! With that alone, he's done much to pay for the misfortunes he inflicted on us. And I'm not even mentioning the enormous service he rendered the country by not giving in to Arachna's invitation. If that bold, inventive man had joined forces with the Witch, the two of them together would have saddled us with misfortunes beyond count. Urfin is a far cry from that dull-witted coward, Ruf Bilan!…"

That very day, all the rooms of the palace were purified of the fog, using Urfin Jus's method, and that method was promoted among the masses. But from time to time, the fog did seep back into rooms through chinks that no one had noticed. And, of course, the primary means of fighting the Yellow Fog remained rafaloo leaves: all the inhabitants of the Emerald City and the surrounding areas now wore them.

Overriding Faramant's desperate opposition, Strasheela issued a decree allowing the townspeople to remove their green spectacles. The City's residents accepted this with delight: now they could see about fifty paces all around them, and that in itself was a relief. Only the Guardian of the Gates kept his spectacles on, and as he roamed through the streets, he bumped into passersby. The day was like an impenetrable night to him, yet the stubborn Faramant still did not want to breach Goodwin's mandate.

Hundreds of infirmaries opened up in the woods and fields of Emerald Land for the animals and the birds. Rabbits, pumas, wolves, foxes, bears, squirrels — all of them formed into long lines before the nurses... The usual chirping and melodious singing was no longer to be heard among the rows of birds. Crows, nightingales, swallows, jackdaws, and robins glumly stuck their beaks into the ground, as it were.

An inviolable truce was observed among all the species of animals in the lines. If some predator attempted to harass another that was weaker, he would receive a severe reprimand and a mark on his brow in indelible paint: from then on, he would not be received at any of the infirmaries. Threat of such a punishment had an excellent effect, and the most savage predators became as gentle as sheep.

Position in line was also observed with great strictness. If any tousled sparrow or sly, gossipy fox attempted to slip in ahead of the others in line, the smart-alecks were driven away in disgrace.

When the animals and birds had their green filters affixed to their nostrils, they lay or stood motionless in some secluded corner for about two hours, to give the glue a chance to dry. The health of the four-footed and winged patients began to improve at once.

Chapter 15

A NEW AFFLICTION

When Ruf Bilan returned after his second embassy to the Emerald City, he reported to the Witch his lack of success. "The peoples of Magic Land cat-e-gor-ic-al-ly refuse to recognize your power, mistress!" said Bilan.

"Ca-re-... Ca-te-ri-... What does that mean?"

"I'm sure I don't know, my monarch. Strasheela the Wise loves those long words very much. It apparently means: under no circumstances."

"He would say it like that! In my day, people didn't use such learned words."

It was the all-knowing Gnomes who learned about and reported to Arachna the methods the people had come up with to fight the Yellow Fog. They even brought her samples of rafaloo leaves. (The Gnomes made use of them themselves when they penetrated into the poisonous air zone.)

"Rafaloo leaves... Hmmm!..." The Fairy thought it over for a long time. "Suppose I were to order you to pick all the leaves from all the rafaloo trees? Then the people would have nowhere to obtain replacements for those that wear out and no longer do the job."

"What are you saying, esteemed mistress?!" exclaimed Castalyo. "There are thousands of rafaloo trees in Magic Land, and millions of leaves on them. How could we ever handle such an impossible task?!"

"Yes, too bad, too bad... Well, no matter! The Yellow Fog will prove itself yet!"

And prove itself it did. Not long after the people had come to cope, and just barely, with the coughing, it became evident that the Yellow Fog had a harmful effect on the eyesight. The eyes became inflamed, and it was difficult to get the eyelids unstuck in the morning without soaking them with water. People had found it hard enough to see through the fog before, but now their field of view became even more restricted. A continuous gloom began at a distance of fifteen or twenty paces, and that was downright dreadful.

Strasheela turned to Boril and Robil for help. The doctors had not gone back to Underground Land, but had remained in residence in the Emerald City and continued their scientific researches.

"We have a means of combating the eye inflammation," said Boril. "We'll put special drops in the patient's eyes... *But*...!" Here the chubby doctor raised his finger. "But this will help only if the cause of the illness has been eliminated. For how can the drops cure it if the poisonous fog is continuing to act on their eyes?"

Robil jumped into the conversation now. "Spectacles!" he said with an air of importance. "They'll have to wear spectacles that fit closely against the skin. The particles of fog won't be able to reach the cornea, and we'll be able to treat the eye inflammation with the drops."

Boril ran over to embrace his companion enthusiastically. "My colleague, you're a genius!" cried Boril. "You're an absolute, one-of-a-kind genius! And your suggestion will be easy to implement: in our village we've saved several thousand pairs of those glasses that we stopped wearing about four years ago when we no longer needed them."

"But they're dark glasses," objected Strasheela. "The eyes may be protected, but people won't be able to see anything."

"No problem!" explained Robil. "They're made of ordinary glass and covered over with dark paint. We'll simply wash it off."

Without uttering a word, Strasheela took two more medals out of the cabinet and pinned them to the doctors' chests.

Within an hour, all the wooden couriers that could be found in the City were scurrying toward the Ore-Diggers' village, carrying bags and baskets with them. Their Corporal obtained the key to the place where the spectacles were stored, and he gave them the order to pack them in with the greatest care.

It was decided they would also make use of the green spectacles of Faramant, who immediately swelled up with pride and stuck his nose high into the air. "I told you so! I told you so!" he kept repeating. "Oh, what a great wise man Goodwin was! He foresaw everything, even the Yellow Fog!"

But utilizing the green spectacles meant that a great deal of work would have to be done on them: leather eye-shields would have to be attached. Every cobbler in the City was called into service for this.

Town criers made their rounds of the City, proclaiming the Monarch's decree:

> *The Yellow Fog has caused an af-flic-tion of deadly ep-i-dem-ic proportions: inflammation of the eyes. In the function of pro-phy-lact-ic measures* ("What on earth is that?" the townspeople asked one another), *all residents of the City and outlying areas are advised as follows:*
>
> *§1. Whoever has spectacles with eye-shields is to wear them and not to take them off.*
>
> *§2. Those who are at home are to bind their eyes with linen or gauze bandages, and to wet them as often as possible with cold water.*
>
> *§3. The eyes must be kept open as little as possible.*

§4. As of tomorrow, clinics will be open at which those suffering from eye inflammation may receive drops for them.

§5. All apothecaries are to set to work at once to produce eye-drops in the largest possible quantity.

§6. Production is to begin on spectacles with eye-shields that will not let the lethal fog in; the deadline for their distribution to the people will be announced later.

§7. The Triply-Wise Strasheela, Monarch of Emerald Land, hopes for con-sum-mate dis-ci-pline on the part of the people and total ad-her-ence to his orders.

"What a lot of big words!" the townspeople whispered with admiration when they heard the heralds. "What wonderful, long, hard-to-understand words! No, we can't lose with a monarch like him — he'll get us out of our difficulties!"

Chapter 16

STRASHEELA'S MOMENTOUS DECISION

With the aid of the prophylactic and curative measures undertaken by Strasheela and his staff, of which the twice-decorated Doctors Boril and Robil were now members, the people were more or less able to cope with the eye inflammation. The animals and birds, however, felt miserable. Men could protect the creatures' lungs from the poisonous fog by attaching rafaloo leaves to their faces. But spectacles for all of them would be downright impossible to lay in — the more so since it would be necessary to fashion the spectacles in every conceivable shape and size.

The one piece of advice that they would be able to follow was transmitted to all the animals and birds via the avian network: simply to keep their eyes open as little as possible. So life in the fields and the forests virtually died out. The herbivorous animals were still not too badly off: they could nibble on grass even with their eyes tightly closed. But the predators, who could not get along without true, sharp vision for pursuing their prey, were soon staggering, so emaciated were they. Insect-eating birds — flycatchers, swifts, goldfinches, cuckoos — sat on the branches, bristling up glumly, and only the indefatigable woodpeckers, holding their eyes shut, gouged the bark of the trees, livening up the forest with their noisy drumming.

And during these days of hardship for the land, other alarming phenomena soon began to be observed, though at first only the most perceptive people paid any attention to them. The Yellow Fog had been blanketing Magic Land for over three weeks. It has already been mentioned that the sun in the sky looked like a dull crimson ball, and that its rays had lost their strength. Since they were barely able to penetrate the fog, they could not provide the same amount of warmth as before, and this became more and more evident with each passing day. The ears of wheat did not develop properly in the fields, and they withered away. The fruit in the orchards were no longer succulent, and they hung from the branches all withered and scraggly...

The country was facing a crop failure such as no one had ever seen before throughout the millennia. Of course, the people could survive a single crop failure by relying on the surpluses that they had accumulated, but what about the animals and birds? And this crop failure would not be followed by another spring. Magic Land was headed for disaster. The wicked Arachna was dealing it a mortal blow.

* * *

Some honored guests from Violet Land had arrived in the Emerald City: these were the Iron Woodman, who was oiling his jaws and his joints unceasingly with a golden oil-can, and Lestar the mechanic and his assistants. A detachment of Deadwood Oaks carried a few armloads of bamboo pipes that the Winkies had fashioned. Lestar had once heard from the one-legged Sailor, Charlie Black, about how steam heat worked, and he had now decided to equip Strasheela's palace for the forthcoming cold spell.

Lestar reported that production of spectacles with eye-shields was under way in Violet Land as well. This had been done after Strasheela sent a special courier with three pairs of glasses as samples. Work on them was in full swing, being carried out by skilled craftsmen, who abounded so among the Winkies. Lestar reported also that the air in the Violet Castle and in the Winkies' dwellings was being purified every day using Urfin Jus's method: it was a great help in the fight against the Yellow Fog. Strasheela and his staff were very happy to hear this news.

A few days later, the Courageous Lion arrived, limping after his long journey. Coughing uncontrollably and holding his inflamed eyes shut, he told them that he had successfully moved his family and his subjects to Rose Land, under the protection of the kindly Stella. He had resolved to set out for the Emerald City himself, to verify the vague rumors that had reached him about the troubles afflicting Magic Land, the result of intrigues by a wicked sorceress.

Doctors Robil and Boril undertook their treatment of the King of Beasts at once. The Lion felt much better after they had insufflated his lungs and put drops in his eyes several times. But his bandaged paws, the green filters over his nostrils, and the enormous glasses that he wore had caused him to lose his kingly appearance, and this made Strasheela laugh.

When the doctors were through with all their procedures and let the Lion be, the latter said: "We had a snowfall. That's what Fregosa the Cook calls it, and she heard about it from Ellie when the girl told her about Kansas."

"Snow? What's *that?*" asked Faramant. (This question was hardly surprising: an unending summer had prevailed in Magic Land for the last few thousand years.)

The Lion explained: "Snow is soft white flakes that float down from the sky. They resemble fluff from a poplar tree, but they're cold. However, they melt when they fall on an animal's fur or on the ground, and turn into little drops of water…"

The Crow jumped into the conversation. "I saw a great deal of snow," she said, "when I flew over the World-Encompassing Mountains looking for a path for Ellie and the Giant from Beyond the Mountains. It really is white, but it's not quite so soft as the Lion says. Snow lies on the mountain slopes, and it's so hard that a person can walk on it without making it collapse."

Everyone turned toward the window without even thinking, to look at the gleaming snowy peaks that were clearly visible from the City during cloudless weather; but alas! — everything was hidden by the turbid gloom.

Kaggi-Karr continued: "Ellie also told me that where she lives in the Outer World, there comes a time once a year when a lot of snow falls down from the sky and the weather turns cold. People say, 'It's winter.' When it's winter, the cold makes the water turn hard, and they call it 'ice.' But the people easily live through the winter, because they have warm dwellings and warm clothes."

Strasheela gave a sudden start and, putting his finger to his forehead, he began to mumble: "Clothes... dwellings..." Everyone looked at the Monarch in amazement, and he said, after ordering everyone to be silent: "I'm going to do some thinking!"

Strasheela's head swelled up to monstrous proportions, and *rusted* needles and pins stuck out from it — as one can see, the lethal fog had had its effect on them as well. Taking advantage of this convenient circumstance, the Woodman oiled them.

Strasheela's pondering continued for a long time, and no one dared interrupt it. Then the Monarch declared solemnly: "We must summon Annie and Tim here!" Then he began to develop his idea in detail. "The people from beyond the mountains have brought much benefit to Magic Land. Who built the Emerald City? Goodwin did. It's true that he turned out not to be a wizard at all, yet in spite of that, we and the Woodman and the Lion are all indebted to him for our present high positions. And Ellie? How much good she conferred upon us! She did away with the two wicked witches, Gingema and Bastinda, and she and her uncle, the Giant from Beyond the Mountains, helped us defeat Urfin Jus's Wooden Soldiers. Ellie brought the Underground Ore-Diggers up from out of their Cavern and freed them from the domination of their cruel kings. No need even to say anything more about Ellie, because we all know about her great deeds. It's better that I remind you about how Annie and Tim secured peace for us with the warlike Marrans and ended the sly Urfin's power once and for all..."

Strasheela caught his breath after his long speech and concluded in a tired voice: "That is why I repeat, I emphasize, and sum-ma-rize: only Annie and Tim can save Magic Land. They'll teach us to build warm houses and sew winter clothing. And maybe... I say, maybe, they'll even be able to defeat the wicked Arachna."

Thunderous shouts of approval drowned out the Monarch's final words. All the members of the Supreme

Council were so convinced of the might of the people from beyond the mountains, that it seemed to them that all the danger had already passed. All that remained was to think of a way to get the news to Annie and Tim, and how to convey them to Magic Land.

The problem was a serious one, and everyone gave it their deepest consideration. After a long period of silence, Rujero spoke up. "My friends," he said, "there's only one way for us out of our dilemma. We must send Oyho the Dragon to fetch the kids. He's already taken Ellie and Fred to Kansas, so he knows the way, and we can rely completely on his loyalty and his quick-wittedness."

It was difficult to offer any objection to such a practical suggestion, and everyone voted "yes" and then got right down to working out the details. Which would be better: sending a letter, or sending a messenger?

A letter would not take long to write, but there was no way of relating in it everything that was necessary to cover, and besides, words on a sheet of paper are far less convincing than direct speech. Strasheela looked at Kaggi-Karr. She understood what his look meant, and shook her head.

"My friend, I'd be very happy to set out for there, but you've forgotten that once I'm past the borders of Magic Land, I lose my power of human speech. What good is a messenger that can't talk? We'll have to send a person."

Two candidates were nominated for this: Faramant and Lestar. Annie knew both of these candidates, and the two of them were able and eager to talk. But the mechanic's presence in the Emerald City was more urgent, since he was getting ready to install central heating in the palace. "Let Faramant be the one to go," was the unanimous vote.

The Guardian of the Gates was not about to refuse. Such a long journey seemed dreadful to him, especially one through the air, on the back of a dragon. But at the same time, it was tempting for him to have this chance to see the Outer World — he alone, out of tens of thousands of inhabitants of Magic Land.

There was no time to lose: every extra day brought closer the onset of winter, that unknown and terrible phenomenon of nature, which now threatened Magic Land for the first time in long ages.

Oyho, like the other dragons, had taken refuge in the Cavern from the Yellow Fog. It would be senseless to summon him to the Emerald City, as this would lose them several precious days. But Faramant himself would travel too slowly on his short legs if he were to journey to Blue Land on foot. So Lestar and his aides quickly fashioned a light litter, and two Wooden Couriers were designated as bearers. Fleet footed and tireless, they would transport Faramant to the Cavern in about forty hours, and there, the Ore-Diggers, in obedience to their monarch Rujero's written order, would fit the little man up for his long journey. At the very last minute, Kaggi-Karr the Crow decided to accompany Faramant, and no one had any objection to this. It would be more enjoyable for them, in any event, to travel together, and the lightweight Crow would hinder neither the Couriers nor the mighty Dragon.

And so the Wooden Couriers, with a rapid, springy step, bore away Faramant, who was settled comfortably on the litter. A third Wooden Courier ran on ahead, shouting continually: "Gangway! Gangway!"

By this time, it was not easy to make progress on the Yellow Brick Road. It was jammed with countless herds of animals intending to seek refuge in the Cavern. They did not know if the people would let them in there, but they had heard that there were never any cold spells down in Underground Land. Hares, raccoons, and rabbits were traveling along the Road; antelopes lifted their proud heads above the rest of the crowd, while bisons and elk trod the ground heavily.

Tigers, lynxes, hyenas, wolves, and foxes were making their way along the sides of the Road. The beasts of prey had their own idea. They knew that they would not be allowed down into the Cavern, but they counted on migrating to the land of the good Fairy Villina, where summer still prevailed as before; it was the birds that had brought them word of this. These same birds had already long been taking refuge from the frosts in the domains of Stella, Villina, and Arachna.

The wicked Enchantress was enraged when she saw her own forests and meadows being overrun more and more every day by animals and birds from regions that were in the grip of the fog. But there was nothing she could do to her uninvited guests, for there was already a large accumulation of them.

The people's resistance likewise infuriated Arachna dreadfully. It was persisting far too long, and she had been counting on a speedy victory. The Yellow Fog was doing its pernicious work, all right: it was corroding the lungs of people and animals, making their eyes water, weakening their vision... But those clever people were finding equally clever means of fighting the affliction. They were breathing the tainted air through rafaloo leaves, and the poisonous droplets were not penetrating into their chests. They were protecting their eyes by means of spectacles with solid side-shields, and the fog merely collected on the glass. They were purifying the air inside their houses using the method devised by Urfin Jus, the same Jus who had refused to serve *her*, the mighty Arachna, and was instead doing her so much harm in the realization of her plans.

Although the roads were covered with a veil of fog, progress along them was almost as rapid as before: every twenty or thirty paces, there stood a post with a sign on which was written which path led where.

No, it was not so easy to subjugate people after all!

Chapter 17

ON JOHN SMITH'S FARM

Filled as they were with vitality and strength, mechanical racers Caesar and Hannibal had accomplished the long journey from the Violet Castle to the Kansas farm and Annie and Tim rushed into the delighted embraces of their parents[7]. Ellie was immediately summoned home from college, and the intrepid travelers' accounts of their adventures occupied everyone for several days. Ellie bitterly regretted that she had persuaded the court to show leniency to Urfin Jus and, instead of punishing him severely for his crimes, to limit it to mere exile. "If only I'd known that he'd be able to dupe the Leapers... That he'd take over the Emerald City again!...If I'd only known ..." she said mournfully.

"But everything did turn out happily," said Annie, consoling her. "And he'll never seize power again! Tim and his volleyball shattered all his dreams forever, and not even one drop of blood was shed when that happened!"

The listeners could not help smiling as they pictured in their minds the amazing spectacle of the Marrans rushing forward for a fight to the death and then changing, just like that, into eager gamers and, instead of striking blows at their enemies, hitting the ball.

After that, Tim and Annie began school, and their studies occupied their time completely. Grammar and arithmetic, penmanship, American history and geography... Classes in the morning, homework in the

---

[7] See the story *The Fiery God of the Marrans.*

evening. Little by little, their thrilling adventures faded away in their memories.

At the end of the school year, an event occurred that made everyone on the farm extraordinarily happy: Captain Charlie Black came to pay a visit to his relatives. The one-legged Sailor had traveled to the Smiths' house several years before, when Annie was still very young. But she recognized her uncle at once, for Charlie had changed very little. Still the same trim, muscular physique; his face was slightly more sunburned, two or three wrinkles had joined those already on his forehead, his hair was a little grayer, but, as always, there was a lighted pipe in his teeth. As before, his wooden leg tapped against the road, leaving round marks in the dust.

Charlie Black had just returned from his latest voyage to the isle of Kuru-Kusu, where he engaged in barter with his friends the cannibals. The Sailor brought his relatives many gifts: large seashells in which one could hear the distant roar of the ocean when holding it up to the ear; wooden figures of gods with whimsically painted faces; stuffed parrots with brightly-colored feathers... Nor did Charlie forget the children from the neighboring farms. Tim O'Kelly received a taut bow and arrows, and when school was out for the day, the boy would disappear onto the prairie, chasing partridges and prairie dogs.

Needless to say, Charlie Black had barely set foot on the hospitable soil of the Smith farm when he learned about the journey that Annie and Tim had made to Magic Land.

"I swear by all the typhoons of the South Seas!" exclaimed Charlie, puffing vigorously on his pipe. "I see that the younger sister is no less fortunate in her adventures than the elder. But stop, drop anchor! Let the little girl herself give an account of everything that happened, down to the smallest details, and let Tim correct her if she mixes anything up, and let Artoshka sit beside me, look me in the eyes, and vouch for the truth of the story by wagging his tail!"

Everyone complied with Charlie Black's wishes. For several evenings, he sat with the children on a large rock out on the prairie, listening to a long account of the Fiery God of the Marrans, alternating between delight and indignation, and peppering his speech with sailors' expletives. "And where do you have the Fox King's Silver Circlet now?" he asked his niece when the story was finished. "You did bring it home with you, didn't you?"

"What for?" asked the girl with surprise. "You know it wouldn't retain its magical power in Kansas. I left it with the Iron Woodman, in the Violet Castle."

"Too bad, too bad," frowned the Sailor. "Silver and rubies are always valuable."

"Now, Uncle, money isn't all there is to life!" Annie objected boldly. "Here, we might receive so many dollars for it, but *there*, it may well stand my friends in good stead in some important undertaking..."

"Perhaps you're right, little one," the old Sailor concurred. "May I be swallowed by a whale!"

The mechanical mules, which Charlie had examined on the first day of his arrival, filled him with delight. He stroked their silky hides, felt their strong muscles beneath them, fingered the mules' silky manes, and talked to them tenderly — to which they brayed loudly in response.

Caesar and Hannibal played a role of no small importance on John Smith's farm. Mary, the modest old mare, was now getting a rest, and all the field work fell to the lot of the mules. Attached as a pair to the plow, they turned up the field and pulled the heavy harrow, and they continued to toil right up to the time when the harvest was taken in.

The mules handled every task with such ease and speed that John had much free time. He hired himself out plowing and reaping grain for the neighbors, and this gained him a steady income. The farmer doted on his obedient, tireless helpers and put them in the stable only on days when the sun wasn't shining. And how many letters of gratitude Annie wrote at his dictation to Fred Canning, who was now a full-fledged engineer at the Osbaldiston Brothers' Machine Shop in Minnesota.

Of course, Charlie Black went for rides on the mechanical mules, and not just one time either! After saddling Hannibal, the Captain, who, like all sailors, was a skilled horseman, pranced along the smooth prairie road, while Annie, clinging tightly to Caesar's mane, squealed with delight as she rode alongside him. "Faster, faster!" cried the girl, setting the speed control as fast as it could go.

Charlie Black's stay with his relatives was approaching its end when an event occurred which changed all his plans and drew the one-legged Sailor into a new series of astounding adventures.

Chapter 18

AN EMISSARY
FROM MAGIC LAND

One day, Charlie Black, Annie, and Tim sat out on the prairie until late twilight. Tim entreated the Sailor most insistently to take him with him on his voyage. "It doesn't matter if I'm only eleven, Captain," said the boy. "See how big and strong I am. Match me against a fifteen-year-old, and it'll remain to be seen who comes out ahead. I'll make a first-class cabin boy, yo-ho-ho!"

Puffing on his pipe, Black made a joke of it: "And won't you be sad to leave your little girl-friend behind, Tim? She'll miss you so much!"

Tim frowned and repeated some words that he had heard the grownups say: "Men are obliged to seek their fortunes in foreign climes, while it's the lot of the women to keep the home fires burning."

The Captain laughed until tears were coming from his eyes. "Well said, I swear by the icebergs! But I'll tell you what, my man: I'll again be dropping by these regions unexpectedly in about three or four short years. By then, you'll be grown up, and I'll take you right on as a sailor."

This promise did not suit Tim very much, and he was about to argue the point further, when all at once the far-sighted Sailor's attention was drawn to a dark spot in the evening sky. It quickly grew larger as it approached, and became a silhouette that formed the strangest outline. Against the background of the sunset, they could make out an ugly, crested head at the end of a long neck; enormous wings were flapping at the sides of its body, while a small cage could be seen on its back.

"It's a dragon!" cried Charlie. "I swear by the ocean deeps, it's a dragon! Ellie and I saw one exactly like that in the Cavern, while we were walking through the underground passage."

"It must be Oyho!" exclaimed Annie with delight.

"Of course it's Oyho!" agreed Tim. "He's the only one who knows the way to Kansas!"

The Dragon, its yellow-white belly flashing, described large circles over the Sailor and the children, who had leaped to their feet. The head of some person who was wearing a sharp-point hat, was sticking out between the bars of the cabin and looking the people over.

"Faramant!" Tim began to shout in his happiness. "Annie, it's Faramant!"

He waved his arms, inviting the Dragon to alight on the ground. The monster landed with a great deal of noise, a little door opened in the cabin, a rope ladder fell out, and a little man wearing a green tunic and green spectacles began to scramble down the ladder. But before he had gone two rungs, a black bird darted out of the cabin and headed joyfully toward Annie's arms.

"Kaggi-Karr!" exclaimed Annie. The girl hugged the Crow and tenderly stroked her ruffled black feathers. "Kaggi-Karr, *dear* Kaggi-Karr, how glad I am to see you!"

The Crow cawed quietly but affectionately.

The little man in the green spectacles finally jumped off the bottom of the ladder and cordially greeted Charlie Black and the children. "I'm very pleased to see you, Giant from Beyond the Mountains," he said, "and I'm happy to see Annie and Tim. I flew here on Oyho the Dragon on a mission of unusual importance…"

As soon as he heard his name mentioned, the Dragon turned his hideous head with the large, intelligent eyes in Annie's direction, and the girl walked over to him and stroked his scaly neck. Oyho struck his long, wriggling tail with pleasure against the ground.

Faramant briefly and efficiently stated the events that had been occurring in Magic Land during the last few months: the reawakening of the wicked Fairy Arachna after a sleep of five thousand years; her intention of reducing the inhabitants of the land to slavery; the proud refusal of its freedom-loving peoples; and, finally, the detrimental effects of the Yellow Fog that the Witch had inflicted upon them.

"All our hope now lies in Annie and Tim," the Guardian of the Gates concluded his melancholy tale. "They helped us in the struggle against Urfin Jus and the warlike Marrans. And now we think they'll teach us how to combat the winter that's approaching our fields and forests..."

When he had heard Faramant to the end, the Captain shook his head and said: "You're dreadfully mistaken, my friend, if you think you can defeat this winter merely by building warm houses and putting on warm clothes. Among us, winter comes and goes, and it's followed by spring and summer. But among you, if I understand your words correctly, this winter will endure forever unless the Yellow Fog disappears. And it won't disappear as long as the evil Arachna is alive. The problem, therefore, is this: it's either victory over the Witch, or the death of Magic Land. And let my wooden leg take root in the ground if I don't take a hand in this matter and make an effort to save your marvelous, inimitable country!"

"Hurrah!" the children cried out with shrill voices, and they ran over to the selfless Sailor and threw their arms around him.

"And what, indeed, could stop a globe-trotting vagabond like me?" the Captain went on. "I'll write to my mate that the ship should set sail for Kuru-Kusu without me, while I set out on a new journey on dragon-back! I just must try out this new means of communication!"

Faramant wiped away tears of happiness that flowed down from beneath his green spectacles, while the Crow, for her part, flew joyous loop-the-loops in the air.

"Have I understood you right, esteemed Giant from Beyond the Mountains?" asked the Guardian of the Gates timidly. "Are you determined to fly to our country and take on the wicked Arachna in battle?"

"Yes," retorted the Sailor quickly.

"Then my mission has been crowned with success such that we hadn't even dreamed of," declared Faramant, positively beaming. "Just think, the Giant from Beyond the Mountains himself doing battle with

124

the Witch for our welfare. Oh, now I'm certain of success before we even start!"

"Aren't you exaggerating my powers?" said Charlie Black with a smile as he removed his now extinguished pipe from his mouth to light it again.

"Oh, no, no, I'm not, mighty friend and protector!" asserted Faramant ardently.

"You will be taking us with you, won't you, Uncle Charlie?" inquired Annie cautiously.

"You?" The Sailor gave a sly grin. "We'll have to think about that just a little."

"What is there to think about?" said the girl, outraged. "Oyho flew here to get *us*, not you! You just happened to be here on our farm."

"All right, all right," said Charlie, brushing the matter aside. "We'll have to discuss all of this with your parents. But in the meantime, you'd better think of where we're going to put the Dragon during his stay here."

Faramant said that Oyho had timed his flight especially so that he would reach this region late in the evening and not cause a stir among the local populace. He had created up quite a furor the last time, when he had flown Fred and Ellie home. They had done it wrong then, and nearly half the people in the state had run out to the field where the Dragon touched down.

Fortunately, Tim knew of a deep ravine not too far away, one that no one ever visited. They hid the Dragon there and bade him lie quietly, promising to bring him food every night.

All night long, the lights remained burning on the Smith and O'Kelly farms, and all night long, neither grownup nor child closed an eye. Deliberations were under way regarding whether they should or shouldn't let Annie and Tim go away to Magic Land a second time. There was no discussion about Charlie Black's wish to set out to battle with Arachna: Charlie was a grown man who could answer for himself, and life had hardened him to dangerous enterprises.

By the time morning came, the Smiths and the O'Kellys had come to a unanimous decision: since the children had already set out once before for Magic Land by themselves on two mechanical mules and returned home safely, then that made it all the more possible to let them go now, under the supervision of Captain Black — especially when it would be done on such a dependable means of transportation as a tame Dragon. They took into account the fact that they were not talking about a mere pleasure trip, but the rescue of an entire country from ruin.

For all that, however, Annie, and especially Tim (whose headstrong nature was well known throughout the area), were absolutely forbidden to enter into any confrontation with the Witch, and they were to stay as distant as possible from anything that was dangerous. The children promised to do so, but in a manner that was suspiciously light-hearted.

When the first rays of dawn illuminated the part of the sky near the horizon, all of them were out like a light, for they were exhausted by their sleepless night.

Three days were needed for preparations. Though the one-legged Sailor's knapsack and his pockets still seemed to constitute an inexhaustible reservoir of tools, as before, it was not enough for the serious goal that Charlie Black had set for himself. He rode into the nearby town and purchased a pile of heavy sheet iron, along with shears that would cut through metal. At a machine shop, the Captain ordered several dozen springs of the finest steel, from the largest and sturdiest to the smallest and flimsiest. The order included an enormous supply of nuts, bolts, and monkeywrenches of many different sizes. Charlie Black paid more for it than the normal price, and prior orders were put aside to fill this one.

Whenever anyone asked him why he was stocking up on such a large quantity of metal, the Captain would only smile mysteriously.

Oyho the Dragon lay quietly in his hiding place. Ellie, whom the Captain had informed about the arrival of the messengers from Magic Land, came in secret to see him. But Ellie's reunion with Kaggi-Karr and Faramant was an especially joyous one. Kaggi-Karr was unable to express her feelings in words, but she snuggled up to the girl so tenderly that everything was understood without the least difficulty. And Faramant conveyed warm regards to her from Strasheela, the Iron Woodman, the Courageous Lion, and all her other friends. He told her about the dreadful events that were shaking the country, and toward the end he relayed Strasheela's invitation to Ellie to come to the Emerald City as a teacher after she had finished college.

Strasheela promised to put up a building for Ellie's school such as the world had never seen before. The plan for it was already inside the Monarch's head, and the Deadwood Oaks were beginning to get the building materials ready, but at that particular moment, of course, they were perturbed by the misfortune at hand. But they would overcome this misfortune, and the school would be built. Ellie smiled and promised to think over this flattering proposal.

When they parted, Faramant gave Ellie his green spectacles: a souvenir from Magic Land. For his own part, it was an enormous sacrifice: it must be remembered that in obeying the Mighty Goodwin's dictate, the Guardian of the Gates had not removed his glasses for many years, and he was so used to them that they seemed to be part of his face.

Each night, Tim and Annie wheeled an entire handcart of food of various kinds for the Dragon: a cauldron of porridge, five buckets of boiled beets, two sacks of grain, and many other odds and ends.

While the shop was busy filling Charlie Black's order, the Sailor did not sit around idle. The consummate craftsman built a spacious cabin to replace the diminutive cage in which Faramant and Kaggi-Karr had flown: four people and all their baggage could fit comfortably inside it. There was no question of their taking the mechanical mules along with them. First of all, too large a cabin would be required to accommodate them; secondly, and most important — the mules would be unable to recharge themselves with solar energy in Magic Land because of the Yellow Fog, and that rendered them useless.

The hour of departure came at last. All the residents of both farms reported to the secluded ravine in the dead of night. The Dragon's colossal form loomed black in a flat area next to the ravine. Oyho had eaten a double ration of food in preparation for his flight, so that he would not get hungry in midflight. The cabin was attached to the body of the winged reptile by means of sturdy straps, while the bundles of sheet iron, springs, and tools were situated nearer the tail. The Dragon was going to be called on to carry a heavy load, but for a being of his enormous strength, it was nothing at all.

There were the final passionate kisses, hugs, good wishes and urgent instructions. Before climbing up the rope ladder, the Sailor asked his niece: "You haven't forgotten to bring Tilly-Willy, have you?"

"No, Uncle, he's in my knapsack."

Tilly-Willy was the heathen figurine that the Captain had given Annie. Of all the idols that he had brought with him from the isle of Kuru-Kusu, this one was stood out from the others in ugliness. As for the secret purpose for which Charlie Black was taking him along, more will be said later.

Tim O'Kelly was the last to climb into the cabin. Under his arm he carried the little dog Artoshka, who had likewise joined this strange expedition that had been fitted up to rescue Magic Land from the machinations of the wicked Arachna.

Oyho flapped his mighty wings, dust and dried grass began to rise in a whirlwind around the people who had come to see the others off — and the Dragon had already vanished into the darkness of the night sky.

Chapter 19

A FLIGHT ON DRAGONBACK

The company of travelers slept peacefully for a few hours on their comfortable little couches, accompanied by the steady swaying of the cabin. When Charlie Black and the others awakened, many tens of miles of the journey were already behind them. The Captain and his companions ate breakfast and then they began to look out through the little windows in the cabin. But it was possible to make out very little from the enormous height that Oyho was maintaining, and the children grew bored. The Sailor began to relate to them a long story about some adventures that he had had in South Africa when he was still young.

Oyho the Dragon continued his transportation of the humans with his mighty wings, and the Great Desert soon appeared before them. Being an invincible and formidable obstacle to those who were on foot or on horseback, the Great Desert effectively partitioned Magic Land off from the rest of the world. But Oyho easily and speedily flapped his huge leathery wings, and he feared neither the sands nor Gingema's Black Rocks.

The Black Rocks! How many recollections the passengers in the cabin had of them! As he looked out the window, Charlie Black recalled how the trio of himself, Ellie, and Totoshka had been dying of thirst beside one of the Black Rocks, and how Kaggi-Karr the Crow had rescued them by bringing them a clump of Magic Grapes. The Crow must clearly have been thinking about the same thing, because she looked so expressively at the Sailor, as if to say: "I remember, I remember everything, and it was nothing, really!" Charlie stroked Kaggi-Karr tenderly, and then he clasped her to his breast.

Tim and Annie, for their part, when they sighted two little black spots amid the yellow sands, talked about the way the girl had almost perished in that place last year, and if it hadn't been for Hannibal's strength and endurance, Annie would have been stuck there forever.

Then beneath the Dragon's wings appeared the World-Encompassing Mountains, yet another creation of the Mighty Wizard Hurricap. An impenetrable chaos of mountain chains and deep valleys with secrets as yet unfathomed stretched out below them, and Annie and Tim thought with admiration about how nimble and sure-footed their mechanical mules were, being able to surmount such barriers. Laughing, the boy and the girl gave each other their word that from now on, they would cross the World-Encompassing Mountains only on dragon back, or, at the very least, on giant eagles like the one that they had encountered during their last journey.

Snow-covered peaks and glaciers drifted by below them, but they were no longer dazzling to human sight. Their whiteness and gleam were now hidden beneath the layer of the Yellow Fog that extended over the mountains. Of course, it did not interfere with visibility here.

But a totally different picture awaited our heroes when they finally came out into Magic Land. In itself, the fog did not appear to be particularly dense, but from the height at which Oyho was flying, the ground could not even be seen. The mighty reptile flapped his wings with great force, but the yellow murk surrounded the Dragon on all sides, and he did not appear to be moving at all.

Kaggi-Karr and Artoshka had begun to talk while Oyho was still flying over the mountains. The Crow's ability to speak proved to be most extremely useful to the travelers, for Kaggi-Karr had traveled the whole length and breadth of Magic Land and knew it intimately. She made her way out of the cabin, perched on Oyho's head, and began to give him directions.

First of all, Kaggi-Karr suggested that the Dragon descend and fly over the ground at a low altitude. Objects on the ground became visible, and it was possible to determine the true direction in which they were headed. "Turn right! Straight ahead! To the left!" directed the Crow, and Oyho obediently followed her instructions.

The passengers looked down. Annie clasped her hands together in dismay and burst into tears. What had happened to Magic Land?! Where were the gay meadows covered with tall grass and beautiful flowers? Where was the dense foliage of the green groves concealing ripe, juicy fruit, where multicolored parrots squawked at one another in sonorous voices as they leaped from branch to branch? Everything down below was so monotonous and dead.

Vast clearings were covered with snow, snowflakes lay on the bare branches of the trees, while a cold wind drove piles of flying leaves from one place to another. No animals or birds were anywhere to be seen, and the golden and silver fishes were concealed beneath the sheets of ice that clothed the clear streams.

Even Faramant was affected by the picture of gloomy desolation that was unfolding before the travelers. He had left Magic Land only six days before when he headed over the mountains, yet what ominous changes had occurred there even during those few days! What supremacy the winter had gained over nature in that region that had once been so bright and sunny!

A long, smooth strip appeared among the forests not far away. The perceptive Kaggi-Karr guessed that this was the Yellow Brick Road, although it was covered over by snow. "Forward and to the right!" she directed the Dragon. "Now we won't stray from our path."

"And how they're waiting for us!" sighed Faramant.

Oyho was beginning to pick up speed, when all of a sudden an enormous figure in a blue cloak became visible on the Road, standing out clearly against the background of white snow. Faramant grabbed Charlie Black by the arm and, with a tongue that slurred from terror, he murmured: "That's Arachna!"

The Sorceress had flown to Munchkin Land just to admire her handiwork. She was walking along the Yellow Brick Road, holding under her arm the Flying Carpet, which was now rolled up, and she was laughing wildly with delight. When she had inflicted the Yellow Fog on Magic Land, even she had not foreseen that it would have such a devastating effect. The Witch guffawed, and the sounds of her voice reverberated through the denuded forest like claps of thunder.

The sinister figure of Arachna was quickly left behind, and once again everything below them became barren and silent.

This unexpected encounter demonstrated to Charlie Black how difficult the struggle would be with the wicked Enchantress, who was of such phenomenal dimensions. But this thought did not frighten the one-legged Sailor — on the contrary, it only inspired him to put forth the most ruthless, merciless struggle against the Witch.

"You just wait, you accursed one!" mumbled the Captain. "When I loose Tilly-Willy on you, then *you'll* be the one to start jumping about in terror, I swear by the typhoons of the Eastern Seas!"

"What are you talking about, Uncle Charlie?" asked Annie in surprise. "Can our little idol really frighten a giantess like that one?"

"It's all right, little one, don't be in a hurry," said Charlie with a smile. "Everything in its time!"

The next morning, the Dragon landed in the central square of the Emerald City.

Chapter 20

THE SUPREME COUNCIL

The arrival of Charlie Black and the children turned into a full-scale holiday for the residents of Emerald Island. The City had lost its former splendor: the roofs and the pavement were covered with snow, and they no longer glittered with emeralds; the fountains had gone dry in the squares, and the gaily-painted houses looked downright dull in the yellow murk.

But as the word spread instantaneously about the City that the Giant from Beyond the Mountains was now there, it produced an effect that was downright magical. The cold, which grew in intensity with each passing day, forced the townspeople to huddle together in groups. Women and children, old men and old women, took refuge in Strasheela's palace, where Lestar was just barely able to manage the central heating. Those for whom there was no room in the palace gathered together in small rooms, trying to warm them with the heat of their bodies. People left their houses only in cases of extreme necessity, for instance, when their turns came to go out into the woods to cut firewood for the palace. When that happened, the woodcutters dressed themselves in all the clothing they owned.

Now, however, young and old alike spilled out onto the squares and streets of the City; hats flew into the air, and cries of delight rang out, acclaiming the Giant from Beyond the Mountains and the two illustrious children who were his companions. The people, in their innocence, thought that the situation would begin to improve at once, that salvation would be quick to come. But the day of salvation was still far off. Pedestrians continued, as before, to move about within a limited circle of visibility, constantly walking over to signposts and reading the directions written on them; their mouths were still covered by rafaloo leaves, and spectacles with side-shields continued to protect their eyes. And to top it all off, there was this unnatural, devastating frost, which penetrated to the very bone.

When Strasheela received his welcome guests, he came right out of the palace, and this was noted in the Chronicles as a sign of unprecedented honor, one which the Monarch of Emerald Land very occasionally accorded to visitors. In addition to that, when he hugged Annie with his soft, limp arms, Strasheela performed several steps of some strange sort of dance, singing out as he did so: "Eh-hey-hey-hey-ho! I'm with Annie again, again, again!" However, the Chronicler maintained a bashful silence regarding this last fact: it would not do, after all, to preserve for posterity the little weaknesses of such a remarkable statesman as Strasheela the Wise.

No sooner had they concluded this solemn ceremony and greeted the rescue expedition that had arrived from beyond the mountains, than an extended session of the Supreme Council was called to order in the Throne Room. This time, in addition to the usual members, it was attended by eminent townspeople and even a few of the Deadwood Oaks, among whom one could spot Corporals Batis and Daruk and Lan Pirot, the former General of the wooden army, who now taught dancing to children in one of the City schools. He had no work to do at the moment: owing to the tragic events that had occurred, all the schools were closed.

Strasheela opened the session. He did not give a report, but confined himself to brief observations: inasmuch as everyone present was current on the situation, there was no need for lengthy discussion. Then Strasheela invited those who so wished, to come forward and join in.

Charlie Black was the first to take the floor. "I'm a man of action, not an orator," said the one-legged Sailor, puffing on his unlit pipe through force of habit. "Therefore, I'll get right down to concrete suggestions. For our battle against Arachna, we're going to need a mobile fortress, one that would offer us an ongoing refuge against the Witch's attacks, and from which we can make sorties of our own, in accordance with the rules of military science. Building such a shelter would be long and difficult, especially since we have another vital task ahead of us, which I'll discuss a little further on. And so I propose that we use for this purpose — the house trailer in which Ellie flew to Magic Land!"

The Captain's suggestion was accepted unanimously.

"I'm the one who constructed that trailer long ago for my sister Anna and her husband John," Charlie went on, "so I know that it still has many years of service ahead of it. We'll put it on wheels, and *then* just let the Witch try to harm our garrison!"

Applause and shouts of "hurrah!" filled the room. Annie and Tim spoke up at once, saying that they had seen the trailer the previous year, and had found it to be in excellent shape.

Far from putting the matter off indefinitely, as is generally done in certain institutions (even some that are most highly respected), Strasheela instructed Corporals Batis and Daruk to assemble their workers at once and to proceed quickly to Munchkin Land to fetch the trailer. Lan Pirot, who had grown bored through lack of occupation, volunteered to lead this detachment. The wooden men, who were tireless and indifferent to the Yellow Fog, would march day and night and would bring the trailer to the Emerald City in about six days. Batis, Darook, and Commander Lan Pirot set out at once to fulfill their mission.

"Now for the second problem," Charlie Black continued his address. "I know, from what my niece Annie has told me, that she left with the Iron Woodman a magical Silver Circlet that makes its possessor invisible. It's essential that we fetch that Circlet here. Tim O'Kelly, after making himself invisible, will infiltrate Arachna's domain, do some reconnaissance there, and perhaps he'll even be able to swipe her book of incantations. Then we'll instantly remove magically this pernicious Yellow Fog from Magic Land."

"Allow me to make a disclosure," said the Iron Woodman, rising to his feet where he sat. Nervously turning over and over in his hands the funnel that served him for a hat, he said: "We'd personally be happy to use the Silver Circlet for the purpose that you mention, but unfortunately..."

"You lost it!" cried Annie, jumping up and down in her distress.

"Yes, to our great sorrow," confessed the Woodman. "Here's how it happened. My Cook, Fregosa, had a pet fallow deer named Auna. One day, Fregosa put the circlet on Auna's head, just for fun, but she inadvertently pressed the little ruby star, and the deer vanished. It was in vain then that the poor woman, who was quite alarmed now, called out to her pet so that she could take the Circlet off her. The deer ran out of the palace, and not even a trace of her was found…"

Annie burst into tears, and Strasheela, the Lion, and the Woodman could do nothing to console her. She really loved that extraordinary gift from the King of the Foxes.

"Yes, that's an enormous, heavy loss," said Charlie Black sorrowfully. "But it's a good thing I wasn't relying *only* on the Circlet, and I've come up with an additional means of fighting the Witch." Then he asked Faramant, "Did you remove the piles of iron and the springs from Oyho's back?"

"Yes, the Deadwood Oaks did it at my command, and they carried the whole pile down to the basement."

"Very good! You see," the Sailor turned to the assembly, "my idea is to construct an automated Giant, who will be our major weapon in our fight against the Fairy Arachna. And to do this, I've brought along all the necessary materials: sheet iron, springs…"

The delight of all those present reached phenomenal proportions. The glass in the windows rattled from their shouts, the floor trembled from the stomping of their feet. It took much ringing of the chairman's bell on Strasheela's part to restore order. When the people had quieted down, Charlie asked Lestar the mechanic: "May I count on your help? The job is an urgent one, and we'll need a lot of people."

Lestar ardently assured the Sailor that he himself and all his assistants would be at the Giant's disposal. "We'll only take two or three hours of sleep a day," exclaimed the mechanic, "but then it won't take us long to build a Giant who will match Arachna in strength! And while we're on the subject, we've brought many different kinds of tools with us from Violet Land, and these will come in handy now."

"Annie," asked Charlie, "where do you have Tilly-Willy?"

"Here he is, Uncle." The girl took the figurine out of the knapsack and handed it to the Sailor. Charlie Black held it up high so that the members of the Council could see it as clearly as possible.

A cry of dismay rang out. The idol looked positively ghastly. There was a baleful and sinister expression in its oblong, slanting eyes. A deep furrow cut through its low forehead. Its huge mouth bared its teeth in a wicked grin, and enormous white fangs stuck out from it. Its whole expression breathed out an implacable savagery and hatred toward the entire world.

The spectators were overwhelmed as they contemplated Tilly-Willy, and a six-year-old boy who had come into the conference room seeking his father, let out such a desperate scream that he was taken from the room at once.

"Like it?" asked Charlie in an ironic tone.

"Such monsters have never been seen in our country," declared the Lion with conviction. "Even the Saber-Toothed Tigers didn't look that dreadful."

"Well, we'll use this fine boy here as a model for our automated Giant. Can you imagine what a monster he'll be when he's thirty yards tall?"

"Yes, he'll look most impressive," concurred Strasheela.

Part III

TILLY-WILLY
THE IRON PALADIN

Chapter 21

THE BIRTH OF
TILLY-WILLY THE GIANT

A workshop was organized in the roomy basement of the palace, where the joiners' benches still stood that Urfin Jus and his assistants had used while producing Deadwood Oaks. A multitude of lamps illuminated the premises. The air in the basement was cleaned by means of fires, and the lamps provided all the light that was needed.

Work went into full swing. Charlie Black made drawings, and then he made use of these drawings to cut out from the sheet metal the pieces to be used for the body, the head, the arms, and the legs of Tilly-Willy, the Giant-to-be — they had given him that name in honor of the little heathen idol. Black's work demanded great precision: the parts that had been cut out had to be bent into shape by means of wooden mallets, in such a way that they received the proper curvature, and would begin to assume human shape after they were riveted together. The slightest error in calculations would lead to irreparable after-effects.

The situation was made complicated by Tilly-Willy's enormous dimensions. Charlie Black and Lestar were resolved that Tilly-Willy would have to exceed Arachna in size. Only then would the Witch feel any fear of her mighty adversary, and that would lead to her defeat and destruction.

Four to five sheets of iron went into the manufacture of each arm. Seven to eight were needed for each leg, while his enormous body required no fewer than twenty sheets. Fortunately, Charlie Black had brought a sufficient quantity of material with him from Kansas.

For twenty hours or more each day in that workshop, drills screeched, hammers pounded, iron rods turned red-hot in the forges, and the smiths forged rivets. So hot was it beneath the low arches of the basement, that the men became covered with sweat, and sometimes they even fainted. But not one of them put his labors aside — they all worked with dedication, for they realized that the salvation of their land depended entirely on them.

And so the colossal thighs, shins, and forearms of the future Giant materialized in various corners of the basement. They were reminiscent of metal tunnels, and the diminutive Winkies could maneuver freely inside them, tools and all. It remained for these parts to be cleverly joined to the other members to produce the actual legs and arms.

In the mechanical Giant's huge head, they cut large oblong holes for the eyes and an opening for the mouth. They decided to assemble Tilly-Willy's body outdoors: if they did so right there in the basement, there would be no way they could get it out through the door.

But making the Giant's body, head, and extremities was only part of the job, and not even the most important part! Tilly-Willy was expected to walk and run and to wield weapons — the sword and the shield. For this, it was necessary to stuff him with a multitude of gears, levers, and springs, both large and small, which would do duty as the Giant's muscles; this demanded a great deal of skill as well as time. Fortunately, the Winkies had long been renowned as exceptional craftsmen, and in recent years, they had had excellent practice in taking apart and putting back together the Iron Woodman with his complex mechanism.

The work continued at an accelerated pace, for there could be no delaying: the cold was getting more intense by the day. The most crucial part of the job — the installation of the gears, the levers, and the springs — was undertaken by Charlie and Lestar, who got only two hours of sleep a day and were soon so exhausted that they could barely stand on their feet. To avoid being overcome by sleep while they worked, they drank extracts of nuts from the nukh-nukh tree.

The work finally reached the point where the final assembly of the enormous mechanism could be undertaken. Nothing less than the courtyard would do for this. They were able to drag the individual portions of the arms and legs out through the door, but the head would not fit through, and so it was necessary to make a large breach in the wall

Bonfires were burning in various parts of the courtyard, and the workers ran over to them continually to warm themselves. The bonfires were useful as well for cleaning the air in the courtyard, and more than once the workers had good words to say about Urfin Jus: it was not particularly convenient to work with the face covered with rafaloo leaves that reminded one of a muzzle. Carpenters had already prepared ladders and tall platforms that could be rolled about from place to place. Blocks and tackles hung down from a sturdy cross-bar that was attached to two tall vertical poles.

They began the assembly by suspending Tilly-Willy's body from the cross-bar on sturdy ropes. In order to hoist it to the necessary height, 170 people, at Charlie Black's command, pulled on the ropes wrapped around the pulleys, with even the Iron Woodman himself participating.

The body was the most important and the most critical part of the automated Giant. The control of all his movements was concentrated there, and for this purpose, the builders placed a comfortable cabin right inside Tilly-Willy's middle, to which one could gain access through a narrow little door. A soft, revolving armchair was fastened down to the floor of the cabin. While seated in it, the person controlling Tilly-Willy's movements would be able to reach all the levers and buttons that activated the springs. As it turned out, the only person capable of doing so would be Lestar, that most accomplished mechanic of Winkie Land. It was he who had thought up many of the gizmos and devices, and he had installed them himself. Here, his small size came in handy. It was helpful, too, that Lestar still had sufficient strength and endurance.

After the body had been suspended in mid-air, the workers began to attach the arms, the legs, and the head to it. A veritable spider-web of ropes surrounded the assembly rig, with scaffolds hanging down from them in the smoke and the gloom. And craftsmen armed with drills and chisels, hammers and pincers, swarmed about on these scaffolds.

The hum of voices, the screeching of pulleys, and the pounding of hammers blended together in the foggy air. Tilly-Willy's immense figure assumed more and more of a human shape.

The moment of triumph came at last when all the mechanical work was done, all the springs and devices had been set in place, and Tilly-Willy the Giant was standing there heavily on his own two enormous feet. An entire barrel of oil was needed to oil all his springs and joints.

Now it was the painters' turn. The painting of the Giant's head was entrusted to the finest masters, real artists in their craft. They took a good look at the little idol that had been brought back from the isles of Kuru-Kusu, and then did their level best!

Anyone who looked at Tilly-Willy's savage face, his wicked slanting eyes, his dreadful tooth-filled mouth with the enormous fangs protruding from it, started in horror. The craftsmen painted his body, his arms, and his legs in the manner of the armor of a medieval knight. All that was needed, to make the resemblance complete, were a shield, a sword, and a spear. But an enormous sword had already been forged, one that was so heavy that even forty men could barely budge it from its spot. And under the solid iron shield that they had made, hundreds of people could take shelter from the rain. It would have been good to prepare a spear for Tilly-Willy as well, but knights' spears were carried by squires, and for this reason it was necessary to dispense with a spear. Where could one possibly find a suitable squire for such a Giant?

Tilly-Willy's creators were very happy with their creation. "Yes," said Charlie Black, "when Arachna gets a look at our little man here, her heart will sink right to her feet."

"And for my part," said Lestar, "I'll try to make our little man pursue the enemy just like a wolf chasing a hare."

The "little man" Tilly-Willy was not mute. They had installed in his throat a siren that could change in pitch from the lowest to the highest. And when they started it up for the first time in order to test it, it caused a dreadful commotion in the City. Wild, penetrating sounds drove all the residents from their houses. The people thought that the end of the world had come, and in their terror they rushed about in the streets, jostling one another in the yellow gloom. It took the town criers, running here and there all over the City, to calm the populace. Charlie Black, in his contentment, rubbed his hands, puffed strongly on his pipe, and swore by the hurricanes of all the latitudes that the automated Giant would prove himself indeed.

The time came to launch their military operations against the Witch. Several days before work was completed on the Giant, the conscientious Deadwood Oaks had brought in Ellie's house trailer on their shoulders. It was fitted up with wheels that had been prepared for it in advance, the door and windows were fitted tightly, the furnishings inside it were refurbished — and they set out on the road at once!

Since it was beyond the capability of the tiny horses of Magic Land to manage the heavy van, Strasheela's Staff decided that their mobile fortress should be pulled by Deadwood Oaks. They assigned them another important task as well: winding up the automated Giant.

The springs that activated the Giant's arms, legs, and neck were so powerful that they responded only to the Deadwood Oaks' strength. So a few of the wooden men clambered up ladders that had been placed against Tilly-Willy's body, and they placed wind-up keys into special openings. The keys turned with a squeaking sound and the springs hummed from the stress, but once they were wound up as far as they would go, they would function for several hours.

Former General Lan Pirot was designated Supreme Commander of all the Deadwood Oaks that participated in the march. He had shown himself to be a capable supervisor.

Chapter 22

THE IRON PALADIN'S
FIRST STEPS

The garrison of the mobile fortress was constituted as follows: Strasheela, the Iron Woodman, Din Gior, Faramant, Doctor Boril, Kaggi-Karr, and the guests from beyond the mountains — Charlie Black, Annie, Tim, and Artoshka. There was no room for the Lion, with his huge bulk, inside the trailer, and so, very much against his will, he would have to stay behind in the Emerald City. Lestar, too, was a member of this military detachment, but it would be his fortune to travel inside Tilly-Willy's midsection.

A few round glassed windows had been constructed in the Giant's belly and his back, so that one could inspect the locality through them; Lestar could see everything that happened both before him and behind. And those enormous eyes in Tilly-Willy's head, which could rotate in their sockets, were specially designed to terrify enemies. That was what Tilly-Willy's creators counted on in the beginning, but it did not turn out that way in actual fact, as will be told later.

Everything was now ready for their departure on their long and perilous journey. Pouches and baskets were filled with provisions, canteens of drinking water were stowed away under the benches, and the poisonous air was purified using Urfin Jus's method. It was imperative that this latter job be done: just try breathing through rafaloo leaves for many days on end in the close confines of a van! The poisonous droplets of Yellow Fog could not penetrate the mobile fortress, so solid were its walls, its floor, and its roof. For ventilation, Lestar drilled a few holes in the walls and protected them with

147

the tried-and-true filters of rafaloo leaves. For personal comfort while they were in the trailer, it was necessary for them to step outside as infrequently as possible, and to shut the door behind them as quickly as they could.

Lestar, after settling comfortably in the cabin inside the automated Giant, pushed the main starter lever. Something began to creak and to grind in Tilly-Willy's innards, springs sproinged, and the Giant began to walk with heavy steps over the frozen ground.

And then a miracle occurred: once Tilly-Willy had taken his first step, he came to life! Of course, such a phenomenon would be called a miracle in the states of Kansas, Ohio, or Connecticut, but in Magic Land, it was a most routine event.

Weren't Strasheela the straw man and the Iron Woodman likewise alive there, moving about and possessing all the usual human feelings and faculties? Didn't Caesar and Hannibal, the mechanical mules, come to life and begin talking the moment they crossed the border into Magic Land? Thus, when Tilly-Willy came to life, all the members of the party recognized it as a happy, but by no means unusual, occurrence.

Tilly-Willy, turning his head, looked about from side to side: his enormous eyes, designed to strike terror into the hearts of enemies, were beginning to see. Then the Giant started to speak, in a deep, resonant voice: "Hey there, give me a mirror. I want to look at myself. It would be interesting to know how one looks from the outside."

Within a couple of minutes, the largest mirror that could be found in the palace had been brought down, carefully wiped clean, and suspended from the crossbar beneath which Tilly-Willy had been put together. In a finicky manner, the Giant selected the spot from which the viewing was best, and he took a long look at his face. Then he burst into booming laughter. "Ah, me! How great! How lovely!" exclaimed Tilly-Willy, delighted. "Do any of you people have such expressive eyes, I swear by the hurricane!"

Those who heard him laughed in spite of themselves: so it seemed that at the time of his creation, the Giant had taken over Captain Black's sailors' vocabulary! How remarkable, even in this extraordinary land...

Tilly-Willy went on: "What nice cheeks I have, what a captivating chin! You people are nothing but pathetic little freaks compared with me... But where's my Daddy, Charlie, through whose ideas you people were able to build such a charming little boy as me?! Oh, do let me see you as quick as can be, Papa Charlie!"

The Sailor stepped forward, rather embarrassed yet at the same time proud at the words uttered by his mechanical offspring. But since it would be difficult for him to be seen so far down below, he climbed up onto the highest of the flights of steps that the Winkies had erected. "I'm glad I was able to oblige you, my son!" he shouted through a megaphone. "We tried so hard..."

"Daddy, please get rid of that tube," requested Tilly-Willy. "My splendid ears can hear every word you say, even without it, may the sharks eat me alive!"

Charlie Black burst out laughing again. "Do you know what a shark is?"

The Giant, unperturbed, responded: "It's probably something like that Witch, Arachna, the one that you built me to fight against. But don't you worry, Dad: you did a splendid job with me. I realized that even at the moment when I received the capability of controlling my own feelings. Let all of you know that my morale is strong, and that if I'm threatened with danger, I'll fight like a lion!"

The Courageous Lion, who was present at this scene along with all the others, was very flattered by this comparison, and he thanked Tilly-Willy for it.

The Iron Giant said tenderly: "Daddy, my beloved, how much I'd like to clasp you to my loving breast, but I fear that that wouldn't end well. You humans seem to be too fragile creatures!"

"Yes, that's the way we're made," explained the one-legged Sailor. "It'll be so much better, son, for you to express your love and appreciation in words, since that'll be safer for me. And now," said Charlie Black, "you must pass through yonder gate. Forward march!"

After approaching the gate, the Giant came to a halt, not knowing what to do. "Papa Charlie, it's too narrow for me. I can't fit under this arch..."

Charlie Black admitted with embarrassment that he had miscalculated, and that it would be necessary to break the arch. "I'll take care of it, Daddy," responded the Giant, and he asked for the heaviest pick. Clutching the tool tightly in his metal fist, Tilly-Willy began, with deft strokes, to demolish the wall. Bricks flew in all directions, and the onlookers took to their heels in whichever direction they could.

A few minutes were all that were needed to effect a breach, and the Iron Paladin stepped out onto the square. The trailer, dragged by the Deadwood Oaks, followed behind him.

As the Giant walked down the street with his sword in his right hand and his shield in his left, his head towered over the fourth floor of the buildings, and the townspeople, looking out their windows, followed Tilly-Willy's progress with joyous acclamations: "Hail our savior! Glory to the future conqueror of Arachna!"

Tilly-Willy bowed pompously in every direction. "Depend on me, citizens! Tilly-Willy may be young, but he won't let you down!!"

Of course, the Giant could not possibly leave the City through the gate, but provision had been made for this: part of the wall had been dismantled ahead of time. The ferry could not possibly support the hero's weight, but he began to wade across, and he remarked, in passing: "I assume that my seams are sufficiently watertight, and I won't get wet inside."

Lestar responded from within the Giant's midsection: "Everything has been done most conscientiously, and you needn't worry."

"Ah, it's you, my supposed driver," Tilly-Willy said ironically. "If I'm not mistaken, your name is Lestar? To tell the truth, I don't really need you, but you might as well stay where you are. A back-up system never hurt anyone..."

Even as he was shooting off his mouth, so to speak, Tilly-Willy lost control of his movements: he slipped on the soft bottom of the lake, flailed his arms, and nearly fell into the water. If that had happened, then Charlie Black and his helpers would have been faced with a task of phenomenal difficulty: raising him from the lake. Fortunately, Lestar did not lose his head. In an instant, he had pushed the proper levers, and the Iron Giant righted himself and strode to the opposite bank, breaking the crust of ice that covered the water.

When Tilly-Willy stepped ashore, Lestar rebuked him gently: "Conceit often leads to tragedy."

"And what is conceit?" asked the Giant. When he had heard the explanation, he said contritely, "I won't get a swelled head again..."

That evening, Lestar told Charlie Black and the other members of the party about Tilly-Willy's childish outburst, which had come so close to putting the expedition in a tight spot. The one-legged Sailor responded about this: "Let me tell you, my friends, that while we were still in Kansas, I decided that our assistant in the fight with Arachna must be none other than a little boy. That's right, that's right, don't be surprised — a little boy *made of iron*, thirty yards tall. Then here, on the Emerald Island, while we were assembling his metal parts into a single whole, I instilled in them the notion that the future Tilly-Willy must be possessed of a boy's boldness, his contempt for danger, his longing to perform heroic deeds..."

"Uncle Charlie," exclaimed Annie with delight, "your plan turned out splendidly! If our Tim were to grow to a height of thirty yards and be made entirely of iron, he'd behave in the exact same way!"

All those who were in the van made up their minds that Charlie Black had achieved what *he* wanted, and that life would now take care of everything else.

Chapter 23

THE QUEEN OF THE FIELD MICE

After the Deadwood Oaks had carefully pulled the trailer off the ferry and were ready to begin drawing it down the Yellow Brick Road, Annie suddenly asked a question which at first glance seemed innocent enough, but which threw the entire company into the deepest consternation. The question was this: "What if Arachna doesn't want to do battle with Tilly-Willy and flies away from him on her Magic Carpet?"

"Indeed, we hadn't thought of that at all," admitted Charlie Black. "The Witch can fly about twenty miles in a single hour, while we, God willing, creep along and cover that distance in a whole day. And then, *where* are we going to seek her after she's flown away?"

"The Magic Television will help us in that," said Strasheela, slapping the box on its polished side.

"It won't help the least little bit," responded Charlie ruefully. "It doesn't function in the Yellow Fog."

They all began to think. Then there was a knock at the door, and in walked Lestar, who was worried. When he had seen that the van was for some reason not moving, he had climbed down from Tilly-Willy's belly by means of the rope ladder and come to inquire about the reason for the delay. And when he learned what the story was, he, too, became sad.

Chapter 23: THE QUEEN OF THE FIELD MICE

Tim said with a sigh: "What a shame that the Silver Circlet is missing. I'd sneak into Arachna's place and grab the Carpet, and that would be the end of the matter!"

Everyone was silent again. Then Annie clapped her hands together. "*I* know how we can deprive the Witch of her Carpet!" she cried out joyfully. "The *mice* can chew it to pieces!"

"What's that?" asked Tim, troubled. "Are you out of your mind?" Then, catching sight of the silver whistle dangling down on Annie's breast, he began to shout in a loud voice: "Call on Ramina? Is that what you mean?!"

"Of course!" replied the girl. "Just keep a tight hold on Artoshka."

Annie blew on the silver whistle that the Queen of the Field Mice had once given to her older sister, and Ramina, accompanied by several of her ladies-in-waiting, appeared at once on the floor of the van. Artoshka barked at the mice, but Tim kept a firm grip on him.

"Hello, your Majesty," said Annie, greeting the little Queen.

"Hello, my dear," replied Ramina. "I'm happy to see you, and Tim, and the Giant from Beyond the Mountains, and even the little dog, my eternal enemy, and I find it very pleasing that you're all in good health. Once again we meet in a time of misfortune for our land. My tribe is suffering the greatest hardships..."

"I hope that none of your subjects has died?" asked the girl sympathetically.

"Not so far. We've taken refuge in the underground passage that leads away from the ancient tower, which I'm sure the Giant from Beyond the Mountains has told you about."

"Yes, yes," exclaimed Annie excitedly.

"You were the one who pointed out the passage to us at the time," added Charlie Black. "After that, we had a nice battle there with a Sixpaw."

"Anyway, we've found refuge in the underground corridor. There's no Yellow Fog down there, but unfortunately, there's no food either."

"Your Majesty," said Annie, "we've come to Magic Land to combat the Yellow Fog, and we're asking you to offer us your help!"

"What help can you expect from creatures as small and weak as us?" asked Ramina in surprise. "We've seen the Giantess Arachna. She was walking through the field where my subjects were in procession, and she was lost in thought and not looking down at her feet. The Witch inadvertently stepped on our column, and with the sole of her foot she crushed 140 mice to death, among which were some highly esteemed individuals!"

Strasheela and his friends offered their most heartfelt condolences to the Queen, and then Charlie Black told her about Tilly-Willy the Giant, who could match strength with Arachna. He placed Ramina and her ladies-in-waiting in the palm of his hand and lifted them up to the window so that they could feast their eyes on the automated Giant. The mice trembled with fear when they beheld the Iron Paladin's savage face.

"But we're powerless against Arachna so long as she possesses her Flying Carpet," said the Sailor. "Our Tilly-Willy is too slow, and he won't be able to catch up to the Witch if she escapes from him by air, so the mouse tribe is faced with the urgent task of destroying the Magic Carpet."

Ramina was overjoyed. "That's something that's well within our power!" she exclaimed in her squeaky little voice. "We'll chew on the rug, and chew on it in such a way that not even little pieces of it will be left."

Strasheela and his friends clapped their hands, and Artoshka, taking advantage of this moment, almost slipped out of Tim's hands.

"But the road from our hideout to the wicked Fairy's domain is a long one," continued Ramina. "There are many obstacles along the way: broad, swift-flowing streams, mountains, ravines with steep sides... We'll need a companion, one who's strong and agile, to help us in the dangerous spots."

Her eyes fell on Tim O'Kelly, and the flattered boy agreed at once to set out. To tell the truth, the one-legged Sailor was very leery of sending the little boy off alone on a long and perilous journey, but there was no other course open to them. Neither he, Charlie, nor the Iron Woodman, nor Din Gior was suitable as an escort to the mouse tribe: they had all become too sluggish. Nor could the Captain entrust such a mission to Faramant or the Doctor: they both lacked the necessary strength and were getting on in years.

"All right, my lad," the Captain decided at last, sighing deeply, "go — but I conjure you by all the masts of my ship, be careful! Be off, my friends, and may you have tail-winds behind you!..."

While they were getting Tim ready — preparing rafaloo-leaf filters and protective glasses for his eyes — the Mouse Queen questioned Annie and Charlie Black about her good friend Ellie, about how well she was doing in school, and about her health. She also inquired about how ex-Wizard Goodwin was getting along, and how he had made out after retiring from the magician business. When she learned that Goodwin now ran a little grocery store, the majestic Mouse shook her head in disapproval.

Tim was now standing at the threshold, his tightly-stuffed knapsack on his shoulders; in the knapsack he had stashed away a stock of food and a change of underclothing, and a sharp hatchet with a sturdy handle dangled from the boy's belt.

"You can't travel on foot, Tim," said Strasheela. "Time is of the essence, and we've got to make the most of every hour. Faramant, give Tim Rujero's Magic Carpet."

As he handed Tim the Carpet, with its inventory number still attached to it, the Master of Requisition admonished the boy for a long time to treat the priceless object with as much care as possible. In his own inventory he wrote: *Carpet given out for temporary use by Tim O'Kelly. Reason: order of Strasheela the Wise.*

Tim O'Kelly exited the van, and he spread the Carpet out on the ground and seated himself on it, while Ramina and the other mice found themselves comfortable spots under his shirt, in his bosom.

"Carry me, Carpet, to the entrance to the underground passage that begins near the farm of Lin Raub," intoned the boy. It was the Queen of the Mice who indicated this exact address to him.

The Carpet rose into the air and flew off in the required direction. As he followed it with his eyes, Faramant made a sign to the Deadwood Oaks, and the trailer began to move slowly from its spot.

The detachment of bold warriors headed toward the south. They would follow the Yellow Brick Road as far as the Great River, but then they would have to leave it and search for Arachna's retreat, which was in the wild mountains somewhere between Blue Land and Stella's domain.

It was tedious to sit there in the jouncing trailer as the Deadwood Oaks pulled it along at their leisurely pace, and Annie turned ingratiatingly to the Sailor. "Uncle Charlie, I still remember that amazing story you told me about Lord Bumcherleigh and Professor Vogel."

Sensing some sort of a trick, Charlie responded in a grouchy tone: "What good is that? Who's stopping you from remembering it to your heart's content?"

"It's good to recall old things, but hearing something new is even better," said the girl with a cunning smile, and then, caressing her uncle, she asked him: "Tell me about something else, for you yourself have been boasting about living through all different adventures."

The Sailor began to weaken: "Ah, you fidget, what a boot-licker you are! What do you want me to tell you about?"

"Tell me how you lost your leg!" suggested Annie. "No doubt that happened during a battle with pirates?"

"It was almost that," agreed Charlie Black. "All right, then, lend me your ears." And Charlie Black launched into his lengthy account.

Chapter 24

THE GREAT MARCH
OF THE MOUSE ARMY

The flight of the Magic Carpet to the tunnel where the mice were hiding, lasted an hour; if Tim had traveled this distance on foot, he would have wasted an entire day. After he had landed, the boy said, with delight: "What a remarkable thing this Rug is! If only I had it in Kansas!" Then he rolled the Carpet up and placed it under his arm.

The Mouse Queen, sticking her head up from under his shirt, indicated the direction to him in her squeaky little voice, and the boy soon found himself near the entrance to the underground passage. Here, he lit a small lantern which Faramant, in his foresight, had given him, and then he clambered down the steep slope.

"Walk as carefully as you can, friend Tim," Ramina advised him. "Otherwise, you'll step right on my subjects."

This advice was well to the point. By the light of his lantern, Tim saw an uncountable horde of mice, and it filled the underground passage completely. They swarmed about everywhere, they peeked out of every crevice, and they hung in veritable clusters from the walls, clinging with their little claws to projections in the rock. Mice were cheeping angrily, fighting with one another for space, but when they saw their Queen and her retinue, they fell silent at once.

Taking a place on Tim's hand (which he held stretched out in front of him) as if on a rostrum, Ramina turned to address her tribe. After giving them a brief report about the rescue expedition that had arrived from beyond the mountains, the Queen concluded: "We must aid the humans in their fight with the cruel Arachna. Only then will light and warmth return. Our task is to deprive the Witch of her Magic Carpet, or else she'll escape her retribution, and the Yellow Fog will continue to hang over the land as before."

"Your Majesty," Tim addressed Ramina, "I've just come up with a good idea. Let's take on the small carpet as many mice as it will hold and fly to Arachna's retreat, and our detachment will make short work of the full-sized Carpet."

"I'm afraid you're mistaken, Tim, my friend," countered the Queen. "It won't be enough to gnaw the Carpet to pieces: there are Gnomes who will quickly gather up the shreds of magical wool and re-spin it, and the Carpet will be woven anew. In order to prevent it from being restored, it'll be necessary to eat it up completely, and for that, *all* my subjects will be needed."

Tim scratched his head when he heard this explanation, and then he said: "All right, let's get started! But aren't you afraid that the mice will perish when they drink in the poisonous fog?"

Chapter 24: THE MARCH OF THE MOUSE ARMY

"It won't have its full effect before a week, a week and a half, and we'll try to reach Arachna's domain by that time."

As one can see, Ramina had an answer ready for everything.

Tim was afraid that there would be no discipline during the march, but as it turned out, the mouse army was very well organized. It was separated into divisions, the divisions into regiments, the regiments into battalions, and the battalions into companies and platoons. Each sub-unit was commanded by an experienced, highly decorated mouse with the rank of lieutenant, captain, or colonel, and their commands were obeyed without question.

The army staff determined the sequence in which the divisions and the regiments would move, and messengers transmitted this sequence to all the sub-units.

Tim marched first, carrying the Queen and her army staff in his shirt and his pockets, and behind him ran the adjutants and the messengers. The boy was anxious that he would not be able to find his way in the fog, but the Queen set his mind at ease: "A Fairy is not going to get lost in the fields and forests of her own country. As soon as you begin to stray from the right direction, I'll feel it at once and tell you."

The army moved in perfect formation, company after company, regiment after regiment, right up until nightfall. Tim was already about to drop on his feet from weariness when Ramina, spotting a wheatfield, gave the signal to halt.

The mice immediately began to run here and there around the field, crunching the dried, withered grains in their sharp teeth. Tim likewise had some supper and went to sleep, wrapping himself in the Magic Carpet.

The next morning, the crimson sun had barely begun to glow through the Fog, when the march was resumed. The second day on the move proved to be more difficult than the first. More than once, they encountered broad, swift streams cutting across their path. Tim grasped his hatchet, cut down a few trees, and threw them across from one bank to the other. By making use of these bridges, the mice quickly surmounted the obstacles and re-formed into columns on the opposite bank: strict discipline was maintained in Ramina's army.

The third day of the march began with the most adverse weather, as a snowstorm broke out. A cold wind swept over the plain, blowing white flakes of snow into the air.

A snowstorm in Magic Land! Who could have imagined such a thing even a month ago in this land of eternal summer? Yet here was the wind howling, bending the shrubbery, breaking branches off trees and casting them down onto the legions of mice.

There was no question of staying there at the spot where they had spent the night, since they might well freeze to death, so Ramina ordered that the march continue. The messengers, holding their tails up high and getting enmeshed in the snow, dashed around from one sub-unit to another. Platoons and battalions assembled in rows, wrestling with the wind and trying not to lose their formation.

Tim O'Kelly, the leader of this extraordinary gray army, marched forward. He covered his back with the Magic Carpet, and snowflakes stuck to his spectacles. As he walked along, he thought: "If only Mom could see how I've kept my promise to avoid danger in Magic Land..."

Ramina, unerringly sensing the proper direction for them to travel in, gave the boy directions as to which way to turn.

How much peeping and commotion there was, how many heroic actions were performed among those uncounted swarms of tiny gray creatures! Here, an elderly mouse fell into a pit that was invisible beneath the snow, and her neighbors, breaking ranks, held out their legs and their tails so that she could cling to them and pull herself up out of the trap. There, two big, strong mice pulled along a young mouse that had grown weak, holding him up on either side and urging him not to lose his spirits.

It was the adjutants and messengers who had the hardest time of it. They plied continually back and forth among the columns, picking up those who had dropped behind and returning them to their place in the formation. One can only envy them their devotion and bravery.

One messenger saved an entire battalion, which had strayed from the path and gotten stuck in a gully with steep sides. By following the messenger's instructions, the battalion was able to rejoin the main forces.

An adjutant named Split Ear carried on his back for a whole mile a mouse named Blackie, who had cut herself on a twig, until he caught up with Tim and turned the wounded mouse over to him. Nor was this the only mouse that was entrusted to the boy's care. His pockets were filled with wounded, exhausted, and frozen mice. Mice were seated at his breast, on his shoulders, on his hat, and they peeked out from his sleeves...

This cruel struggle with the frost and the storm lasted for several hours. Ramina's troops made many a sacrifice, and there's no telling how it all would have ended if the wind had not finally begun to die down. It became warmer, and the crimson sun began to glow.

The Queen ordered a halt for feeding and bivouac for the night. Before anything else, a roll-call was taken of the various battalions. The army had lost 785 warriors and commanders, who had either frozen to death or vanished without a trace. This figure was not too great for a host that numbered many thousands, but if misfortunes such as these were to be prolonged, then there was no way to avoid thinking about it...

On the fourth day of the march, the path itself became much worse: the mice had reached a mountainous region where they could not move as quickly as they could on the plain. And yet the mice still had to make haste: the fate of the whole land depended on the success of their undertaking.

It was imperative that the speed of movement of the fortress-van be coordinated with that of the mouse army. If Charlie Black should reach the wicked Sorceress's cave ahead of the others, the Witch would simply fly away, and then it would be very difficult both for the mice and for Tilly-Willy the Giant to track her down.

A tall mountain with steep slopes loomed up in the path of the mice, and the gray army needed several hours to scale it. Taking advantage of this circumstance, Tim decided to fly back to the one-legged Sailor with a report. He took the Mouse Queen with him as well.

The Carpet bore the boy quickly to the van, which had already left the Great River behind and was penetrating more deeply into the southern region. Tilly-Willy was walking behind with clumsy steps; the Deadwood Oaks wound him up twice a day.

Annie, Charlie Black, and all the others were glad to hear from Tim and Ramina that the mouse army was on the move, and they felt sad when they learned what losses it had suffered in the previous day's storm. The snowstorm had likewise caught the area where the van was moving, but of course it had not caused any harm to the garrison.

According to calculations made by the Iron Woodman, Kaggi-Karr, and Ramina, it was evident that the mobile fortress was making better time than the mice, and so they would have to hold back for a day or two so that they would not frighten the Witch away prematurely. Tim stocked up on provisions and sharpened his hatchet; then he placed Ramina in his pocket, and they set out on the return trip. When they reached the mouse army, they found the last platoons rolling down the mountain that had cost them so much trouble to scale.

The next day of the march proved to be extremely arduous. Their path was constantly cut across by chasms with perpendicular walls. They were able to go around some of these, and Tim threw bridges across others by cutting down trees that grew by the edge of the ravine.

But then they encountered a gorge that was impossible to detour, and which had no trees growing along the edge. What could they do now? Carry the mice across on the Flying Carpet? No, that would take far too much time. The Queen proposed that they fashion a living suspension bridge. A few hundred of the biggest and strongest mice, grasping the tails of their comrades with their front paws, formed a living chain, and Tim threw it across the abyss.

The mice swarmed over this live, quivering bridge, company by company, peeping with terror and trying not to look down. Everything went without a hitch, except when the head of Blackie, the wounded mouse, began to spin, and she almost went plunging to the bottom of the chasm. But a friend of hers grabbed hold of her just in time.

When the crossing was completed, Tim used the Carpet to pick up the members of the bridge. This was their last and most difficult obstacle. The subsequent leg of their journey led through areas that were flatter. And after four days of forced marches, to the inexpressible delight of the entire army, from general down to mouse private — the blue sky appeared above them: they were in Arachna's domain. This did not happen a moment too soon: many of the mice were already coughing, while the eyes of others were beginning to water.

Now that the region of the Yellow Fog was behind them, the mice could breathe freely. All the same, particular caution was called for here: Gnomes might be lurking about in the area. Once the Gnomes learned of the invasion of the mice, they would go and report it to the Witch, and everything would be lost. Luckily, the ground here was very soft, and the mice quickly dug themselves many burrows and found a safe refuge in them from the eyes of others. Tim, for his part, flew back to the trailer for another conference with Charlie Black.

Chapter 25

TILLY-WILLY — INVENTOR

By the purest chance, Ramina's army did not encounter a single Gnome during their journey, and thus Arachna learned nothing about the coming of the mice: that would have compelled her to be wary.

But the scouts did inform the Witch that a strange house on wheels was approaching her territory, a house drawn by wooden men, and well defended: it was under the continual escort of an iron giant with a savage face. Arachna decided to learn about what her enemies had in mind and just how dangerous they really were.

Taking Ruf Bilan with her, the Witch clambered aboard the Flying Carpet and took to the air. About a mile from the spot where the people were to be found, as stated by the Gnomes' reports, the Sorceress landed and, hiding in the woods, she sent Bilan out as a scout.

A half hour went by. Then, not far from Arachna's hiding place, dried leaves could be heard crunching under the feet of Ruf Bilan as he made his way back, and the fellow himself soon appeared. The little man was walking unsteadily, his face pale with terror, and his lips twitched convulsively. At last he forced himself to say: "What I saw, mistress!... What I saw..." And then he fell silent.

"Well, *tell* me, you sniveler!" the Fairy bellowed at him.

"There's a... a giant," began the scout, stammering. "He... he's b-bigger than y-y-you are... And his face... Ah, what a f-face! I hid myself well in the bushes, but when he l-l-looked in m-my direction, his d-dreadful eyes s-s-seemed to be looking right through me... And th-there's a one-l-legged m-man that he c-calls 'Papa!' I b-barely g-got away from there..."

"Imagine my depending on such a dunce!" said Arachna with contempt. "You walked and walked, yet you didn't find out a thing. I'll just have to go myself."

The Witch walked at first at her full height, but then she crouched down, and finally she took to moving among the trees in a crawl.

At last, some sort of rumbling and crashing sound could be heard. Arachna moved as close as she could, and here is what she saw: Tilly-Willy was hacking a passage through the forest for the van. He was standing with his back to the Witch, leaning forward a little, and his gigantic sword was flying back and forth in his mighty arms like a reed. With each stroke he made, a stout tree fell over, and the unflagging Deadwood Oaks lugged it to the side. Arachna did not get a look at the Giant's face, but his mere size and strength inspired the greatest respect in her.

"No," said the Witch to herself, "it wouldn't do for me to come to blows with an iron fellow like him. But what does it matter? I've got the Magic Carpet, so that imbecile will have to chase me around the country on his own two feet." If the Witch could only know of the indomitable horde of mice that was advancing upon her cave in a mighty avalanche!...

Arachna returned home gloomy and meditative. While on the way, she devised plans for delaying her enemies' progress for the longest possible interval. Arachna ordered the Gnomes to maintain a ceaseless surveillance over her foes and to report to her every evening on their whereabouts.

The layover of the van, as agreed upon between Charlie Black and Ramina, lasted for two days. During the very first night, an important event occurred in Tilly-Willy's condition, and it influenced the whole course of the campaign.

Lestar was sound asleep in his comfortable armchair when the muffled voice of the Iron Paladin was heard from above: "Lestar! Master Lestar! Answer me!"

No response. The Giant raised his voice higher. "Lestar, listen, I'm calling you!"

"Mmmm..." answered the mechanic in a sleepy voice. "What on earth has happened? Who is it?"

"It's me, Tilly-Willy! Why didn't you answer me?"

"Can't you see, my friend? I was asleep — and I must have been sleeping pretty soundly at that!"

"Asleep?" inquired the Giant. "What is this 'sleep?'"

"Sleep?" Lestar stammered. "It's very hard to explain. It's like this. A person lies down, his eyes close, and he goes off into a sort of torpor, he stops seeing and hearing things, and consciousness doesn't return to him for several hours. That means that he's awakened."

"But listen to me," said the Giant, growing anxious, "that's downright dangerous. An enemy can approach a sleeping person, and he can do anything he wants to him, even kill him!"

Chapter 25: TILLY-WILLY — INVENTOR

"It's not as bad as all that," said Lestar with a smile. "If there's an enemy in the vicinity, people just don't go to sleep, or else they post sentinels. Without sleep, a person can't function: sleep restores his strength and his fortitude."

"What imperfect creatures you humans are," commented Tilly-Willy. "You waste such a heap of time unproductively! As for me, at night, when everything is quiet, all kinds of interesting ideas come to me. Today, for instance, I came up with a little scheme which, in my opinion, will be most useful, I swear by the masts!"

Now the Iron Paladin had not been wasting the days that they spent in traveling. He would talk with Lestar for an entire hour on various topics, though primarily on technical matters. He had learned a great deal, and his store of words had increased quite noticeably. Lestar, therefore, became fired with enthusiasm, and he jumped up and down in the chair. "What sort of little scheme? Tell me!"

"I've thought of a way to make me self-winding," said Tilly-Willy. "Those Deadwood Oaks, who putter around me with ladders and make squeaking noises with the keys — may a hurricane drown them, for they get on my nerves dreadfully! Here's what I was thinking: if you were to install a few more springs and levers, and arrange it in such a way that it can be pulled two ways..."

With this, the Giant launched into a discourse that was so technical that you and I wouldn't understand even a word of it, so there's no point in quoting his words here. Let us say merely that the essence of his suggestion was as follows: one arm, as it rose and fell, would wind the other; the left leg would wind the right, and vice versa.

Lestar was thrilled. He even opened the little door and leaned outward in order to hear better. Then he began to shout: "Listen, my boy! You're a mechanical genius!"

"What do you mean, a genius?" replied Tilly-Willy modestly. "I simply have a lot of free time, which you humans waste on various nonsensical things like sleeping and eating."

Lestar, unable to restrain himself, ran to the trailer, and he roused Charlie Black and told him about the Iron Paladin's ingenuity. The Sailor in turn was delighted.

The next morning, day had hardly broken when the work began. The necessary springs and levers were on hand among Black's equipment, and the reconstruction of the mechanical Giant proceeded swiftly, with Tilly-Willy himself giving most useful instructions. The job was finished by the end of the second day, and Lestar said to the Giant: "My dear Tilly, everything is now ready! From now on, you won't be needing my services, so we'll be parting company!"

"What do you mean?" asked the Giant, surprised.

"I mean that I'll no longer be sitting inside your belly and burdening you with my worthless self."

"But that's ridiculous!" said Tilly-Willy, distressed. "Your weight is a mere bit of fluff to me, and walking along the roads without my driver and, I dare say, my mentor and friend will be most boring! There won't be anyone to exchange words with. I beseech you, esteemed Lestar, take your place again!"

The craftsman, smiling, climbed back into the cabin.

Tilly-Willy's intellectual development proceeded rapidly after that, but it cost his mentor, Lestar, very dearly. During the day, the Giant walked along behind the van, but at night, when he had plenty of time to think, he gave the mechanic no rest. Question followed question, just like those a child of three might ask, and there was no end of them.

"What is the sun, and why does it move across the sky?"

"Where do rivers come from?"

"Why is the night dark?"

"Why does the wind blow?"

"Why does my Dad have only one leg?"

"How do people live beyond the mountains?"

And so on, and so forth.

The good-natured Lestar wore himself out trying to the utmost of his abilities to illuminate Tilly-Willy in his thirst for knowledge, and he ended up falling asleep in mid-sentence...

From this time on, it was a rare night when Lestar was able to get his full quota of sleep, and he tried to make up for the lost hours during the day, when the Giant left him in peace. Yes, the task of the little mechanic from Winkie Land — being young Tilly-Willy's tutor — became a most demanding one.

Chapter 26

THE TACTICS OF ARACHNA THE WITCH

Let us return to the point when the re-equipping of the Iron Paladin was finished. The military detachment of Strasheela and Charlie Black, with its might and combat-effectiveness immeasurably increased, took to the road once more. Now that they were approaching Arachna's domain, the greatest caution was called for. Charlie Black could not, of course, carry out reconnaissance with the help of the Carpet, but the detachment did have one very experienced fighter, Kaggi-Karr. She flew on ahead several miles, surveyed the road, darted about everywhere, and then returned to the others with valuable information.

If they encountered a ravine across which it was necessary to lay a bridge, the Iron Paladin went into action. He chopped down huge trees and laid them in place, following Lestar's instructions.

It was only a short time before our heroes learned the hard way that Arachna was aware of their approach. The van was riding along through a forest glade when all of a sudden, at its narrowest point, the Deadwood Oaks tumbled down into the ground, making a great deal of noise as they went; the front wheels of the vehicle tumbled downward, and a broken axle began to creak. The passengers slid along the now tilting floor, hitting the walls and banging into one another. The groans of those who were bruised filled the air, not to mention the desperate yelping of Artoshka, who was being crushed under the Iron Woodman's weight.

"We've fallen into a trap!" cried Charlie Black. "No doubt about it, this is Arachna's handiwork!"

While the people were trying to get back on their feet, Tilly-Willy arrived on the scene of the accident. He pulled the van up out of the trap and set it down on the level ground. He asked at once, in an anxious voice: "Papa Charlie! Are you still in one piece? Nothing broken?"

"No, no, my dear boy," replied the one-legged Sailor appreciatively. "All I got was a bump on the head."

"What's a bump?"

It was necessary to explain that phenomenon to the knowledge-hungry Giant. Only then did Charlie and Lestar the craftsman undertake to make a new axle and repair the broken wheel. Boril set dislocated arms and legs and rubbed scratches with curative balm.

Chapter 26: THE TACTICS OF ARACHNA

The repair of the van was not completed until evening, and then they decided to stay put for the night. "Yes, we got off pretty easy," said Black. "It could have been much worse. From here on in, we'll have to keep a sharp lookout for the Witch."

"It won't do for us to fall into pits," expounded Strasheela with an air of importance. "A pit is a bad thing, while level ground is very good. If we travel all the time on the level ground, then we'll never fall into a pit."

Everyone agreed that Strasheela was right, but unfortunately, his advice did not allow for the possibility of detecting pitfalls that had been camouflaged.

The next day, the detachment stopped to spend the night in a valley, on the bank of a deep river. Charlie Black, Annie, Din Gior, Faramant, Boril, and Tim (who was spending the night in the van with the others) were asleep, exhausted by the bumpiness of the journey. Only Strasheela and the Iron Woodman, who did not know what sleep was, continued to talk, and their topic of conversation had for many years been one and the same thing: which is better, brains or a heart.

During their heated debate, the friends heard a muffled noise of some sort resound in the distance, and at once the ground began to shake. "There's been an avalanche somewhere," observed the Woodman, and then he continued his proof that if a person has a loving heart, then brains are of no consequence.

About an hour went by. Charlie Black was dreaming that he was sailing on a ship, and that water was bubbling around the sides. Then the Sailor awoke, and was amazed to hear the actual sounds of water bubbling and splashing under the floor of the van. He opened the door and looked outside: from what he could make out in the darkness and the fog, there was water lapping all about them!

"Mayday!" Charlie shouted. "It's a flood!" Din Gior, Faramant, Boril, Tim, and Annie leaped to their feet.

"Lestar, of course, is asleep up in his cabin," said Din Gior speculatively, "and it won't occur to Tilly-Willy to come to our assistance on his own. He doesn't understand what a desperate plight we're in. I'll run to him."

Taking his splendid beard, which Annie had, most conveniently, arranged in three plaits the night before, and throwing it over his shoulder, Din Gior exited from the van. He had to wade over to Tilly-Willy the Giant through water up to his breast, but the Long-Bearded Soldier successfully made his way to the Giant's foot and began to pound it with his fist.

"What happened?" shouted Lestar, after waking up; he had just managed to doze off after another conversation with his pupil.

"Take a look outside and you'll find out!" responded Din Gior.

By that time, Tilly-Willy himself realized that something was wrong, and he carefully picked Din Gior up and placed him on his shoulder.

After slamming the door behind Din Gior as the latter departed, Charlie Black reprimanded Strasheela, the Iron Woodman, and Lan Pirot (who had now shown up with a report) because they had not sounded an alarm in time. Strasheela and the Woodman justified themselves by the fact that they were landlubbers and did not know the sounds of water, while the former General reported that the stream had overflowed its banks very suddenly, and they had already been in the water before his companions even knew what was happening.

However, it was pointless to look for people to blame for this oversight, for everyone knew perfectly well the cause of what had happened. The noise that the Woodman and Strasheela had heard was the sound of an avalanche, one arranged through the courtesy of the Witch, to dam up the stream. The waters continued to rise, and the van began to float, bobbing along on the waves. But there was not even one little chink in it, so no water seeped inside.

"Hurrah!" cried the delighted Tim. "Our fortress has turned into a ship, with Charlie Black as its Captain! Command me, Captain, and Cabin Boy Tim O'Kelly will perform his duty!"

But to Charlie, it was no laughing matter. The situation was becoming perilous. The van might become so entangled in floating debris that it would be impossible to extricate it. And the Deadwood Oaks could not hold it back: being made of wood themselves, they floated right along with the van.

Luckily, Tilly-Willy came to the rescue. He walked over to the drifting fortress and, before doing anything else, he inquired about Papa Charlie's health and general state; only then did he take hold of the shaft with his enormous hand. It ceased moving at once.

The night was so dark that it was necessary to wait until morning before they could make a decision. The garrison in the fortress somehow managed to hold out until the weak, turbid dawn. Charlie then decided that they should make their way to dry ground: smashing the dam that Arachna had erected would mean losing a great deal of precious time.

The Crow flew out on a scouting mission. She returned a half hour later, reporting the presence of a flat shore onto which it would be an easy matter to pull the van.

The Captain had brought with him from the City a supply of rope. He threw one end of it to the Deadwood Oaks, and the latter tied it to the shaft and to the wheels. Tilly-Willy splashed through the water, pulling the van along behind him. The Crow flew on ahead of the Giant, pointing out the proper direction to him.

"Land! Land!" the passengers in the van cried out, just as Columbus's sailors did once, a long time ago.

The Deadwood Oaks, headed by Lan Pirot, crawled out of the water soaking wet, in pitiful shape, with their paint peeling off, but with all their strength intact. When everything was in order once again, the little detachment continued on, along the road that the Crow had reconnoitered.

"Yes," said the Sailor, worried, "that Witch is a dangerous adversary, for she's very cunning and resourceful. What surprises might she be preparing for us even yet?"

They did not have long to wait for her newest surprise. The following evening, as the caravan was making its way through a rocky gorge, the ground suddenly began to quiver, and large rocks tumbled down the slopes of the gorge. Rumbling and crashing down on uneven spots, fragments of the cliff shattered to pieces and flew through the air with the speed of projectiles fired from guns.

Tilly-Willy, with amazing agility, protected the van with his enormous body and held his huge shield out in front of him, to receive the blows of the cascading rocks.

The bombardment lasted for several minutes, and during this period, the Iron Paladin was able to disperse dozens of projectiles, any one of which could have smashed the van to smithereens and destroyed the people inside it. The rocks hit the shield with a dreadful din, deafening the fighters who were holed up within the mobile fortress.

The cannonade at last fell silent. Thanks to Tilly-Willy's resourcefulness and dexterity, they came through the whole business without suffering any great damage. One of the van's wheels was totally demolished, Algen the Deadwood Oak had a hand broken off, and the shield showed some rather sizable dents. After they had changed the wheel (for Charlie had some spare ones on hand) and giving Algen a new hand, the expedition made haste to leave that perilous spot. When the van left the gorge, the travelers observed Arachna flying along above them in the fog, wrapping herself in her blue cloak to protect herself from the cold.

"It's evident that Ramina has not yet fulfilled her military mission," said Strasheela. "Since the Witch is flying on her Carpet, that means that the mice have not devoured it."

"It's not all that easy a thing to do," said Charlie Black with a sigh. "I'm hopeful that they're on the watch, and merely awaiting a favorable moment."

At their first resting-place, Strasheela got it into his head to reward Tilly-Willy with a medal for the selflessness that he had shown during Arachna's assault. The wise man of straw always kept a supply of medals with him, and Faramant, Chief of Requisition, took care of them. But they needed a long time to get across to the young Giant just what a medal was and what it was awarded for. When Tilly-Willy finally understood, he said: "And does Papa Charlie have a medal? Judging by what Lestar has told me about his heroic deeds, I swear by the storms of the southern latitudes, he should have a whole bunch of medals!"

Strasheela smacked himself on the head in desperation. If the Monarch of Emerald Land had been able to blush, he most certainly would have done so when he heard this forthright question. "Ah, what a lout, what a blockhead I am!" exclaimed Strasheela, pulling out the pins that had been protruding from his head and which had gotten stuck in his straw hand. "What was I thinking of before? During his first visit, the Giant from Beyond the Mountains rescued the Emerald City from the domination of Urfin Jus, and he freed me and the Iron Woodman from captivity… At that time, of course, my craftsmen had not yet fashioned any medals. But where have my brains been *now*? Now, when the Giant from Beyond the Mountains has again hastened to our assistance, exposed his valuable life to danger, taken on a dreadful opponent in combat?... And I, unfortunate nincompoop and dolt that I am, never once thought of commemorating the services of this self-less man with the Order of the Star and Emeralds? My dear friend, pardon my blunder and accept these awards..."

Despite Charlie Black's protests (which, however, were hardly very strong!), the Monarch pinned to the Sailor's jacket the three highest decorations of the whole land, all of them made of gold and adorned with emeralds. Not until then was a medal finally fastened to Tilly-Willy's iron breast.

"Too bad there's no mirror around," sighed the Giant. "I'd like to see how this trinket looks on me..."

The next obstacle in their path was a lofty heap of boulders. Arachna had gone to no little trouble to pile up a whole mountain of enormous lumps of rock. But in the end, her labor was all for nothing. After about three hours of work, Tilly-Willy cleared the path. Now that they had passed these mountains, the van came out onto a level plain, and the party stopped and waited for news from Ramina.

Chapter 27

THE FATE OF THE MAGIC CARPET

The army of mice had for several days been occupying their burrows by the border of Arachna's territory. During the day, the mice hid cautiously from the eyes of outsiders, and at night, they moved out in regular columns to feed in the Witch's fields, which were not touched by the toxic fog.

Every day, patrols posted in secluded spots saw the Fairy fly away somewhere on her Magic Carpet, not to return for several hours. After two meetings with the Giant from Beyond the Mountains, Ramina knew that the Witch was engaging in military operations against her enemies, but without any particular success. During the night, the mouse scouts penetrated all the way to Arachna's retreat via secret paths, and returned with the report that the Carpet was hidden within her cave and that there was no way of gaining access to it.

But after one rainy day, the Carpet had gotten soaking wet during its time in the air. It had been laid out to dry in the yard before the cave. It was still there that night, and it was this joyous news that the party of scouts reported to Ramina.

Messengers set out at once for the fields where the mice were feeding after their day's fast, and they spread the mandate: "All sub-units are to assemble in formation and to assume the positions designated in the disposition."

Before half an hour had passed, the divisions and regiments were ready to go into action. In the darkness of the night, the tiny gray bodies of the mice blended right into the ground.

Regiment after regiment crept silently up to the Carpet from different directions. Nothing was heard but the rustling of tiny feet, though the sound of soft commands was heard too from time to time. The two elderly Gnomes who were guarding the Carpet were sound asleep, and so was Arachna, exhausted after her labors of the day.

Ten thousand mice ran forward and converged on the Magic Carpet, and hundreds of thousands of sharp white teeth penetrated its fabric. The wool began to split, and the first holes appeared here and there.

The Queen had given her tribe this strict command: "You must do your work diligently, and don't limit yourselves to tearing the Carpet apart into its individual shreds of wool: these shreds themselves must be swallowed, repellent as that is. The task must be completed by morning, and nothing must remain where the carpet was, except empty space."

The mice tried their very utmost. Platoon leaders kept a close watch to assure that not even a single shred of wool remained in the yard. If a mouse were unable to swallow a piece of thread because it was too long, then one of her companions would bite off the excess.

The Gnome guards snored away peacefully, and the Carpet came more and more to resemble a sieve. Finally, rubbing their paws against their stuffed bellies, the mice began to move away from the Carpet. But many shreds remained there.

The wise Ramina had foreseen this. Her adjutants scampered away from the area, and before long, fresh divisions that had been held in reserve threw themselves on the remnants of the Carpet with renewed strength. It was comical to watch two mice grasp a long piece of thread, each of them pulling it toward himself, and then see the thread give way, and the two friendly competitors roll over on their backs, kicking their feet in the air.

Ramina's mandate was carried out with military precision: by morning, the Carpet was gone — but the gray army was unable to budge from where it was, so heavily were the mice weighted down by the fabric that they had swallowed.

Arachna awoke earlier than usual that morning : it was as if something were prodding her in the side, compelling her to walk out of the cave. And after one look at the spot where the Carpet had been spread the night before, the Witch was stunned. In the place of its lively colors, she saw something gray, something quivering, something vaguely outlined.

It did the Enchantress no good to look about for the guards. The Gnomes had long since become aware that the Carpet had disappeared and, knowing that a fearful punishment awaited them for their negligence, they had taken refuge in a hiding-place somewhere. Arachna took a few steps forward. The gray blanket began to stir, to assume definite form.

"Mice!" gasped the Witch. "My Carpet has been eaten up by mice!"

It would have been the simplest thing for her to throw herself on this living mass and stomp on them with her feet. But Arachna, like many women, was afraid of mice. The reader must not be surprised at this, though, and should recall that even elephants, the giants of the animal kingdom, are likewise afraid of the little gray beasts.

"Cats will help me," thought Arachna.

She dashed into the cave, fetched her book of magic, and quickly began to mumble an incantation to summon cats.

At that time, a great many wildcats had gathered in Arachna's domain, coming in from the neighboring regions to take refuge from the Yellow Fog. Red, striped, black, bitten and scratched in fights with rivals, cats by the hundreds raced forward from all directions at the Witch's summons, holding their tails high and meowing loudly.

Something happened now that the Gnome Chronicler recorded with both amazement and delight.

The mice wished with all their might to be as far away from the cats as possible, and since the cats were advancing upon them from everywhere, the only path of salvation lay in the sky. The mice's stomachs were filled with wool, but even there, the magic wool had not lost its lifting power. And was a great deal of this power really required to lift a mouse into the air?

In obedience to the mental commands of their new masters, the magical bits of wool did their duty, and an uncountable horde of mice rose into the air, with their Queen at their head. Instead of tasty prey, the savage cats found only the bare ground, and they entered into a savage brawl among themselves.

The mice, using their tails as rudders and now giving deliberate commands to the magical shreds of wool, moved away from Arachna's cave. They peeped merrily as they flew, and exchanged impressions with one another regarding the convenience of this new mode of travel.

And did our mice remain airborne for long? Unfortunately, they didn't. Little by little, they returned to being ordinary land-bound creatures destined to move about on four legs. But by then, the magical wool was dispersed about the whole land, and even the industrious Gnomes could not possibly hope to gather it all back together.

And thus was Arachna the Witch deprived of her Flying Carpet. She understood now with full clarity that a showdown with the Giant that accompanied the van was inevitable. As long as she had possessed the Magic Carpet, she could have slipped away from him via air, but now, she and Tilly-Willy -alike were earthbound. Once again, Urfin Jus's sinister prediction came to her mind...

Calling together about two dozen Gnomes out of those who had not yet had time to scatter in flight, Arachna sent them out on reconnaissance. Their task was to find out where the fortress on wheels was, and whether or not it were headed straight for the cave. Arachna herself began to prepare a weapon — an enormous club — from an ironwood tree, a species renowned for its sturdiness.

Chapter 28

A NEW ALLY

When Tim flew back to the place where his friends were encamped and reported that Arachna's Carpet no longer existed, there was jubilation all around, and even the Deadwood Oaks, in their elation, performed an ungainly dance, which greatly distressed Lan Pirot, that connoisseur of dancing.

"Now the Witch won't get away from us," stated Strasheela self-confidently. "She was able to fly, but we couldn't. So we had no way of catching her. Now we're still unable to fly, but she can't do it either, and that means we *will* catch her."

Everyone agreed with Strasheela's opinion, except for Charlie Black. "I'm afraid it's not quite like that," observed the Sailor with anxiety. "Of course, our chances of victory are now much higher. Our boy, Tilly-Willy, is developing not by the day, but by the hour, like something straight out of a fairy tale. All of you can observe how, literally right before our very eyes, he's growing more clever, smarter, and more intelligent. However, I'm afraid he won't be able to overtake Arachna if it ever comes down to a pursuit. The Witch is light on her feet and capable of making great leaps, and at any given moment, she can change the direction she's running in. Our boy is just too ponderous for that..."

Everyone grew melancholy when they heard Charlie's sensible words. "What can we do, Uncle Charlie?" asked Annie.

"We'll have to look for an ally who's as agile as Arachna and as strong as Tilly-Willy. And I think a Giant Eagle would be ideal as such an ally."

"You mean Carfax the Eagle?" exclaimed Tim and Annie in astonishment.

"Exactly, Carfax the Eagle," confirmed the Sailor. "From your stories of your adventures last year, I've gotten the impression that he's a most noble bird, one who won't stand for lies and deceit. Don't forget, the Eagle left Urfin Jus the moment he became aware of the latter's odious intentions. Carfax treats mankind well, and he asked for nothing in return when he carried you across that gulf that was too much for your mules. And like all the inhabitants of Magic Land, he'll be interested in anything that would put a speedy end to that hateful Yellow Fog."

"That's true, very true, Captain," cried Tim. "I'll fly right out to seek Carfax's assistance."

But Annie was outraged at this. "It's always *you* who do everything, *you* who go everywhere," said the girl angrily. "*You* led the army of mice when they marched, *you* flew out on reconnaissance. When is it going to be *my* turn?"

"You know, Annie," said the Sailor, jumping in, "seeking Eagle Valley will be a dangerous undertaking. Flying on a Magic Carpet is not the same thing as riding on a mule. And who is it who gave her parents a solemn promise not to involve herself in any dangerous adventures?"

"Didn't Tim also do that very same thing? Answer me *that!*" The Captain had no response for this. So Annie went on: "Aha, I got you! Say what you want, but *I'm* the one who's going out to fetch Carfax. Anyway, he'll listen to me first."

"And why is that?" asked Tim in surprise.

"Because I'm a woman!" declared Annie in a triumphant tone.

Everyone burst out laughing, and the question was decided in Annie's favor.

To make her solitary journey less devastating, the girl took her dog Artoshka along with her.

Annie was a little frightened when the Carpet, in obedience to her command, rose into the air, flew along over the woods and fields, and then, as it approached the mountains, began to gain altitude. But the girl and the dog encouraged one another, and soon they were less afraid.

Above the mountains, the sun shone much brighter than it did down below, the air there was cleaner, and Annie and Artoshka felt great. A labyrinth of snow-covered mountain peaks floated by beneath the Carpet. Annie observed that the snow line extended further down the mountains than it had the year before. The girl inferred correctly that it had grown colder up in the mountains, just as it had in all of Magic Land. Nothing but fog was visible in the depths of the mountain valleys, but our aerial travelers firmly believed that the Carpet would take them wherever they had to go.

And it did exactly that. When Annie stepped off the Carpet, she saw not far away a gigantic nest as tall as a three-story building. The head of an enormous nestling was peeking out of the nest. Soon, the air began to hum with the sound of flapping wings, and a Giant Eagle came in for a landing. That Eagle was Carfax himself.

The Eagle at first looked at his little visitor with surprise, but his memory was good, and he recognized her.

"Greetings, noble Carfax," said Annie with a bow.

"Welcome to our mountains, my girl," replied the Eagle in a hoarse, deep voice. "I assume you have come to see me on some very important matter, or else you would not have entrusted your life to that insignificant shred of cloth."

Annie took exception to this evaluation of the Carpet, and she said that it was quite suitable for someone her size. "However, that's not what I'm here about. It's indeed a very urgent request that brings me here.

Tell me, are you Giant Eagles bothered by that fog that's hanging over the earth?"

"What can I tell you?" answered Carfax meditatively. "Up here, we can live with it, but down in the valleys, it's become extremely difficult to find goats and aurochs, and in recent times we've had to go hungry a lot."

"Then you'll want to learn how it all came about!" exclaimed the girl. And she told him about Arachna's lengthy sleep, about her awakening, and about how the wicked Fairy, in order to reduce the peoples of Magic Land to slavery, had conjured up the Yellow Fog.

"My uncle Charlie Black, my friend Tim O'Kelly, and I — we've come to your country at the request of its inhabitants. We've taken on Arachna in battle and we've achieved some success, but we don't have enough strength to win a decisive victory. And if you don't help us, the Yellow Fog will continue to hang over Magic Land." The girl concluded with excitement.

"From what I understand of what you've said, this Arachna is like Urfin Jus, who seized power over the Marrans last year?"

"How can you say that?" said Annie, beginning to laugh in spite of herself. "Urfin is only small fry next to Arachna, as my Uncle Charlie would say. Even when he captured the Emerald City, the sun continued to shine as before and the sky was still blue. But now, Magic Land has been deprived of both sun and sky, and it's well on the way to total ruin. And since you mention Urfin, let me tell you that he's been neither god nor king for a long time, for the people figured him out and drove him into exile. And he's become a good man — he declined to enter the Witch's service, and he thought up a way to deal with the Yellow Fog."

"I'm glad about that," said Carfax. "All right, I'm ready to do battle with Arachna, since there's no way of avoiding it."

"You won't have to fight her alone, because you'll have Tilly-Willy the mighty Iron Paladin on your side. He's very strong, but — how should I say it?" — the girl began to stammer — "he doesn't have enough speed and agility to defeat Arachna."

After hearing this explanation, the Eagle said: "Let's not waste any more time talking — let's get to work. You'll fly on my back rather than on that piece of rag, for you'll be far more comfortable there. The only thing I can't understand is how you'll be able to climb up onto me: there are no staircases here in Eagle Valley."

"Don't you worry about that," said Annie with a smile. She sat down on the Carpet, took Artoshka in her lap, and quietly commanded it: "Carpet, lift me up onto Carfax's back." Within a few seconds, both girl and dog were in place.

"It's evident that even that rag is good for *some*thing!" said the Eagle, quite astonished.

He directed the nestling to wait quietly until its mother returned from the hunting expedition that she had flown out on, and he soared noisily up into the air.

Chapter 29

THE BATTLE OF THE GIANTS

The arrival of Carfax at Charlie Black's camp showed that Annie had carried out her important mission successfully. The first thing the girl did, after touching down with the Carpet, was to stick out her tongue at Tim and to cry out triumphantly: "You said I couldn't do it! So *there!*"

"All right, all right," grumbled Tim. "I give up!"

Charlie Black and his detachment greeted the Giant Eagle with great joy, and Tilly-Willy said politely:

"I'm very glad to see you, most esteemed bird! I'm hopeful that together, you and I will overcome the wicked Arachna!"

Carfax was taken aback at the Iron Giant's savage countenance, but being a wise and gracious bird, he did not say anything about it. On the contrary, he sang the praises of his large, slanting eyes. "No doubt you can see very well with them," said the Eagle, and Tilly-Willy felt inordinately proud.

"My beauty is of rare degree, I swear by the icebergs!" he exclaimed. "But that's something *everyone* in Magic Land knows!"

Now that all their martial forces were mustered in one place, it was possible to begin their actual military operations. But before advancing at full strength upon Arachna's cave, it was necessary to determine if the Sorceress were actually there. The assignment of going to gather the latest intelligence fell to Tim's lot, though Annie was likewise bursting to go into action. This time, however, the girl was on her own, for no one took her side, not even Artoshka.

Tim and Artoshka flew off on the Magic Carpet, and after about two hours, they returned disappointed: Arachna was gone. The boy had tried to seek out at least one Gnome in order to question him, but it was as if the little people had vanished right into the ground. In spite of this, the excursion was not a total loss. Artoshka stated that if they let him follow the Witch's trail, he'd hunt her down no matter *where* she was hiding.

Strasheela said: "You probably have very good eyesight if you expect to see the Witch's tracks. But what if she goes onto the rocks, and no tracks are noticeable?"

Artoshka burst out laughing. "We dogs have a sense that enables us to follow trails even in total darkness: it's our sense of *smell*." Strasheela shook his head doubtfully.

Chapter 29: THE BATTLE OF THE GIANTS

Since the dog could pick up the trail only at the place where it began, it was decided that the whole company would proceed to the cave. Tim, flying over the area repeatedly on the Carpet, reported that progress to the cave would be rough, and that the van would not make it through at all. Regrettable as it was, it would be necessary to abandon their mobile fortress. So they drove it into some bushes and camouflaged it with branches.

The very first steps they took along the stony path were enough to show them that going to meet the enemy on foot, with their rafaloo-leaf filters over their lips, was a far cry from traveling in a comfortable vehicle. Charlie Black was glad now that he had not brought with him from Kansas a cannon and a supply of powder and shells, though such an idea had come into his head. How could they have pursued the elusive Witch through mountain defiles and ravines if they had been encumbered by a heavy, clumsy weapon? And rifles of any caliber would have no more effect on Arachna than a child's fire-cracker.

Going was rough for the convoy even without the cannon. However, it was good that the detachment included more than two dozen Deadwood Oaks, commanded by Lan Pirot. These wooden powerhouses carried on their shoulders all the cargo from the van: their provisions, the bedding, and the tools. They headed the procession, keeping their eyes open for ambushes and pitfalls, and they threw any large rocks from their path.

Behind them walked Charlie Black and Tim, with Artoshka in his arms. (The dog had to conserve his strength for the forthcoming pursuit of Arachna.) Then followed the Iron Woodman; he had to carry Strasheela, because the poor fellow was constantly stumbling and falling, and that held up the progress of the column. Din Gior and Faramant accompanied the stocky Doctor Boril, with his medical bag hanging, as always, at his side. Din Gior carried the Magic

Television, which they had decided not to entrust to the Deadwood Oaks, and Kaggi-Karr was perched comfortably on Faramant's shoulder. Finally, behind all of them and making up the rear, majestically strode Tilly-Willy the Iron Paladin.

Carfax made up this little army's air force. The Eagle carried Annie on his back. He turned his sharp gaze to every side, but all was peaceful around them.

How our heroes rejoiced when they crossed the border into Arachna's domain! Above them spread the blue sky without a single cloud, a sight that they had not seen for a long time. The bright sun shone bountifully on them with its rays. Waves of invigorating fresh air filled their lungs, which were out of the habit of breathing freely. Casting away the now-hateful cords that held their rafaloo leaves on, the people congratulated one another, and even the Deadwood Oaks gave way to loud rejoicing: their bodies, which had grown damp through lack of sunlight, would now quickly dry out. Tilly-Willy alone looked totally dumbfounded at the sky: in all his short lifetime, he had not yet seen daylight in all its splendor.

Since the detachment had been marching for several hours and the day was declining, they decided to stop where they were until morning: suppose they were to approach Arachna's cave in the dark, and the Witch set an ambush for them?

How pleasant this night was in the warm, fresh air, under the big, bright stars in the dark blue sky!

Stretching out on his hard bed and looking upward, Charlie Black said angrily: "And that confounded Witch deprived Magic Land of all this loveliness! For that alone she deserves to die!" Annie, Tim, and Artoshka, for their part, passed a splendid night, ensconced comfortably under Carfax's soft wing.

At daybreak, the entire diverse company set forth once again, and after about three hours, they approached Arachna's retreat. It was empty. There were no Gnomes in evidence, for they had all hidden somewhere.

Before they embarked on their final showdown with Arachna, Strasheela came up with the idea of looking at her on the Television. So they set the Magic Box down on a flat rock, and all of them crowded about in front of the screen. Strasheela uttered the magic words, the frosted glass burst into light, and Arachna appeared in it. Wrapped up in her blue cloak, she was hiding out among a jumble of wild cliffs. From the look on the Witch's face, it was evident that malice and fear had mastered her completely. She was looking about her in every direction, fearful that her enemies would discover her even in this secret hiding place. Not far from Arachna lay an enormous club, which the Fairy could easily pick up at any moment.

"Uh-oh," said Faramant. "The dear thing has armed herself quite thoroughly."

Tilly-Willy disagreed. "Against my sword, that wooden object won't count for a thing, I swear by the foremast!"

After unsuccessfully searching the cave for Arachna's Magic Book, our heroes set out again, leaving all their cumbersome baggage behind in the yard in front of the cave.

Artoshka ran ahead of the others, his nose planted to the ground. He was following the Witch's trail, not deviating from it, and did so as easily as a person walks down a city street. It was difficult for Lestar and Tilly-Willy to follow behind the little black ball as it rolled along through the bushes, the tall grass, and the accumulations of rocks, so Kaggi-Karr flew along above him and served as a reliable guide for the Giant. The line of Deadwood Oaks and humans stretched out behind them in a long chain, while above them, Carfax slowly flapped his enormous wings. This time, he carried no one on his back: during the battle, he would have no time to remember any rider and take care of him.

Every half hour, Strasheela used the Television to verify whether or not the Witch was still in her hiding-place. Arachna was still there, but her behavior had become more and more uneasy. She was gazing attentively at the sky: had she already observed the Eagle there? Charlie Black made a signal to Carfax to descend closer to the ground, and the Eagle switched to a low-altitude flight.

"Arachna's trail is now fresher and more distinct," reported Artoshka to the commanders. "We're getting close to the Witch's hideout."

But the road became worse and worse. They encountered many gullies in their path, both wide ones and narrow ones. The Deadwood Oaks threw bridges across the narrow ones, using logs that they had carried with them, but the wide ones they had to go around. Tilly-Willy, walking at the head of the column, had to exercise extreme caution: the slightest fumble on his part could lead to a fall and to serious damage. And this would spell the failure of the entire campaign.

"Confounded Witch!" panted the short-legged Boril, barely able to keep pace with his companions. "Where are you hiding?"

"Why don't you stay here, Doctor?" Charlie Black suggested many times.

"Not on your life! Medicine must always be at its post!" And the brave little doctor continued to trudge along, dripping with perspiration.

All at once, the enormous black form of Arachna loomed up on the summit of the mountain: the Witch had become aware of her enemies' approach.

The situation of Charlie Black's detachment became dangerous as they found themselves under fire. The Witch continually bent down, picked up large rocks in her powerful hands, and hurled them enormous distances. The rocks shattered into pieces, and one such piece had already smashed the body of one of the Deadwood Oaks. The missiles that were aimed at Tilly-Willy, the Iron Paladin deftly fended off with his shield.

Captain Black noticed nearby something resembling a pointed-topped stone tent, which had been formed when two slabs of rock fell in such a way as to prop up against one another. Charlie and his comrades-in-arms took refuge from Arachna's fire under the heavy arches of this "tent." "When giants are fighting," he said, "it's better for us dwarfs to stay out of the way. Our blows would have no more effect on them than insect bites."

The Sailor took up a position near the exit to the tent so that he could observe more comfortably the scene of the battle. He saw Tilly-Willy the Giant advancing inexorably up the mountain slope, and the Witch hurling enormous rocks at him. With his heart in his mouth, Charlie followed the fragments of rock hurtling downward, making a rumbling sound and bouncing up and down. They were so large that the shield would be unable to turn them aside. But each time, Tilly-Willy ducked adroitly to the side, and the missiles bypassed him.

"Storms and waves!" the Sailor began to scream wildly, waving his arms. "The Eagle has finally entered the fray!"

Carfax had long been awaiting a favorable moment, and he suddenly struck Arachna's back from the air with his powerful beak, with such force that the Witch almost lost her balance and dropped the rock that she was about to throw. The Enchantress turned furiously to face this new foe, and she picked up her club from the ground and tried to stun Carfax.

But the Eagle, in spite of his immense size, was very agile, and he skillfully dodged her blows. While Arachna was contending with the Eagle, Tilly-Willy continued his progress up the slopes with enormous strides. Every one of his springs was creaking and groaning, his mechanical muscles were wound up as far as they could go, while Lestar tapped his little feet impatiently against the floor of the cabin and kept repeating feverishly: "One more little step! Now another! Put some effort into it, my little one!..."

The Giant continued steadily upward, shouting out threats: "Thunder and lightning! What I've got in store for you, you accursed Witch, once I get up the mountain!..."

Struck by the unspeakable savageness of Tilly-Willy's face, and the wicked gaze from his slanting eyes, Arachna became rigid with terror. But the Iron Paladin moved ever faster in his climb. Charlie Black had shown himself to be a great expert in military affairs when he summoned Carfax to do battle with Arachna. It was not easy for the mighty Sorceress to fight on two fronts. When she turned to face Tilly-Willy and tried to knock him down with her huge rocks, the Eagle attacked her from behind, tormenting her with his beak and his sharp talons, and buffeting her with his wings. No sooner did the Fairy turn back to Carfax than the Giant put more of the mountain behind him, unhindered.

The Witch was beginning to understand the hopelessness of her situation. Ah, if only she had the Magic Carpet! Then, once she'd escaped the Champion of Iron, she'd battle the Giant Eagle one-to-one in the air, and even now there is no way of knowing who would have come out the victor. But the scraps of the Carpet had been dispersed throughout the entire land, and so this bitter combat would have to remain on the ground.

There was only one course open to Arachna: to seek refuge in flight. She managed to stun Carfax for a moment with a deft blow of her club, and then she made her way along the mountain slopes with enormous leaps, away from the now unspeakably close Tilly-Willy.

The huge figure of the Witch suddenly vanished from the sight of Charlie Black and his friends, who were observing the scene of the combat. This threw the Sailor into despair. Seizing the Carpet from Tim's hands, Charlie leaped onto it and commanded it to carry him to the scene of battle. But the Carpet merely made some spasmodic exertions and rose barely a few inches from the ground: the Sailor was simply too heavy for it.

Tim, who was watching this scene with great interest, ran over to Charlie Black and exclaimed: "Excuse me, Captain, but I'll have to be the one to fly it!"

"All right, lad," agreed Black sullenly, "you're the lucky one." And he gave up his spot to the boy.

The Carpet ascended at once, and it carried the delighted Tim O'Kelly to the peak of the mountain. It was a staggering, unforgettable sight that met the boy's eyes there. The Witch, her blue cloak now torn to shreds, was dashing from one mountain slope to another with all the dexterity of a chamois. Relying on her long club, she leaped across gullies and made detours and loops, trying to confuse her pursuer.

She might just possibly have succeeded if it hadn't been for Carfax. The Giant Eagle was circling about over the Witch's head, aiming his beak at her face, striking her back with his wings, and grasping at her shoulders with his talons.

Behind her, using all the strength of his mechanical muscles to their utmost, the Iron Paladin with the dreadful eyes and the dauntless spirit of youth, was pursuing the fugitive with light, springy leaps.

Looking over the labyrinth of ridges and ravines from high up, Carfax saw, far away, an enormous rocky crag surrounded on three sides by chasms. The Eagle had long been familiar with the Crag of Doom — he and his brother eagles had driven mountain goats and aurochs onto it many times, and there the animals met their deaths. "The Witch's path must take her there, and nowhere else," the Eagle resolved.

So no matter how hard Arachna strove to move aside from this perilous path, Carfax did not leave her this possibility. She could not go left nor could she go right, but only straight ahead, and every step, every leap brought the wicked Fairy closer to the spot where retribution would inevitably be accomplished.

And there, at last, was the Crag of Doom!

As Arachna realized the trap that her mighty adversaries were driving her into, she howled wildly with rage and fear. Turning to face Tilly-Willy, the Witch desperately lifted her huge club into the air.

And so began a most extraordinary battle. Tim O'Kelly shrieked with delight as he watched it, and he fidgeted about so much on his little Carpet that on ten occasions he would have flown right off it, had not the Carpet itself, showing great foresight, lifted up one edge or another.

The two giants, with all the agility of walking-sticks, fought one another with their respective weapons: Arachna with her truncheon, and Tilly-Willy with his sword. And who knows if the Iron Paladin would have won the day or fallen in battle if he hadn't had Carfax to help him? The infuriated Eagle, forgetting altogether any danger to himself, tormented the Witch viciously with his talons, and he struck her in the face with his wings and prevented her from seeing her opponent.

The long-awaited moment of victory came at last!

Tilly-Willy with a deft stroke sliced the Enchantress's club right in half. Only a useless piece of wood remained in Arachna's hand, and, flinging it at the Eagle, the wicked Fairy gave out one last deathly wail of "Urfin was right!" and plunged into the chasm. A cloud of white steam rose up from the bottom.

"Victory! Victory!" proclaimed the Eagle in a loud voice.

"Victory!" thundered Tilly-Willy, which Lestar echoed in a weak voice from his cabin. Lestar was happy as never before in his life, despite being quite battered by the tumult that he had been forced to experience in the Giant's belly during the pursuit and the fierce combat.

It is impossible to express in words the joy that Charlie Black and our other heroes felt when Tim O'Kelly, after returning on the Magic Carpet, reported to them the outcome of the final battle. [In all the excitement, it had not occurred to any of them to follow the battle on the Magic Television.] Before long, the victors themselves returned: the Eagle, who had suffered many wounds, and Tilly-Willy the Iron Paladin, that Giant with the savage face and the kind heart, now covered with dirt and with deep dents in his breast and his sides.

What praise, what kind wishes the people showered on the intrepid, self-sacrificing Carfax! The Eagle said: "Don't thank me, my friends. The Yellow Fog is a mortal threat to me as well as to the rest of you, and that means I was fighting not only for my friends, but likewise for myself and my own tribe. But now I'll be returning to my family: they're waiting for me with impatience and anxiety. On the way, I can drop Annie off at Arachna's cave: why should the girl exhaust herself needlessly?"

Before mounting onto the Eagle's back, Annie blew on the whistle, and Ramina appeared before her. "Rejoice with us, your Majesty," said Annie. "The wicked Arachna is dead, and the mouse tribe played an important role in her destruction."

The girl took the infinitely delighted Queen in her hand, and the Magic Carpet bore her up onto Carfax's back. As they flew away, Annie saw her friends setting out in a merry column on the journey back.

Chapter 30

THE YELLOW FOG IS GONE!

Annie followed Carfax with her eyes until he had become nothing more than a black dot on the distant sky and then disappeared altogether. Ramina, too, took final leave of the girl: she set out to her people to lead them back to the places that they had inhabited since time immemorial in Emerald Land.

Annie stepped nervously into Arachna's abode, and then she stopped short and stood there in amazement: the whole cave was filled with little people. There were old men who were looking upward and tearing at their white beards, neat little old women wearing white bonnets and embroidered aprons, not to mention young people and very tiny children carrying large, beautiful toys in their hands.

The Gnomes stepped aside to make way for Annie, and an imposing old man in a red cowl stepped forward: this was Castalyo, Chronicler and eldest of the Gnomes.

"Welcome, dearest Annie!" said the Gnome with a bow.

"You know my name?" exclaimed the girl in amazement.

"We know everything about you," explained Castalyo in a grandiose manner, "O newcomers from the Emerald Island and visitors from beyond the mountains. We have spent many a night under your van, listening to your conversations and becoming acquainted with the plans you were making for your military campaign."

"And you revealed them to Arachna, of course?!" cried the girl with indignation.

"We did nothing of the sort," the Gnome denied calmly. "We maintained neu-tral-it-y, as your friend Strasheela the Wise would have loved to express it. The fact of the matter is, back in ancient times, an oath was exacted from our tribe: we were to serve Arachna, to obey her in everything, and to do nothing that would be harmful to the Sorceress. *But*," and the old man smiled slyly, "there was nothing in the oath that required us to fight her enemies, and so, we *didn't* fight."

Annie marveled at the Gnomes' cleverness, and she asked, "But why did you keep yourselves hidden from us until now?"

"Because you would have insisted that we cooperate with you, and that was something we couldn't do. But now that Arachna is dead and the oath is no longer in force, we're completely at your disposal."

"You mean you know already about the Witch's death?" asked Annie, her amazement increasing more and more.

"When you went to Arachna's mountain hideout, didn't you see some little gray columns along the way?" Castalyo smiled as he asked this.

"I did, but I didn't pay any attention to them. I thought they were just ordinary rocks."

"They were us, the Gnomes, wrapped up from head to toe in gray cloaks. We're unsurpassed as experts in the art of camouflage."

"Yes, I'll have to agree with you there," admitted the girl.

"And as soon as Arachna fell in battle, the joyous news traveled from one post to another, even faster than your avian network."

"My goodness! I can only be glad that when the Witch was fighting us, you people observed neutra...lity." Annie stumbled on this difficult word. "I can imagine the nasty tricks you could have played on us."

"Have no fear of that!" Castalyo emphasized proudly. "But let's get down to business. I presume that you, as Arachna's conquerors, will be searching for her Magic Book so that you can remove the wicked spells that she cast?"

"That's right, noble grandfather."

"That being the case, I will now show you our mistress's hiding place..."

The hiding place turned out to be in the furthest, darkest corner of the cave. It was a niche hollowed out of the wall and covered over with a flat piece of rock that blended right in with the rest of the stony surface. Little buttons activated hidden springs, and there was no way that anyone could have found them without the help of the Gnomes.

When all the essential operations had been performed and the niche was open, Annie pounced eagerly on a thick parchment book with a red binding. "Thank you, thank you so much, noble grandfather!" exclaimed Annie eagerly. "But how did you learn the Witch's secret?"

"Well, as I've already told you, there's nothing that can stay hidden from our eyes. Most laughable of all was our mistress Arachna's unshakable faith that her hiding place was known to her alone." The old man began to chuckle, and his laughter was taken up by the other Gnomes.

"I thank you again and again, my friends," said Annie, and then, laughing, she added, "But to be frank with you, I wouldn't like to have spies like you around *my* house!" The Gnomes laughed again, this time even louder.

After several hours, Charlie Black's detachment returned from the mountains. How Annie's friends rejoiced when they saw in the girl's hands the secret book — the goal of their fierce combat. If the book couldn't be found, then all their efforts would have been for nothing, and inexorable doom would have awaited Magic Land.

While the yard in front of the cave was ringing with the merry hum of voices, Ruf Bilan crawled out from some inconspicuous hiding-place. The traitor's face was ashen with shame and fear. Bowing humbly before Strasheela and the Giant from Beyond the Mountains, Ruf Bilan begged them not to punish him too severely for his latest treason. "It's not my fault," murmured the terrified renegade. "When I awoke from my long sleep in the Cavern, an Underground Ore-Digger began to re-educate me, but at that time..."

"Gnomes sent by Arachna took you away," Strasheela interrupted Bilan. "We know all about it. We know that you fell into the Witch's hands, and she was able to remodel you as she saw fit." Then the just monarch added, "That fact lessens your guilt."

Bilan threw himself at Strasheela's feet. "You mean you're not going to kill me?" he exclaimed, delighted. "Oh, I'll be able to justify your kindness!..."

"Yes, but the way you are now, you're a disgrace to your tribe. You'll have to be put to sleep again..." Noticing the dread on Bilan's face, Strasheela reassured him: "You'll only be put to sleep for a short time, for a month or two, and after that, you'll be re-educated the *right* way. Depart now for the Emerald City and report it to Rujero that I want him to make a decent person out of you."

"By the masts and sails!" exclaimed Charlie Black, "that's well thought out, Strasheela, my friend!"

After bowing low and showering him with expressions of gratitude, Ruf Bilan set out to face a new sleep. When his form disappeared behind the nearest hillock, Castalyo stepped out of the crowd of Gnomes and addressed Strasheela respectfully: "Triply Wise Monarch of the Emerald Island, we have long heard of your great virtues, and we ask that you accept us Gnomes under your distinguished auspices."

"What does that mean?" asked Strasheela in surprise.

"It means that we want to become your subjects. Of course, we admit that we don't merit such an honor, but we'll gladly pay any tribute that you see fit to exact from us."

Strasheela leaned back pompously, leaning on his splendid walking-stick, which he had been able to hold on to during the march. He found the Gnomes' request flattering. "Hmm... hmm..." he said. "Your announcement is quite unexpected, but it appears that it is not con-tra-dic-ted by any attendant cir-cum-stan-ces."

This vague phrase elicited the greatest admiration on the Gnomes' part for Strasheela's erudition. Their former mistress had never used such long words!

"Are we to understand, your Grace, that you are willing to grant our request?" inquired Castalyo timidly.

"Yes, certainly," Strasheela consented graciously. "And as for tribute... I've heard that you've been maintaining a detailed chronicle of our land here?"

"That's right, your Grace," replied Castalyo proudly. "We've been keeping it for five thousand years."

"In that case, continue to keep it into the future, and that's what the tribute will consist of that we shall impose upon you."

"Hurrah! Long live the Triply Wise Strasheela!" shouted the Gnomes in a chorus.

"But of course you'll offer us the fruits of your labors," Strasheela concluded kindly.

"Then allow us to make a gift to you of all the volumes of our Chronicle that have been preserved for the past five thousand years. Among us, they just lie about in a useless pile, but when they're in the Emerald City, historians can read them and write long, learned works..."

And so the library of Chronicles was packed away and loaded onto the strong backs of the Deadwood

Oaks. The Gnomes have scrupulously adhered to their promise to continue their Chronicle, right down to the present day. In time, the 579th volume of the *Universal Chronicle of Magic Land* was forthcoming, and those who are interested may read in it a description of some strange and unusual events that occurred in Magic Land, under the title *The Mystery of the Deserted Castle.*

By general consent, Charlie Black was granted the honor of removing Arachna's spell and getting rid of the Yellow Fog. It was he, after all, the Giant from Beyond the Mountains, who had created Tilly-Willy the mighty Iron Paladin and had had the good sense to enlist the aid of Carfax. Without those two giants, victory over the Witch would have been impossible.

It was decided that the solemn ceremony to remove the witchcraft should be held on the border of Arachna's old domain, at the place where the Yellow Fog began. There, they would be able to see at once whether or not the magic words had had the desired effect.

After a few hours of traveling, the convoy stopped at the edge of the region of sunlight and the area where the Yellow Fog held sway. Before them stretched a murky gloom which exuded dampness and cold. On this side, birds twittered in the trees as they flitted from branch to branch, magnificent flowers lifted their little heads from among the grass, and butterflies of many hues fluttered about; on the other side, however, the ground was covered with snow, the trees stood bare, and the forest was dead and deserted.

Everyone's heart was pounding as Charlie Black, looking in the book, began to pronounce the magic words in a loud, clear voice:

"*Uburru-kuruburru, tandarra-andabarra,*
Faradon-garabadon, shabarra-sharabarra,

Disappear forever, accursed Yellow Fog, from Magic Land!"

And then, O wonder! it was as if some huge hand pulled back the curtain of fog, and on the side where there had just been an icy desert, the blue sky unfolded in all its splendor, and the bright sun began to shine!

Our heroes' delight can not even be described. Annie and Tim hugged one another, Charlie Black threw his pipe high into the air and dexterously caught it again, Doctor Boril waved his medical bag, Lan Pirot gracefully performed the "Reindeer Dance" which had won him first prize in the City Dancing Contest. Artoshka barked deafeningly, forgetting that he was able to talk, and Kaggi-Karr executed some crazy aerobatics. The Deadwood Oaks launched into a happy bout of noise-making, while that overgrown boy Tilly-Willy began to sing gaily the first song of his life, whose words and melody he had composed himself.

Magic Land was thus saved from doom, and the warm sun would once again shine on it without cease, trees would bear luscious fruit all year round, and people would work happily in the fields throughout the whole year, taking in bountiful harvests.

Charlie Black built a bonfire, and when it was blazing hot, he threw Arachna's Magic Book into the flames. "Let the evil incantations contained in this confounded book disappear forever!" said the Sailor. "If we don't destroy it, who knows whose hands it might fall into and what harm might be done to the people!"

The flames slowly leafed through the pages, which had grown stiff through the millennia, and finally it blazed up in a smoky, stenchful fire. And when nothing but ashes was left of the ancient pages of witchcraft, a sudden gust of wind picked them up and carried them far away.

"And thus let all evil perish in Magic Land, and in the whole world!" said Charlie Black triumphantly.

Chapter 31

HOMEWARD BOUND

It was in the happiest frame of mind that our heroes prepared to seek out the van, which they had left not far from this very spot.

"Captain," volunteered Tim, "I'll fly on ahead and get everything ready for when the rest of you arrive."

But when the boy sat down on the Carpet and commanded it to betake itself to the van, the Carpet did not even stir. It did no good for Tim to repeat the command again and again — his efforts gained him nothing.

"What on earth has *happened* to this thing?" cried Tim, outraged.

"It's really very simple," explained Strasheela. "Arachna is dead, her Magic Book has been burned, and so all her witchcraft has died with them."

"And now we're left with this useless shred of carpet here!" The boy even kicked the Carpet with his foot.

"You ought to be ashamed of yourself!" Annie rebuked him. "This wonderful little Carpet rendered us so much service, and that's how you show your gratitude!" Annie rolled the Carpet up and put it under her arm. "I'm going to keep it as a souvenir of our adventures."

"All right, give it to me. I'll carry it," said Tim, ashamed now, and he relieved the girl of her burden.

Faramant took his inventory book from his pocket, leafed through a few pages, moistened a pencil with his saliva, and jotted down the following note: *Second-hand Flying Carpet, dimensions 4x3 cubits...* In the margin, he wrote an additional note for the sake of clarity: *Written off, as its magic power is spent.*

After putting his notebook away, Faramant explained pompously: "Every business requires organization. Whom are they going to ask when they take inventory and notice something missing? The Master of Requisition, of course!"

The travelers made their way over snow-covered areas, and all around them, amazing things were happening. Steam was rising from the ground, babbling streams were flowing down the hillocks, buds were quickly swelling up on the branches of the trees, and here and there in the little glades, the green tips of blades of grass were making a timid appearance.

Under the miracle-bringing rays of the hot sun, it was spring again in Magic Land!

Overtaking the people as they flew, birds were filling the air with song: nightingales, robins, goldfinches, siskins. These unwilling guests of Arachna's were returning from her former domains to the nests where they were born, and from whence they had been driven by the Yellow Fog. Squirrels and opossums leaped from tree to tree, and to the side a bear was trudging clumsily by, looking fearfully at Tilly-Willy's dreadful face.

The observant Giant noticed the little bear's terror, and he recalled that not only the bear, but other animals as well, jumped fearfully into the bushes the moment they caught sight of him. Tilly-Willy stopped and called out to the bear to come over. The latter did not dare disobey, and approached in spite of himself. Not daring to look the Iron Paladin in his dreadful eyes, the little bear glumly kept his eyes lowered.

"Listen, my friend," Tilly-Willy addressed the bear gently. "It seems you're afraid of me?"

"N-no, I'm n-n-not af-f-fraid," mumbled the bear in a trembling voice. "W-why sh-should I b-be af-f-fraid of y-y-you?"

"That's exactly what I think," concurred the Giant. "After all, I have performed services for the country. So why don't you want to look me in the eye?"

"L-l-leave me a-l-lone, l-l-let me go..." And the bear suddenly quickened his pace and scuttled into the nearby underbrush.

With bewilderment and resentment, Tilly-Willy followed the bear with his eyes. "So *that's* the thanks I get from them..." he said mournfully.

Seeing Tilly-Willy's unhappiness, Strasheela decided to console him with his characteristic wisdom. "You mustn't become upset, my friend," he said softly. "On the contrary, you should be proud that your eyes contain such mag-net-ic power..."

"Man-ge... What's that?"

Strasheela repeated the word. "It's a power that's far from being given to everyone," he explained. "Have you ever seen any person with eyes like yours?"

"No," said the Iron Giant.

"There you are! Your face, and especially your eyes, contain inimitable in-div-id-u-al-it-y, and therein lies your su-per-i-or-it-y to all things, living and non-living!"

Captivated by these long and sonorous words, the simple-minded Giant forgot his grief and exclaimed happily: "Now I won't even pay any attention to the fear those simpletons show!"

"That's the way to do it!" Strasheela said, cheering him up.

The travelers continued on. Nature was coming back to life right before their eyes.

Kaggi-Karr, who was accomplishing her journey on the Iron Paladin's shoulder, flew suddenly from her spot, all flustered. "No, I can't do it any more!" she cried. "I must set about at once to perform my duties!"

"And what duties are those?" asked Tim innocently.

"Is it really possible you don't know that I'm Magic Land's General Director of Communications?" retorted the Crow with annoyance. "I've even been awarded a medal for my services, but being that I'*m* no show-off, I'm not in the habit of wearing it." With those words, the Crow tilted her eyes sardonically at Boril's breast, which was adorned with his two medals.

"Excuse me, your Excellency," said the boy, somewhat embarrassed. "I *am* a newcomer here, and so I wasn't aware of your high standing."

Flattered at being addressed with such a high-sounding title, Kaggi-Karr informed the company of her plans. "I'm going to send my couriers out at once, in all directions," said the Crow. "All the people, all the animals, and all the birds must be informed as quickly as possible that the Yellow Fog is gone forever, and that they may now return home. I'll send messengers down to Underground Land, to the Munchkins and the Ore-Diggers. I'll call back all those who took refuge from the Yellow Fog in the lands of the good Villina and Stella. Let things return to normal in Magic Land with all speed!"

Annie and Tim looked with respect at this rumpled bird, on whom so much depended and who endeavored to confer as much benefit as she could on the residents of Magic Land. But Kaggi-Karr was already somewhere off in the distance, giving commands to the swallows and sparrows that had flown in at her summons.

Each new day of travel brought amazing changes with it. The snow and ice had long since disappeared, grass was quickly sprouting from the ground, the trees were covered with dense foliage and were attracting bees with the aromas of their superb flowers.

Annie, Tim, and Charlie Black were thrilled as they recognized the delightful landscape of Magic Land. They themselves had raised all this beauty from the dead, and so their happiness was particularly heartfelt.

Herds of antelope, bison, and deer overtook and passed the travelers. Fiery-red foxes were hiding in the underbrush, watching for some unwary rabbit that they might sink their teeth into. Lizards were emerging from their deep burrows, where they had been hiding out from the frost.

Kaggi-Kárr received reports several times a day from her signalbirds. All the news was encouraging. The Marrans had already left the Quadling Country and returned to their own valley, where they had begun their sowing. When they departed from Stella's domain, the Marrans had insured their munificent hosts that from now on, a state of eternal friendship would exist between them, and that their relations would never be darkened by even a shadow of hostility.

The Munchkins and the Ore-Diggers had likewise left the gloomy Cavern and returned to their comfortable domiciles, which were now warmed by the rays of the hot sun. Of course, the animals that had also sought sanctuary in Underground Land followed along right behind them. Staggering from hunger and squinting in the bright light that they were no longer used to, the elks, the buffalo, the antelopes, the hares, and the raccoons were dispersing through the forests in all directions, returning to the spots that they had inhabited previously.

Strasheela inquired most considerately about the fate of Urfin Jus. How had the former king endured those hard weeks of snowy captivity in his dismal solitude? Had his health suffered in any way?

The Magic Box showed the Monarch of the Emerald City and his friends a cozy valley in the foothills of the World-Encompassing Mountains, Jus's bright, newly painted cottage, and vegetables springing to life in his garden.

The gardener was digging up the beds, throwing dirt aside with powerful sweeps of his shovel. On his face was a gentle, peaceful expression that had not been characteristic of him at all in the past. It was as if the old petulance in Urfin's eyes had never even existed. Beside him, on the hemp, Guamoko the Great Horned Owl was perched majestically, and to all appearances, he was beginning to recover after a long fast.

"…There you are, Guamokolatokint, my friend," said Urfin, continuing a conversation with the Owl. "Now do you agree that I've turned out to be a prophet? Arachna is deceased now…"

"But how can you prove that, Master," objected the Owl, extremely flattered at being addressed by his full name — something that happened so rarely! "Maybe the Witch simply came to her senses and returned the sunshine to the people as a gesture of good will?"

"Good will? Ha-ha-ha!" Urfin burst out laughing. "A lot of good will *she* had! No, it's entirely clear to me that Strasheela the Wise came up with some totally unexpected method of taking care of that villainess!"

Urfin Jus's words carried Strasheela away, and his head began to swell because of this praise. Then the gardener continued: "Believe me, I'm really dying to know just what he did come up with. Perhaps I could send you to check it out. You have no objection, do you, Guamokolatokint?"

"With pleasure, master. I'll find out everything!" replied the Owl cheerfully, infinitely happy at Urfin's simple flattery.

Strasheela did not listen to any more of their conversation, and he turned off the Television. "I can see that that former u-surp-er has done a complete turnaround," he said. "We'll have to invite Urfin to come back to the Emerald City. He's been punished enough for his past crimes, so he might as well live among people again. His conduct during this entire business with Arachna has been beyond praise."

The convoy continued on its journey, and at last it crossed the border into Emerald Land. Strasheela and his friends were no longer traveling in the van. They had turned it over to the care of the Deadwood Oaks and were now proceeding on foot, reveling in the rebirth of nature.

They began to encounter the first farms. Their occupants had made it back from the City, where they had taken refuge from the cold and the Yellow Fog. The farmers were at work in their gardens and in their fields. The people were again happy, as before, and only their gaunt faces bore witness to the difficult time that they had just lived through. And with what enthusiasm they greeted their liberators! The Giant from Beyond the Mountains, Annie, Tim, Strasheela, the Iron Woodman, and, most of all, Tilly-Willy, the kind-hearted Giant. His dreadful face no longer held any fear for them: everyone knew that it was only a mask, designed to frighten the wicked Fairy.

And now the towers of the Emerald City appeared. The delighted travelers could not tear their eyes away from them.

The Emerald City had always been renowned for its splendor, but to our heroes, it seemed to have grown even more magnificent — though it was unlikely that this was really possible. The emeralds on the walls, on the towers, on the gates, and on the roofs of the houses were sparkling with an unusual luster, as if the rain had washed them clean of dirt. Green and red tiles of the roofs alternated in picturesque disarray, and the Emerald City as a whole resembled a heavenly plaything created by the hand of some exceptional craftsman.

The travelers crossed the lake on the ferry, which had long been back in service. The Iron Lad waded across the lake, but this time he did not stumble: his gait was firm, his movements confident.

Tilly-Willy took up residence in the largest of the City's parks: the City did not have a single house that could accommodate him. This park was soon ringing with the sounds of children's voices from dawn to dusk: the boys and girls in the City were very much attracted to the amiable Giant, and though they were rather surprised that he was so big, they were not the least bit frightened by his face. And the Iron Lad was always happy to play with them: games were a most serious and necessary thing for someone his age.

A happy shock awaited our travelers when they came up to the City gate. The small gate, as always, was closed. Annie rang the bell three times, the gatekeeper's window opened, and out peeked Faramant. He was wearing his green spectacles! It turned out that the Guardian of the Gates had departed from the convoy an hour before, leaving his companions behind, and resumed his usual post, the one that he had occupied for many years, in the sentry box.

"Who are you and why have you come to our City?" asked Faramant severely, though a smile was hidden in his eyes.

"I am the Triply Wise Strasheela, Monarch of Emerald Land, and I come to occupy the place that is mine by right."

"I am the Iron Woodman, Monarch of the Winkies, and I come to enjoy the hospitality of your remarkable City at the invitation of my friend Strasheela."

"I am the Giant from Beyond the Mountains, the Salt-Water Sailor, and I come to your magnificent City to take a rest after our hard fight with the mighty Witch Arachna."

The other travelers likewise introduced themselves in due formality. The small door opened, and Faramant met the new arrivals with his little basket of green spectacles. "The Emerald City welcomes you, newcomers," said the Guardian of the Gates pompously, "but you must put on these green spectacles. Such was the mandate of Goodwin the Great and Terrible, and his word is law!"

The travelers, amid laughter and jokes at Faramant's expense, put on the green glasses, and everything around them began to sparkle in various shades of green, ranging from soft turquoise to dark green and aquamarine.

Then Strasheela, the Woodman, Charlie the Sailor, and the others entered the City, and imagine what happened next!

People were crowded on the porches of their houses and on balconies. Whole clusters of little children were clinging to the rooftops, holding tight to pipes, weather vanes, and carved ornaments, while old men and women looked out of windows that were opened wide. The air resounded with joyous cries, and armfuls of flowers rained down on them from every direction...

And among all this joyous confusion bustled the shaggy form of Kaggi-Karr, the main Mistress of Ceremonies of this triumph, and already hoarse from shouting! It was she who had appeared there the night before, informed the people of the City and the surrounding area of the imminent arrival of Strasheela and his friends, and arranged for them a reception unlike any that had ever been seen before.

The procession, accompanied by thousands of ecstatic townspeople, walked along the carpet of flowers that covered the streets, and it entered the square in front of the Palace. In the midst of this square, as in the former happy times, the City's main fountain gushed and poured forth in multicolored shades, while little golden and silver fishes frolicked and leaped up from the basin.

Strasheela's palace, with its doors wide open and its windows shining like mirrors, was in readiness to welcome its master and his guests. The palace staff had polished the floors until they shone; not a speck of dust was left on the walls and the ceilings, silken and velvet drapes hung down from gilded cornices over the doors, and everywhere were emeralds, emeralds, emeralds!...

Their unbearable brilliance was blinding to the sight, and the wise Faramant had been three times correct in insisting that our friends put on their green spectacles. Baluol the Chef, wearing a white apron and a white pointed cap, greeted the guests by the door of the Throne Room with an enormous cake on a golden platter, and tables had been set with a multitude of varied and most exquisite dishes.

The Courageous Lion awaited his friends inside the Throne Room. The esteemed King of the Beasts had grown too old to go out on long, dangerous journeys, but he was most happy to see Annie, the Giant from Beyond the Mountains, and all the others alive and well. He wept with joy, and wiped away his tears with the tuft at the end of his tail.

But Annie was truly staggered when gaunt, lanky Doctor Robil walked over to her with a courteous bow. He was in his parade dress, with his medals pinned to his breast, and there in his hand was the Silver Circlet which, according to the Iron Woodman's story, had been lost along with Auna, the tame fallow deer.

The matter was very simply explained. When the Yellow Fog enveloped the land, Auna, still invisible, returned to the Violet Palace to seek the protection of her mistress Fregosa, and the Silver Circlet was removed from the fugitive's neck. Unfortunately, this happened *after* the Iron Woodman had set out for the Emerald City, and the precious talisman remained behind in Winkie Land right up to the disappearance of the Fog.

The delighted Annie quickly put this elegant adornment on her head, but of course she had no thought of pressing the little ruby star and making herself invisible. Why should she play tricks like that among her circle of friends?

Tim said: "What a pity that we didn't receive this object sooner, before we set out to fight Arachna. I would have stolen into her cave and grabbed the Magic Book."

Annie disagreed. "In my opinion, nothing at all would have come of that. The Book was safely hidden, and without the help of the Gnomes, you'd never have been able to find it. And even if you *had* found it and we'd removed the Yellow Fog from the land, we don't know what would have happened after that. The wicked Fairy may have had other incantations even more terrible, and she might have inflicted on the country something much worse than the Yellow Fog."

Everyone agreed with Annie that as it was, everything had turned out just fine. Even without the help of the Silver Circlet, Magic Land was free forever of Arachna, and the mighty Sorceress would never again threaten the inhabitants.

"Anyway," said Annie with a laugh, "I won't leave the Silver Circlet with you again. You were too careless as guardians. But what is this, my friends? I don't see Ramina! Where is the kind Ramina, our first ally in the struggle against Arachna?"

Kaggi-Karr, a trifle embarrassed, admitted that she was at fault: in all the bustle, she had completely forgotten the Queen of the Field Mice.

"We'll rectify that mistake," said the girl with a smile, and she blew the Magic Whistle. Ramina appeared at once on her outstretched hand, wearing her parade outfit — a gleaming gold crown on her head. Annie and Ramina greeted one another affectionately.

Those participating in the triumphal banquet took their seats at the festive table, while at one of the open windows of the palace, framed against a background of shining, snow-capped mountains, the ugly but wise head of Oyho the Dragon appeared. The devoted beast was waiting for the saviors of Magic Land, ready to take them back to their beloved far-off homeland.

THE END

THE MYSTERY OF THE DESERTED CASTLE

INTRODUCTION

Chapter 1

THE MEN FROM
ANOTHER PLANET

Magic Land and its capital, the Emerald City, were inhabited by tribes of little people — the Munchkins, the Winkies, and the Quadlings — and these people had very good memories when it came to things that they considered marvelous.

One such thing that was marvelous to them was the arrival among them of a little girl named Ellie, when her house crushed the wicked Witch Gingema to death like an empty eggshell. For good reason, they had called Ellie "the Fairy with the Death-Dealing House" from that time on.

It was no less marvelous for the residents of Magic Land when they first beheld Ellie's sister, Annie. She likewise gave them the impression of being a wonderful fairy. She had galloped in on an unusual species of mule that fed on sunlight, and she wore on her head a Silver Circlet that turned anyone invisible who put it on and pressed down on its little ruby star.

Many, many other marvelous events took place in Magic Land and gave its residents something to

217

talk about. There was only one marvel about which they knew almost nothing — how their country had become magic in the first place! For it had not always been partitioned off from the rest of the world by a Great Sandy Desert and surrounded by the impenetrable World-Encompassing Mountains. Not always had an eternal sun shone upon it, with its birds and beasts talking human-style.

It had become magic in accordance with the wishes of the great Wizard Hurricap.

In those days, Hurricap was already old and thinking of retiring, and he wanted peace and solitude. That is why the mighty Wizard built himself a castle at a distance from Magic Land proper, close by the mountains. With the utmost severity, he forbade the inhabitants to approach his domicile, or even to remember his name, Hurricap.

The inhabitants, surprised as they were at this, nevertheless believed that Hurricap really did not need anyone else. Centuries and millennia went by. The peaceable little people, adhering to the Wizard's mandate, tried their best to put him out of their minds, and they never saw him again. So Hurricap's miracles began to fade gradually from their memories.

In contrast to all this, the good residents of Hurricap's land were unable to find anything marvelous in what was evil, and thus they did not retain it for very long in their memories. Think of how much misery Urfin Jus had inflicted on them in his efforts to conquer Magic Land, first with his Wooden Soldiers, and then with a large army of Marrans! But what happened after that? No sooner had Urfin thought over his lot and declined to assist the wicked giantess Arachna, than the good residents at once forgave him for his crimes and began to regard him as a good person. They reasoned: a person who performs even one good deed will not get it into his head to return to evil acts.

And the most curious fact was — that's exactly how it *did* happen later on.

After their friends from the Outer World — Annie, Tim, and Charlie the Sailor — had helped them defeat Arachna the Witch, the people gazed happily at the sky, which was bright, bright blue, and which no longer held even a trace of the Yellow Fog that Arachna had visited upon them. The celebrated inhabitants of Magic Land lived once again in peace and happiness, not expecting danger from *anywhere*. Yet danger was indeed approaching, and — who would have thought it? — it was coming from the clear sky itself.

A formidable interstellar spaceship from the planet Rameria was already nearing the Earth. It was racing along through outer space at an unheard-of speed — 150,000 kilometers per second. And, as Kau-Ruk, the extraterrestrials' Celestial Navigator, wrote down in the log, "it plowed the interstellar desert for seventeen years." During that time, the spaceship traversed an enormous distance, one which light, that fastest mover in the Universe (capable of traveling at 300,000 kilometers per second), would have taken nine years to cover. That's how great the distance was between Rameria and Earth.

But the alien astronauts were not even aware of their flight. For them, time had come to a standstill as nearly all of the ship's crew had been reduced to a state of *anabiosis* — which is the term applied to a prolonged sleep accompanied by super-cooling — and placed in special in-flight sleeping modules. There, the astronauts slept tranquilly for a good seventeen years.

Time had lost its power over these men — and that was a real miracle. If these astronauts were to be roused after a thousand years, even then they would awaken in exactly the same state as when they had first drifted off into slumber.

To the uninitiated, the sleeping modules looked like enormous refrigerators with a multitude of cells, with each cell containing a crew member. The polished surfaces of the cells gleamed like mirrors, and if one were to look closely at them, he would notice red, blue, and green regulatory valves sticking out here and there, and would see little multicolored lights flashing on and off — the lights of the control apparatus.

During all this, Kau-Ruk the Navigator, seated in his cosmic observatory, calculated the ship's position in space and plotted its course on a star-chart. In addition to Kau-Ruk, three other men were up and around: General Baan-Nu, Commander of the spaceship, who checked the readings on the instruments in the ship's deckhouse; and Lon-Gor the Doctor, who kept his eye on the condition of the sleeping crew, checked on temperature and humidity, and regulated the amount of oxygen and the supply of the refrigerant, which was liquid helium. Finally, there was Mon-So the Pilot, the General's loyal right-hand man, who carried out his orders most meticulously and had never once tolerated any kind of objection or argument.

The silence in the in-flight sleeping modules seemed eternal. Once in a while, the unrelenting alarm siren would go off in the Doctor's cabin. When that happened, Lon-Gor would slip swiftly but with noiseless steps to the area where the modules were located, turn the necessary valve — green, red, or blue — and all would be silent again.

Mon-So had nothing to do, with all his pilots asleep in the modules; he did not enjoy reading books, so he played tic-tac-toe with himself in his cabin. Mon-So sometimes roamed the corridors of the ship or kicked a ball there, but only when all the others were asleep. He was goalkeeper of a soccer team, and he simply could not function if he broke training.

(Everyone on Rameria was practiced in one sport or another.)

The quartet of astronauts, while keeping the space-watch, engaged in special in-flight gymnastics every morning, even here on board the ship. Now and then, Kau-Ruk arrived at these sporting activities late, when he was engrossed in some interesting book. It would not necessarily be a story dealing with the history of a nation or with some unusual personage, or one containing adventures: Kau-Ruk read books on technical subjects with no less enthusiasm.

"Kau-Ruk is the most capable man in your whole crew," Guan-Lo, Supreme Ruler of Rameria, had told the General before take-off. "There is only one reason why I have not designated *him* Commander of the starship: he is lacking in drive." Nevertheless, he did designate Kau-Ruk the Navigator as Deputy Commander.

Chapter 2

THE AWAKENING OF ILSOR

For Baan-Nu the Commander, Mon-So the Pilot, Kau-Ruk the Celestial Navigator, and the ship's Doctor, the time did *not* pass imperceptibly: they aged exactly seventeen years during the flight. Of course, age was reckoned differently on Rameria: the people there lived three times as long as those on Earth. Thus, the four astronauts who maintained watch on the ship remained, by Ramerian count, young and in the prime of life.

THE MYSTERY OF THE DESERTED CASTLE

No other people besides the non-sleeping astronauts broke the silence of the enormous spaceship; its cabins, its work areas, its engine rooms, and its corridors were empty, and thus the ship gave the appearance of being deserted.

In fact, there was one other person on board the starship who was not sleeping, or, to be more precise, found himself in the process of being awakened. That person was Ilsor, General Baan-Nu's manservant. He was awakened at the General's behest. Baan-Nu had reached a state of utter exhaustion, and he had grown so tired of going without his servant that he had long been finding fault with everything around him: to him, the doors slammed shut too loudly, the ball-point and felt-tipped pens wrote badly, the food (which they extracted from cans) did not taste good, and his bed was altogether too hard.

The Commander would even have forced Doctor Lon-Gor himself to become his servant rather than be willing to wait the few more weeks or so when the spaceship's entire crew was due to be reawakened. He was not accustomed to dressing himself and to taking care of his own personal appearance, and consequently, his disheveled red beard had grown to a fantastic length; the jacket that he put on over his overalls (obviously to serve in the capacity of dress-coat) lacked buttons; the overalls themselves had no zipper and were pleated like an accordion; and the General's elbows were in tatters because he was constantly catching them on some sharp corner or hook. In addition to all that, Baan-Nu did not go to much trouble to distinguish his left and his right boots: the right boot invariably ended up on his left foot, and this was extremely uncomfortable, even for the General.

Lon-Gor spent a long time turning first one valve, then another, as far as they would go, and then he sat tight while all the multicolored lights winked non-stop, indicating that a complete thaw was in progress. Finally, the shining, polished cell opened, and Mon-So and Kau-Ruk, as per the Commander's order, picked up Ilsor, who had been immured inside it, and bore him from the module to the Doctor's cabin.

"All right, you lazybones, get up!" said the General joyfully, over and over again, when they had brought him there from the compartment, under Lon-Gor's direction. Ilsor awakened slowly, rocking back and forth a little on his suspended air mattress (which was something like the hammocks used by sailors in their forecastles).

Ilsor occupied a special position: not only was he a good servant to the General, but an outstanding inventor as well. It was his design that they had followed when they built the spaceship in which the Menvits were now flying toward the Earth. It was called the *Diavona*, which in the language of the Chosen Ones meant "the uncatchable."

Ilsor was still asleep. He gave a sudden start, but he did not awaken, and his eyes didn't open. He could sense only that Baan-Nu was bending down toward him.

The voice of the ship's Doctor reached Ilsor as if coming from a barrel. Lon-Gor was repeating several times: "Reawakening takes time, reawakening takes time."

The General clearly did not believe that his servant needed this much time, because he made a most impatient gesture: he stretched out his arm to Ilsor and shook him with all his strength by the shoulder. His servant was supposed to leap instantly to his feet the moment he, the General, addressed a word to him. However, realizing in the end that there was little point in shaking him like this, Baan-Nu withdrew.

Chapter 3

THE ARZAKS
AND THE MENVITS

Ilsor still did not grasp the fact that he was on board the spaceship. He awoke, and he seemed to behold life on Rameria once again, pursuing its normal course right there before his eyes. He saw his far-off home planet. He saw his people, the Arzaks, and their houses, which resembled pieces of rock, in the Silver Mountains. It wasn't only the mountains there that were streaked with silver — no, a soft, effervescent white light bathed the entire planet of Rameria. The soil, the grass, the trees, the bushes — all of them were silvery, and it seemed that one needed only to touch the leaves, and they would begin to jingle!

The Arzaks were most hospitable — and as trusting as children. Their eyes were very alert, and always opened wide. And the Arzaks were *talented.* Among them were many artists, doctors, scholars, writers, designers and engineers, and teachers. Not only did the Arzaks know a great deal, but they simply could not resist sharing their achievements with their neighbors the Menvits — and sharing them with the greatest pleasure.

But the Menvits were a treacherous people.

The Menvits had a Supreme Ruler named Guan-Lo, who was also a wizard. He was the possessor of a commanding hypnotic gaze, and he could compel any person to do whatever he wished. The moment anyone began to protest, Guan-Lo looked him in the eye — and the person immediately fell silent. The Supreme Ruler had inherited this wizardly skill from his forefathers under the most awesome secrecy, and he taught it to the Menvits. After all, it had not taken him long to draw attention to the fact that the Arzaks were a talented people. "It would be nice," thought Guan-Lo, "to put that talent to work for us."

Even before that, the Supreme Ruler had realized that the Arzaks were a well-bred folk, and that while conversing with other people, they looked them directly in the eye. And nothing is easier than bringing witchcraft to bear while looking people directly in the eye. "You'll pay for your fine breeding, my dear friends," said Guan-Lo, positively purring with contentment. "You're all slaves already, and I presume that you'll be serving us most faithfully."

He began to talk the other Menvits into believing that they were the chosen race of the Universe, that there was nothing that they couldn't do. Other rational beings were created for the sole purpose of deferring to them. And convince them he did! The Menvits proclaimed themselves the Chosen Masters, while the Arzaks were nothing but slaves.

And that was a very melancholy page in the history of the Arzaks!

First of all, the Chosen Ones deprived the Arzaks of their musical, expressive language. That is to say, they began by teaching the Arzaks the Menvit language — and not merely enough of it to communicate in bits and pieces. The Arzaks had long since known it well enough to communicate with the Menvits. Now, however, the Menvits strove to get the Arzaks to learn Menvit to perfection, as if it were their own tongue. For the most part, no great effort was even called for. The Arzaks, who were inquisitive by nature, displayed on their own an enormous interest in the language of their neighbors. Not recking of any danger, they committed everything to memory, and within a short time, they could speak both their own tongue and that of the Chosen Ones with equal fluency. At that point, the Menvits forbade them to speak Arzak, and they closed down the Arzak schools.

But that's not all they did!

They pretended that they were going to entertain the Arzaks, and they arranged a banquet on the grounds of the Ruler's palace. And it was there, at that banquet, that they used their wizardly commands against the Arzaks.

Ilsor could well recall the Menvits' first command, for it was invariably one and the same: "Look into my eyes, look into my eyes, and obey me, alien!" With this command, the pretended banquet began. The Arzaks, well-bred people that they were, looked them in the eye — and every one of them was bewitched. They were ordered to forget their native language altogether, and so they forgot it.

Then a misfortune even more calamitous befell them. The Chosen Ones commanded the Arzaks to forget that they were a free people — and the Arzaks forgot that, too.

They were still the same inventors, scholars, and artists as before. And they still made their ideas into realities, for they were used to working not only with their heads, but with their hands. In this manner, not only outstanding field equipment, machines, and extraordinary works of art, but also the technology of interstellar travel and the Menvits' spaceships — all these things were created by the Arzaks' hands. However, strange thing! their discoveries and their knowledge were utilized henceforth by the Menvits. The latter occupied all the important positions in industry and agriculture all over Rameria. They called themselves engineers, doctors, pedagogues, agronomists, even though the only role they played everywhere — in the fields, in the factories, in the institutes — was that of supervisors.

It was the Arzaks, of course, who were really all the things that the Menvits claimed themselves to be; but whenever they discovered, invented, or created anything, they promptly forgot all about it. It was as if they acknowledged on their own that there could be no greater pleasure in life than to fill the role of a work force: they laundered, they scraped, they wove, they grazed livestock, they grew grain, they operated machines, and, above and beyond all that, they were servants and cooks. And they genuinely believed that they had no other business in life except performing the kind of labor that the Chosen Ones considered menial.

That was the very thing that Guan-Lo the Wizard was striving for.

Commander Baan-Nu was one of the Menvits. He displayed all the characteristics of the race of the Chosen Ones. He was a very tall, strapping fellow, and he carried his large, round head proudly on his broad shoulders.

The Menvits were a strong, handsome people. In addition to their passion for physical culture, they had a special preoccupation with dress. It absolutely had to be something smart and becoming, or else the Menvit would fall into such a bad mood that a thousand comedians would not be able to get him out of it.

Baan-Nu's face might even have been considered pleasant were it not for the icy expression that froze his very eyes, making them appear fixed and motionless.

The Menvits were confident of themselves, but such an expression does not evolve merely from looking down on other people with disdain. The Menvits had committed many a wrong against the Arzaks and imposed their will upon them, and the more misdeeds a Chosen One committed, the colder his eyes became.

Ilsor knew all about the hypnotic effect of a Menvit's glance, when a person standing before a Chosen One loses his will completely and follows behind him as an obedient slave, forgetting about everything in the world except for one thing: that he's a slave, and the person before him is his master.

Among the sleeping astronauts on the ship were a number of Arzaks: they were metalworkers, drillers, electricians, builders, and other slaves, without whom the Menvits would be unable to establish their base on Earth. It was Ilsor who would be directing the labors of the Arzaks under the still-uncertain conditions on Earth, and, besides being General Baan-Nu's servant, he would also be chief technician as long as the work was in progress.

The Menvits trusted Ilsor. He was infinitely good. He was the most obedient of the slaves. There was no job that he couldn't handle. And he would never run away anywhere, because he simply did not have it in him to do such a thing without asking their permission (or so the Menvits thought).

Ilsor was finally awake, and he leaped from his bunk. "General," he said, making a deep bow to Baan-Nu, who was just then entering the Doctor's cabin. "I am pleased to serve you."

"I know," replied the General, nodding condescendingly, though in his mind he was rejoicing because Ilsor would shortly have him looking his best again. "I know," he repeated, "you're devoted to me to the very end."

Ilsor bowed his head as a sign of acquiescence, but he decided that this was not enough, and he made haste to bow once again.

Chapter 4

ON BOARD THE SPACESHIP

The astronomers of Rameria, observing various planets through super-powerful telescopes, had become interested in the Earth — or Belliora, as they called the Earth in their own language. They established that Belliora was no different from Rameria in its make-up.

The emissaries from the planet Rameria were to verify if life existed on Earth. But the flight of the *Diavona* was not planned as a scientific expedition. No, the Menvits were flying to Earth with a military objective in mind: to subdue this new planet.

The braking engines were already on, a fact that Ilsor could guess from the gentle vibration of the ship. Doctor Lon-Gor undertook the task of reawakening the whole crew. At once, the various modules of the spaceship, which had hitherto appeared lifeless, were crowded and swarming with people. Stretching and yawning, the astronomers, the geologists, the engineers, and the pilots emerged from them, reawakened after their seventeen-year sleep. Only the Arzak laborers remained in their spots, for they were not permitted to leave their modules for the time being. The ship now resembled an aroused ant-hill, with men buzzing here and there in all directions.

As soon as the awakened men had more or less shaken off their grogginess, Baan-Nu called the Menvits together in the observation room of the spaceship. "My esteemed brothers!" he addressed the assembled men solemnly. "We have been entrusted with a major assignment — the conquest of the flourishing planet Belliora. It's got to be flourishing, for that's what our astronomers have predicted."

On Rameria, there existed toys — figurines with nodding heads that the Arzaks carved out of stone for the Menvit children. And now, just like those obedient figurines, all the astronomers nodded their heads in unison in agreement with Baan-Nu.

"Our assignment is very simple," continued the General. "We're to land anywhere on Belliora and begin building a city."

Baan-Nu would not have spoken in such simple terms if it had not been for the Navigator. The Commander was always tempted to indulge in colorful descriptions of dangers, both past and future. But Kau-Ruk did not understand tall stories.

The Navigator was seated comfortably in his armchair, and he was shaking his head, not like an obedient figurine, but in a manner expressive of doubt. He listened attentively to the Commander. "And what if Belliora is inhabited?" he asked.

"According to our preliminary data, there's no one there," responded Baan-Nu.

"But what if there is?" the Navigator insisted. "The astronomers *have* established that Belliora is flourishing. That means that it might well have creatures on it resembling men."

"Then so much the worse for them!" said the General heartlessly, with all the self-assurance typical of conquerors. "We'll destroy the majority of the inhabitants, and the rest of them we'll reduce to slaves, just as we've already done with the Arzaks." Then he added, with vexation, "And let them serve us with the same devotion as the Arzaks do!" Kau-Ruk bowed his head as a token of his concession, for he did not want to antagonize the Commander.

"But that is not the point," declared Baan-Nu, in a calmer tone. "Belliora is now before us. Our ship will orbit it many, many times. Belliora will be observed through telecameras and photographed. Physicists will take samples of the air at various altitudes and determine the magnitude of the atmospheric pressure, and mathematicians will calculate the strength of the gravitational field. All right, everyone, let's get to work!"

For a start, technicians, Ilsor among them, put on space-suits and went out through the air-locks to take a look at the starship's metal sheeting. The first thing they saw was that its once mirror-like surface was covered with depressions and ruts — marks of its collisions with streams of space-dust and fragments of meteors. It was as if some mysterious engraver had been working it over, centimeter by centimeter, for seventeen long years, covering it with enigmatic designs. These depressions now came in handy, for the men made use of them as they began using sprayers to apply a fine heat-resistant coating to the ship's plating. Without this, the spaceship might burn up when it entered the Earth's atmosphere. It was Ilsor who had anticipated the need for this coating, which would not only protect the ship from burning, but would also make it undetectable by radio waves in the event that stations sending out such waves should exist on Earth.

Chapter 5

SOME EVENTS INVOLVING URFIN JUS

While the flight of the Extraterrestrials was in progress up in the sky, life was pursuing its normal course down in Magic Land. All the usual day-to-day events were going on there, and one of these involved Urfin Jus.

It was not only his place of residence that Urfin had changed. He had previously lived in the woods of Munchkin Land, and he now inhabited a valley in the World-Encompassing Mountains. No, the major change had occurred in Jus himself, as a person. He had become totally different, as if the man had been reborn altogether. The expression on the face of this new resident of Hurricap's country was no longer severe. And insofar as a man's character is reflected in the things he makes, then nothing less than a miracle had occurred with Urfin. In the place of the grim, somber toys that had once frightened children, he now fashioned the gayest dolls, animals, and clowns, and he gave them away to the Gnomes.

Urfin himself had received a gift from the Iron Woodman. A telescope had been assembled for Jus in Winkie Land, so renowned for its craftsmen. Jus built a tower onto his house and fastened the telescope down to it with nails, and then he took to observing the heavens in the evenings. And thus did it happen that he noticed the *Diavona* in his telescope.

Of course, from such a great distance, he could not make it out as a spaceship, but only as a tiny, flashing star. He might not have paid any attention to it if the star had not been shining before his eyes in all the colors of the rainbow.

Jus continued to observe it for several nights. With each passing night, the color red predominated more and more in its luminescence, and the star grew larger. Something unprecedented was going on here.

Urfin was puzzled, and he continued his observations. The idea of a spaceship did not occur to him. Such a thought would never even have entered his head. But one of the reasons why the light was growing stronger was because Kau-Ruk the Navigator was turning on the *Diavona's* braking engines, one after the other: two, five, ten, and finally all of them were on. The Extraterrestrials were approaching the Earth, and that is why they were slowing the ship down from its super-speed. This was essential if they were to begin orbiting the Earth.

Chapter 6

THE UNKNOWN LAND

The *Diavona* went into orbit around the Earth, sweeping gradually closer to it. The automatic on-board telecameras were aimed at Belliora and turned on without delay. The blue outlines of the unknown planet appeared on the observation screens, both in the Commander's deckhouse and in the room where the Menvits gathered. The aliens looked at the indistinct spots which were the strange (to them) oceans, seas, dark mountains, yellow deserts, and green valleys and forests. The long flight had dulled the Extraterrestrials' feelings, but now they began to feel worried, and an alarming thought began to flash from somewhere in their subconscious minds: "Is anything waiting for us here?"

Baan-Nu flicked on the switch that controlled magnification, and images of big cities with high-rise buildings, factories, airports, and ships quickly began to flash on the screen.

"Attention!" the order quickly rang out. "Camouflage immediately!"

Like an octopus, the *Diavona* discharged a dark camouflaging cloud through a special hatch in the body of the spaceship, and the vessel was enveloped completely. From now on, no telescope would be able to detect the enormous Ramerian starship. Rather, any astronomer on Belliora would see only a dark, shapeless mass, and not even the wisest sage would be able to guess its significance. The alien spaceship now approached the Earth in complete safety.

The emissaries from Rameria, wasting no time, examined the views of Belliora. And the more they

233

saw, the gloomier their ashen faces became. Baan-Nu and his subordinates beheld railroads, canals, cultivated fields, mighty fortresses, and enormous ships in the roadsteads of large ports, with the barrels of guns looking ominously skyward from their decks. In spite of all efforts, doubt and indecision awoke in the eyes of the aliens, who had long been conditioned to the idea that the Earth was uninhabited.

"No," declared the General glumly, "it'll take more than one blow to force *that* civilization to its knees. We can't land just anywhere on the planet now. They'd rake the *Diavona* with gunfire before we could even open a hatch." As a Menvit conqueror, Baan-Nu assumed that Belliora would receive the cosmic newcomers not in peace, but with war. That's how the Ramerians would have dealt with any strange ship that landed on *their* planet.

The Menvits decided to find a quiet spot far removed from the big cities, the seaports, and the mighty fortresses. There, they could remain in hiding for the time being, until the workers, under Ilsor's direction, assembled the helicopters: reconnaissance flights would be easier in those than in the giant spaceship.

The ship proceeded to make more and more circuits of Belliora. The observations continued. Samples taken of the air showed that the atmosphere of the Earth differed little from that of Rameria and was quite suitable for the Newcomers to breathe. This, at least, came as a relief: living in space-suits on a strange planet for months, maybe even years, would have been impossible.

At last, the Ramerians had a stroke of luck. Amid an endless expanse of sandy desert, they distinguished a large wooded plain surrounded by a range of tall, snow-capped mountains. The spaceship flew over the plain several times. The telecameras worked without interruption. There was no doubt about it. In the midst of the woods and fields, they could see villages with tiny houses, and in the center loomed a remarkable city whose towers and walls glowed with a mysterious but very beautiful green light. And nowhere was a single citadel or fortress in evidence, nor were the steel muzzles of any cannon sticking up into the air, the sight of which had affected the Menvits so unpleasantly during their first orbits of the Earth.

Baan-Nu and his subordinates were happy now for the first time. The General extended his hand toward the telescreen, with its view of the peaceful villages and the marvelous city, and he declared contentedly: "This is a suitable land. Our base on Belliora will be here."

Little did he know that that land was magical!

Part I

FIRST DAYS ON EARTH

Chapter 7

URFIN JUS — GARDENER

The remarkable red-shining star gave Urfin no rest. His thoughts returned to it from time to time, and in the evenings, he would sit at his telescope for hours on end. But try as he might to locate it, it was nowhere to be found.

The star had vanished without a trace. Of course, on occasion he did notice some sort of dark cloud moving now through the sky, but he attached no significance to this.

Urfin was presently on friendly terms with the residents of Magic Land, but he was in no hurry to report anything to them about the star that intrigued him so much. After all, he understood nothing about it himself.

A long time had passed since Strasheela the Wise had kept his word and invited Urfin to move to the Emerald City and live among other people. Urfin had not expected to find this invitation so gratifying to him. However, he had already been living for many years in the World-Encompassing Mountains, and he was used to his cozy valley with its clear stream and did not want to leave his vegetable garden.

Living alone was as natural for him as eating and drinking. As before, he had no interest in being like other people, and he wore clothing of a different color — not blue or violet, but green. He did this not because of any nasty disposition, but because he was simply unsociable by nature. He shared his society with Guamokolatokint, the old Great Horned Owl, and exchanged a few words with him every day.

"Well, now, Guamoko, my friend," Urfin generally asked him every morning, "has any news arrived by magpie express?" Then he and Guamoko would slowly, and with many pauses, discuss the news that the wise Owl had retained after receiving it from the other birds.

"The Iron Woodman has paid a visit to Strasheela the Wise," said Guamokolatokint sedately. "The Courageous Lion is also on the road, but he's grown old, and his legs carry him slowly. He trudges along, then he sits down and takes a rest."

"And how is our Supremely Wise one?" asked Urfin.

"He's complicated his life again. He's come up with some sort of library, and he's reading serious books."

"That's his privilege," sighed Urfin.

Urfin had always been competent as a joiner. There was a time, to be sure, when the tables, chairs, and other articles that he had fashioned out of wood had replicated the maker's quarrelsome disposition, and tried to poke the people who bought them, to trip them up — in a word, they caused people no end of trouble. No one would buy these recalcitrant articles, and Urfin was forced against his will to raise vegetables in his garden, for how else was he to live?

So Urfin became a gardener, and he worked quickly, but somehow always in a state of boredom, without any real interest. At that time, work had brought him no pleasure. But now, Urfin had begun to think about himself and his past deeds and was to all intents and purposes born anew, and everything around him changed. Some unusual products began to emerge from his labors. Everything went so well with him that even he was surprised. He renovated his house in the valley and painted it in the gayest colors that he could find on his farmstead. And he felt himself drawn to taking up vegetable-gardening again. And not just to keep himself busy!

Ever since the day when he had received Strasheela's invitation and realized that the residents of Magic Land were no longer the least bit angry with him, he had never given up on the desire to develop something new for them.

Urfin had boldness and perseverance to spare, and he grew such extraordinary produce in his garden that even Guamoko the Owl, who at first felt skepticism toward Urfin's undertaking, later became filled with unbounded admiration for him. "Here's a wonder indeed!" he hooted, flapping his wings. "It's fantastic! It's evident, master, that you still know how to do magic!"

Here was a golden carrot, and blue cucumbers as transparent-red as pomegranates, and plums and apples as sunny as oranges. No, it can't be denied that he produced some truly elegant fruits. And most important, these were attractive not only because of their colors, but also because they were sweet, sizable, and delicious.

Clearly, it was more than mere chance that had attracted Jus to vegetable-gardening. Producing vegetables and fruits for other people proved to be most interesting in its own right, and much good presently came out of it.

As soon as these glorious fruits were ripe, Urfin loaded a wheelbarrow to the brim with them and carted them off to the Emerald City. And it became a real Food Festival. Everyone who possibly could, hurried to it from all corners of Magic Land.

Moreover, Urfin did not want to offend anyone, and he wished to make his gifts to all the residents and visitors alike. So he filled his wheelbarrow many times with loads of fruit and raced back to the City.

But this delivery was a long and arduous one. Then the residents of Magic Land placed one of the wooden couriers at Jus's disposal. The fleet-footed runner never tired. He delivered Urfin's gifts with amazing speed.

Urfin got the vegetables and fruits ready for the courier. He harvested them, digging them up and rinsing them off with sparkling spring water, after which the hot sun quickly dried them. Jus placed the fruits most carefully in the wheelbarrow. The people of the Emerald City would not let him leave until he had eaten a whole mountain of pies, which were especially delectable when baked by the housewives of that remarkable City.

Chapter 8

THE YELLOW FIRE

The Food Festival became a yearly institution, and people came to await it with the same eagerness that they awaited their birthdays. This was because, wonderful as life is in Magic Land, every single day is still just like every other. The sun rises high into the sky each time, and once the day's wonders are over, it sets once more behind the mountains.

It happened on the eve of this year's festival. The preliminary period had arrived almost imperceptibly, and it would continue for several days, to give all the enthusiasts enough time to travel to the Emerald City, and to give Urfin the Gardener enough time to get his fare ready. The fruits and vegetables had turned out extremely well, and there were such vast quantities of them that Jus was afraid of not being able to transport them all to the Emerald City in time for the opening of the ceremony. Long rows of tables, which had been hauled from the houses of the City's residents, had been set up adjacent to Strasheela's palace.

Urfin and the wooden courier who was helping him transport the vegetables, plied back and forth between the World-Encompassing Mountains and the Emerald City. As they passed through Munchkin Land with their wheelbarrows full to the brim, they left in their wake the delicious aroma of ripe fruit infused with sunlight. How could the Munchkins possibly look indifferently at this colorful palette of fruits and vegetables in the wheelbarrows?

They leaned almost all the way out of the round windows of their houses, and it was even strange that they didn't fall, the way they clung to the window-sills with their feet. They continued to talk with one another, their voices choking with anticipation. "Oh, oh, oh," said one Munchkin, "blue cucumbers again. How splendid they are!"

"Who cares about cucumbers?" exclaimed another. "The yellow nuts are the real sensation. I saw a whole cartload of them myself! My mouth is watering already."

"I like the apples and the oranges," a woman's shrill voice sang out. "The way our Urfin grows them, his apples are afire like orange suns, while his oranges are as red as apples."

"Ah, I could eat my fill of those!" a little Munchkin boy assured them in a tinkling voice.

The piles of radiant, aromatic fruits grew higher and higher on the tables in the Emerald City, and the supply of them in Jus's garden never seemed to diminish.

THE MYSTERY OF THE DESERTED CASTLE

The Munchkins washed their clothes out thoroughly and adorned them with festive collars, while their wives put on skirts that were flared in a bell shape, and sewed new bells onto the hats — in a word, they prepared for the Food Festival as if it were a ball. And people in all corners of Magic Land were preparing for the festival with equal care. "I'm going to be the prettiest," said one little girl. "Mama has said that my lace collar is very stylish."

"No, *I'm* going to be the handsomest," a male Munchkin contradicted her. "I've got the brightest-shining bells on my hat. And boy, do they ring! I'll be able to dance to my own melody throughout the entire festival, and I won't even need any other music."

"I still haven't sewn mine to my hat," said another Munchkin man. "I'd better not wait too long."

"No, don't wait too long, don't wait too long," replied the other Munchkins in their excitement.

The bells on their hats jingled, and there was an incessant sound of tinkling in their homes. Time was indeed upon the Munchkins this very night to set out on their journey.

Thanks to Strasheela's shrewdness in the field of engineering, a few changes had come about in Magic Land. The most notable, of course, was still the conversion of the Emerald City into an island. But in spite of the artificial lake that had been dug around it, the residents continued, from sheer force of habit, to call their capital, not the Emerald Island, but the Emerald City.

Other places in Magic Land were affected as well by the innovations of Strasheela the Wise. Thus, the inhabitants no longer had to wonder how they were going to cross the Great River — a bridge now spanned it. And it was no longer frightening to travel through the dense forest, even at night — thanks to hanging lanterns that shone in the dark along the entire length of the Yellow Brick Road, whose movement and reddish light frightened away all the wild beasts.

However, in order to make it on time, the Munchkins would have to get moving very soon, for their steps were quite short and they had a long road ahead of them.

Needless to say, they slept fitfully that night, just like children on Christmas Eve. And for that reason, they awoke at once when they heard the bells on their hats begin to jingle.

But they always placed their hats on the floor for the night, in order that they would be silent. Who was tinkling the bells? Mice, perhaps? The Munchkins took a look under their hats, but there were no mice to be seen.

At that time, an incessant droning resounded outside, and it grew louder by the moment. The Munchkins ran out of their houses. A huge fiery globe was flying through the air in the direction of the World-Encompassing Mountains, making a dreadful din as it went.

"Is that a meteor?" asked Prem Cocus, bewildered. "But meteors don't drone," he said, answering his own question. "Look!" he cried, stretching his arm toward the sky and directing the Munchkins to turn their eyes that way.

The globe disappeared, and was replaced by a quivering yellow fire similar in form to two or three crowns attached together, or to several inverted sheaves.

To the Munchkins, this was nothing less than dreadful, and they, too, began to tremble. "Tinkle-tinkle" went the bells on their hats.

The droning sound continued to grow stronger and stronger. Clouds of yellowish-white smoke rose into the air from the World-Encompassing

Mountains. A whirlwind began to howl, and trees bent all the way to the ground.

At that moment, the fire went out. The droning gave way to a loud roaring sound from the mountains, repeated several times as its echoes reverberated.

"Quick, quick, to the Emerald City!" urged Cocus. "This is terrible! It's terrible, and baffling. Perhaps our monarch..."

"Strasheela the Wise will figure it out," the Munchkins decided, still trembling, and the bells on their hats jingled in rhythm with the people's words.

Chapter 9

THE LANDING

The aliens were in a hurry to land before morning. They assumed that the people of Belliora would most likely be sleeping at night, just like those of Rameria, and that their own arrival would thus go unnoticed. How could they possibly have known that on this night of all nights, the people of Magic Land were not sleepy?

After the ship had completed its final orbit around the Earth, it began its descent in a smooth trajectory. Kau-Ruk the Navigator sat at the control panel. His movements were efficient and precise. He gazed intently at the radar screen that enabled them to see in the dark, as the contours of the unfamiliar locale showed up on it.

It was important not to overshoot the mountain range, or, more precisely, the place at their foot where the Extraterrestrials had observed an enormous castle with black gutted windows and ramshackle roofs. To all appearances, no one was living in this edifice, and it might serve as a good shelter for a start.

Commander Baan-Nu prepared to present himself to the new planet in all his splendor. His beard had long since been exquisitely cut and combed, strand by strand, by Ilsor, and the servant was already helping the General to pull on his ceremonial dress.

The Menvits' ceremonial outfits consisted of suits made of a closely-woven silk-like material. Their sheen almost brought life back into the pale, immobile faces of the Menvits. The medals adorning the Menvits' suits were neither riveted nor pinned on, but were embroidered in gold, silver, and black thread. They were in the shapes of suns, moons, and stars; their lower parts were set off by stripes — one, three, etc. — and in the center of the medal, one could see images of the constellations and the planets that surrounded Rameria. The Menvits were rewarded in accordance with the following rule: the more exalted the rank of the person wearing the suit, the more medals he had, and the more beautiful the medals themselves were. Boots made of soft, light leather, with fasteners to keep them shut, went with this ceremonial outfit.

As soon as the outlines of the castle appeared on the radar screen, Kau-Ruk swung the ship around with flair so that it pointed toward the Earth. He actually enjoyed demonstrating his skill and surprising everyone with it, and he felt it a shame that there were no spectators to see it up in the heavens. But outwardly, the Navigator remained totally imperturbable.

The ship slowly came in for a landing. For a moment, the spaceship hovered in the air above the castle itself, supported by a fiery column of several coronas of quivering yellow flame, before beginning to settle slowly to the Earth. At this point, folding supports slid out from the ship, making the vessel look like a gigantic tripod.

When the columns of smoke and dust had cleared away, the Menvits made their final tests of the atmosphere and, convinced that everything was in order, they opened the exit hatch. The cool night air, saturated with the fragrance of grasses and flowers, coursed into the confines of the spaceship, intoxicating the Extraterrestrials.

They lowered a ladder. General Baan-Nu was the first to descend to the Earth. He did not let a certain brand-new red portfolio out of his grasp, and for safety's sake, he had fastened it to his arm with a chain. In the portfolio was a manuscript. This was the General's most precious possession. He intended to write a history of the conquest of Belliora, and he had already begun the composition of it during the flight. The General meant to use his work to glorify the military prowess of the Menvits, and, most of all, to glorify himself.

The ship stood at the foot of some magnificent mountains, whose snow-covered peaks melted into a sky dotted with stars. Nearby were noisy forest thickets, from which, like a lullaby, came the nighttime chirping of birds. As the Commander stepped onto the soft, damp grass carpet, he felt a rising tide of that irrepressible joy that every conqueror feels, and his heart even stood still for a moment, then began to beat faster and faster. Baan-Nu had to unfasten the zipper of his collar. "The most distinguished of the Menvits will be living in this spot," said the General to himself. "And there will be plenty of slaves everywhere."

As he turned back toward the ship, he saw that nearly all the others had already descended. The Menvits were pacing proudly back and forth in their outfits with the medals embroidered on them, and sometimes they stared into the eyes of some Arzak who was dawdling. "Come, get a move on!" this glance commanded, and the Arzak began to hustle like a wound-up toy.

The Arzaks bustled about, doing their customary work, which was: arranging a comfortable life for the Menvits. One of them pitched an inflatable tent and covered its floor with air-mattresses. Another was preparing dinner and serving drinks. Still others dragged branches from the woods and covered up the tent. To camouflage the spaceship, they pulled an enormous net over it, one with leaves and branches painted on, so that it resembled a multicolored rug.

One group of Menvits carefully carried a large panel from the ship with a portrait of Guan-Lo on it, and they placed it on a small mound. The General approached the assembled Menvits and, turning his eyes toward far-off Rameria, he solemnly intoned: "In the name of the Supreme Monarch of Rameria, the Worthiest of the Worthy, Guan-Lo, I proclaim Belliora joined forever to his possessions! *Hurrah!*"

"*Hurrah!!!*" the Menvits joined in as with one voice. "*Hurrah!!!*" The Arzaks remained silent. They cast furtive glances, filled with longing, toward the direction in the sky where their home planet was.

"Navigator," the General addressed Kau-Ruk in a rather cold tone. Although he was in a cheerful enough mood, he was nonetheless unable to overcome his feelings toward Kau-Ruk, whom he did not especially like because of his efficiency and his excessive degree of independence. "At daybreak," said the General, "you're to go out on reconnaissance." What he was thinking was, "The first reconnaissance is always the most dangerous, so cope with *that* assignment, if you're so smart!"

"Keep an eye on everything, in the most attentive manner," he commanded, "but don't be yawning now."

"Roger, my General," responded Kau-Ruk, and not at all in the manner that was acceptable among the military ranks of Rameria — but then again, the Navigator always did things his own way. He knew a great deal, and for this reason he did not resort to sorcery, as the other Menvits did.

"There's no reason why I shouldn't rest now myself," said the General, stretching and yawning, "and besides that, nights on Belliora are cool."

One of the slaves offered Baan-Nu a tray of fruits that he had taken the liberty of picking from a nearby grove.

"All right, Ilsor," the General addressed his servant, munching contentedly, "is everything ready for my rest?"

"Everything is ready, my General," replied Ilsor, bowing so low that his body hung down as if on hinges.

As the General looked at his servant, bent as he was in such an absurd position, he suddenly burst out laughing. "What's the matter, Ilsor? Are you walking on air from the sheer happiness of finding yourself on such a splendid planet?"

"Yes, my General," concurred Ilsor. "How can I *not* be happy at what makes *you* happy?"

"Well said!" Baan-Nu smacked Ilsor on the shoulder, and then he headed for the tent.

Arming himself with a pair of binoculars, he made the rounds out of every window in the tent, one after the other, running his eyes lazily over the mountains and observing the nearby trees most carefully when he came to the forest — for an enemy ambush might well be planted there! But since he could make out nothing but silhouettes of birds, he stretched out peacefully on the pile of mattresses, which Ilsor had taken the trouble to cover with fluffy white furs of some species of animal resembling a snow-leopard; an enormous canopy, also of white fur, separated the General's bed from the rest of the tent, where the other Menvits had spread themselves out.

Baan-Nu placed his portfolio under a fur pillow, which Ilsor obligingly lifted up a little for him. When he was sleeping, the General would hide nothing that he valued highly in a safe — for one might obtain the keys to a safe; he knew of no place that was more secluded than the head of his bed.

When the Commander of the Menvits had dozed off, Ilsor picked up his binoculars, but he did not put them away — he, too, took a look through them at the vicinity. Then he went over to the group of Arzaks, who had gathered together to spend the night directly under the open sky.

"My friends," he said very softly, "don't lose hope." Then, in a loud voice, he gave instructions in his capacity as chief technician: "In the morning, we're going to get started assembling the helicopters."

Not one of the Chosen Ones suspected what Ilsor really was. "The most industrious servant, with a fine knowledge of technology" — that was the sum total of the knowledge that the Menvits had of him.

But what they *didn't* know!

Ilsor was more resistant than the other Arzaks to the hypnotic gazes and the commands of the sorcerers. He had stronger will-power. He had succeeded in assuming the pose of an obedient slave before the magic took effect. Therefore, he could listen in on the Menvits' most confidential discussions, and the Menvits were not the least bit wary of him, for they found him compliant, and that meant that he must be completely spellbound. From the conversations of the Chosen Ones, Ilsor understood all of what had happened on Rameria.

The Arzaks had faith: only Ilsor could help them; he would come up with some means of liberating them, and so they chose him to be their leader. Ilsor never gave up on the idea of freedom for the Arzaks.

His other concern was for the earthlings. Judging by the structures in the photographs, which had not escaped the leader's gaze, Belliora was inhabited by intelligent beings. These beings knew nothing about the danger hidden in the Menvits' glances. To warn them was Ilsor's primary duty, although he had no idea how he would go about this.

Chapter 10

THE RECONNAISSANCE

At daybreak, Kau-Ruk and a group of pilots set out on reconnaissance. Quietly they passed the patrols, which consisted entirely of Menvits and which stood watchfully at their posts. In temperament, the pilots were closer to the Navigator than to any of the other fighting men — imagine if their squadron had been under the command of Mon-So, the General's loyal henchman! Taking some Arzak slaves along with them, the pilots moved forward lightheartedly. To them, reconnaissance was something akin to a recreational outing.

The first thing they decided to do was to inspect the castle, not knowing that before them stood the former residence of the wizard Hurricap.

Circling round it, the Newcomers came to a stop in front of the closed door, whose upper edge came to an end beneath the ceiling. They made continual wisecracks about it: "What a mansion! Places like this are fitting only for monarchs and ghosts!" "All right, now, let's push against it with out shoulders. One more time, now. It surely won't be able to resist our shoulders."

The hinges of the door were quite rusted, so, as it happened, the strength of the slaves was needed to force the door to swing inward. As the Menvits entered the premises, dozens of disturbed owls of all species darted out the empty window-frames, while a swarm of bats began to flutter around.

Chapter 10: THE RECONNAISSANCE

The Ramerians were astounded at the dimensions of the castle, at the height of the chambers, at the colossal rooms. The pilots continued to make light of it all: "Why don't you take a chance and settle down here for a few days — that way, you'll no longer even notice what a monarch is like!"

There were many interesting things to be found in the confines of the castle. The Menvits saw cabinets as tall as a five-story house, and inside them were saucepans and bowls resembling swimming pools, enormous knives, and books large enough to encompass an entire forest glade.

The Newcomers could not begin to understand why anyone would put up such a colossal building in the first place. They recoiled in spite of themselves at the vastness of these dimensions. Of course, they had read fairy tales when they were children, and the first thought that came to their minds was: "Could it be that an Ogre once lived here?"

With the help of the slaves, the Menvits opened one of Hurricap's books, thinking that this might shed some light on things. But no matter how conscientiously the aliens leafed through it, they saw nothing but blank paper: the text had quite disappeared from the pages. How could the Menvits have guessed that the good Wizard himself had done this: when enemies approached, the books would not show what was written in them. The Menvits quickly lost interest in the books.

As they looked over the rooms, the furniture, and all the household utensils, Kau-Ruk exclaimed in surprise: "Do such giants really live on Belliora?"

He even tried to sit down in Hurricap's armchair. The Arzaks, standing on one another's shoulders, formed a human ladder, and the Navigator climbed up them and thus gained access to the chair. As he stood against the back of the chair, which was as hard as flint, he felt as awkward as a person in the vicinity of an enormous

stone statue of an animal. There were many such stat-
ues on Rameria — the remains of the ancient culture of
the Arzaks.

"Just think," said the Navigator to the pilots as they
looked up at him, "if even *some* of the inhabitants of
this planet are of ample enough size to occupy this chair
comfortably, then we Menvits are the veriest midgets
next to them."

Suddenly, the situation seemed laughable to Kau-
Ruk. "Won't I make Baan-Nu happy," he thought. "A
ghost coming with the castle, in the bargain." But as the
Navigator pictured in his mind the small houses that he
had seen on the observation screen in the spaceship, he
said to himself in disappointment, "One won't frighten
the General very much with the ruins of a castle."

The detachment of pilots-turned-scouts continued
on. Overwhelmed by all that they had seen, they were
by now quite dejected. But the men were in good spirits again when they stepped out of the gloomy forest
into a charming glade, then another, and yet another
after that. All around them spread green meadows with
masses of large pink, white, and blue flowers shaped
like great big bells. Tiny birds, hardly larger than bum-
blebees, flitted about through the air, displaying their
extraordinarily brilliant plumage. They were chasing
insects.

Shaggy bees, which were flying about too, were no
less attractive, with their brightly contrasting yellow and
brown colors. They were singing their endless and monotonous bumblebee song.

Red-breasted and golden-green parrots screeched
in their raucous voices as they greeted the sunrise. They
looked at the men as if they understood everything they
were saying. Had the Menvits been able to guess the
truth, their amazement would have known no bounds,
because the parrots really were conversing. "Wake up,
wake up," said some, "it's a beautiful morning!"

"What's that I see, what kind of people are those?"
asked others in bewilderment.

Schools of swift little fishes darted about in the clear brooks. "If all of Belliora is like what we've seen so far," exclaimed the extraterrestrials in delight, "then it's really a splendid place!"

Chapter 11

THE AVIAN NETWORK

Since they had landed at nighttime in the vicinity of the deserted castle, where there was no human habitation for tens of miles in any direction, the Newcomers felt perfectly safe, and it was almost as if they were not on Belliora at all, but back home on Rameria. It was not by mere chance that they named their camp near Hurricap's residence "Ranavir," which in the Menvit language meant "safe refuge." The Menvit wizards, having made slaves of the other people, believed so much in their own magic that they assumed that events could develop only in the manner that they themselves wanted. They had no way of knowing that events were already developing in Magic Land — and not entirely in accordance with what the Newcomers would wish.

Many things, it is clear, had been determined by none other than the master of the huge castle himself. Yes, it's true that the wizard Hurricap had vanished without a trace, but sorcery never simply disappears like that. Consider, if nothing else, the gift of human speech that Hurricap had bestowed upon the birds. The birds listened attentively to the humans and were up-to-date on various events, and with their songs and their chirping they carried news to all corners of Magic Land. Because of their ability to understand one another, the birds and the humans had become friends. The people never molested the wild denizens of the fields and forests, and the latter in turn became invaluable aides: they conveyed important news in plenty of time, and more than once they had given warning of danger. Now, too, the Extraterrestrials aroused the curiosity of the birds more than anything. While the Menvit scouts were admiring Belliora's landscapes, the feathered inhabitants of the forest were flying from tree to tree — and *not* just for the purpose of feeding on little worms and bugs!

Kau-Ruk did not admit it to himself, since it appeared to be a lot of gibberish, but nevertheless he could sense surveillance on the birds' part. He noticed that the feathered ones were not flying randomly in all directions, but behaving differently: not moving about in isolation, but conducting themselves as part of some larger movement. They were interacting with one another, as if carrying out some sort of definite plan. And they were showing interest in the Newcomers, clearly in the manner of scouts, flying about and observing the aliens. The Newcomers thought they fancied certain definite, though rather improbable, words issuing from their beaks: *Kachi-Kachi, Kaggi-Karr, Strash-eela.*

The Menvits, sorcerers though they were, had no understanding of the avian network. But the first morning had hardly passed after their arrival on Earth, before the alarming news was sweeping through the dense thickets. Branches were quivering first here, and then there. From tree to tree, from nest to nest, the agitated and vociferous messengers dashed. "Get up, get up!"... they excitedly roused all those who were still asleep.

"Some strange men have appeared in our land," cried the larks and the mockingbirds in all different voices, both frantic and leisurely, chirping and twittering back and forth. "They've come out of some huge machine. They're swarming about the old castle. They've set up a box that they draw water from."

Chapter 11: THE AVIAN NETWORK

The Newcomers were so reminiscent of Ellie's countrymen that the birds took them at first for people from beyond the mountains. "Hello," said the feathered ones, "are you from Kansas?" But the Newcomers remained silent.

The Ramerians had been at work since daybreak. The astronomers had set up a large telescope on top of a mound, the botanists studied the plants, and the geologists investigated the soil. In fact, it was the Arzaks who did all the work, while the Menvits merely shouted at them and issued orders.

On Baan-Nu's instruction, the Arzak laborers set to work on restoring the unoccupied building. Hurricap the Wizard had erected the castle in the twinkling of an eye. But his magic art had stood the test of many centuries, and not very much restoration was called for. It was necessary to fit the windows with glass, to repair the roof, to re-lay the floors here and there, and to paint the walls and the ceilings.

They manufactured plastics on the spot from mixtures that they had brought along with them, and they boiled them in vats. They made do with very little, with things that they had ready to hand — the clay that they added to the mixture was available in the World-Encompassing Mountains, and they borrowed Hurricap's own vessels.

They smoothed out this molten viscous mass into the window-frames, and it hardened, forming glass of flawless transparency with bluish, yellowish, or reddish tints. Through those sheets of glass, concocted in those boiling caldrons, one could see everything from the interior of the castle, but those looking in from the outside could make out nothing.

Special self-molding casting machines stamped out shingles that resembled red ribbed tiles, and these were fastened to the roof. Plasterers, like house-painters, worked with atomizers, which began the job of sealing up cracks, rifts, and openings with a special putty. After a while, the putty dried, and they covered it with gray paint — and it became indistinguishable from stone or from chunks of rock. In this way, the Newcomers sought not only to patch up the castle, but to give it an appearance that would remind them more or less of Rameria. For the houses on Rameria were shaped like chunks of rock, and had windows of many colors.

The Arzaks worked with great speed, but nonetheless, their Menvit overseers continued to drive them.

Ilsor directed the assembly of the helicopters, whose dismantled parts had been stowed on board the *Diavona*. Only a small supply of fuel had been transported from the home planet, but the geologists counted on obtaining what fuel they needed right here on Belliora, and they were already beginning to make exploratory expeditions. They brought back samples several times, but Ilsor rejected them. "We need better quality," he proclaimed to the geologists.

In truth, Ilsor was in no hurry to pave the way for the Menvits, and he knew that the fuel that they had brought with them would not last for very long. He had already visited the outskirts of the villages of the Ore-Diggers and the Munchkins, and he saw what inoffensive people lived there.

Hiding among the branches, the birds watched the Newcomers, who, judging by their observations, were behaving in a most inexplicable manner. Some of them — tall in height, holding their heads up proudly, with imperious gestures and loud voices, wearing outfits with medals embroidered on — were giving orders to the others, who were dressed modestly in loosely-fitting green suits made of a rough material resembling sackcloth. In build and strength, the men in the sackcloth-like suits were inferior to those with the medals. They had gentle eyes, and to the birds, they appeared to be totally defenseless.

Chapter 11: THE AVIAN NETWORK

The birds listened to the Newcomers' conversations, but they couldn't understand a word of it. "How strangely they mumble," thought the feathered ones.

They strove to get as good a look as possible at what was being done to the ruined castle. Their attention was drawn to a certain mysterious bulky object resembling an enormous house with round windows, with light shining out through a screen net. Throwing caution to the wind, a few swallows and wrens flew right up alongside the spaceship — and they paid dearly for that! One of the tall Newcomers raised his arm, holding in his hand an object reminiscent of the long flashlight that the birds had seen among the cigarette-lighters, pistols, and other objects that Charlie the Sailor had. The Newcomer pressed a button — and out flashed an irresistible beam of bright light that incinerated the birds in an instant!

The swallows did not even have time to dash back to their abodes in the mountain caves. The wrens, who could run better than they could fly, made quickly for the bushes, but that dreadful beam of light scorched both them and the green branches of the shrubbery. Nothing came out of the beaks of the fleet-footed birds but a cry resembling the sound of a flute or a person singing. That song which since time immemorial has made people call the wren an organist.

The feathered spies did not know that they were looking at a ray-gun, but they *did* know now what they could expect from their uninvited guests. They made haste to hide themselves in the forest, and never again did they get caught, for they exercised the greatest caution whenever they were observing the area near the castle.

The birds assembled impromptu on the branches of a wide-spreading oak tree to deliberate on what to do. They promptly decided to make out a report and dispatch it to the Emerald City.

THE MYSTERY OF THE DESERTED CASTLE

Esteemed Monarch Strasheela, wrote Kachi, a parrot whom the years had made wiser, in the report, *I hereby inform you of events of extreme importance. It may be that the years have made me too cautious, but it appears to me that a danger now threatens us that is even more terrible than the war with the giantess Arachna. Newcomers have arrived in our land and taken up residence at the castle of Hurricap. They have an enormous machine with round windows, which they originally came out of. Most important: they have a sort of flashlight that doesn't shine, but which kills by burning. Our boldest scouts — the swallows and the wrens — have already perished. Rack your brains, Monarch. When danger threatens, something must be done about it.*

A golden woodpecker memorized the text of the message and raced quickly to the northeast, in the direction of the Emerald City. He flew along at top speed, and his golden feathers flashed like fire in the blue sky. The woodpecker had no fear of getting tired, for he would proceed only a few miles and then transmit the text, word for word, to a blue jay. The latter, with fresh reserves of strength, would take to his wings like a ship at full sail, and would pass the wise Kachi's words on to another bird, and so it would travel on along the network.

The services of the illustrious Kaggi-Karr, who had first thought up the avian network, were known to everyone in Hurricap's Land. It was by taking her advice that Strasheela the Straw Man had received brains from Goodwin the Great and Terrible and become monarch of the Emerald City: such was the command of that humbug wizard Goodwin when he left Magic Land.

For the abundance of useful counsel that she had given him, Strasheela had rewarded the Crow with a medal, of which she was very proud. For this reason, she considered herself the most important bird in the whole kingdom — the Queen of the Crows.

A short time went by, and the last messenger at the end of the network, a horned lark — so called from his two elongated black feathers that resembled little ears — reached the gates of the Emerald City.

Chapter 12

AN IMPORTANT DECISION

Faramant, standing by the gate, was hard put to hand out green spectacles, and he had very few of them left, despite having provided himself with several extra baskets of the glasses — that's how many people sought admittance to the Emerald City.

The first news of the unusual events that were unfolding in the mountains, came from the courier who was working with Urfin Jus. Then the lark arrived. And after all the others, the tired Munchkins trudged in.

By that time, the other residents from all corners of Magic Land were on the scene, and a general pandemonium ensued.

The lark with the little black ears relayed the wise Kachi's report to Kaggi-Karr the Crow. Then the Munchkins related in horror their account of the roaring sound from the mountains and the yellow fire. In their excitement, they interrupted one another: "It was a red globe!" "It was not, it was more like a meteor!" "It was *not* a meteor, it was humming!"

When she had heard everything, Kaggi-Karr, quite alarmed, reported quickly to Strasheela. She sought out the Monarch in the Throne Room of the Emerald Palace, which was now called the Library.

The Library was another of Strasheela's ideas. Way back when he first knew Ellie, he had heard that places exist where people store and read books. Strasheela had come across a few books in Goodwin's storeroom behind the Throne Room, among the fantastic birds and fishes, the Mermaid, and the other marvels that the Great Humbug had employed when undergoing his transformations. Several books were on hand in Ellie's trailer-van. Of course, these books alone were not enough to make up a real library, for they could all fit on two shelves, which Strasheela himself had affixed to the wall with nails.

But then the Gnomes had come to his rescue. They brought in their multi-volumed Chronicle, and that filled up every shelf in the storeroom behind the Throne Room. The books were a real treasure in Magic Land. The enthusiasm with which the Monarch of the Emerald City read them, compensated for the small quantity of them.

The most interesting of the treasures that he found was *The Encyclopedic Dictionary*. In it were written so many diverting facts about the things that surrounded the inhabitants of Magic Land, as well as many other odds and ends, including information about items that Strasheela had never seen, such as a bus, a lighthouse, the theater.

The assiduous monarch devoted hours to his self-improvement. He had plenty of time, for he had no need to eat, drink, and sleep. These activities really cause people so much bother in the Outer World!

His brains, which were made of bran mixed with needles and pins, had served their master well and faithfully for many years now. They had prompted a great many successful ideas and actions in him, and for this reason, his subjects had bestowed upon him the title "The Triply-Wise Strasheela."

Ever since the *Encyclopedic Dictionary* had fallen into the Triply-Wise Monarch's hands, Strasheela's learned head had become a veritable storehouse of all kinds of knowledge, and he proudly styled himself an "en-cy-clo-ped-ist."

He had a weakness for memorizing long, erudite words and then, when the opportunity arose, heighten the effect by pronouncing them syllable by syllable.

Who, if not Strasheela, could be expected to provide an answer regarding the events of such a baffling night?

When he had heard all of the Crow's report, Strasheela was genuinely troubled, and he decided to summon the members of the Supreme Council to report to him at once in the Library. Aside from the Monarch, the Council included Din Gior the Long-Bearded Soldier, who was his Field Marshal in times of war; Faramant, Guardian of the Gates; Tilly-Willy, the Iron Paladin, and, of course, Kaggi-Karr, Chief of Communication. Also attending the Council was the Iron Woodman, monarch of Violet Land, who at the time happened to be staying as a guest of his friend.

Tilly-Willy, although he could have squeezed his way inside the premises, preferred to sit on the ground outside the palace; his head fit perfectly against the open third-floor window.

By human reckoning, the Iron Paladin was only a couple of years old, a mere child. But the remarkable creations of Magic Land develop much faster than elsewhere. Thus, for quickness of wit, Tilly-Willy would be the equal of any second-grader. In technical matters, his understanding was on a par with that of Lestar himself, that most eminent of the craftsmen of the magical kingdom. The lad Tilly-Willy remembered his creator, Charlie the Sailor, so strongly that he never ceased to miss him. And he was happy at any excuse to talk about the Sailor; he would then be less melancholy, for it was almost as if he were really visiting his Dad, Charlie.

When the one-legged Sailor had built Tilly-Willy in preparation for the fight against the Witch Arachna, he had created a real monster. He had given the Iron Paladin an unusually savage face, like that on a certain diminutive idol from the isle of Kuru-Kusu. But though dreadful fangs protruded from the little Giant's mouth and his eyes were all slanted, he smiled in a friendly manner, and his gaze was not the least bit hostile. The Giant had a kind heart, and no one was afraid of him.

He entertained the little children and carried them on his shoulders, and they shrieked with delight. The children loved Tilly-Willy, and they did not even see his enormous white fangs, just as they overlooked shortcomings of any kind in their parents, in their friends — and in anyone who was dear to them.

Tilly-Willy looked gently at the members of the Council through the open window. The thing that everyone found *most* frightening was the news of the death of the birds from a single fiery ray that shot noiselessly from what looked like an elongated flashlight. That ray was unexplainable, something that they knew nothing about.

"With people who brandish such a dreadful weapon, we've got to be very, very careful," said Strasheela.

"But what's happened?" asked the Woodman. "Where did those men come from?"

"From the yellow fire, the one that roars," proposed Kaggi-Karr.

"Hold it, hold it," said the Monarch, waving his hand. He began to leaf through his favorite dictionary. "Meteor... globe... fire... rumbling... thunder," and he looked up the words, flipping the pages.

"Perhaps they came here by chance, like Ellie's house?" suggested the Iron Woodman. "Could it simply be an ordinary tornado that brought them?"

"Tornado… house…" Strasheela read further. He looked up the words "volcano" and "earthquake." "No," said Strasheela with a shake of his head, "there's nothing here that'll help."

A thought flashed through the mind of the Guardian of the Gates. "Maybe we should get as close a look at that machine as we can, though as circumspectly as possible."

"That's the very thing I plan to do," said Strasheela pretentiously, heading for the Magic Television, which was a gift of the fairy Stella. "I believe that this box will now perform its most useful service of all for us."

The Television lay on a special side-table in the Throne Room, and on both sides of it, right and left, hung the shelves of books.

"*Birelya-turelya, buridakl-furidakl,*" Strasheela intoned. "*The edge of the sky turns red, The grass turns green instead. Little box, little box, be obliging, show us what's happening at Hurricap's castle.*"

The screen lit up. Before the eyes of the astounded spectators appeared the Newcomers, looking exactly as related by the lark. They were walking back and forth in a haughty manner and giving orders in sharp voices to other men who were bowing down submissively before them, men with pleasant-featured faces. The viewers assembled there wanted to listen in on the Newcomers' conversation, but the speech that came across to them was in some unknown tongue. Strasheela and his friends, as they looked at the screen, noticed a multicolored translucent net. When they gazed more closely at it, they could make out a massive dark shape beneath the net; it had a round door in its side, and a long ladder stuck down from it.

"How on earth did such an enormous thing get into our country?" inquired Faramant. Then he said with conviction, "Definitely not from the sky. It couldn't have fallen from the sky. It's too heavy."

"Then what was it that was flying and humming?" asked Din Gior.

"Give me a chance to think," said Strasheela, "and I'll solve the mystery."

Strasheela began to think hard, and the exertion caused the needles and pins to stick out of his head again; it was at such moments that the Wise Monarch thought with unusual clarity. After a long period of contemplation, Strasheela said: "That mysterious thing is not a cart, for it has no wheels. It's not a boat, because there's no river near Hurricap's castle. It's not a meteor, because a meteor flies through the air, but doesn't roar. In my opinion, it's an airship. And it was in that that these bizarre men arrived."

"Glory to Strasheela the all-Wise, I swear by the typhoons of the South Seas!" The Giant did not say this particularly loudly, but even this was enough to make the glass rattle in the halls of the palace. No one was surprised to hear nautical oaths, which were unusual in magical regions, coming from the mouth of the iron lad. Tilly-Willy had never, in fact, laid eyes on the sea, but he had heard a great deal of nautical expletives from his creator, the Sailor, at the time when the one-legged Charlie was fashioning the Giant. The expletives had been planted firmly in Tilly-Willy's enormous head, and he made frequent use of them.

"I swear by the wizards and the witches! Masts and sails! The wind and the waves! May the first storm sink me! May the thunder tear me apart!" All the Giant had to do was open his mouth, and expressions like these would come tumbling out continually.

"As to where the Newcomers have flown in from," continued Strasheela, "that I don't know. It definitely wasn't from Kansas. If such people were to be found in Kansas, Ellie would have told us about them."

Chapter 12: AN IMPORTANT DECISION

"We'll have to undertake a careful reconnaissance," said the Crow, "and then we'll be able to decide what to do."

"But a reconnaissance will be dangerous," said the Iron Woodman. "The Newcomers are on their guard, and they think nothing of killing inoffensive birds."

"The scouts will have to be smart, observant, and completely undetectable by the enemy," Strasheela emphasized.

"I know of no one who would be more fitted for reconnaissance than the Gnomes," said Kaggi-Karr.

Once more, Strasheela appreciated the quality of the Crow's mind, and everyone agreed with him.

"It's necessary to notify the Gnomes now, so I'll fly at once to their cave."

But Kaggi-Karr had hardly uttered a word when the glass began to rattle again. "A thousand devils!" said Tilly-Willy. "Here's what we'll do: *I'll* go see the wee little Gnomes, and I'll gather as many of them together as we need and take them where they have to go. I can accomplish this in no time, I swear by the reefs around Kuru-Kusu and by the anchor!"

The members of the Council accepted the Giant's suggestion without any debate: it was difficult to think of a better course of action. He could walk at a speed of forty miles an hour. Moreover, like Strasheela and the Iron Woodman, he had no need to rest and sleep, which meant that he could continue to move without stopping.

The preparations required only a short time: Tilly-Willy took with him a basket filled with soft moss, and, to be on the safe side, they gave his joints a good oiling — which took a whole barrel of machine oil. Then off the Iron Paladin went down the Yellow Brick Road.

Chapter 13

URFIN IS OFFENDED

In view of the extraordinary nature of all the events that had occurred, the Food Festival for this year was canceled.

From the moment when the Newcomers had taken up residence in Magic Land, the normally happy life of its inhabitants had been disrupted. The Winkies found it hard to sleep — they were doing so much winking that their eyes never stuck together long enough for sleep to come. And the Munchkins stopped eating — they were constantly munching and thus forgot to swallow their food. What kind of Food Festival could there possibly be? Not one person was in any condition for it.

Urfin, of course, was deeply hurt by all this, for he thought that everyone had forgotten about Mr. Jus. He ran home so that he could catch a glimpse from there of whatever it was that was roaring so monstrously in the mountains.

Hiding in the darkness, he got a look at the Extraterrestrials' ship, which resembled an enormous house with round windows. Then he returned to his own unhappy thoughts: "All that's needed to happen is for some sort of little men to arrive from another planet," the famous gardener reflected, "and then no one needs Urfin any longer. Well, I'll take all the fruits and eat them myself!" He addressed Guamoko: "Bring a Luscious-Wuscious Date-Melon here. They can wage war to their hearts' content, but you and I are going to have ourselves a feast!"

The wise old Owl rolled a Luscious Melon over, one that was approximately five times as big as he was. Urfin carried a table out of the house, and with some difficulty he lifted the fabulous fruit up onto it. As Jus cut the melon with a huge knife, its fragrant juice oozed out of each section of it in great big drops, and Guamoko's mouth began to water. Then, sitting down at the table, they dug greedily into the succulent, sugary pulp.

"You really outdid yourself this year, Master," was the Owl's final comment (which was music to Urfin's ears) when they had finished off the melon. "I've never eaten anything so sweet." Urfin Jus did not answer. He threw himself under the covers and went right to sleep.

And what a dream he had! A horde of Newcomers was descending upon his house and garden from all directions, and they stretched out their tentacle-like arms and roared: "Where is that Urfin? We want a Food Festival!" To prevent the food from falling into the aliens' hands, Urfin began to polish off melon after melon, and the faithful Guamokolatokint rolled them over to him, one after the other. Urfin stuffed himself so full that he could not even move, and then the Owl cut up a melon himself and thrust the chunks straight into his mouth. "I'm about to burst!" cried Urfin, and he woke up.

Jus ran outside. Everything there was peaceful: there were no Extraterrestrials anywhere in the vicinity, and the remnants of the Luscious Melon were lying there undisturbed on the table. Guamoko was perched on the table beside the melon rinds. One eye of his was already awake. Seeing his master, he pretended to be still sleeping. Urfin always made him to do some job each morning: for instance, to peck out caterpillars, or drive birds away from the garden. But this time, the renowned gardener was not after the Owl. Jus began to fix up his wheelbarrow, mending it here and washing it there, and then he loaded it with fruit.

"All right, Guamoko, you can stop pretending!" he grumbled at the Owl. "I saw one of your eyes open."

"That doesn't mean anything," responded the Owl. "I'm sleeping."

"Have it your way. I'll go alone, then." And Urfin rolled the wheelbarrow away.

"You're wasting your time, master," Guamoko hooted after him as only Great Horned Owls can, without opening his eyes. "They still won't be holding the festival to honor your fruits. It's the wrong time for it!"

Urfin knew where he had to go: everyone in Magic Land, from north to south and from east to west, was aware that the Newcomers had taken over Hurricap's castle.

Chapter 14

THE GNOME SCOUTS

Day quickly followed day, but the Arzaks lost count of them. They toiled without stop, and they had long been measuring time in terms of how many bricks they had laid, how deep the wells were that they had dug, and how great the number of trees that was they had sawn down.

From morn to night, Ilsor directed the work, and between jobs, he waited on the General.

They had already built repair shops, and they completed setting up stations to monitor weather conditions and assembling the flying machines.

The small but swift helicopters were required to move about at night. Thanks to their new noiseless construction, they gave off a dry whirring sound when they flew, such as one hears when wings are flapped. In the darkness, who would even pay any attention to some vague, winged silhouettes whirring in the sky among the feathery clouds? One would most likely take them for nocturnal birds setting out in search of prey.

Sometimes, Baan-Nu personally oversaw the progress of the work. At such times, Ilsor followed behind his master as noiselessly as a shadow: he carried around a notebook and pencil and he reported deferentially on how the work was progressing, and provided explanations for a few deviations from the original plans. Thus, in accordance with what Ilsor felt to be best, landing-fields were prepared for the helicopters. These were extremely simple, and therefore reliable, construction projects. In fact, they were not even that. They were nothing more than ordinary round clearings in the forest, with the trees chopped down below the roots. The helicopter stood in the middle of this clearing. Above it stretched a translucent sheet of camouflaging material, made up to look like a large color photograph of that place, a clearing made by cutting down the trees and bushes. The sheet quivered at the slightest breeze, enhancing even more the resemblance of this picture to a real live forest. It could be easily removed at any moment to uncover the helicopter: all one had to do was pull on the cord.

The camouflaging sheet protected the helicopter from the scorching rays of the sun, but if the weather should turn bad, it could also protect it from the rain. Beside each landing field stood a tent for the pilots, where they could drink a cup of tea between flights.

In spite of his impatience, Baan-Nu was happy with Ilsor. Work proceeded at a feverish pitch under the leadership of this most intelligent and most obedient of the Arzaks. The workers accomplished genuine miracles in their attainments.

The Menvits, in addition to their supervision of the Arzaks, had another concern. They began every morning with callisthenics. They ran, jumped, gyrated on horizontal bars, and chased a ball around the meadows, trampling the soft, silky grass of Hurricap's Land and magical flowers: white, pink, and blue. They loved competitions of all kinds, and they held them even here, while preparing for war against the earthlings. One type of competition, the Extraterrestrials' favorite, was the muscle contest. The winners were the ones with the most developed physiques: the ones with the strongest muscles (which rippled beneath their skin like little globes) and who knew best how to use them.

Baan-Nu, for the most part, spent his time inside the castle. The restoration of Hurricap's ruined domicile was nearing completion. The General's suite, with its private office, and the living quarters for the Newcomers, had long been ready. Fireplaces had been set up to provide heat; now the nighttime temperature in the halls of the castle could be maintained at the same level as in houses on Rameria, and the Menvits were no longer chilled to the bone.

The General secluded himself in his office with his red portfolio that he never let go of. "In accordance with your designated policy, O mighty Guan-Lo," Baan-Nu continued his favorite labor each time with these same words, "I hereby continue my historical book *The Conquest of Belliora*. It is now Day Such-and-such since Belliora first had the fortune of receiving the most distinguished representatives of the planet Rameria, headed by the most illustrious General Baan-Nu."

The General even became befuddled from the strain of writing down such profound words. After rereading his last line, he stood up and assumed an "illustrious" pose: resting his chin in his hand, he lifted his eyes toward the sky. Then, wiping his forehead with a handkerchief made of the finest lace, Baan-Nu took up his pen once more and got started on the chapter proper: an account of just how he was going about conquering the planet. He did not forget to sing the praises of the Earth's natural environment. "A sweet-smelling garden in bloom," he noted, "A little corner of paradise here, such as one can only dream about."

Chapter 14: THE GNOME SCOUTS

Then he turned to its horrors. As you can see, he could never even have imagined such dense forests. "The conquest of Belliora must begin with her primeval woods. Wild animals in gloomy, gloomy thickets… they roar, trumpet, meow, and bark." Baan-Nu wrote this down, getting carried away by his own fantasies. "At night, it is a veritable symphony of howls. And their eyes? A mass of flashing green fires burning brighter than the emeralds in the towers of that extraordinary city. Such emeralds exist only in the pictures drawn by our children."

Baan-Nu himself concocted various dreadful things with claws and hooves, and he described savage single combats in which he always came out the winner. The General was silent regarding the cannon, the warships, and the fortresses that he had seen from the spaceship, reasoning thus: if I write about those things, then I'll surely have to give an account of the military operations I've undertaken against them, and that will call for the truth, not fabrication.

The General likewise said nothing about the inhabitants of Hurricap's Land, aside from the fact that they were protected by giants. Baan-Nu began an account of a skirmish with one giant whose house the Menvits had occupied.

He only had time to write about the giant's saucepans that were as large as basins and cupboards as tall as five-story buildings — when someone in a most unceremonious manner tore the sheet of paper from his hands, with its description of this momentous historical event, and made off through an open window. The General was so startled by this theft that he barely had time to notice the black plumage of a bird. Diamond rings still flashed in his eyes, and he was ready to swear that he had seen them on the bird's legs. But he was not altogether certain. He did not even attempt to grab his ray-gun from the drawer in the table. Pulling a fresh sheet of paper from his portfolio, he again applied

273

his pen feverishly, and described his battle with a dreadful dragon-bird with diamond rings on its legs.

This little episode with the bird did nothing to mar the mood of triumph that Baan-Nu was experiencing. It was as if the General had already acquired everything on Belliora and had conquered it all. Baan-Nu's fantasy, which was getting well out of hand, played no small role in this. He liked this new planet more and more, and he made excellent progress on his manuscript, for which reason his eyes blazed with the fire of self-assurance. The Menvit could not hide it, even when Ilsor entered the office with lemonade or coffee on a tray. The General clapped his servant on the shoulder ever more condescendingly and asked him at such times: "Well, Ilsor, didn't we do a good thing in coming to Belliora?"

"My opinion is the same as my master's opinion," the slave replied submissively, and he bowed as a sign of great subservience.

"Yes, yes, Ilsor, I know," said Baan-Nu with a smile. "You're the most faithful of servants."

The leader of the Arzaks bowed again and again, to hide the smirk on his face.

Ilsor, too, thought continually, but *not* of glorifying the Ramerian General. More than once, he had made excursions beyond the confines of Ranavir the moment Baan-Nu had fallen into the conqueror's tranquil slumber (and conquerors always fall asleep early).

Ilsor made it as far as the Ore-Diggers' village. He approached the nearest of the houses ever so quietly and stood beneath the window. He heard the whirring of a loom, which sounded more like music, and then he saw the weaver himself — a stocky, lively, self-satisfied old man. The weaver walked over to a little old woman, who was evidently his wife. He handed her an empty saucepan. Obviously he was bringing up the subject of dinner. No doubt he loved his loom, but he did not for-

get about his food either. The Arzak listened very attentively to the old people's conversation.

"Fry me a young chicken, won't you, Elvina?" said
the weaver. "You *have* bred a whole lot of them."

"It's too early," answered Elvina. "They're not old
enough yet."

If only Ilsor could have understood even the least
little bit of their conversation! But the words he was
hearing sounded just as unintelligible to him as the Newcomers' conversation sounded to the birds. The leader
of the Arzaks realized what a great barrier lay between
him and the earthlings. How could he talk to them if he
didn't know their language? It would be difficult for
them to understand one another.

Ilsor made another excursion in the other direction,
as close as he could go to the World-Encompassing
Mountains, and he happened upon Urfin's dwelling.
This time, he could not grasp a single word in the language of the earthling as he talked with the Great Horned
Owl. But he was startled by the discovery that he did
make: that the earthling and the Owl were having a conversation with one another!

"Could that be a trained bird?" said the Arzak leader
in surprise. "But he doesn't seem to be repeating words
he's memorized, like a parrot. No, he's conversing in his
own right, he's thinking!"

Tilly-Willy proceeded quickly, as promised, to the
cave of the Gnomes, who, since the death of Arachna
the Witch, had been free people in Magic Land. In accordance with Strasheela's command, their sole obliga-
tion, a pleasant one at that, consisted of continuing to
maintain their Chronicle.

The Iron Paladin stretched himself out at full length
on the ground as comfortably as he was able. Heavy
though he was, his springs, which had been installed
by Charlie the Sailor and the Winkie craftsmen, were in
perfect working order, and Tilly-Willy could lie down

and get up so deftly and adroitly that not even a squeak was heard.

The Paladin, in the softest voice that he could manage, called out to the eldest of the chroniclers: "Hey, Castalyo! My old friend! Thunder and lightning! Gnomes! Come out of the cave. I have to speak to you, may a shark eat me alive!"

The Gnomes did not wait to be called a second time. They crowded about the Giant, whose eyes moved about here and there. "The people in the Emerald City are asking a great service of you," said Tilly-Willy to the Gnomes. "Strasheela regards you as the finest scouts to be had anywhere. You must try to find out the whole truth about the Newcomers."

"The wish of Strasheela the Wise is to us as good as a command," replied Castalyo. "But we'll go there of our own free will. How could we possibly stand aloof when misfortune is threatening the Emerald City?"

It was the work of a moment, and the little men had assembled. The would not take with them any knapsacks with spare clothing or any traps for snaring rabbits — there was no need to, since they were not going on a march, but on a special assignment. The scouts could do without anything that might hinder their reconnaissance. At the time of their assignment, they had gathered to wash their clothing in the streams, and even in times of peace, the Gnomes loved to dine on nuts and berries. All the same, the scouts placed their toothbrushes and soap in their pockets, for they liked very much to wash themselves. Most important, they did not forget to put on their gray hooded cloaks. When a Gnome wrapped himself up from head to toe in one of these cloaks and lay down, somewhere in a pit, rolled up in a ball, or stood like a column by the roadside, he was indistinguishable from a gray stone, such as lie about in such great profusion in the thickets of Magic Land. Castalyo was right when he repeated: "We're unexcelled masters of camouflage."

Several hundred Gnomes climbed into the basket with its soft bedding of moss — as many as would fit in. Castalyo, as always, assumed command over them.

The long-legged Paladin put an enormous distance behind him, and delivered this most observant of armies to the woods before the ruined castle. The Gnomes scattered in all directions, and before long, they had infiltrated the Extraterrestrials' territory in many different places.

Not one of the Newcomers guessed it, but no matter what the Arzaks did, under the pressure of the Menvits — whether it was constructing landing fields for the helicopters, digging wells, or preparing food — attentive, beady little eyes were observing them everywhere. The Gnomes peeked out of bushes and from behind rocks, and they climbed up onto the various kinds of apparatus that had been unloaded from the *Diavona*. These daredevils, under the leadership of Castalyo, even penetrated into the spaceship itself and inspected its layout, though they understood nothing about it.

A sound of "scrape-scrape!" could be heard from time to time in the Newcomers' encampment, but even the most meticulous Menvit overseer would have taken this for some insect rustling or creeping by, and thought nothing more about it. It was the Gnomes, recording their observations on tiny pieces of paper, and their pencils were minute — no one but their owners would be able to use them.

The Gnomes' messages were very convenient for the birds, who delivered them without delay to the Emerald City. Castalyo rolled up pieces of paper into tubes and attached them with blades of grass to the legs of the couriers: a mockingbird, a waxwing, and a golden woodpecker. But it would have no simple matter to decipher them if it had not been for the inventive mind of Lestar the craftsman as well as that of Rujero, who together had thought up a way of constructing a microscope out of a few magnifying glasses and a few drops of water. Even Strasheela, during his most strenuous exertions, when the needles stuck out of his head and bristled like a hedgehog, would be quite unable to read them.

Tilly-Willy found himself a place to hide in the depths of the forest at a considerable distance from the castle. There, at some unremembered epoch, Hurricap had built himself a pavilion in which to rest whenever he was on an outing. Tilly-Willy too, bearing Strasheela's dispatches, settled in the pavilion, and he kept a careful eye on the road lest he be observed by some Extraterrestrial or other who happened to wander in that direction. If worst came to worst, the Paladin was to take the Newcomer captive: he would seize him and bear him away to the Emerald City.

As before, all orders were written down by the Field Marshal or the Guardian of the Gates, acting for the Monarch. Strasheela could now read well, but the art of writing eluded him altogether — for such things sometimes happen in Magic Land.

Strasheela and his friends were up to date on everything that was happening in Hurricap's castle, but they could not figure out why the Extraterrestrials had come to this secluded country of theirs. Many a time, Strasheela and the Woodman would sit down before the screen of the Magic Television and watch the aliens most attentively, both those who were working and those who were commanding them, but they could make no sense out of anything.

All the while, the Gnomes followed the Newcomers everywhere. Two words came up especially often in the Extraterrestrials' conversations: "Menvits" and "Arzaks." It took very little time for Castalyo's keen mind to guess what these words meant: the "Menvits" was what the masters were called, while "Arzaks" referred to the slaves. The word "Rameria" was also uttered quite frequently, at which time the person saying it generally looked upward, at some point in the sky. Castalyo, attempting to follow the Extraterrestrial's eyes, also looked upward, and since this generally happened at night, he often saw the Moon before him. For this reason, the eldest of the Gnomes deduced that "Rameria" was what the Moon was called in the Newcomers' language: from there, in Castalyo's opinion, they had flown to the Earth.

Chapter 15

THE ABDUCTION OF MENTAHO

There had once been a time when people dwelt in the enormous Cavern beneath Magic Land. They were known as the Ore-Diggers because they excavated metals and precious stones from mines. But they were called the *Underground* Ore-Diggers because they lived and worked underground.

For many centuries, the Underground Ore-Diggers had toiled by the sweat of their brows, and yet lived in poverty. This was because they were ruled by seven indolent kings, who did no work themselves but who loved to live in luxury — and not only themselves, but also a whole army of attendants whom they accustomed to a life of leisure.

To the Ore-Diggers' good fortune, Ellie and her cousin Fred appeared in the Cavern one day, after losing their way during an excursion into the mountains and following an underground river to the Ore-Diggers.

It was then that the power of the seven kings ended. Strasheela the Wise came up with a clever trick: he persuaded the Ore-Diggers to have the monarchs drink the Soporific Water. The kings awoke innocent as babies, and they were taught to believe that they had formerly lived the modest lives of tradesmen: one had been a weaver, another a smith, a third a sower of grain...

The Ore-Diggers had left the Cavern and built villages in the vicinity of those of the Munchkins, under the hot sun of Magic Land. They took up agriculture, like the other residents of Hurricap's land, and only small brigades of workers now took turns going back down underground to mine copper, iron, and other metals that no state can do without.

Mentaho had once been the most arrogant of the Underground Kings, and frightfully proud of his exalted origin. But the ex-king, who had become a weaver, and his wife, the elderly Elvina, lived now in a clean, modest little house on the outskirts of the Ore-Diggers' village, and they had grown very attached to it. It was they whom Ilsor had seen during his reconnaissance trip.

During the day, Mentaho sat at his loom, and if he was not sitting, then he missed his singing very much, and he was always repeating: "There's nothing finer than the work a weaver does." In the evenings, he went out to chat with his neighbors. Elvina bustled about the farm, dug in the garden, and bred chickens and ducks. They were both very happy with their fate, and they had forgotten completely that they had once worn royal robes and commanded hundreds of people.

One morning, Mentaho and Elvina were having a quiet breakfast, when all of a sudden the door of the house was flung open. A stranger dressed in a leather outfit, bending double because he was so tall, squeezed into the room. He looked at them with a commanding stare that Mentaho and Elvina were unable to resist. They lifted their eyes toward the stranger, and, struck dumb with terror, they looked fixedly at him. The could not even cry out.

The newcomer was Mon-So. He swept up Mentaho with one arm (and the weaver was of considerable size), while he seized Elvina in the other like a feather, and, nudging them, he took them outside. The weaver and his wife saw a mysterious vehicle parked there before their porch, but they were given no time to look it over. The abductor forced the old people into its cabin and snapped the door shut, and the vehicle rose into the air. Elvina was downright terrified, and Mentaho too was distressed, for anything unknown always frightened him.

But some time went by, and Mentaho began to do a little reasoning. He had ridden dragons many times, and what was happening right now to him and Elvina was similar to such a flight. "Don't be afraid, old girl," said Mentaho. "This contraption, this beast that's carrying us is surely like a dragon. It's unlikely that its driver is going to do us any harm. What point would he have, doing it in the sky? They're taking us into captivity. Though I can't understand what they need *us* for." Her husband's words calmed Elvina a little. The old lady even peeked furtively out the window at the fields and forests that were vaguely visible below.

They flew along for an hour or more, and only then did the helicopter, driven by Mon-So, ended up at Ranavir. The vehicle descended smoothly, and Mentaho saw the castle. Of course, this could be none other than Hurricap's abode, which the Newcomers had taken over.

Mentaho and Elvina were taken straight to the office of the Extraterrestrial General. A ray of light coming in through the rose-colored window glass shone on the graceful figure of the Menvit, with his gold- and silver-embroidered medals. For this reason, perhaps, the Extraterrestrial appeared so resplendent to Mentaho and Elvina, and his face, his hair, and his beard were positively aglow.

"Mission successfully accomplished, General," reported the pilot.

"Good, Mon-So. Bring them closer."

Baan-Nu appeared to be taken aback when the prisoners approached him. He even began to feel suspicious that the people who had been brought to him were not captured Belliorans at all, but Arzaks in disguise — the only thing different about them was the color of their skin, and the two races resembled one another like brothers.

All possibility of error was ruled out, since it was the loyal Mon-So who had carried out the mission. All the same, the striking resemblance between the Belliorans and the Arzaks disconcerted the General.

Mentaho could feel Baan-Nu's steady gaze upon him, but for some reason he was afraid to look at him himself in response. But he knew that one must look danger in the eye, for only then will it become less dreadful. So, taking a deep breath, he lifted his head. Mentaho did wrong, for looking him in the eyes turned out to be the most dreadful thing of all. The weaver could no longer tear his eyes from the General's face. Some kind of mysterious force had taken hold of him, and he stared and stared against his will into the Extraterrestrial's eyes, as if awaiting some command that he was prepared to obey.

"What's happening to me?" thought Mentaho. "Why do I feel so strange? It's as if I no longer see anything or hear anything, and my will is no longer my own. I seem to be asleep," and here he did, in fact, yawn. "It can't be, it can't be," Mentaho commanded himself, and with his last reserves of strength he fought against sleep. The Menvit was not even thinking of giving any commands; he was merely reflecting, and his eyes just happened to be resting on Mentaho's face.

The General continued to reflect on the striking resemblance between the Arzaks and the captives.

Could their ancestors have been transported from one planet to the other back in the distant ages?

"We'll have to go into action," Baan-Nu commanded to himself. "It's necessary to subdue the earthlings without delay. Isn't it likely that the Arzaks will see them as kinfolk and take their side? But that could never happen. They're slaves, and they're submissive." In his annoyance, the General grew more and more gloomy. He coldly ordered Mon-So to take the prisoners away. Mentaho and Elvina were confined in quarters resembling a storehouse where parts of machines were kept. There, the old people sat through the rest of the night without any sleep, and they sighed and thought over what fate had in store for them. Only toward morning did they drift off into slumber.

Chapter 16

THE SPEECH MACHINE

Mentaho awoke in a cozy little room. Everything in it was set up for comfortable living: there were two beds, a table in the middle of the room with several chairs around it, a small cabinet with dishes, and that was all. No, it wasn't quite all. When Mentaho turned around, he saw in a corner behind him some sort of bizarre object that sparkled like a small grand piano, and an indistinct rustling and a light twittering sound could be heard coming from it. The weaver did not spend a lot of time thinking about it, for he was hungry, and a substantial breakfast was waiting for them on the table.

The captives hurried over to where the food was. Taking a seat in one of the chairs, Elvina could not restrain herself, and she asked: "Where on earth are we, my lord?"

"Where on earth are we, my lord?" someone repeated after them. Elvina and Mentaho looked about them, but there was no one else in the room but them.

They ate their breakfast in total silence. When they had finished eating, Mentaho entered that splendid frame of mind that he always entered whenever he had eaten good food, especially if it consisted of pies with whipped cream — and that was the very thing that had been served to them today. He leaned back in his chair and said contentedly: "Don't be afraid, old girl. You and I are going to continue living!"

All at once, the machine that resembled a grand piano sputtered and clicked, and a voice exactly like that of Mentaho poured out of it: "Don't be afraid, old girl. You and I are going to continue living!"

"Good heavens, what ever is that thing?" exclaimed Elvina in fright. The machine, in a high-pitched voice, likewise exclaimed: "Good heavens, what ever is that thing?"

Mentaho began to think, and all at once the answer struck him. "I've figured it out," he explained to Elvina. "It's a speech machine."

The machine immediately imitated his words. Mentaho walked over to the window. It was covered over by a thin but sturdy metal net. There was no doubt about it — they were prisoners.

Then the machine, sputtering and clicking three times, began to speak in different voices: "Don't be afraid, good heavens, I've figured it out, old girl. You and I are going to continue living, Speech Machine... My lord, where..."

The machine was putting sentences together in the language of the earthlings, using the words that it had heard and rearranging them this way and that, like a child's blocks on the floor. Some of the sentences made no sense at all, while others came out sounding well-reasoned.

The ex-king and his wife understood now why they had been abducted. The Newcomers wanted to learn, with their help, the language of the earthlings. The quick-witted Mentaho was beside himself. If it was necessary for the aliens to know the language of the inhabitants of Magic Land, that meant that they planned to settle there for a long time. Mentaho recalled the gaze of that Chief Newcomer, the one that he and Elvina had been taken to see. Chills began to run up and down the weaver's skin. There was no hiding from a gaze like that.

"I'll have to do my best not to look him in the eye," Mentaho resolved. "I'll have to look around and try to understand everything, or my name isn't Mentaho."

"You won't take *me* in!" the former king said aloud.

"You won't take *me* in!" the sound of his voice was heard again.

"What are you getting so excited about?" said Mentaho, unable to stand it any longer.

"What are you getting so excited about?" responded the machine.

"All right, we're going to beat you," said Mentaho, giving up. The machine muttered these same words, and then there was silence once more.

The Speech Machine had too small a store of the earthlings' words, and it waited for the captives to begin talking again. Mentaho did not feel like doing his captors any favors, and he would gladly have maintained silence indefinitely, but there would be times when he had to talk with his wife, whether he wanted to or not. The Extraterrestrials had been very clever, capturing both the husband and his wife.

The Speech Machine was not the only thing that was waiting. General Baan-Nu was waiting for a report about the captives. As always, he was engaged in his favorite occupation — he was writing his historical book *The Conquest of Belliora*.

"And so," wrote the General, beginning a new page, "I continue from the time when the dragon attacked me…" Baan-Nu began to think. This time, the news of the work of the Speech Machine with the captives aroused him far more strongly than his own fantasies. But the latter would have become inexhaustible if the General had only known how close he was to the source: there were real dragons wandering about in Hurricap's land!

The Machine gulped down the earthlings' words greedily, and by evening its vocabulary had attained several hundred. Then something new became apparent in its workings. It began to guess the meanings of some of the words, saying, for example, the word "bread," and after it they heard *nobar*; after "water," it said *essor*.

"In other words," mumbled Mentaho, "bread is `nobar' and water is `essor' " The weaver's memory was being enriched with ever new words of the Menvit language. He now understood that it was to become their interpreter.

"I'm still not going to do the Newcomers any favors," he said defiantly, though he continued to memorize words. "Suppose I break this Speaker?" Mentaho turned one of the chairs legs up and prepared to smash it on the Machine. But the former king caught himself just in time. For all that, he was still the Newcomers' prisoner. If he didn't comply with them, what would they think of doing next? Mentaho was afraid most of all for Elvina, for he loved his wife very dearly.

"All right," exclaimed the weaver angrily, "if it comes to that, I'll learn their confounded language! It may even come in handy."

There was a clicking sound in the lock, the door opened, and in walked a person. He placed some refreshing drinks and some sandwiches on the table and then, pointing to himself, he uttered his name: "Ilsor."

"Ilsor," repeated the Machine in the corner. If it had not been for his very pale skin, Mentaho and Elvina would have taken Ilsor for a resident of Magic Land: he had the same open face and kindly eyes that inspired trust in other people. Mentaho told him his own name and Elvina's.

Ilsor opened the door and took a quick look around, then he beckoned to Mentaho to follow him. Elvina was about to come along with them, but Ilsor shook his head silently. The Chief Technician of the Arzaks took Mentaho outside to a dense thicket in the vicinity of the castle and pointed to a pile of gray rocks that were sticking up like columns of uniform height.

"Don't lose heart, Mentaho!" came a whisper from somewhere down below. "Keep your chin up!"

Recognizing expressions typical of the Giant from Beyond the Mountains, Mentaho looked closely at the rocks. One of the columns stirred and began to move about, and the weaver saw at his feet a tiny old man with a long white beard.

"I'm Castalyo, the elder of the Gnomes," the little old man introduced himself. "I bring you a message from Strasheela. To your share, Mentaho, has fallen the honor of being the eyes and ears of the earthlings in the enemy camp." Mentaho was struck dumb by this. "Try to understand the aliens' language," the tiny man continued. "We must know what the Newcomers' intentions are."

Ilsor beckoned to Mentaho to follow him once again, and he took him back to Elvina. The weaver wanted to say "thank you" to Ilsor, but he didn't know how to express this in Menvit. Then he pointed with his hand at the tray with the refreshing drinks and the sandwiches and cried out, "Nobar! Essor!"

That same day, the news spread among the Extraterrestrials that the Bellioran captive was making notable progress in his study of the Menvit language.

Chapter 17

THE RADAR INSTALLATIONS

After the disappearance of Mentaho and his wife, the Ore-Diggers and the Munchkins began to use small wooden bolts to lock their houses at night. Though such protection was not very reliable, they nonetheless felt more secure with it. The altogether timid residents, those who wanted to be completely safe, transferred themselves down into the Underground Cavern.

The Extraterrestrials caught on to the fact that their presence at Ranavir was no longer a secret to the earthlings. How could it possible remain hidden when some dozens of men, the crew of the mighty spaceship, were constantly roving about the surrounding forests?! And when the Arzaks were working, there were flare-ups of fire that could not be concealed, as well as the clattering, the noise, and the rumbling that reverberated through the mountains and echoed in every direction. So the Newcomers ceased even to attempt to hide themselves. Their whirring helicopters appeared over the land during the day, as the men took surveys from them and prepared maps.

The Emerald City drew the Extraterrestrials like a magnet. Sometimes the helicopter hovered over it for a long time while the Menvits admired its beauty: there was nothing at all like it on Rameria.

Parties of geologists set out from Ranavir — for the fuel that the helicopters needed. They obtained new samples, as before, from the World-Encompassing Mountains, and Ilsor continued to state with dissatisfaction: "Low quality. It won't do." To Baan-Nu he explained: "We can't make anything good out of something bad, General. Why risk the safety of the helicopters? And there's plenty of time — the people are peace-loving."

In the western spurs of the World-Encompassing Mountains, the geologists discovered two abandoned mines, and not far from them were some small mounds of rocks that had been extracted from these mines. It was not at all difficult to establish that these had been obtained from the mines at an earlier date. Among the polished rocks they found transparent green strains of that same mineral that gave its name to the splendid city of the earthlings.

They reported this priceless find to Baan-Nu, and you should have seen the way his eyes began to flash when he learned of the existence of the Emerald Mines.

They set about immediately clearing out the mines and strengthening the supports of their underground galleries. Before two days had passed, two dozen Arzaks, working under the supervision of a Menvit geologist, obtained the first emeralds. Several of these were the size of walnuts. The General was afraid even to believe this stroke of good fortune: on Rameria, emeralds were no less precious than diamonds, and the valuables that they mined now disappeared into his strongbox. As he admired their play of colors during the evenings, Baan-Nu thought of the countless treasures to be found in the Emerald City. He was not aware that, side by side with the real emeralds, the ingenious Goodwin had set gems made of simple green glass. "When I transport all these treasures away from here," dreamed Baan-Nu, his eyes sparkling, "I'll become a rich and powerful man back on Rameria."

Mentaho and Ilsor saw one another every day. When Ilsor, with a smile, appeared at the door of the little room where the captives were secluded, he greeted them thus: *"Téru, mérui!"* Mentaho already knew, from the Speech Machine, that this meant: "Hello, my friends!"

"Téru, téru," replied the weaver, *"em nóto Karóssi!"* Which meant: "Hello, hello, I'm glad to see you!"

The leader of the Arzaks and the former king looked at each other with sincere feelings of friendship. But in spite of that, the conversation went badly. Ilsor reported to the General that the Speech Machine was taking too long to perform the function required of it, and he suggested that he work with him personally. "The Bellioran must have the opportunity of conversing in Menvit on a steady basis," he said. "That is my plan: stimulation is needed. A life that's devoid of stimulation will not be conducive to open conversations."

Baan-Nu approved of Ilsor's plan and gave him permission to act on his own. The obedient servant found out what Mentaho was enthusiastic about. That very day, the weaver sat down at his loom; both were happy, and both began to sing: the loom whirred with pleasure, and that sounded like music, while Mentaho hummed a little tune to himself.

Mentaho increased his command of the language at once. He studied conscientiously, and in response the machine gave him "10," "11," "12," which were the highest grades possible among the Menvits.

"You were right, Ilsor," said the General. "It's true: much stimulation does indeed mean many words."

"And when they know many words," agreed the servant, "you're that much closer to your goal, which is the establishment of your predominance."

"I know of another means of arousing people's enthusiasm," stated Baan-Nu with assurance. "It's infallible, and it achieves excellent results."

The General pulled two transparent emeralds from his strongbox. Then, in the prisoners' room, he set them down before Mentaho. "All right, now, take a look at these," he said, impatiently pushing the precious stones toward the weaver.

The Machine translated it at once. The weaver looked at the emeralds. "Uh-huh!" he said. The Machine was silent.

"Do you like them?" asked the General.

"Uh-huh!" repeated Mentaho, nodding his head.

The Machine was unable to translate this word "uh-huh," and the weaver did not say anything further. Baan-Nu sat there puzzled. When he saw the bored look on Mentaho's face, he realized that his little stones were having no effect, and he grew angry. "What's this?" he asked Mentaho. "You mean you're not even interested in looking at emeralds?"

"Uh-huh," the weaver responded once more.

The General decided that this word "uh-huh" must be a very important, though untranslatable, word among the earthlings.

By now, the former king knew the Menvit alphabet by heart, and he read through an A-B-C book and then set about reading an anthology of Menvit literature. Before very long, with Ilsor's help, he had learned to converse fluently in the language of the Newcomers. Ilsor operated the Speech Machine, and he made it memorize more and more new earthling words, with a speed that was nothing short of amazing. He also made it inform Mentaho about how these words were pronounced in Menvit. Elvina, however, fell hopelessly behind, for the old woman simply had no desire to learn the language of their uninvited guests.

When, in Baan-Nu's opinion, the captive had absorbed the Menvit language sufficiently, and the Speech Machine could provide smooth translations (in accordance with the amount of information stored inside it), the General, accompanied by Ilsor, made an appearance in the secluded ones' room to have a talk with Mentaho.

Baan-Nu began by questioning the prisoner about his country. Mentaho exhibited the greatest care: he had already received instructions from Strasheela on what to say and how to say it. There was no need to tell him that the land was Magical. And he was strictly forbidden to mention the fabulous fairies Stella and Villina. Nor could he bring up the fact that birds and beasts could understand human speech. The existence of Strasheela and the Woodman were likewise to remain a secret.

"Tell me, Mentaho," asked the General, "what is the name of this country where we now are?"

The Machine sighed, blinked, and squeaked as it diligently translated now into one language, and now into the other.

"It's called Goodwinia, most esteemed General," answered the weaver in Menvit.

"And why is it called that?" was the next question.

"It's named after Goodwin, who was famed for his military exploits," said Mentaho without batting an eyelash — though, of course, he said this in his own language, since it was still difficult for him to create his own sentences in the other idiom.

"Was Goodwin a king?" asked the General. When he received an affirmative answer to this question, he inquired: "So that means that you used to have wars?"

"What wars we had!" boasted Mentaho. "Goodwin's army was famous for its exceptional bravery. It won victories over the mighty kingdoms of Gingemia and Bastindia." The weaver was hoodwinking him, but he was using real names to avoid becoming confused himself.

292

"Do you have cannons?" the Chief Newcomer continued his interrogation.

"We have only one cannon," Mentaho admitted truthfully, "but what a cannon it is! With only one shot it can flatten a whole army of wooden soldiers."

"What kind of soldiers?" The General did not understand. Mentaho realized that he had said too much, and he remained silent. Baan-Nu decided that the Speech Machine had made an inaccurate translation. But in any event, the Extraterrestrial was growing less and less pleased with this conversation.

"Well, has Goodwin continued to rule the land?" he inquired.

"No, lord General. He flew off to the Sun."

"And how did he fly?"

"This way, in an air…"

"An airship?" asked the General.

"That's right," responded the weaver.

The announcement of Goodwin's interplanetary journey (for that is what Baan-Nu understood the flight to mean) threw the General into despair. He made a wry face, but he continued with his questions.

"Tell me, Mentaho, my friend, who used to live in Ranavir?" It was in desperation that Baan-Nu called the weaver "friend," so upset was he. "Such an enormous castle…"

Mentaho figured it out: he was being asked about the former occupant of the castle. But he knew nothing about Hurricap. However, the weaver kept his head. "Well… it's like this," he said, waving his hand vaguely. "The builder of this castle was Hurricap."

"Are there giants in Goodwinia?" Baan-Nu asked this most vital question with a pounding heart.

"Where could they possibly have gone?" said Mentaho matter-of-factly. "Yes, they're still wandering around."

The Ramerian suddenly broke out in a cold sweat. But since he still did not know the details, he continued the conversation. "Do the giants have their own kingdom?" he asked, with as much composure as he could.

"No, the giants lead solitary lives," related Mentaho. "They're so savage, you see, that they can't live together. Whenever they meet, they begin to hurl rocks at one another."

Although King Mentaho, under the influence of the Soporific Water, had been transformed into a weaver, his personality was absolutely unchanged. He lied in a downright inspired manner, in full possession of himself, and he looked the other person right in the eye as he spoke — eyes that were oblong and severe, and which were now opened wide in amazement at the weaver's story.

Mentaho lied as only a king can!

The chief Menvit fell silent, overcome by dismay. He even forgot about his gaze, for otherwise he would have been able to order Mentaho to do whatever he wanted him to — for example, to speak only the truth.

The next time he met with Mentaho, Baan-Nu changed the order of his questions, and threw them at him at random. But the same names were repeated in the weaver's responses. "No," reflected the General, "it's impossible to admit that this frivolous man, this scatterbrain, is lying. But of course, he must be making it all up. His strength of character may be extensive, but to my mind, he's simplicity itself."

Ever since their landing, Baan-Nu had recalled many times that Guan-Lo, Ruler of Rameria, was awaiting some signal from him that Belliora had been conquered. It was necessary to make haste now.

The Extraterrestrials began by surrounding Goodwinia with a chain of radar stations. Baan-Nu ordered that the radar installations be set up about fifty kilometers from one another. This, in his opinion, would ensure the defense of the border between Goodwinia and the Outer World.

Chapter 17: THE RADAR INSTALLATIONS

Cannon were unloaded from the *Diavona*, but the radar installations had to be built from scratch.

While the Arzaks were putting the installations together, Menvit helicopter pilots flew up onto the loftiest peaks of the World-Encompassing Mountains, where they cleared areas of obstacles and set up turntables for the cannon. A rotating radar antenna would detect the approach of any living being, an electronic device would relay a radio signal to Ranavir, and in addition to that, the self-loading cannon would be aimed at the live target.

The labors were presently completed. But the installations were not activated at once. They were kept on hold for an entire hour, to give the helicopters enough time to fly back to the camp.

One of the pilots learned for himself how efficient the system was that they had just installed. The door to his helicopter began to sag unexpectedly, and he spent more than an hour in readjusting it. The pilot was so occupied with his repair work that he did not keep track of the time and forgot about the cannon being on hold; thus, when he finally took off after the others, a discharge was fired right at him. The pilot was wounded, but fortunately he was not killed, and he landed the helicopter with great difficulty at the bottom of the ravine. How surprised he was later when an emissary from Baan-Nu (Ilsor, of course) came to see him at the shelter, where he lay all bandaged up, and instead of a rebuke, he brought him notification that he would be decorated with the Order of the Moon.

This in no way meant that Baan-Nu valued the pilot's extreme absent-mindedness so highly. No, it was because, thanks to him, he felt reassured: now no one could enter, undetected, the country where the Ramerians had landed. Also, if the residents of Goodwinia themselves should suddenly decide that they needed help, none of them would be able to make it in secrecy to the Outer World.

Chapter 18

GORIEK'S ENCOUNTER

In accordance with the instructions of Strasheela the Wise and his friends, Mentaho gradually won the Newcomers over. Ilsor was a great help to him in this. He extolled the Bellioran captive lavishly to Baan-Nu. "He's intelligent, capable, and receptive," he said. "Mentaho is rendering us an invaluable service with the artlessness that is natural to him."

The ex-king and Elvina even received permission to walk about unguarded in the area around the little house where they lived, and the door was kept unlocked. This relative freedom of movement was very opportune, for it enabled them to meet more often with Castalyo. The frequent walks that the weaver and his wife took in the forest aroused no suspicion. The elderly couple were merely going out to pick mushrooms. Mentaho made no secret of the fact that he loved to eat, and the fastidious Elvina, wearing a clean apron, never forgot to carry a basket with her and to fill it with mushrooms.

As the saying goes, two heads are better than one. Mentaho was cunning, and Ilsor was intelligent. And so one day Ilsor gave Mentaho an idea for something that would thoroughly disenhearten the Ramerians, and Ilsor was talked about afterward as the earthlings' best friend. It was a genuine military stratagem, and when Castalyo wrote about it to Strasheela, the latter was transported to an ecstasy that can not be described. He even broke out into a dance, as in the olden days, and he sang out: "Ey-hey-hey-ho! We've got a remarkable friend! Ey-hey-hey-hey-ho!"

Ilsor had long since taken note of the Paladin, Tilly-Willy. Being an inventor in his own right, he was amazed at the skill that had gone into the creation of this iron man, and at how superbly his mechanism had been constructed.

Ilsor's advice was simple. Tilly-Willy began to make appearances on the country's roads, endeavoring to cause the Ramerian pilots to take notice of him as often as possible. But they encountered him in different places on each occasion — it was an easy enough matter for him to cover great distances because of his long legs. Most important, he made himself look different each time: now he would be steelgray in color, now yellowish-bronze, then green with black spots, like an enormous lizard. At other times he flashed on his shoulders some sort of brightly-colored cape that covered him from head to toe.

The pilots were convinced that these were different giants that they were seeing. They brought the General new and different photographs of the immense paladin. But the transformation was accomplished in a very simple manner. Inside Tilly-Willy, in a cabin where a human being could fit in, sat Lestar, who was not only the most outstanding craftsman of Winkie Land, but also the Iron Paladin's first friend. He had with him a whole array of paint jars and sprayers. Tilly-Willy would show himself to one Ramerian pilot, and then he would hide in the forest beneath the trees while Lestar quickly painted him another color. Thanks to this ploy, Baan-Nu and his subordinates thought that people of enormous size and strength really did dwell in the vicinity of Goodwinia.

Mentaho confirmed that it was these very giants who had assisted King Goodwin in achieving his remarkable victories. Believing now in the existence of these giants, Baan-Nu decided that the Newcomers would have to conduct themselves much more carefully for the time being: it would not do at all to make such a giant angry! Engaging in combat before they were ready for war did not fit into the aliens' plans.

And yet one of the hostile steps that were being taken with regard to Goodwinia was noticed by the Earthlings. In the World-Encompassing Mountains — in the northern part of them, to be exact — was a spot inhabited by giant eagles. This secluded area was known as Eagle Valley. In accordance with age-honored custom, the eagles limited the population of their tribe to exactly one hundred. Each new chick was brought into the world only if one of the older members of the tribe passed on. For this reason, the right to hatch a nestling was granted to the she-eagles only through a system of strict succession.

There were serious reasons for this. The eagles fed on the meat of mountain goats and aurochs, and, naturally, these animals did not breed rapidly because they were constantly being destroyed by the giant birds.

At one time, the leader of the eagle tribe had been Arrahes. He wanted to appropriate the turn of another eagle, Carfax, to hatch a chick. However, the noble Carfax had emerged victorious and himself became the leader of the tribe. From his seed had sprung an eaglet named Goriek. In size and strength, Goriek was almost the equal of his father. And like many of those of his youthful age, he was rather too presumptuous.

Eagles possess unusually keen eyesight. From a great height, they can make out even tiny objects on the ground for many miles in every direction. Needless to say, the cannon installed on the bare rocks could not possibly remain hidden from their eyes. But only if they happened to be watchful eyes. Goriek, though, was not paying attention. He was pursuing a large, fleet-footed aurochs, and so absorbed was he in his hunt that he completely forgot about caution. The aurochs was moving about among the chasms, easily overcoming the steep mountain slopes, and it leaped from cliff to cliff. The young Eagle, pursuing the aurochs, had no intention of letting the mighty animal go, and even a sudden flash of metal from some unknown object on the rock did not stop him.

The radar went into action, the cannon rotated. Fortunately for Goriek, it happened that the invisible ray fell on the aurochs, which at that moment was climbing up an exposed slope. The cannon, following the ray, turned around, and the animal, struck by its discharge, tumbled down into the abyss. It also grazed Goriek, who at that moment had caught up with the aurochs, and injured his wing. In a dreadful thirst for revenge against this unknown foe, and fired by anger and pain, Goriek began to ascend along the side of the mountain in enormous bounds. And before the cannon could reload, he pounced upon it with all the fury that he was capable of.

The giant Eagles, even in their youth, are possessed of extraordinary strength.

Goriek tore out the cannon, turntable and all, and hurled it down into the chasm. The cannon shattered to pieces with a deafening clamor. Then Goriek seized the radar installation in his beak, and soon nothing was left of the sensitive apparatus but fragments.

After a long search, the father and mother found Goriek on the cliff, and they dragged him home with great difficulty through the mountain gorges.

Chapter 19

GINGEMA'S BLACK ROCKS AGAIN

Signals to show that the radar installations were in good working order were received at Ranavir twice every twenty-four hours. And one day, when they failed to come in, Mon-So, commander of the squadron, set out to learn what was wrong. He found one of the installations totally destroyed: nothing was left of the radar apparatus but a pile of shattered components, and the cannon was gone altogether. The pilot found two eagle feathers on the mountain slope, and their dimensions stunned him: each of them was as long as a man is tall. It all became clear: only the birds could have been responsible for this.

Earlier, while still engaged in clearing space for the radar stations, the Ramerian pilots had seen giant Eagles a number of times during their flights over the mountains; but from their distance, they had been unable to get a close look at them. Whenever a helicopter headed toward those remarkable birds, the latter had withdrawn from them with lightning speed. Kau-Ruk had had the most success: he had managed to fly closer than any of the others, but even he failed. Of course, he did appear on other occasions, hovering over Eagle Valley in his helicopter, and he saw the birds soaring up to their huge nests and observed them hunting aurochs and mountain goats in the distance.

Mon-So's report made a painful impression on the Menvits. So their system of border defense turned out to be not at all as dependable as its creators had believed. Receiving this unpleasant piece of news was not in accordance with Baan-Nu's plans.

"I'm outraged at your absent-mindedness," roared the General, rebuking both the pilots and the engineers. He was so angry that his eyes, which were normally oblong, grew round as buttons. "Today, one of our installations was lost to our system," he shouted. "What guarantee do we have that tomorrow we won't lose a second, and a third?"

The pilots and engineers remained silent. Then the stellar Navigator, Kau-Ruk, took the floor, after being lost in concentrated thought. "The fact of the matter is," he said, "that there are extraordinary eagles living in those mountains."

"Well, what of it?" asked Baan-Nu, not seeing the connection.

"They do their hunting in the places where our radar is set up. The cannon can't help but hit such enormous birds."

"What are you leading up to?" rumbled the General.

"The cannon will hit them, and the Eagles will tear them out," said Kau-Ruk. "A wounded Eagle of such a size is possessed of truly awesome strength."

"I suppose you're right," said Baan-Nu, agreeing with the Navigator in spite of himself. "But what can we do about it?"

"There's only one way out," explained Kau-Ruk. "We must remove the system to some place outside Goodwinia. During our reconnaissance flights, we saw that the country is surrounded by a chain of Black Rocks. They are equally distant from one another. As for the reason why these Rocks have been placed there, we can only guess. No doubt they're road markers. Or, more likely, they're altars on which the ancient Belliorans offered sacrifices to their gods..."

It was Gingema's Rocks that Kau-Ruk had in mind, but the Newcomers from the distant planet could not possibly know that they were magical. The wicked Sorceress had placed them there in the desert a few centuries ago in order to block the way to Magic Land to anyone from the outside world, whether he were traveling on foot or on horseback. Only inhabitants of Magic Land itself could walk, fly, and ride freely by. Of course, the Witch had not foreseen helicopters, which flew over the stony barriers without hindrance.

"I propose that we set up our radar stations on those mammoth rocks," the Navigator suggested. The others found his suggestion to be an intelligent one, and they adopted it at once.

The Newcomers quickly set to work. The General designated Mon-So as the one responsible for carrying out this task.

The same number of helicopters took to the air as the number of cannon available, plus one additional vehicle for the squadron commander — he had to oversee the work, and thus be able to move about freely from one point to another. They did not take any of the Arzaks along with them. Two Menvits sat in each helicopter: one pilot, and one engineer. The cannon were allocated in advance: the Menvits knew precisely which one to carry to which point, and the helicopters took off like bees emerging from a hive, each of them flying out to its own destination.

The sun rose higher and higher in the sky, and it was as if the color were drained from its face and passed to the clouds, while the heavenly body itself turned paler. Beneath its rays, the fog dissipated, and only here and there in low-lying areas were its whitish masses still spread out. There below them were the cannon, their muzzles sparkling with dew. The radar stations were not moving, not vibrating, but it was as if they were straining themselves, and they were reminiscent of winged horses ready at any moment to begin prancing. The sun seemed about to awaken them with its rays. But they were not really asleep and were not going to awaken — they had merely been turned off.

The helicopters hovered over the installations. The engineers descended on rope ladders and attached cords to the brackets on the radar equipment, tying sturdy knots. There remained the task of carefully lifting them up and transporting them to the Black Rocks. They had selected the tallest and most accessible of Gingema's Rocks.

The helicopters' propellers cut easily and noiselessly through the air, as if they were swirling in it. The transfer operation promised to go through without a hitch. The commander could not restrain himself, and he flew back to Ranavir for a few minutes to report to the General that the fulfillment of the mission was proceeding at a good healthy clip. He felt like making Baan-Nu happy.

The General was finishing his morning callisthenics. He was doing some "shadow-boxing," and was bounding joyfully all over the field. Perhaps that was how his next battle with a monster was supposed to look, one that he had not yet put into writing in his *Conquest of Belliora*.

The squadron commander exchanged greetings with the General and painted the situation in the most glowing colors, and then, with words of encouragement from Baan-Nu, he flew back to direct the continuation of the work.

Flying over the Black Rocks from a great height, Mon-So saw that the cannon had already long been in place. Now the helicopters, hovering over the Rocks, would be pulling up the ropes. The engineers would climb up the ladders, and they would all return to the base, for a reception and congratulations.

"It's wonderful, terrific," Mon-So almost sang to himself. Yes, to the squadron commander, his pilots would now be sitting at the head of the banquet table, just like the old days on Rameria when they met with success. And Ilsor would be waiting on them. Baan-Nu had promised him that gift. Mon-So was already thinking of the festive bill of fare that he would be ordering, and he had even turned his vehicle back in the direction of the base, when all at once his two-way radio began to speak in a chorus of voices. It was his pilots, who had observed their commander up in the clouds, and they interrupted one another continually in their calls for him to come down to them. "These Rocks are like magnets!" they moaned.

Mon-So was dumbfounded as he scrutinized the situation below. Something inconceivable was happening. Some of the helicopters seemed to be leaping over

Rocks, while others were going around in circles like maniacs. Now and then, as if they had grown tired, certain vehicles would behave normally, which is to say they would hover like balloons over the Rocks; but their passengers the Menvits, on the other hand, were behaving like performers in a circus. At first they would bounce up and down, so high that they were almost on the roofs of their helicopters, and then with a leap they made it back into their cabins, only to be drawn out once more. Then it was the same thing all over again. The whole episode kept repeating itself, until they were all exhausted.

Some of the helicopters were hovering in the air empty: the engineer and the pilot together were turning somersaults on the ropes, like acrobats.

When Mon-So saw this, he was quite beside himself, and he could not return to his previous state of mind. He needed time to calm himself down, and he resolved to look into the behavior of the vehicles and the crew. The squadron commander promised himself that he would have all guilty parties suitably punished. He began to descend toward one helicopter where the pilot and the engineer were both resting after their desperate leaps over one Rock.

"Mon-So, my colonel, listen to me!" the pilot's voice reached his ears. "My partner fastened the installation to the Black Rock and was climbing back into the helicopter. But that's when it all started. He managed to get halfway up the rope, and then he went crashing down. He tried to climb up again, but it was as if something were pulling him downward. I resolved to help him. I began to pull the engineer up, rope and all. But I'd only pulled him up halfway, when my buddy released his hands and crashed down onto the Rock."

It was the same thing further on. The pilot landed the helicopter next to the Rock and dragged the engineer into the cabin. Then he pulled the steering column toward himself, and the helicopter rose into the air.

However, they had hardly begun to fly over the Black Rock itself, when the pilot was drained of his strength and let go of the steering column. His vehicle, describing an arc, leaped over the Rock and landed again on the other side.

Mon-So laughed a little at the pilot, but all the same, he threw him the end of a rope so that he could tow the rebellious helicopter away. Once the cord was fastened tight, both helicopters rose into the air without any hindrance. Then Mon-So felt a sharp jerk — the cord was drawn taut, and the second helicopter was hanging on it like a rock — the pilot had apparently released the steering column once again. Mon-So pushed the accelerator pedal down to the floor. The propellor began to turn with such unrestrained force that the helicopter itself began to turn in the opposite direction. However, they did break away from the mysterious pull and gained altitude, but the poor pilot was unable to regain consciousness. Mon-So, pulling the second helicopter behind him with the cord, managed to land both helicopters at a spot far removed from the Stone. He pulled the pilot and the engineer out of the cabin and, cursing himself, he smacked them on the cheeks. At last he managed to revive the unfortunate men.

"Ah, Mon-So, my colonel," said the pilot as he opened his eyes. "Listen to me. My partner and I can remember nothing from the moment I let go of the steering column. I recall only being pressed back in my seat by some great force, but not a thing after that."

In a similar manner, by attaching one helicopter to another, Mon-So helped all the Menvits out of their predicaments — he certainly could not leave them there forever on the Black Rocks.

When they reported to Baan-Nu about what had happened, the latter thought that an epidemic of some terrestrial disease had broken out among the pilots, and he ordered that they all be placed in the isolation ward.

But once the pilots had rested up from their futile leaping and their fright, they displayed no further signs of illness.

"It's nothing dreadful," the General decided. "They got too much sun, that's all. It's a much greater shame that the installations aren't working." In his haste while rescuing the pilots, Mon-So had forgotten to hook up the power supplies to the radar stations and the cannon.

Not one of the pilots who had been to the Black Rocks had any desire to return to that perilous spot. Nor were there were any volunteers among the other pilots either.

Though he would not admit it to himself, even Mon-So was a little afraid to fly there. He would be running the risk of getting stuck and being forced to tarry alone in the desert among the Rocks. The pilots had little liking for this most dedicated executor of the General's commands, and he did not believe that any of them would exactly hasten to his rescue. Nor would Baan-Nu himself be likely to save him!

The General gave thought to the matter of what further steps were to be taken with the installations, and until this problem was resolved, the radar system would remain inoperative.

Part II

ANNIE, TIM, AND THE NEWCOMERS

Chapter 20

MANKIND THREATENED
BY DISASTER

Oyho the Dragon made the trip from Magic Land to Kansas a third time. His companions Faramant and Kaggi-Karr were exhausted by the journey, and they fell asleep.

As he had also done the last time, Oyho timed his arrival so that he would not alarm the local populace. He landed at night near the familiar ravine where no one ever went, and he concealed himself there.

Faramant and Kaggi-Karr found the Smith farm without any difficulty. The family had long been asleep when the Guardian of the Gates knocked timidly at the door. The arrival of unexpected guests, especially when they come from Magic Land, is always a surprise, and this one, naturally, threw the sleepers into an uproar.

Annie delightedly clasped the happy Kaggi-Karr to her breast and stroked her, and she embraced the Guardian of the Gates. Farmer John received the travelers with great warmth. Only Mrs. Anna looked with anxiety at the Crow and at Faramant, with this feeling in her heart: this flight of emissaries from Magic Land had not come about by mere chance, and for her, it portended nothing good.

Faramant and Kaggi-Karr felt dejected when they realized that they had not caught Ellie at home, even though she was employed as a teacher not far from her parents' house. She had just taken her pupils on a field trip to another state. "That's a shame," sighed Faramant. "Each time, I think we'll be seeing her for one last time, and now we don't get to see her at all."

Then, in order not to let himself get all upset, the Guardian of the Gates changed the subject and launched into an account of the Newcomers who had taken over Hurricap's castle. The Extraterrestrials had not come to Earth with peaceful intentions. They had surrounded the World-Encompassing Mountains with a string of self-firing cannon, which would not let a single living creature by.

"Carfax's son, Goriek, was hurt by one such cannon," said Faramant, "but he did the right thing: he threw the cannon down into the gorge."

They listened to him with the keenest sympathy for the people of Magic Land, who had once again fallen into misfortune. "But how did you manage to get to Kansas?" asked Annie apprehensively.

"On Oyho, as always."

"But he wasn't wounded?" Annie looked worriedly at the Guardian of the Gates.

"He's safe and sound," replied Faramant. "He's lying in his gully, waiting for someone to bring him a dozen buckets of porridge and baked potatoes: the poor thing got pretty hungry during the journey."

The farmer promised to feed the Dragon, and Faramant went on: "We made it here without any incident. For some reason, the Extraterrestrials have given up using their cannon and are showing no interest in them, at least for now. That's what Strasheela says."

Annie gave a start. "Strasheela, illustrious old Strasheela! How ever is he getting along there? And the kind Woodman and the Courageous Lion? How are all my friends doing?"

"So far, nothing bad has happened to them, but there's no telling *what* evil awaits them unless you, Annie, and Tim..."

Mrs. Anna, not waiting for him to finish, jumped into the conversation. "I *knew* that was what you were leading up to! You've come for help again."

"All right, Anna, all right," the farmer said, calming his wife down. "It appears that the matter this time is much more serious than before. We'll have to ask the O'Kelly family to come over. Including Tim, needless to say."

John walked over to the neighboring farm, while Mrs. Anna became submerged in melancholy thoughts, and Annie quietly questioned Faramant about the Emerald City, about Strasheela, the Woodman, the Lion, about Tilly-Willy, about the Munchkins, the Winkies, the Leapers... Mrs. Anna, too, was curious to hear the news, but her mind gave her no peace.

Tim and his parents were shortly on the scene. During the two years that had gone by since his last return from Magic Land, he had grown considerably, and he was now almost as tall as his father. Sensing that new adventures were in store for him, Tim greeted Faramant and Kaggi-Karr joyfully.

Faramant now had to repeat what the Smiths had already heard.

Richard O'Kelly declared proudly: "There are hundreds of millions of us on Earth. Do you really think we can't deal with a handful of alien invaders?"

Faramant interrupted him. "And suppose dozens more spaceships come zooming along in the wake of the handful?" Annie gazed fearfully up at the stars.

"Fortunately, in our fight against the Menvit aliens, we have allies: the Arzaks."

A long silence ensued. Then Mrs. Anna asked: "But my esteemed Faramant, how do you figure that Annie and Tim can be of any help to you in your fight? They're merely children — already mature, it's true, but children all the same."

"To tell you the truth," said the Guardian of the Gates, "we weren't counting only on the children, great as our hopes are in them. We were thinking of inviting also the Giant from Beyond the Mountains, that wise, highly experienced man. As it happens, Tilly-Willy has a very tender heart (and who would have thought it possible in an overgrown iron kid like him?). He misses Charlie the Sailor, and he's ready to talk about him from morning to night."

"It's nice that he's got such a good memory and is so thankful," replied Mrs. Anna. "But my brother is sailing the Pacific Ocean, and it's unlikely that he'll be here with us again in any of the months ahead. When you set out on the return journey to your amazing country, though, I'm going to ask you to take a certain object to Tilly-Willy, something that Annie and I have been keeping for him for an entire year…"

"Mom!" Annie put her finger to her lips and looked slyly at Mrs. Anna, who fell silent.

"Once again, things haven't turned out the way we would have liked."

"That means the Giant from Beyond the Mountains won't be able to participate in our struggle," sighed Faramant. "Still and all, I'd like to ask you to let Annie and Tim come back with us. We'll protect them from danger and won't let them actually fight the enemy themselves, but their advice can be invaluable to us…"

Farmer Smith jumped in before his wife, who was about to say something. "Listen, Anna," he said. "It's twice now that our kids have been summoned to Magic Land. The first time around, the danger threatened only Strasheela and the Iron Woodman. The second time, danger hung over all of Magic Land because a wicked witch sought to ruin it. But now, this third time, the matter is immeasurably worse: a dreadful misfortune is threatening the entire world. We could never forgive ourselves if we didn't help out, if we kept Tim and Annie here."

Both mothers understood, and they gave their children permission to go.

Once agreement had been reached, Farmer John said: "And now, my dear ladies, I've got good news for you. Our children won't be embarking on it alone. We'll send for Alfred Canning. I'm sure he won't refuse to join in the struggle against the extraterrestrial Newcomers."

"Yes, yes, he'll help," exclaimed Mrs. Anna. "He's now an engineer, an inventor, and he's come up with a whole lot of devices of all different kinds. What are his mechanical mules, compared to them?"

"Fred will definitely help," the farmer agreed. "And at the same time, he'll keep an eye on our kids."

When the women learned that Fred Canning would be taking part in this perilous expedition, their hearts at once were greatly eased.

Chapter 21

A CHEERLESS BANQUET

Alfred Canning received the following telegram:

Come quickly, relatives on Emerald Island seriously ill, drastic remedy needed.
John Smith

The telegraph operators did not understand a word of this, since they were ignorant of the Emerald Island, and so secrecy was maintained. But Fred Canning guessed that danger of some sort was threatening Magic Land, so he took an extended leave of absence and showed up two days later at the Smith farm.

The young engineer thanked John Smith for his confidence in him. "Perhaps my knowledge will come in handy," Fred assured him earnestly. "There's a whole swarm of formulas running through my head. I've invented an explosive of which one pinch will blast an entire mountain to smithereens."

Tim's eyes began to sparkle with eagerness. "Freddy," exclaimed the boy, "it would be a good idea to put some of that explosive under the Newcomers' ship, don't you think?"

"That we'll have to see about," replied Fred, not committing himself.

"But we've got to, we've got to!" insisted Tim. "I'll even put it under the ship myself. I'll put on the Fox King's Silver Circlet, and then I'll be ready for action!" And Tim told him about the magic Circlet that Annie had received as a gift from Keensniffer XVI, King of the Foxes.

"Listen, Tim. If you can't put such wild ravings out of your head, then you can just stay behind in Kansas."

Alfred said this so forcefully that Tim calmed down at once. Yet all the same, he asked: "Freddy, will we be taking the explosive with us?"

"No, of course not. We'll prepare it on the spot. The necessary substances can be found there as easily as here. Still, we'll have to provide ourselves with some firearms."

Canning purchased a box of rifles and about two dozen revolvers; an abundance of cartridges was supplied along with them. The load turned out to be considerable, but for Oyho it was like nothing at all.

And so the night came when the Smiths and the O'Kellys said goodbye once again to their children and to Alfred Canning. Only a few words were said, but there was great emotional anguish hidden behind them, for worry and anxiety would be with the Smith and O'Kelly families for long, long weeks to come.

Oyho set his course for Magic Land. The travelers took their places in a roomy cabin on his back. It was the same one that Charlie Black had fashioned at the time of the last flight.

This time, they did not take Artoshka with them. His temperament was rambunctious, and he might by chance start barking and thereby spoil everything.

During the journey, Alfred was constantly recalling his chemical formulas, and he discoursed on them for a long time. Tim and Annie could not understand a word of them. Not surprisingly, the children quickly fell asleep, between this long, monotonous discoursing and the even swaying of the cabin.

It was evening when the tame Dragon landed at the foot of the World-Encompassing Mountains. At this point, the magic started, and Kaggi-Karr began to talk. Tired of her forced speechlessness, she extended a warm greeting to Annie, Tim, and Fred.

"It would be senseless to continue our journey by night," warned Kaggi-Karr. "We might blunder right into the Newcomers' flying machine."

The travelers settled down for the night, but before they did so, Annie could not restrain herself from trying out the Silver Circlet with the little ruby star, to see if it were still in working order. The Circlet functioned flawlessly, and our heroes drifted off to sleep, lulled by the rustling of the forest.

In the morning, Oyho flew ever so silently from one forest clearing to another, concealing himself from alien helicopters. But he did not encounter a single one of them, and he presently brought his companions down safely at the gate of the Emerald City.

Strasheela had been planning to announce to the whole City, the whole country the arrival of Annie, Tim, and Alfred, to have a gala parade march from the gate to the palace, complete with music and speeches. But his Field Marshal, Din Gior, had talked him out of this. The Long-Bearded Soldier, who well

315

understood the necessity of maintaining military secrecy, expressed the need for caution.

"Any unexpected festivities will alert the Newcomers," he said, "and compel them to investigate what's going on. And it'll be a disaster if they find out about the people from beyond the mountains." Strasheela displayed his intelligence and canceled all his preparations for the splendid reception of his guests at the City gates.

However, once they were under the protection of the high palace walls, the Wise Monarch ran things as he pleased, and he gave free rein to his wildest fantasies. He himself dressed up splendidly. On his new velvet tunic, which was tightly stuffed with fresh straw, dazzling buttons flashed, little silver bells tinkled under the wide brim of his hat, and the toes of his red morocco-leather boots stuck high into the air, while his breast was bestrewn with medals. Some of these he had conferred upon himself, while others he had received from the Iron Woodman, monarch of Violet Land, and the venerable Rujero, ruler of the Ore-Diggers. There were even medals that had been sent by the good fairies Villina and Stella.

The broad smile had not worn off Strasheela's good-natured face.

For this festive occasion, the Iron Woodman, too, had been brightly polished, and he had his golden ax on his shoulder. The Courageous Lion, whom old age had not prevented from making the scene at the Emerald City (though he could walk only slowly on his tired old legs), was wearing a golden collar of the type that kings are assumed to wear. Field Marshal Din Gior, whose beard reached all the way to the ground, stood there in his ceremonial dress-jacket, bearing his staff that sparkled with precious stones. Doctors Boril and Robil, dressed in black capes that flashed with medals, held their medical bags in their hands (in case anyone should faint at the banquet!). Present, too, was the monarch of Munchkin Land, Prem Cocus.

To the side, like an enormous monument, stood Tilly-Willy the Iron Paladin, who was dreadfully disappointed that Charlie the Sailor was not among the newcomers. Tilly-Willy admitted secretly to Annie that he had been awaiting his creator the whole time since Faramant and Kaggi-Karr had set forth for the outside world, and he had grown so excited that some of his springs had even weakened, and bolts had begun to clank when he walked.

"But that's no good at all," said the girl tenderly to the Giant. "A knight must always be strong…"

"I know that," the Giant sighed resonantly, "but there's not a thing I can do about it. Come on, Annie, let's you and I talk about my Dad, Charlie."

Annie smiled, and she drew from her traveling bag a large rectangular package. "Guess what this is," she said. "The person you miss so much couldn't fly to Magic Land in person, Willy, but he did send you a present. Take a look, and you'll see Charlie as if in the flesh!"

Annie took from the package a large photograph of the one-legged Sailor. Charlie Black had been photographed on the deck of his boat in the middle of the raging sea. Black was clenching his same old pipe in his teeth, and his eyes were smiling.

The Iron Paladin's happiness knew no bounds: he looked at that beloved face without a letup, holding the photograph up first to one eye and then the other, gazing at it close-up and then at a distance… "Thunder and lightning!" cried the Giant in his excitement. "By what magic was Charlie able to be transferred onto this sheet of paper, to remain on it for always?"

"That's something I can't explain to you," admitted the girl. "I just don't know."

Tilly-Willy asked Annie to sew together a sturdy leather case for the portrait, to prevent something as fragile as a photograph from wearing out too quickly... So Annie sewed a case out of Six-Paw hide — it was unlikely that any material could be found that was stronger than *that* — and from then on, the portrait of Charlie the Sailor was kept safe and sound in the Iron Giant's cabin.

At the banquet, Annie, Tim, and Alfred were received most hospitably (with bread and salt) by Baluol the chef, who was now fatter than usual and was wearing a white apron and a white pointed cap. The monarch had read about this fabulous (from his own point of view) custom in the *Encyclopedic Dictionary*, and he wished to make it all pleasant for his guests.

After the banquet, which, truthfully speaking, was not particularly merry, Strasheela asked his newly-arrived friends from the outer world to step into the Throne Room to view the Television.

Stella's magic rosewood box was working splendidly, as always: it displayed the Menvits and the Arzaksto the viewers' eyes. The slaves at Ranavir were enclosing the territory of the castle with barbed wire, with loudspeakers, bells, and antennas hanging down from it.

Fred, being an expert on technical matters, understood that what they saw before them was a warning system, which would no doubt give out a fiendish racket if anyone should try to infiltrate the Newcomers' stronghold.

"Look! There's Ilsor!" said Strasheela with a start. "He's the General's servant — and our friend." Annie, Tim, and Fred could not help taking a liking to Ilsor's trim figure, his handsome face with its spirited black eyes and its shock of dark hair.

When Strasheela asked it to, the Television showed them the spaceship *Diavona*, which towered into the air on its three high supports. Fred marveled at the cosmic vessel's imposing appearance.

Fred Canning spent that night immersed in deep thought, and he did not close his eyes even for a moment. Tim and Annie, with their lack of concern typical of children, did rest. Strasheela, who never slept, sat on his emerald-studded throne and reckoned mentally how many prime numbers 64,725 could be factored into.

Chapter 22

THE SECRET OF THE EMERALD

All the while, work in the emerald mines was proceeding at a full pace. The General had already stashed away in his vault the first small box filled to the brim with precious stones. But it must be related that prior to that, something quite unexpected had occurred. Rebellious tendencies had begun to appear in the behavior of the Arzaks who were working on extracting the emeralds.

The Menvit geologist who supervised the Arzaks in the mines saw to it at the end of the day that the slaves did not hold back on any of their haul. He directed his hypnotic gaze into the black and brown eyes of the Arzaks as they approached the box, one after the other, and he instructed them by hypnotic suggestion to place the emeralds in the box. "Do as you're told, slave, do as you're told," his command emanated. "The emerald doesn't belong to you, so give it up." The Arzak's hand would unclench itself of its own accord, and the clear green stone would roll from it slowly down into the box.

Then one day, as it happened, the overseer issued an order to one of the Arzaks who had not yet sur-

319

rendered his emerald. "Go down into the mine, slave," he said, "and bring up the folding chair."

But instead of going down into the mine, the slave suddenly retorted: "The chair can wait till tomorrow!"

The words of the Arzak who had dared to talk back to him, fell upon the Menvit like snow upon his head, and he was even at a loss as to what he should say to him now. Meanwhile, several other Arzaks who had not yet turned in their emeralds expressed their approval of their companion's response, while all the others looked on at them in utter confusion.

A few minutes passed, and all the Arzaks had placed their emeralds in the box, but there was no way the Menvit geologist could live down the episode. He found it unpleasant to look at the slaves who had become witnesses to his disgrace. Then he directed a hate-filled glance into the eyes of the disturber of the peace, and he quietly but distinctly he repeated his order: "Do as you're told, slave, do as you're told. Bring me my chair, at once!"

The Arzak quivered, and then he began to hustle and quickly disappeared into the mine. Five minutes later, he reappeared with the chair in his hands. The Menvit felt calmer: he was not powerless after all before his slaves.

Before the sun had gone down, the Arzak miners trooped back toward the castle gates, quietly discussing what had just happened. Most bewildered of all at this unaccountable change of behavior was the culprit himself who had triggered off the incident.

When the Arzaks told Ilsor all about it that night, he pumped them for all the details, and when he learned that in the first instance, the Arzaks had been holding emeralds in their hands when they answered, and that in the second case, their hands had been empty, he said: "I remember reading something in the ancient sages: *a snake, after looking at an emerald, at first begins to weep, and then goes blind*. I thought it was all nothing but a fairy tale. But here's what we'll do... We'll experiment one more time."

The next day, every Arzak placed in the box all the emeralds that they had mined — all except one, who concealed a small stone in his boot. Those who had surrendered their emeralds walked as far away aspossible, while the one who had hidden the talisman on his person purposely hung around right where the overseer could see him. Finally, the Menvit noticed that one of the Arzaks did not have his tool in his hand.

"Where's your pick?" the geologist addressed him.

"In the mi... I forgot... " the Arzak replied, stammering, and he looked him inquisitively in the eye. The overseer, too, did not turn his eyes away from those of the slave.

"Go down and get it," he said.

The Arzak lowered his head and trudged along slowly, and then he obediently plunged into the mine as fast as his legs would carry him. When he returned and took his place in the column of miners, who had meanwhile formed into a line, he could not restrain himself, and he whispered quietly to his neighbor: "It's good! It works!"

"Then why did you run so fast to obey his order?" asked his neighbor.

"So that the master won't guess our discovery."

That very evening, all the Arzaks knew about the marvelous green stone that freed the slaves from the necessity of obeying the Chosen Ones. In order to counteract the Menvits' magic spells, it would be necessary to obtain a stone for each of the Arzaks. So work in the mines built up to a feverish pace, much to the geologist's joy.

Baan-Nu could not help being pleased when he saw with what speed the boxes were being filled. But the Arzaks were happiest of all: never before had work given them so much pleasure, for, say what you like, they were working toward the goal of freeing their people.

Chapter 23

URFIN AT RANAVIR

As for Urfin's first trip to Ranavir, it was not a success. He did succeed in penetrating the territory of the Extraterrestrials' base. But he left his wheelbarrow of fruit and vegetables back at the fence, to minimize the risk.

Urfin was not going to knock at the door of Hurricap's castle, for without his fruits, he had no reason for being there. But Jus stole furtively all around the wizard's home, hiding behind every corner. And he peered in through the windows — for he did very much want to know how the Menvits lived — first through the yellow one, then the rose-colored and the blue ones. But he could make out nothing but the glass.

As he headed toward home, the gardener grabbed his wheelbarrow and returned to the castle by a roundabout way — and this one just happened to lead through the area of the Emerald Mines. Urfin hid behind a low mound of rocks that had been worked off. The working day in the mines had just ended, and he saw the friendly faces of the Arzaks, with their pensive eyes, near at hand.

Observing which road that the slaves were taking as they returned to the castle, Urfin ran on ahead of them and, shaking out his wheelbarrow, he arrayed his splendid vegetables right in the miners' path. The Arzaks, as if bewitched, came to a halt before this miracle, and when they tried some of the vegetables, they entered an extraordinary state of mind, like men who had fallen into a fairy-tale where all hopes become realized.

Urfin began to visit the Emerald Mines often. He was struck most of all by the circumstance that when the Arzaks were leaving the mine after their toils were over, they appeared more lively and in better spirits than they had at the beginning of their work-day. It was as if they did not grow tired, as if they were, in fact, resting down in the mine. One the other hand, once they took out the emeralds that they had quarried and given them up to the Menvit geologist as he stood by the entrance with the little box, they again grew listless and walked along without looking at one another. "There's magic in those emeralds, no two ways about it!" observed Urfin.

The second time, Urfin Jus approached Ranavir openly with a wheelbarrowload of vegetables. The sentinel seized him at once, and so he appeared before Baan-Nu. Ilsor (whom Urfin, in common with the other residents of Magic Land, knew about) played the role of interpreter.

"Answer me," said the General, "who are you and why have you come here to us?" He made no attempt to hide his interest in this Bellioran who had come to see the Menvits of his own free will.

"I'm a gardener," replied Urfin, "I cultivate fruits and vegetables of size that's unequaled anywhere. And I'm prepared to bring some of them to my lord General's table every day. In return for my services, I ask only one little trifle. One emerald for every ten cartloads." For Magic Land, where there were as many emeralds as there are stars in the sky, this was a truly modest payment.

When they had finished talking, the gardener placed before Baan-Nu his grapes, his melons, his strawberries, and all sorts of other things that he had brought in the wheelbarrow. And as the General sampled the fruits, one after the other, his mistrust of the Bellioran disappeared. Baan-Nu even agreed to his request of paying for them in emeralds — resolving, however, to take them back from the gardener once he had conquered Goodwinia.

From then on, Jus wheeled several loads of magical fruit every day to the Menvits in their kitchen. Before long, news reached the Emerald City of Urfin's duplicity, of his agreeing voluntarily to supply the General and the other Menvits with vegetables from his own garden. Of course, he was not doing this for nothing — he received a magnificent emerald for every ten cartloads. In addition to that, the Newcomers had promised not to molest him once they had conquered Goodwinia, and perhaps all of Belliora.

Chapter 24

ALFRED CANNING'S FIRST VICTORY

The residents of Hurricap's country did not cause Baan-Nu any misgivings. He remained in the dark regarding Magic Land's more remarkable beings — Strasheela, the Iron Woodman, Tilly-Willy, and others. What *did* bother him was the giants. And if an army with cannon and guns should yet appear from the Outer World, well, *that* was something to think about. But the General firmly believed that no army of any size could approach unobserved.

All the same, Baan-Nu felt that it was essential to take certain precautions. He ordered that Ranavir be surrounded by a barbed-wire fence, leaving only a few entrance ways here and there. At those places, the workers fitted up an alarm system comprising loud-speakers, bells, and antennas: the shrieking of sirens would let them know if anyone were trying to get through.

During the first days of it, they had a few false alarms: the sirens went off, but there was no one to be found in the vicinity. If the Menvits had been a little more observant, they would have noticed the comical little faces of the Gnomes in the bushes and behind the large rocks. But they knew nothing about them. They were at a total loss as to what had set off the alarm system.

After the Gnomes had had enough of teasing the Menvits, they dug a long tunnel-trench under the wire, and then wandered noiselessly, as always, about the territory inside the base.

When Alfred Canning, back at the Emerald Palace, looked over the Gnomes' report, a hilarious idea regarding false alarms came to him. After thinking it through thoroughly, he added a few words to Strasheela's next set of orders. These concerned mainly Kaggi-Karr.

Soon after, the alarms began to sound at every one of the Extraterrestrials' entry points. The sirens roared deafeningly and disrupted everything with their racket. The Menvits dashed toward the fence, their ray-guns in readiness. Every Extraterrestrial had drawn one and the same conclusion: "Belliorans are attacking the base." But there was nothing to be seen near the barbed wire.

The racket ceased when they reached the fence.

The Menvits inspected the entire barrier, meter by meter — but still there was nothing! Bewildered, they turned back. But they had not gone a hundred paces when the noise resumed. The same business was repeated several more times. Finally, from the quivering of the leaves in the forest, the Newcomers understood: "Birds!"

Yes, all this commotion, all this pandemonium had been accomplished by waxwings and swallows. Flocks of them flew down onto the alarm system, which instantly began to wail. Kaggi-Karr was in command of the feathered ones' attacks. The raids continued many times, but the birds remained impossible to catch. The occupants of Ranavir contended with it for a long time, until at last the birds gave up on their commotion as the daylight declined.

At that point, the bats entered the game. They lived by the thousands in caves not far away. And what happened now! The wailing of the sirens did not die down all night long, even for a second, and no ears were able to tolerate it. The Ramerians lost their sleep.

So General Baan-Nu, turning blue with anger at his own helplessness, ordered the Arzak workers to turn off the alarm system. And so Alfred Canning pulled off the first victory — admittedly not a very significant one, but a victory all the same.

Chapter 25

HOW DOES ONE FIGHT MENVITS?

The Iron Woodman, the Courageous Lion, Alfred Canning, Din Gior, Faramant, and Kaggi-Karr, not to mention the Monarch himself, were in attendance at an urgent conference called by Strasheela. Tilly-Willy was peering in through the window from the outside, and no one knew that Annie was seated there comfortably within his cabin. The participants were deliberating a difficult problem: how could they combat the Menvits and emerge victorious? There was no possibility of entering into open warfare with the Newcomers: the Extraterrestrials' ray-guns were far superior to the ordinary guns and revolvers that Canning had brought in from the Outer World. The best thing to do would be to make use of one of the wonders of Magic Land.

Faramant proposed that they unleash Arachna's Yellow Fog on Hurricap's castle and the territory around it. Tim still recalled the magic words that the Witch had employed to accomplish this. This, of course, was due to a lucky chance: Charlie Black, before burning her magic book, had read aloud the incantations that it contained, and the boy had a good memory. "The cold spell that the Fog'll bring with it will make the Newcomers catch cold," said the Guardian of the Gates, "and when they're in their weakened state, then we'll be able to deal with them easily."

The others liked this suggestion: it was not simple, yet it would not call for too great an effort. In any case, it was worth a try. So Tim was summoned to the Throne Room.

Strasheela turned on the Magic Television. Alfred directed Tim to utter the magic words before the screen as the image of Ranavir appeared on it.

"*Uburru-kuruburru, tandarra-andabarra,*" Tim began, and then suddenly he began to choke with laughter. It struck him so funny to be playing the role of an evil sorcerer.

Fred pounced on the boy. "Who laughs while saying words of malevolent force? You must be totally serious if you want to achieve any results."

But as it happened, Tim simply could not force himself to be serious. All he had to do was utter two or three words, and he would begin to titter. They ended by sending the boy away, and Canning himself read out the incantation, after it had been written down for him on a sheet of paper. It sounded very impressive, coming from his mouth, but it produced no change at Ranavir: the sky there remained blue, and the sun continued to shine as bright as before.

The members of the conference looked at one another, dismayed, and then the Monarch of the Emerald City shook his head dejectedly. "We forgot," he said. "When Arachna perished and the Giant from Beyond the Mountains burned her magic book, all her magic was destroyed with them."

"That means we'll have to come up with something else," said Canning in a businesslike tone. He did not want all the others to grow sad. "One of the greatest marvels that's found in your country is the Soporific Waters," he said. "Do you remember how easy it was to defeat the Underground Kings when we had its help? In spite of their army, their Sixpaws, their dragons... And don't forget that the Arzaks will be helping us. If they can add some of the Soporific Water to the Menvits' food, it'll put them to sleep, and that'll be the end of the matter!"

"Good thinking, my dear Fred," said Strasheela. "I had something like that in mind myself. But," he added with uncertainty, "how are you going to get the water into Hurricap's castle without being detected? You won't be able to carry a lot of the water there..."

"Yes, how?" Canning repeated the question. "That's what we've got to figure out." Silence set in.

"It would seem," said Alfred, immersed in thought, "that the only way we can manage it is by means of piping. We'll have to use pipes to direct the Soporific Water into the well at the castle."

"But that would require digging an underground passageway," said Din Gior.

"Yes, and it would be necessary to exercise extreme caution at all times," Strasheela reminded them.

"Well, what about the mice?" Annie could no longer just sit there in her hiding place. With Tilly-

Willy's help, she left the cabin and entered the Throne Room through the open window. "There are lots of mice, they'll do everything without making any noise, and all we'll have to do is point them in the right direction. Here's Ramina's magic whistle — I've got it on me right now. Do you want me to summon the Queen of the Field Mice?"

"That's one way out," Kaggi-Karr cawed enthusiastically, and she sped over to the girl so that the latter could stroke her feathers. She may have been a respectable, self-important Crow, but she still loved affection. Annie stroked Kaggi-Karr gently on the head, and then she looked expectantly at the other members of the conference.

"We may have something there," Canning finally agreed.

"Hurrah!" cried Annie, almost jumping for joy.

"Hurrah!" Kaggi-Karr cawed after her.

"But we mustn't forget the possibility of the other solution — the extreme one — as well," said Alfred. "If nothing else helps, then we'll blow up the Newcomers' spaceship. We'll prepare a small yet powerful mine. We'll mine the spaceship immediately. And Ilsor will aid us in that perilous undertaking."

Without losing any time, they assembled two brigades — one made up of Winkies led by Lestar, and the other composed of Ore-Diggers under the leadership of Rujero. A squad of Deadwood Oaks carried pipes and all the essential tools.

After the re-education of the Seven Underground Kings, their families, and their retainers, the Soporific Water had seldom been used. Such a thing was done only under particular circumstances, such as when they put Ruf Bilan to sleep for his treachery. There were no prisons in Magic Land, and any wrongdoer got off with a long sleep.

Field Marshal Din Gior notified the men guarding the Sacred Spring that they were to grant admission to Winkie and Ore-Digger maintenance squads. They decided that, for the time being, the real reason for the work would be kept secret, to prevent the Newcomers from learning anything too soon. Rujero and Lestar were ready to lay the pipe. Everything was now up to the mice.

Chapter 26

THE ABDUCTION OF ANNIE SMITH

The operation of blowing up the spaceship, though Canning planned to use it only as a last re-sort, required preparations of its own. Alfred lost no time in searching out the ingredients for his explosives. Accompanied by Annie and Tim, he roamed about the area around the Emerald Island, looking for the necessary minerals.

One day, the whole company crossed the lake on the ferry, which was manned night and day by Dead-wood Oaks, and set out down the Yellow Brick Road. What memories this road brought back to the travelers! Annie thought about how her big sister Ellie, when borne to Magic Land by a tornado, had traveled to the Emerald City to see Goodwin the Wizard. She had been accompanied by the most outlandish fellowship that anyone could ever imagine: Strasheela the Straw Man, a Woodman made of iron, and a Cowardly Lion, and each of them had a fondest wish. Strasheela yearned for intelligent brains, the Iron Woodman wanted a kind heart, and the Cowardly Lion had his mind set on courage. And though Goodwin turned out to be no wizard at all, he was able nevertheless to grant their wishes. Strasheela got his brains, the Iron Woodman his heart, and the Lion his courage, and Ellie returned home by means of Gingema's magical Silver Shoes.

Fred, for his part, while still a boy, had walked along this very road after successfully escaping from the Cavern into the light of day[8]: he had been heading for the Emerald City to report that Ellie was in the power of the Underground Kings, that they were keeping the girl captive and demanding that she restore the Soporific Waters, which had gone dry through the fault of the traitor, Ruf Bilan.

"All right, Annie," said Alfred, interrupting his own reflections, "tonight you'll summon the mice, you hear me?"

"Oh, Alfred," said Annie, delighted, "I hear you! At last I'll get to see Ramina!"

Noticing a mound in the distance that might well be a source of the minerals that they needed, Alfred and Tim hurried toward it, equipped with geological hammers and carrying knapsacks to collect the rocks in. Annie stayed behind in the glade, picking flowers.

All at once, a shadow flitted about above her and a whirring sound was heard, and then a helicopter touched down in the glade only a few paces away from the girl. A tall pilot leaped out from the cabin, and in a couple of bounds he was alongside her. Annie screamed desperately, and she tried to run for it — but it did her no good: the pilot seized her firmly by the arm, and the twelve-year-old girl, though both strong and agile, was unable to tear herself away. In but a moment, the stranger had picked Annie up like a doll, and she was so frightened that she could not even close her eyes tight.

Alfred and Tim, waving their hammers, dashed toward the spot where this drama was taking place.

---

[8] See the story *The Seven Underground Kings.*

But they were too late: the helicopter was already ascending into the air. The black dot disappeared beyond the forest, and Tim and Fred stood there all the while, trembling and following it with their eyes. When they had recovered their senses, they raced back to the City.

Annie was frightened, and she was just barely aware that she was in the cabin of a helicopter, that the door was firmly shut, and that the vehicle was gaining altitude.

The helicopter traveled above the forests and fields of Magic Land. At times, the gleaming towers of the Emerald City became visible, and then they would disappear. Below them flashed farms and gardens, with people working in them. They turned their eyes upward toward the flying vehicle, but of course they had no way of knowing that it was carrying their guest from the Outside World, who wanted to help them but had instead fallen into misfortune herself. It was useless to scream and to cry out for help, not to mention risky (for Annie might unintentionally give away the names of her friends) — Annie realized that.

The pilot turned and looked fixedly at Annie, and then he said something. His tone of voice was not sharp. It was just possible that the Menvit was urging her not to be afraid. In any case, the gaze from his oblong, almost squinting eyes was not a baleful one.

The girl was sorry that she did not have her Silver Circlet with her: what a great help that gift from Keensniffer XVI would have been to her in her present situation! A marvel would have occurred after they had let her down from the vehicle or taken her away to some place or other: in one instant, she would slip from their grasp and make herself invisible, and *then* let her kidnappers look for her! "But I'm just dreaming, as in a fairy tale," mused Annie. "What's not around will never be found."

She lowered her head, and suddenly something cold, which appeared to have slipped off its chain, touched her hand. Annie even jumped to her feet: how could she have forgotten! It was Ramina's silver whistle. Here it was, the key to her salvation!

Annie looked cautiously at the pilot's broad back: had he noticed her movements and directed his attention to the whistle? The pilot turned around, feeling her eyes upon him, and he nodded his head reassuringly at her. No, he was fully occupied, keeping his eyes on the instruments that controlled the helicopter.

She soon had an escape plan ready. The moment she was alone once more, she would summon Queen Ramina: her royal friend would help her out in her hour of need. There was one magical quality in particular of which she was mistress: she could transport herself to any spot in but a single instant. When Ramina had learned everything that was happening to Annie, she would quickly relay the news to the Emerald City.

The helicopter landed at Ranavir. The pilot (who was none other than Kau-Ruk) ordered Annie, by an insistent gesture with his head, to follow him, and so the girl walked obediently behind the Menvit.

The appearance of the young prisoner in the Newcomers' base produced no impression whatever. The Menvits walked by indifferently. Nor did the Arzaks drop the work they were doing. However, when she was alongside one of them, she heard, as if by magic, some words that she understood: "You... don't... worry..."

"That must be Ilsor," the captive guessed. Annie walked along more briskly now. The situation could not be all that bad if she had a friend there among the Newcomers.

The navigator had abducted the captive on Baan-Nu's order. To the General, the events of the last few days, especially the pranks played by the birds and the bats with the alarm system, seemed suspicious.

"Is everything in this land really the way Mentaho says it is?" he thought. Baan-Nu determined to verify the weaver's testimony. In view of the mission's exceptional importance, he entrusted it to Kau-Ruk and ordered him to find him one of the inhabitants who was not from the nearby village of the Ore-Diggers, but, rather, from the Emerald City area. "That'll be more trustworthy," Baan-Nu figured.

Annie ambled along behind Kau-Ruk, trying her best to maintain her calm.

Baan-Nu walked out of the castle, wearing his dress-coat with the medals embroidered on it. Ilsor was already preparing to accompany him. Annie gazed upon his magnificent suit. "He's probably a very wealthy person, some kind of a big-wig," she thought. "I've seen such beautiful outfits only in books."

The General was as severe as he always was, and he did not warm up in the least when he saw the girl's friendly face.

The talk, which was more reminiscent of an interrogation, took place in the Blue House of the prisoners. First of all, Mentaho and Elvina were led out of the room. Elvina, as usual, was planning to go out for a walk, and she had her mushroom basket with her. When they unexpectedly bumped into the visitor from the Outside World, right there on the doorstep, instead of being delighted, they were dreadfully upset. They understood the most important fact: that the girl, like themselves, was a prisoner of the Menvits.

Mentaho was able to get Annie's attention as he pointed to himself, then shook his head and raised his finger to his lips. He pointed afterward to Elvina and again placed his finger against his lips. Annie thought this over: "He probably means that we're to be strangers, or, in any case, that I be silent about something."

That was it precisely.

Baan-Nu began by asking the captive: "Do you know the people who walked out of this place?"

A machine in the corner of the room, one that resembled a small grand piano, flashed and sputtered, much to Annie's amazement, and it began to translate Baan-Nu's questions for Annie and the girl's answers for the General.

"No," replied Annie, "I don't know them."

Kau-Ruk watched the machine with interest and listened intently to the dialogue, while Ilsor reacted to everything with his accustomed calm, though his eyes, perhaps, grew more resolute.

"What are their names?" asked Baan-Nu, resorting to guile.

"If I don't know these people," answered Annie in surprise, "how do you expect me to tell you their names?"

This was followed by the same questions that Baan-Nu had put to the weaver many times. But having heard accounts by Faramant and Strasheela, Annie already knew both the questions and the answers.

She conscientiously related to the General that the land to which the Newcomers had flown was named Goodwinia, that it had received its name from King Goodwin, that other kingdoms that had been united by the fearless king were called Gingemia and Bastindia.

As he heard these familiar names, Baan-Nu relaxed more and more. And when the girl answered his question about the giants in exactly the same terms as Mentaho had done in his own time, the General finally believed in the truthfulness of the weaver who was his captive. After all, how could a simple little girl from another part of the country, if she wanted to deceive him, just happen to come up with exactly the same words as Mentaho?

Baan-Nu was not looking at Annie at all severely now, and his mood was noticeably more cheerful.

"Now that you've learned everything you want from me," Annie asked him politely, "could you let me go home?"

But hardly had the machine translated the request than the General frowned again. "No!" he said spitefully. "You're going to stay here and live with Mentaho and Elvina. I'll order them to take care of you." And the General, accompanied by Ilsor and Kau-Ruk, left the house.

"Fine!" Annie shouted after them. "If Tilly-Willy feels like it, he'll make mincemeat out of all of you!"

The Speech Machine painstakingly translated the girl's last words, but fortunately, no one heard them now.

Chapter 27

THE QUEEN OF THE FIELD MICE

When the captives were alone once more, Annie looking slyly at Mentaho and Elvina, said: "Don't be upset."

She blew on Ramina's whistle, and at once the Queen of the Field Mice appeared before her, accompanied by several ladies-in-waiting.

Elvina let out a cry in spite of herself, and she did not even notice that she had stepped up onto a stool: the worthy old lady was afraid of mice.

"Greetings, your Majesty," the girl addressed the Queen politely. "Forgive me for disturbing you, but I'm in a bad situation..."

"Greetings, Annie, my dear!" replied Ramina. "Do you really think you have no right to my attention and assistance? You *are* the possessor of the silver whistle, after all! But how ever did you fall into the power of the Newcomers from another planet?"

"You mean you already know about that?" asked Annie in surprise.

"Of course," Ramina replied calmly. "I was enlightened long ago by my sister queen, Queen Tarriga of the Bats. Her subjects have recently been giving our uninvited guests a nice little concert!" Ramina, unable to contain herself, began to snicker, and her ladies-in-waiting respectfully followed suit.

"I can imagine how worried my friends must be about me now," said Annie, greatly troubled. "They may even think I'm no longer on this world at all..."

"You're exaggerating, Annie, dear," said the Mouse Queen. "Have you forgotten Strasheela's Magic Box? I'm sure your friends are completely up-to-date on everything concerning you. But I'll go and verify that fact right now."

Before Annie even had time to think about it, Ramina disappeared. She left her ladies-in-waiting behind there in the Blue House, and old Elvina looked askance at them in terror.

About twenty minutes passed, no more, but that was time enough for the Queen to go everywhere she wanted. The look on her face when she returned was one of contentment. "Of course, it was exactly as I had thought!" she declared. "The moment Fred and Tim had run back to Strasheela's palace, the all-seeing Box went to work, and your adventures are known to everyone. Your friends hope to rescue you very soon... And by the way, my own people, too, have been given an assignment of national importance." Annie understood at once what kind of assignment that was.

The old couple offered the mice a splendid repast consisting of little pieces of lard and baked breadcrumbs. The banquet lasted right up until nightfall. Then, as Ramina said goodbye, she promised to come and visit Annie during breaks in their nationally-important service, and to provide unbroken communication between Annie and her friends. And Annie could always have recourse to the whistle in the event of emergency.

Chapter 28

THE INVASION OF THE INVISIBLE ARMY

The mice settled in on their Assignment of National Importance, and the underground tunnel began to grow, not by the day, but by the hour. Along behind the hosts of mice, treading on soft, loose earth that had been placed there for the express purpose of muffling their footsteps, came Lestar's and Rujero's brigades, laying the pipes that the Deadwood Oaks were carrying.

The sharp-toothed army was divided up into regiments and battalions, and each unit had its own particular job to do. Some bit into the earth and produced thousands of little tunnels which, after caving in, formed a single large tunnel; others carried the dirt away, meticulously and a little bit at a time, in such a way that no one would notice it, and they disposed of it in the forest, by the roots of the trees. The remaining mice stole into the castle hideout.

Annie Smith was sleeping peacefully in the Blue House, at whose door a sentinel had once again been posted, at the time when the gray hosts were scampering about Ranavir. With amazing dexterity, the mice squeezed like water through unnoticeable holes and cracks, and they penetrated the poorly-secured doors of the rooms and the cabinets.

In the morning, in the Menvits' laboratories, the insulation on the electric wires was completely bitten through. Flasks, measuring glasses, and test tubes containing various substances lay smashed on the floor. Tanks with samples of fuel in them were now full of holes, and the fuel had poured out of them. Only bits and pieces were left of the herbaria that had been gathered of the plants of Magic Land. Of the suits that had been placed on hangers, only the collars were still in one piece: the rest of them lay in shreds on the floor.

Baan-Nu was still asleep when Ilsor came to see him. As he stepped over the threshold into the General's private suite of rooms, he was so amazed that he began to rub his eyes.

"My General, Lord Baan-Nu," Ilsor called out to him softly.

Baan-Nu gave a start, and sleep vanished from him in an instant. A scene of dreadful havoc met his eyes. Of the tiger-skin that had lain on his bed, only some fuzz was left. The General's night-robe had been reduced to a few strips of cloth. His magnificent boots resembled more than anything else the sandals that the ancient Greeks used to wear; the rest of them had been completely eaten away. Ilsor wanted to fetch his dress-jacket for him, but there was nothing in the cabinet but a pile of shreds.

Baan-Nu, still in his night-shirt and not even waiting for spare clothing to be brought to him from the *Diavona*, dashed into his office. His heart sank as he felt a premonition of irreparable disaster. The night before, he had been so tired out from describing his combat with the horde of invisible creatures, that he had not bothered to stash his manuscript away in his portfolio, as he usually did, nor had he hidden it under his pillow. He had dreamed all night long about this combat with the invisible beings, and perhaps this dream had turned out to be prophetic?

When he looked on his desk now and saw nothing there but little piles of confetti, he wrapped his arms around his head with a groan and sank down into an armchair.

At that moment, Mon-So arrived with a report. "My General," he began, "everything in Ranavir has been smashed or torn to pieces that can possible *be* smashed or torn to pieces. Most probably some earthlings came..."

Mon-So did not get a chance to finish, for Doctor Lon-Gor appeared on the threshold. "My General," he said, "bandages have disappeared, thermometers have been smashed, and all my powders have been scattered and mixed together. The earthlings..."

"What earthlings?" screamed the General, unable to control himself any longer. "Why do you turn my head aside with this talk of earthlings? *The Conquest of Belliora*, my book, my life work, is ruined." And he began to wail, much to the perplexity of the Menvits standing there.

The most amazing thing about all this chaos, as it turned out, was that the personal property of the Arzaks had not suffered any damage. [Kau-Ruk's belongings, too, were intact.] Baan-Nu demanded that the prisoners be brought before him. So Annie, Elvina, and Mentaho were led into his office. But the people secluded away in the Blue House knew nothing about it. For that matter, how *could* they have known anything, with the windows of the house covered over by a steel grating, with the door locked from the outside, and with the Menvit guard never once stepping away from the porch...

Chapter 29

STRANGE GOINGS-ON
AT RANAVIR

The day arrived for which Tim had been preparing so long and so carefully. The boy put on his athletic outfit, which would inhibit his movements less, and he wore soft-soled boots that would enable him to move about without making any noise. In his pocket he carried a wrench, screw-drivers, and a small pair of pincers. A dagger in a leather sheath hung from his belt. The Silver Circlet was fastened to his head with a small strap, to prevent it from getting lost in any confusion.

No doubt this covered everything, but Engineer Canning reminded the boy again and again to be cautious. "The Newcomers haven't figured out where Annie is from," said Fred. "But if the Ramerians should capture *you*, they'll know from your size and your strength that you're no native of Goodwinia."

Tim agreed with all these arguments — anything, as long as they'd let him be on his way as quickly as possible! But when Fred advised him: "There won't be any possibility — so bide your time, leave Annie in captivity for the moment," the boy gritted his teeth so stubbornly that it was obvious that in no way would he be carrying out that particular instruction of Fred's. Tim had decided long ago that if Fred did not send him out, then he'd simply make himself invisible and run from the City. He *did*, after all, have the magic Circlet on his head!

"Ah, I'm afraid you're going to cause us misfortune!" said Alfred anxiously as he and the boy parted company.

Tim installed himself at last in Tilly-Willy's cabin, and the Giant speedily delivered him to Hurricap's valley. All along the way, the Iron Paladin asked the boy about Charlie Black. Tim had rarely encountered the One-Legged Sailor in Kansas, but, not wanting to make the Giant unhappy, he concocted stories and told him a whole series of tall tales about Charlie's exploits in the Outside World, which, as he depicted it, was teeming with sorcerers and wizards. The simple-minded Giant expressed his enjoyment so loudly that the rumble of his voice carried for many miles all around. It was a lucky thing for him that he did not encounter a single one of the Newcomers' helicopters along the way.

The Iron Paladin hid himself in Hurricap's pavilion, while Tim, by pushing on the little ruby star, became invisible and strode boldly toward Ranavir. And when Castalyo, eldest of the Gnomes, described the next few days at the Newcomers' base, he termed them the "Days of Madness!"

It all began when an iron barrel of fuel standing on a mound near the landing fields suddenly and unexpectedly began rolling down the slanting rise. It tore along so fast that the pilots and engineers barely had time to get out of its way. To top off the calamity, the barrel crashed into Baan-Nu's private helicopter, which the General had not even used yet, and smashed it to pieces. It had been the finest vehicle in the whole fleet, the most superb and the swiftest.

The General wanted to check out with his own eyes what had happened. But as he was walking past the well, the hose hanging down from it began to unwind of its own accord. A powerful, cold stream of water hit Baan-Nu flush in the chest and face. The General's splendid new outfit, which had only just been obtained from the stores on the *Diavona* after the invasion of the mice, was drenched in no time by the torrent of water.

The General tried to express himself in words, but every time he opened his mouth, water surged into it and choked him. As the stream of water struck the earth, it divided into smaller sprays in which the rainbow shone merrily.

It was Ilsor who put an end to this unpleasant adventure. Diving under the torrent, he seized the hose, which was quivering like a snake. The leader of the Arzaks could have sworn that some invisible hand let go of the hose. Then soft, quickly-receding footsteps could be heard. Ilsor turned the valve and made haste to lead the soaked General away so that he could change his clothes.

Baan-Nu was beside himself with rage. But never till his dying day would he have lived down the burning shame of it all, had he known that the people in Strasheela's palace had been watching this entire scene, from beginning to end. "Atta boy, Tim! Nice going!" exclaimed Faramant, clapping his hands. "You've given him a nice little bath!"

"An ex-tra-or-di-na-ry sight!" said Strasheela pompously.

Canning alone was nervous, and kept saying: "Ah, I'm afraid he's going to cause us misfortune!"

Things seemed to be calming down at the Newcomers' base. A harvesting machine was spreading sand over the enormous puddle that now covered the ground next to the well where the General had received his dunking. Then all at once, Ranavir was again in an uproar — and what an uproar it was! And the culprit in this new confusion was Baan-Nu himself.

To allow for the possibility of danger to the base, a military alarm signal had been worked out in advance, and a secret button was located in Baan-Nu's office.

The General, who was now dry but still disheveled, had hardly pulled on his shorts when, for reasons known only to himself, he felt like checking to see if his subordinates were ready to repel any sudden attack by the earthlings. The alarm sounded…

The Ramerians once more flew into a panic. Each of them raced to the spot to which he had previously been assigned, in accordance with regulations. The Menvits dragged out fire-extinguishers and clicked the triggers of their ray-guns to be sure that they were in working order. Sentinels from a specially designated detachment slammed the hatches of the spaceship shut and then took up positions beside it like sinister pieces of sculpture.

All day and all night, the Ramerians bustled about carrying out the General's orders, and then in the morning, new surprises awaited them.

The tables and chairs in the hall where the Menvits dined were found piled up in a pyramid whose apex reached almost up to the ceiling. All the boots had been removed from the slaves' tent to a forest clearing and arrayed in a circle, looking for all the world as if they were about to take part in a round dance.

The Arzaks laughed as they collected their footwear: someone was clearly playing a prank on them, but wanted no harm to come to them...

Sounds of cracking and clicking were heard during the night on the landing fields, but the sentries could spot no one. All the same, important parts disappeared from the instrument panels of nearly every helicopter...

Baan-nu ordered that Mentaho be brought before him. Glaring at him wickedly, the General said: "Listen, earthling. You must explain the cause of these baffling phenomena."

Mentaho was unruffled. Ilsor had already transmitted Strasheela's instruction to him.

"What can one do, esteemed General? The Days of Madness have begun earlier than usual this year, and I didn't have a chance to warn you about them." And he lifted his arms contritely.

"What Days of Madness?" asked the General with a frown.

"The Days when Things Go Mad, esteemed General! It happens here in Goodwinia every year. We're used to it by now, and we're on our guard."

"What do you mean, 'on your guard?'"

"It means we're very careful when we deal with objects. They stop being obedient and try to do all sorts of nasty things to people. The shovel bangs the digger on the head, the dishes jump off the table onto the floor, the fences run away from the houses into the forest..."

"What a wild country you have," declared the General. "And how long do these Days of Madness last?"

"Normally a day or two, rarely longer," said the weaver. "It's my guess, esteemed General, that the objects have already quieted down. From now on, everything should be peaceful and quiet."

The General dismissed Mentaho, and for a long time he reflected on the fact that there were many wild and unpleasant things on Earth that never occurred on Rameria.

Chapter 30

ESCAPE

After these unexplained events at Ranavir, the Extraterrestrials began to walk about extra alert, looking with caution at objects and expecting new tricks from them. When they opened a door, they leaped through it quickly, fearful that it might bang them on their foreheads or on the backs of their heads.

This time, the General did not believe Mentaho's cock-and-bull story, and, to be ready for any emergency, he ordered that the guards be doubled at every passageway and commanded patrols to comb the territory of the base every hour.

Tim found himself in an awkward position, and he was sorry now that he had overdone it in his efforts to pique the Newcomers. If that had not happened, then he would be able to spirit Annie away without any hindrance. But now that the Menvits were on the alert, the matter was that much more difficult. Still, Tim did not lose hope. Hiding behind the heaps of firewood, he kept the Blue House under continual observation. And in the end he succeeded!

Annie was being taken from the house, under guard, to Hurricap's castle, apparently because the General again needed clarification on some point. Without a second's delay, Tim leaped out from behind the firewood, grabbed Annie by the arm, and whispered: "Let's run for it!"

The Circlet protected from human sight not only the person wearing it, but also everyone who happened to be touching the wearer. The Menvit, who had been training his eyes directly on Annie, was dumbfounded: the captive that he had been taking into the castle had vanished in an instant.

Annie and Tim started to run. But the Menvit, hearing their footsteps, began to shout at the top of his lungs: "They're invisible! Seize the invisible ones! They're here, in this immediate area!"

The alarm on the base was sounded. A detachment of Menvits cut off the path leading to the nearest gateway. Tim and Annie encountered Newcomers everywhere they went. The boy's heart sank in bewilderment, but fortunately, he saw a watchtower nearby, and it was vacant.

"Let's climb up into the tower!" he whispered to Annie.

It was not easy to climb up the narrow stairway together, keeping hold of one another all the while, but the children accomplished it successfully. And just in time!

The Menvits were walking all over in a chain, with their arms linked together, combing the territory of the base. But it was as if the invisible ones had vanished right into the earth.

Mon-So led the search to the vicinity of the watchtower. Noticing that there was no one on guard in it, he sent an Arzak up to check to see if it were really unoccupied.

The Arzak clambered briskly up the stairway onto the upper platform where Annie and Tim were standing silent and motionless. He heard at once their excited panting, but he made a casual hand gesture in the air and shouted loudly toward the ground: "There's no one up here, esteemed officer!" Then he leaped jauntily to the earth.

The searches continued for a long time, but they were fruitless.

"Perhaps the earthlings can make themselves not only invisible, but also intangible?" thought the General, worried. "If that's the case, I can't imagine how we're going to fight them."

As evening approached, the base quieted down: its occupants dispersed to the places where they slept, and even the guards sat down at their posts.

Without a squeak or a sound, Annie and Tim descended the stairway and slipped quietly past the guard at the nearest gate. They made for the pavilion where the Iron Paladin was waiting for them.

Chapter 31

SINISTER PLANS

Baan-Nu called together a secret meeting of his staff. Of the Arzaks, Ilsor alone was present, and only in his capacity as the General's servant.

As Baan-Nu called the meeting to order, he proposed a toast in honor of the great, the invincible Guan-Lo. The attendees stood up, stretched their arms into the air, and cried out three times in hoarse voices: "Hooray!"

"It's time to be done with Goodwinia," declared the General with no other introduction. "Let us begin with the Emerald City, the heart of Goodwinia. We'll destroy everything, but we'll seize the emeralds. We'll show the earthlings what we're capable of. Up to now, all we've done is amaze them, and they've been trying to guess who we are. Now, let them live in terror, let them tremble!"

Ilsor circulated silently among the attendees, serving drinks and fruit, and he caught every word.

"The code name for this operation will be 'Terror.' All the helicopters will be taking part in it. We'll equip them with bombs. After the majority of the inhabitants have been killed, the survivors will submit to our gazes." The General fell silent, and cries of approval rang out at once.

"We'll all be returning to Rameria as rich men," Baan-Nu promised. He did not tell them, of course, that he had resolved long ago to take the treasures of the Emerald City for himself.

"General," Mon-So, commander of the helicopter pilots, addressed Baan-Nu respectfully, "ever since our invisible foe paid us his visit, almost every helicopter has been out of service."

"How much time will you need to repair them?" asked the General.

"If we work at our utmost pace, it won't take any less than ten days," was the answer.

That response made Ilsor happy. It would mean time enough both to report to all the necessary people, and to come up with something.

In a tone of voice that clearly did not allow for any objection, the General said: "The helicopters must be ready on time. You will have everything you need in the way of men to do the repairs and of extra parts. Those personally responsible for the readiness of the vehicles will be Mon-So and you, Ilsor."

"I hear you, General," said squad commander Mon-So, bowing his head. Ilsor, who again felt himself to be chief technician, also made a bow. And on that note, the meeting was adjourned.

Part III

THE SOPORIFIC
WATER

Chapter 32

THE DEADWOOD OAKS ON THE OFFENSIVE

Through Mentaho, Ilsor reported the plans that were brewing for a raid by the Extraterrestrials on the Emerald City.

A midnight Council of War was in session in the Throne Room of the Emerald Palace. It was no longer enough to work only by day. Every minute was of the essence. The only thing that all of them could think about was how to ward off the dreadful threat that was hanging over Magic Land. After a whole day of uninterrupted thinking, the members of the Council were dead on their feet. Even Strasheela's paint had cracked through his strenuous overexertions. Annie had to take her paints and brush and touch up his face. Tears ran down the Woodman's cheeks, due to the emotional strain, and it was necessary to apply a drop or two to them from the oil-can to prevent them from rusting.

Participation in this conference was particularly difficult for Kaggi-Karr. Now one and now the other eye would be veiled under her heavy, swollen eyelids, and only by shaking her head was she able to open her eyes once more.

The first one to have his say was Strasheela. His speech, as always, was distinguished by its brevity and by its wisdom that was unique to him alone: "We must not let the Newcomers have the initiative," he said. "While the pipeline is being laid, we must undertake active offensive operations of our own. We must turn the Newcomers' own tactics against them and force them onto the defensive." Then the Monarch asked, "Does anyone have any suggestions? Be brief. Remember, where there are many words, there's very little wisdom."

Everyone approved of Strasheela's speech, of course, but no one was in a hurry to put forward any suggestions. It was easy enough to talk simply, but another thing altogether to be wise.

It was Faramant who first ventured to break the silence. Extended watches at the gates are just the thing to make for serious reflection, so if good advice is needed, the Guardian of the Gates is the one to ask: he has it, beyond measure.

"We'll have to make a sally right into the Newcomers' base," said Faramant. "The attack will have to be forceful and swift, while the Newcomers' main weapon — their ray-guns — must be powerless to stop it. To put it briefly, I see no other candidates to participate in such a sally, but the Deadwood Oaks."

At this point, Din Gior intervened, for in his capacity as Field Marshal, he was responsible for the success of Magic Land's war machine. "Faramant's idea is a capital one," he said, "but would the Deadwood Oaks be able to carry out the operation? We painted kindly faces on them, and we don't know what effect such a change has had on their intellectual faculties. I offer no objection, but I suggest that we discuss this circumstance further: the outcome of the operation depends on it."

Controversy had arisen, and it was time once again for the Wise One to intervene. Strasheela said: "The one who is good is also wise. A fool can not have a kindly face, for he does not have sufficient intellect for it. It is evident that better candidates than the Deadwood Oaks are not to be found. The only thing necessary to consider now is how to protect them against the ray-guns. The ray will not kill them, but it can set their wooden bodies on fire. What do the members of the Council think?"

"We could dress the Deadwood Oaks in wet cloaks," cawed Kaggi-Karr. Her penchant for offering advice overcame even her sleepiness.

"Cloaks will dry out quickly in the sun or the wind, so that won't do," said the Iron Woodman at last. He had been unable to get a word in edgewise once the members of the Great Council began to talk.

"We'll have to protect the Deadwood Oaks with mirror shields," Strasheela blurted out. As an encyclopedia reader, he had no difficulty in coming up with correct answers.

Canning, not surprisingly, was the next to take the floor, as the discussion turned more and more to a search for technical solutions on the basis of scientific knowledge. "Mirror shields are more than just an excellent defense against the ray-guns," he observed. "If we fashion them in the form of curved mirrors, then we can focus the energy of the rays and direct its path backward — against the Newcomers themselves."

It was now possible to adjourn the Council, since its main objective — anticipating the Menvits with an offensive operation of their own — had been achieved. It was clear who would be carrying it out. It was understood how they would defend them against the Newcomers' weapons. They had come up with a way of turning that weapon against the enemies themselves.

Preparations for the sally did not take much time. While the craftsmen were fashioning brass shields and treating them with mercury, in accordance with Canning's formula, to make them shine like mirrors, the Deadwood Oaks, under the leadership of General Lan Pirot, were learning new formations that would allow them, while on the march, to reflect the radiant energy and redirect it now at one and now at another object.

Lan Pirot's dancing ability and his leadership skills qualified him admirably to teach the Deadwood Oaks exercises with the mirrors while marching in formation on foot. In order not to give away the idea behind the operation, the Deadwood Oaks carried hoops of various colors in their arms rather than mirrors.

The residents of Magic Land observed with interest these dances performed by an ensemble of Deadwood Oaks under Lan Pirot's leadership, though they could not figure out why the Wooden Soldiers were indulging in such idle recreation when the Menvits were threatening to attack. Be that as it may, no one felt any resentment regarding this unexpected but beautiful revelry.

The performance of this ensemble resulted in one more plus. From on board the helicopter that was carrying out surveillance of the Emerald City, General Baan-Nu received a wireless message: Belliorans dancing. "All right, go ahead and dance," thought Baan-Nu as he read through the telegram. "The only dance that's worthwhile is the dance of the conqueror."

The next morning, Field Marshal Din Gior reviewed one last time the troops that were going to take part in the offensive. He gazed at the soldiers' happily smiling faces and frowned. They were already in a very frivolous state of mind. The Field Marshal asked Lan Pirot in a severe tone: "Are you people aware of the gravity of this mission?"

A smile covered the face of the wooden General from the right ear to the left. "Precisely, your Excellency, exalted Field Marshal." And he impatiently performed a few steps of some style of lively dance.

Din Gior could only sigh. If that was how the General was, then what could one expect of the soldiers? "Can you handle it?" he asked once more, glumly.

"Please not to worry, your Excellency," replied Lan Pirot. "If you've thought everything out well, then our success will be complete, because we're going to perform in a way that's above praise." And again, right where he was, he broke out into a dance.

When the bugle sounded, the detachment formed into a column, and all the soldiers lifted their shields up in front of them and broke out into a run down the road leading to Hurricap's castle. They covered the entire distance between the Emerald City and the clearing before Ranavir, without once stopping to catch their breath.

The Newcomers' guard-posts spotted the Deadwood Oaks in plenty of time. The alarm sounded, and detachments of Menvits leaped up, ready to bring to bear their proven weapon, their ray-guns — but the fact that the Belliorans themselves were on the offensive took them aback. "This means that they were able to anticipate us in preparing for war. But succeed or fail, we must ward off their attack. And it won't hurt to teach those presumptuous Belliorans a good lesson." Such were the thoughts running through the Menvits' minds.

By this time, the detachment of Deadwood Oaks had formed themselves into a chain as they ran. The chain closed ranks, creating an enormous semicircle filling the entire glade, covered tightly from above with flashing shields. Without slackening the least little bit, the arc advanced to meet the detachments of Menvits.

When the command was given, the Extraterrestrials turned on their guns — and screams of terror rang out from within their ranks. The rays from the guns, reflected back by the arc of mirrors, struck the detachment of Menvits flush in the center. Before the

Newcomers even realized that it was they who were wounding themselves and scattered in all directions, a few severely burned Menvits lay distended on the ground.

Without losing any time, the arc of mirrors swung around, and the shields deflected the rays from the pistols that had not yet been turned off; the rays struck one of the barrels of fuel destined for the helicopters, and turned it into a huge bonfire. Then they began to dance on the laboratory, and at once columns of smoke rose from it. When what was happening finally dawned on the Menvits, they turned off their fire-guns and made use of their buckshot cannon. The arc broke up into a loose chain once again as the Deadwood Oaks slung their shields onto their backs and began to run in the opposite direction.

When the fires were extinguished and the wounded had been bandaged, the Menvits surveyed the trophies that the foes had left behind: a few blue and yellow slivers that had been knocked from the Deadwood Oaks when they were hit by the shot.

The conquerors' joyful spirits turned to gloom.

The entire wooden army was repaired that same day . Bright new jackets were painted on the Soldiers, with shoulder straps and medals thrown in, and for Lan Pirot, who had been completely repainted and was resplendent, there were gold epaulets and ribbon medallions across his shoulder.

Chapter 33

OPERATION "TERROR"

Strasheela rejected Faramant's suggestion that, for greater safety, the emeralds be removed from the City towers and walls, from the pavement and the roofs of the houses. To deprive themselves of the emeralds would amount to showing fear of their enemies, and be tantamount to throwing themselves on their mercy. "It'll be more fun to fight *with* them," said Strasheela. "We must preserve the glow of their green fire. They'll be a help, so let them have their full play of colors."

"And besides," said Field Marshal Din Gior, agreeing with him, "there can't very well be an Emerald City without emeralds."

Since the idea was impossible, and the emeralds were, in fact, a necessity to help the fighting men, they were not removed, but were, rather, polished until they shone even more brilliantly. Thus in all its splendor lay the Emerald City before the attack of the Menvits. For its defense, they resolved to call on all the inhabitants and all the amazing beings of Magic Land. What could they do against the aliens? They could be valiant, and that was no small thing.

Most valiant of all were the iron and wooden beings in the army of Magic Land: Tilly-Willy, the Woodman, and the Deadwood Oaks under the leadership of Lan Pirot. The Deadwood Oaks had already undergone a baptism by fire with the Newcomers. Tilly-Willy sharpened his sword, which forty men would hardly be able to budge. His enormous shield shone like a mirror, reflecting the sun's rays in the direction of the foe (a good military stratagem that he had learned from the Deadwood Oaks).

The Iron Woodman with his heavy ax, though he was about ten times shorter than his comrade-in-arms the Iron Paladin, was also a good fighter.

Din Gior threw himself wholeheartedly into his work. It wasn't for nothing that he read the chronicles stored in a small room behind the Throne Room and learned almost by heart the descriptions of the famous battles that had been fought in Magic Land in the past. Before all else, he skillfully deployed the available military forces. He set up battle outposts around the City, composed of citizens with rifles and revolvers that Canning passed out to them. Alfred commanded the outposts.

The townspeople learned to shoot rather well: one out of every five bullets hit its target, but for people who had never harmed anyone, such a result was a remarkable achievement.

Watchers were stationed on the walls and the towers. In this manner, the army would learn in plenty of time of the approach of the foe.

Din Gior assigned the basic forces, including the army's iron representatives, Tilly-Willy and the Woodman, to the City. But he had not forgotten about the necessity of reserves, and he designated the Wooden Soldiers, under the command of Lan Pirot, for that purpose. He had them hide carefully in the woods under leafy bushes. For communication, the Field Marshal assigned wooden couriers to run everywhere. But most important of all was a certain something foreseen by Alfred Canning that would assist in the defense of the Emerald City. In accordance with his directions, Annie, along with the wives of the Munchkins and the Ore-Diggers, and every other resident who knew how to hold a needle in his hand, began to sew sacks, stitch by stitch, out of thick gray fabric. This was a military duty comparable to learning to shoot a rifle. The gray fabric had been appropriated in part by Ilsor from the stores of the *Diavona*, and woven in part by Mentaho.

When the sewing was finished, bonfires were kindled in the City and the sacks were held over them in such a way as to fill them with hot air. Once they were filled, the sacks became enormous balloons that hung suspended over the City. While the bonfires were burning and the balloons were being prepared, Oyho the tame Dragon flew through the sky, distracting the attention of the Menvits.

In the Newcomers' base, preparations were under way for the attack on the Belliorans. Arzaks, under such constant vigilance of Menvit pilots and engineers that they could not even stop to catch their breath or blink their eyes, repaired the damaged helicopters: they fixed the broken instruments, installed new parts to replace those that were missing, and loaded the buckshot cannon.

They were the first to notice the winged creature in the air, a creature resembling a lizard. It was flapping its huge leathery wings, with its powerful clawed feet dangling down beneath a scaly yellow belly, and a red tongue was flickering among the long, sharp teeth in its gaping mouth.

"Look!" several of the Arzaks began to shout immediately. "It's a flying reptile!"

Kau-Ruk happened to be out testing his helicopter. He stared intently at Oyho. "Where did that living fossil come from?" he said. He reported at once to Baan-Nu.

"Look up in the sky, General," the navigator addressed Baan-Nu. "Don't you notice something up there?"

"Can that be a dragon?" asked the General in amazement, unable to believe his own eyes. He followed Oyho's flight with a sinking heart.

"Perhaps we should postpone Operation 'Terror?'" Kau-Ruk looked questioningly at the General.

"No!" the General retorted resolutely. "Our military mission can not be put off because of some tricks by the earthlings. We've got to be done with these unlikely earth beings, and the sooner, the better."

The day soon arrived that Baan-Nu had designated for the operation. Helicopters streamed toward the Emerald City. Each vehicle carried, in addition to the pilot, a sharpshooter. The pilots had provided themselves with large boxes to hold emeralds and other valuables. They believed Baan-Nu when he promised them: "After the battle, your boxes will be full to the brim. The first thing you'll do is bring them back to Ranavir and turn them over to me for safe-keeping. Later, you'll take them back to Rameria with you. You'll become the richest men on our home planet."

The vehicles headed toward their goal, and the members of the squadron kept in communication with one another by radio. But at the same time the squadron of thirty helicopters was moving from Ranavir toward the Emerald City, another squadron from the northern part of the World-Encompassing Mountains was racing forward to meet them. These were Carfax's Eagles. The Eagles had been exercising extreme caution ever since the Extraterrestrials' cannon had wounded Goriek. By their very nature, they generally associated very little with humans. But they, too, were residents of Magic Land. Sensing something that was not good in the Newcomers' behavior, Carfax had ordered his brother Eagles to keep their eyes on their uninvited guests. That is why, after observing the by no means peaceful intentions of this detachment of helicopters, the Eagles were now rushing to meet them.

Less than thirty miles remained between the helicopters and the City when Commander Mon-So and the other pilots became aware of dark spots that looked like birds, streaking right in their path far ahead. Sometimes they slipped away, and sometimes they came closer. A vague flapping sound grew louder and louder.

Then all at once, a grayish-black shadow became visible in the mirror attached in front of Mon-So, and it was swooping downward as if straight out of a cloud. The vague flapping turned into a screeching war-cry. Driven by curiosity, Mon-So lowered the side-window of his cabin and poked his head out... And at that moment, he came near to losing it. The wind generated by the flapping of an enormous wing hit him with such devastating force that Mon-So was pressed back into his seat in the cabin. If he had been leaning out only a tiny bit more, he would have been thrown from the helicopter altogether.

More out of fear than from reflecting about it, Mon-So raised the window and guided the helicopter in a manner to dodge the Giant Eagle's wings. Taking a hurried look on either side of him, he observed that the same thing was happening in the vicinity of the other vehicles, and Eagles, with their wings spread wide, were swooping down on the helicopters.

"Well, my colonel," came Kau-Ruk's mocking voice over the walkie-talkie, "what are we going to do *now?* How are you planning to ward off this overwhelming attack? Wouldn't it be better just to drop out of the game straightaway? I don't know about you, but I'm turning back. I want neither to die myself not destroy those proud birds. Combat with Eagles was not part of the plan."

"I forbid it!" screamed Mon-So in a strained voice. "You'll answer to Baan-Nu for that!"

"But can't you understand?!" cried Kau-Ruk, likewise shouting, as the din all around them was by now becoming unimaginable… "A bloody battle would be utter folly. Why should we injure such noble birds, and ourselves perish in the process?"

"You're a coward!" Mon-So almost growled. But Kau-Ruk, not listening to another word, turned his helicopter aside and headed for one of the clearings in the forest.

A ferocious aerial battle now ensued.

The Eagles fell upon the helicopters like rocks, enfolding them in their powerful wings; their enormous beaks loomed larger and larger in the windshields before the pilots, coming from the direction in which the vehicles were headed. The daylight turned dark to the pilots' sight as the shadows engulfed them. Operating by sheer guesswork, the pilots seized levers and turned the steering controls. The sharpshooters scorched those before them with their ray-gun fire. But for the giant birds, it was not the shots that were terrible. It was the rotating propellers of the helicopters, which chopped at them and cut right into their bodies. But when they felt the pain, the Eagles squeezed them even more tightly with their wings. The pilots let go of the steering columns, and the vehicles went out of control. A few helicopters plummeted downward, but the Eagles were themselves torn to pieces along with them.

When Carfax saw his fellow Eagles perishing in this manner, he pounced down on the nearest helicopter and began to buffet it with his wings, digging his claws into the chassis and shaking it so hard that the vehicle turned over completely. After hovering for a moment in the air, it plunged downward and exploded.

Having thus disposed of one helicopter, Carfax jumped onto a second one, and then a third...

Some of the Eagles attacked the helicopters in the direction of the small tail-propellor. Letting out war-cries, they sank their claws in and held on for dear life, wrecking them with their powerful feet and shattering them with their hammer-like beaks.

They asked for no mercy in the battle, and they did not show any. The ray-guns were discharging continuous volleys, it is true – but to no avail. The Eagles, having learned from their bitter experience, no longer approached the windshields directly. They attacked now from below or at the tail-end, and once the vehicle lost control, they did not harass it any further.

The enormous dimensions of the birds and their fury threw the Extraterrestrials into panic. The same panic that they had wanted to inflict upon the Emerald City, with the view to bringing the earthlings to their knees.

Din Gior's army did not have to participate in the battle, but his warriors were the world's most biased observers. They let out cries of joy whenever their Eagle allies met with success – and groans of sorrow whenever one of them died. Tilly-Willy ran a long way after one of the falling helicopters, hoping to strike it with his sword, but the helicopter crashed into an enormous oak tree and shattered to pieces.

Finally, the squadron of Newcomers turned to flight. With bent propellers, damaged engines, and battered chassis, zigzagging and tracing outlandish patterns in the air, the surviving helicopters headed back to Ranavir. The empty boxes that they had brought along to hold the emeralds had long since been thrown overboard. The enemy fled, but the flying army barred their way toward Hurricap's valley, and only about a dozen vehicles succeeded in reaching the retreat.

Mon-So was one of those who somehow or other made it back. His report, and even more than that the sight of the damaged helicopters, staggered Baan-Nu. Fear settled in the heart of even the General, who not so long ago had counted himself invincible. He simply could not understand how this could have happened in such a small country, one inhabited entirely by timid people.

Mentaho the Interpreter assured the General that the Eagles were not planning to attack Ranavir itself. They had no hostile intentions. All the same, Baan-Nu continued to be overcome by trembling, and his fear did not go away.

A few days later, the rulers of the Emerald City and Violet Land, as well as the fairies Villina and Stella, bestowed upon Carfax, representing his army, the highest decorations of their respective realms. Strasheela ordered that a detailed description of this historic battle be set down in the Chronicle. And the Gnomes carried out their duty most conscientiously.

Chapter 34

THE MENVITS' LAST HOPE

The General looked grimly in the mirror, and his noiseless, measured steps died away at once. Going over to an armchair, he sat down heavily in it, as if he were releasing all his cares at the same time as the weight of his body. Never yet since his arrival on Belliora had he felt these cares so markedly. The reverses of the last few days weighed heavily on his shoulders and breast, but their strongest effect upon him was to have given him a headache.

"What can I do? What's happening?" reflected the Chief Menvit. "Our aerial attack on the Emerald City ended in total defeat. Who knows, perhaps while we were creating our technology on Rameria, the Belliorans were uncovering secrets of nature that are beyond us? Why did the Giant Eagles attack our helicopters? Did the people of Goodwinia instruct them to do it? And the invasion of the rodents — was that a chance occurrence or an audacious foray? And why did the human attackers leave behind slivers of themselves? By all accounts, it's clear that the Belliorans have guessed that we want to conquer them. Well, if we can't do it by force, we'll do it by cunning. And it's the Speech Machine that'll help us in it. There'll be no misfire with *that!*"

The General took a little silver bell from the table and began to shake it impatiently. The door opened at once, and Ilsor appeared on the threshold of the office.

"Ilsor," asked Baan-Nu, "is everything ready for the experiments?"

"The Machine is in complete readiness, and Colonel Mon-So has placed two earthlings at Your disposal. There are no obstacles to the experiments, General."

This report calmed Baan-Nu. No more would he fall prisoner to events, but, rather, he would himself subordinate them to his own will. "Let me begin my experiments at once," commanded Baan-Nu. "Except for Kau-Ruk, Mon-So, and yourself, no one must be present."

The participants in this experiment, which was now of such paramount importance for the Menvits, reported to the Blue House, led by the General. "Let's start with Mentaho," suggested Baan-Nu.

Mentaho and Elvina, sensing that something out of the ordinary was being prepared at the Blue House, seated themselves in chairs close by the door. They thought that they would be sent straight out to gather mushrooms. But instead of that, Baan-Nu greeted the weaver with an unaccustomed exclamation: "Greetings to you, most highly-esteemed Bellioran!"

"Will anyone ever understand these Generals?" thought Mentaho, and then he shot out at once in Menvit: "Greetings to *you*, monarch!"

Baan-Nu frowned slightly, and threw a glance Kau-Ruk's way. "Mentaho is overdoing it somewhat," he thought. "'Monarch' is still a bit premature." Then, looking the weaver straight in the face, he commanded him with no further introduction: "Now, then, move your chair toward me, then go over to the Speech Machine and stand there."

Mentaho, who was seated, stared down at his feet, as he always did when talking with Baan-Nu, but he did not understand to whom these last words were directed, nor did he display the slightest interest in finding out.

"Tell me what's bothering you, Mentaho, and don't keep anything hidden," the General bade him, staring the weaver in the face, but avoiding his cunning eyes.

"Bothering me?" said Mentaho, scratching his head in bewilderment. "Why, nothing's bothering me. But it *is* pretty boring here, for Elvina and I have no one to talk to except some box." And the weaver nodded toward the Speech Machine.

"There's no point in even going on with this man," Baan-Nu realized. "Not only has he mastered our language, but he's even understood what we needed him for. So much the worse for him — we'll keep him isolated permanently from the other residents of Goodwinia."

"But we've gotten carried away by our conversation," the General spoke aloud once more. "Take a break, Mentaho. You and Elvina go out and gather mushrooms." The weaver and his wife went out, grasping their basket.

"Let's try it with the ones who are fresh," said Baan-Nu. The guards brought one of the Munchkins into the room. He looked about himself curiously and began to study the medal that adorned the Chief Menvit's breast.

"Greetings to you, worthy son of Earth," the General uttered hospitably, raising his arm over his head. A click was heard, the little light began to flash, and the Speech Machine articulated the General's words in his own voice, but in the language spoken by the people of Magic Land.

The Munchkin smiled broadly and folded his arms, going through the motions of shaking hands, and he said: "And all my respects to you, worthy individual!" The Machine provided a translation at once, in the Munchkin's voice.

Looking the Bellioran in the eye, the General quickly commanded: "Address Ilsor."

When the Munchkin heard the translation of this, his expression went blank. "How am I to distress Ilsor?" he asked.

The Machine translated again, and it was Baan-Nu's turn to be surprised. "You can address a person but not a thing," he said instructively.

Ilsor surreptitiously pressed one of the buttons, and the Speech Machine began to explain, without any outside assistance: "It is possible to distress a person or a thing, and also oneself — as you are doing right now, Commander."

It was only his amazement that enabled the General to tolerate this unheard-of impertinence. His eyes flashed on the Munchkin, who was not acting the least bit subservient. "It is not fitting to talk to a General in this manner," he commented sharply. "Put *that* in your pipe and smoke it!"

The Bellioran's face displayed utter bewilderment. "I'm quite prepared to light up my pipe," he babbled out, "but what I can't understand is, what would a General be doing here, and what purpose would such an action serve for you?"

"What are you babbling about, you run-of-the-mill scramble-head?" cried the General, quite unable to control himself.

The Munchkin was quite alarmed now. "If I ran a mill, I'd be grinding flour. And if I were a scrambler, then I'd have scrambled eggs frying in a frying pan. What exactly are you asking me about? I can see that you're angry. The last thing I want to do is offend you. But give me orders that I can understand, or else I won't know what to do." He said this in a quiet voice and looked at Baan-Nu respectfully and with reverence.

"Mon-So!" bellowed the General at the top of his lungs, "where ever did you get this blockhead?"

Mon-So stood at attention before Baan-Nu and was about to return an answer, but at that moment, Ilsor pressed the button again. The Machine began to squawk, and those present heard its own scratchy voice utter the following: "There he goes calling names, and him a General yet! He's unable to explain what he wants in a way that makes sense, and he calls the *other* person a blockhead."

"Ilsor, turn off that Machine at once! Mon-So, answer me, why have you ceased to perform your duty?

Are you tired of being a colonel? I could demote you to lieutenant!" The General screamed this. "Now bring me the other Bellioran. Ilsor, turn the Machine back on."

The second Munchkin was brought in to Baan-Nu, who was utterly unable to calm down.

"Pick a slip of stationery from the carton!" the General threw abruptly at the Munchkin, looking him significantly in the eye.

The Bellioran's eyes popped, and he began to turn his head frantically about, searching for something.

"What 'garden' am I supposed to pick it from?" he asked the General at last. "I've never heard of any such flower as a 'slip.' We do have a flower called a cowslip, but they grow high up in the mountains. Where do you see any flowers in this room? And what's this thing you say is stationary?" He raised his shoulders as he asked this last question, and then he dropped his arms weakly.

"What in the world is he talking about?" the General addressed Ilsor, shaking his head like crazy.

"It's just random gibberish," the servant replied calmly. "Apparently, the Machine is not allowing for every possible combination. Allow me to ask the Bellioran a question, in order that we may clarify the cause of the confusion." Ilsor looked at the General respectfully as he awaited permission.

"Go ahead, Ilsor," assented Baan-Nu.

"Worthy son of the Earth," said Ilsor, "tell me, who rules the Emerald City?"

"The Wise Strasheela the Scarecrow rules it."

"Ilsor, he's pulling the wool over your eyes. How could any ruler have a name like that?"

When the Machine had translated the General's words, the Munchkin stared Baan-Nu in the face with perplexity. "How am I supposed to pull wool away from the monarch's eyes when he isn't even wearing anything made of wool?"

"What, more quibbling?" screamed Baan-Nu in a rage. "You're going to understand me now, you idiot! We're giving you too many words, and your limited brains are not up to digesting them. It'll be simpler for you to understand the language of direct commands. Take a slip of paper," — and Baan-Nu himself took some paper from the carton on the windowsill — "and draw me your 'scary foe.'"

The Munchkin thought for a moment, and then he drew a Saber-Toothed Tiger with dreadful fangs.

"I didn't *think* you were talking about your monarch," observed Baan-Nu contentedly. "On your feet," he commanded with such force that the Munchkin jumped up almost all the way to the ceiling, yet he was still able to stand at attention. "On the double!" raged the General, his eyes flashing fire. "March!"

The Munchkin, making two little jumps, began to at first walk along in a ceremonial manner, then, at the command "on the double!" he became ruffled and broke into a skip at twice the speed as before, and he promptly slackened when he received the order "March!"

"Watchman," howled Baan-Nu, "give this idiot ten lashes of the cane!"

"But General," said the Munchkin, "since you're such an eminent personage, explain to me what connection there is between watchmakers and canes, and just where he's supposed to stash them for me?"

The Machine winked at the Munchkin and gave out with grumbling sounds in Menvit. The General turned crimson, and without a word he dashed for the door. Kau-Ruk and Ilsor looked at one another, and the navigator shrugged his shoulders. "Why is the General so upset?" thought Mon-So as he hurried after him.

Chapter 35

URFIN ASSISTS THE ARZAKS

Urfin observed and took note of everything. He could not help feeling that the Menvits' adventure with Gingema's Black Rocks was not over, and it returned to his mind time and again.

One day, Urfin set out for the Great Desert. He had no fear of the magic power of the Black Rocks. He had once been assistant to Gingema the Wicked Witch, and for that reason, their magical properties had no effect on him.

Jus took his saw along with him, more from force of habit than anything else — merely to have some kind of tool in his hand. It was of no practical use. This was not because of the enormous dimensions of the stony colossi. One could not cleave stone with a saw, even less if it were magical. A saw would not even scratch them. Urfin climbed up onto Gingema's black creation and sat down as comfortably as he could. He went over the Witch's activities mentally, one after the other. But no matter how hard the illustrious gardener tried, not a single sinister incantation came to his mind, and every potion had been totally forgotten.

But evil is not destroyed by means of other evil. A marvelous thought suddenly struck him. "Suppose I build a big bonfire and heat this little stone up? All witchcraft begins with fire."

And that's just what he did. He brought bundles of firewood in his wheelbarrow. Then he lit a huge bonfire, with the Black Rock right in the middle.

The fire blazed splendidly. Tongues of flame enveloped the titan and made it hotter and hotter. All at once, the inscription "Gingema" started to run, and then disappear. Urfin was genuinely alarmed: what if he had overdone it, and all the witch's magic should now just evaporate? Like a madman he dashed to get some spring water, and then he ran all around the Rock, splashing the contents of his pails and kegs onto it. The black colossus began to moan, and then it went rigid and collapsed, crumbling into small pieces. But the most amazing thing was that every little fragment was adorned with the inscription "Gingema."

Urfin was unspeakably happy. There was nothing more that he could have desired. Making several trips, he carted the pieces of the shattered Magic Rock to his house. From then on, he sought an opportunity to make use of the enchanted fragments.

Jus happily wheeled his wheelbarrow, laden with vegetables, down the forest path. The mere sight of the cucumbers, strawberries, and nuts was enough to gladden even a heart experienced in the ways of gardening. If only there hadn't been the concern, which lay over Urfin's mind like a heavy burden.

"How am I going to get the emeralds from the Menvit leader?" he speculated. "He's accumulated so many of them that it'll be enough to help free an entire people, the Arzaks on far-off Rameria."

As Jus reflected, his thoughts turned to the sheet of paper that the Crow had stolen from Baan-Nu. Kaggi-Karr had surmised at the time that it was a plan for some important military operation that she had intercepted. But when Ilsor explained what the text said, they had found everything in it downright hilarious, both the General and his fictitious adventures. The warrior-visionary's fabrications were of no interest to them and were soon forgotten, but Jus remembered now that the General liked adventure. "All right, then," thought the gardener, "we'll have to arrange an adventure for Baan-Nu with Gingema's Rock."

Small as those magical fragments were, not one of them was smaller than a cobblestone, so how was he to go about presenting such a thing to the Chief Menvit unnoticed? If he left the cobblestone somewhere to the side, the General would not pay it the slightest attention. There was nothing noteworthy about the stone externally, other than the inscription. It was possible to deliver Gingema's present to the castle itself along with the vegetables, so that was no problem. But what then?

However, Urfin needed to take his wheelbarrow from his garden to the castle and back again only a single time before a plan of action ripened in his mind.

Once, while in the kitchen, he had heard from the Chief Cook-and-Manager, who was exchanging remarks with the guard, that the General had accumulated an enormous hoard of emeralds. By that time, Urfin was able to express himself to some extent in Menvit, and he could understand well enough what they were saying to one another.

"Your General may be wealthy," mumbled Jus as if to himself, "but I doubt if his hoard can really compare with the treasure in Hurricap's secret vault."

"And where is that treasure?" the Cook quickly inquired.

"Right here, where you are," explained Jus. "The hidden vault is in the castle, but it's carefully camouflaged. No one knows its whereabouts."

"And how do you happen to know about it?"

"A wandering sage read about it in some ancient book."

From that time on, the Chief Cook and the guard, armed with metal rods, prowled about the castle, tapping the walls and the floor in vain efforts to locate the hidden vault. One fine day, this tapping attracted Baan-Nu's attention. The Cook was brought at once before the General. When the poor fellow was interrogated, it came out that he was seeking a hidden vault.

374

Chapter 35: URFIN ASSISTS THE ARZAKS

"Don't tell me you believe those cock-and-bull stories!" he sneered. However, the idea of the treasure soon grew on him, and he wanted to talk to the gardener himself. An opportunity to do so quickly presented itself. The General kept his eye open for Urfin, and when the latter once again delivered his vegetables and fruits to the castle, he dragged him into his office.

"What do you know about Hurricap's secret vault?" he asked him impatiently. "Where must it be sought?"

Urfin had been waiting for these questions. "All I know is that the vault is located in one of the towers of the castle," the gardener responded, "sealed up by a stone with the inscription 'Gingema' on it. But Hurricap may have put a spell on the treasure. Whether he did so or not, no one in our country has ever made any attempt to look for it."

"Miserable cowards!" thought Baan-Nu. "But then, that's all for the good. Now I can take possession of *all* the treasure!" He said aloud: "Urfin, I'm asking you not to talk about it to anyone else."

In order to make the General's search easier, Jus replaced a few crumbling old stones with sturdier ones inscribed with "Gingema." The plan that Urfin had come up with to despoil the Menvit leader of his emeralds, was something like catching fish with several fishing rods far removed from one another.

The next morning, the gardener left in the kitchen the fruits that he had brought, and then, slipping past the guard, he made the rounds of his stone "fishing rods." In one of the dark corners of the castle he saw what he had been expecting: it was the General; he was contorted in an unnatural posture, and beside him was a candle-holder. The candle had thus far burned down only by a quarter: this meant that Baan-Nu had fallen into the trap but a short time ago.

He was silently straining to pull his hand away from the stone, but he could not. His fear and his greed were locked in combat within him. The fear said: "Call out for help, because you won't be able to pull free by yourself." But the greed whispered: "If you call out for help, then you'll have to divide up the treasure. It's better to put forth a supreme effort and free yourself."

Before the fear could gain the mastery over the greed, Urfin dashed into the General's office and sought out the keys to his strongbox, and in a moment he had poured the contents of the boxes into a sack. He filled the boxes with cobblestones. The gardener found himself pushing a heavily-loaded wheelbarrow as he headed for home, yet wheeling it was easy — in Urfin's hands lay the means of freeing an entire nation.

After hiding the emeralds, Urfin hurried back to the castle, with his wheelbarrow rumbling loudly. The candle by now had gone out completely, yet still Baan-Nu had remained silent, not having lost his hope of freeing himself. When the Chief Menvit heard the noise of the wheelbarrow, he called out to the gardener. Urfin came over to him and assisted the General in freeing himself from the stone. While Baan-Nu was in his office, recovering from his ordeal, Urfin replaced Gingema's stone with the one that had been there before.

For a long time after that, the General and the Chief Cook, unknown to one another, continued to roam about the castle in search of Hurricap's secret vault. Baan-Nu was totally unable to remember the spot where the mysterious force emanating from a stone with an inscription of "Gingema" on it, had held him captive for several hours.entire nation.

After hiding the emeralds, Urfin hurried back to the castle, with his wheelbarrow rumbling loudly. The candle by now had gone out completely, yet still Baan-Nu had remained silent, not having lost his hope of freeing himself. When the Chief Menvit heard the noise of the wheelbarrow, he called out to the gardener. Urfin came over to him and assisted the General in freeing himself from the stone. While Baan-Nu was in his office, recovering from his ordeal, Urfin replaced Gingema's stone with the one that had been there before.

For a long time after that, the General and the Chief Cook, unknown to one another, continued to roam about the castle in search of Hurricap's secret vault. Baan-Nu was totally unable to remember the spot where the mysterious force emanating from a stone with an inscription of "Gingema" on it, had held him captive for several hours.

Chapter 36

AN ANXIOUS WAIT

During these trying days for Magic Land, intense labor, wholly undetected by the Menvit conquerors, was continuing underground. Lestar's and Rujero's brigades lived with but a single nagging thought in their minds: "The water, the water, the Soporific Water. We must get it into the Newcomers' base."

This same thought of the water likewise occupied the gray, whiskered army: the little mouse faces could be seen scurrying about confidently and quickly, as Ramina's subjects applied themselves diligently to their task. As before, some of them dug through the earth, while others bore it as far away as possible.

Rujero and Lestar were not newcomers to this sort of work. As a matter of fact, they had restored the Spring when its waters had stopped flowing, through the fault, admittedly by chance, of a servant of the forces of evil in the person of Ruf Bilan. That affair had occurred while the Seven Underground Kings were still reigning, and the pair had explained to them that the restoration of the water had come about through Ellie's magic.

In fact, Deadwood Oaks, under the direction of Rujero and Lestar, had sunk a column of pipes into the ground until they hit the level of the ground water. But before long, the unstable mountain rocks collapsed, shattering the clay pipes through which the water came up. So they decided to dig a well, and to remove the fragments of pipe while they were at it. The well grew quite deep, and in order to prevent the earth around it from crumbling and then caving in, they fortified its walls with beams. The beams were obtained on the surface, in Munchkin Land. For this, Prem Cocus, the ruler of the Munchkins, played his part to the utmost.

Any action that anyone undertook called for extreme caution. The Newcomers were quite capable of repairing their helicopters and using them to carry out surveillance. The residents of Goodwinia camouflaged themselves when they transported the beams to the site. They covered their cargo with grass, and thus assumed the appearance of farmers transporting hay. Of course, the ones who were laying the underground pipeline were worried. No one knew if the Soporific Water would flow through the pipes. They were relying on Lestar the craftsman — he had a very inventive head on his shoulders, and was very good at coming up with things. But if it didn't, then it was dreadful even to think about it.

Blowing up the spaceship — which Canning had proposed as a last resort — was not desirable. No one had any idea what the consequences of such a catastrophe would be.

Hurricap's castle might well come tumbling down, burying the Menvits under the debris. But the Arzaks would perish along with them. Even if they were alerted in time before the explosion, not all of them would be able to take cover without being noticed. And the Blue House would be destroyed, with Mentaho and Elvina inside it.

There was yet another thing that Alfred was afraid of: that the shock would cause the roof of the Underground Cavern to collapse, burying the ancient palace of the Underground Kings, with its seven colors of the rainbow. One of nature's unique wonders would thus cease to exist.

Nevertheless, Ilsor planted the mine on the *Diavona*.

At this time, the animals and birds began to migrate as far from Hurricap's castle as they could. Fear of the future drove white-tailed deer and black-tailed rabbits onto the same path. Alongside of them, jaguars, which are similar to tigers, and mountain lions — or pumas — ambled softly. Red-maned wolves walked behind giant bears with fuzzy black fur and white markings around their eyes that resembled large spectacles. The antelopes bounded along spiritedly. But the raccoons trudged forward in a leisurely manner, stopping at every stream to rinse berries and nuts in the water. No snapping of teeth was to be heard, nor any baleful snarling. For the moment, the refugees had become the best of neighbors. Birds, seized by the same premonition of disaster, were leaving their forests. And behind the birds and beasts, the people moved along the forest roads. Only the grim owls, nocturnal predators, did not succumb to the general panic and remained at home in their nests.

This abrupt migration did not escape the Newcomers' eyes. As they viewed the evacuation of the woods and villages in the vicinity of the castle, they grew sick at heart. The area where they resided suddenly became like a sinking ship, which every living thing was fleeing in panic.

Why were they seeking safety in flight? Did they perhaps sense some impending natural disaster, such as the eruption of a volcano or an earthquake? The Newcomers would have to be on their guard, in order that they themselves would not perish in this unknown country.

While all of this was going on, the labors under the ground continued at an unslackening pace. And at last the moment arrived when the pipeline for the Soporific Water was linked up with the well-shaft. The mice, who had a keen sense of smell, themselves wished to be lowered into the shaft in cages.

There was nothing left now but to wait. If the Soporific Water penetrated into the shaft, then the mice would go to sleep.

The refugees found sanctuary in Yellow Land, the domain of the good Fairy Villina. Whether or not the escapees would be returning to their own regions or remain there forever — it all depended on the mice.

Chapter 37

THE MICE ARE ASLEEP!

It happened during the night. No one ever knew how, as he had received no permission to go out, but Tim sneaked up to the well. He laid his ear carefully against the wall and did not hear a thing. Or, to be more precise, he heard a feeble whistling sound.

"Could those mice already be breathing heavily in sleep?" thought Tim. He quickly pulled up first one cage, then another, by their ropes. Even in the dark, the sharp-eyed boy could observe that the little beasts were lying there in their cages, their legs spread helplessly apart.

He dashed headlong to the tunnel entrance, and he raced inside and cried out loudly: "They're asleep, they're asleep! They're asleep at last! The water is flowing!"

Rujero just happened to be down there in it. The craftsman ran over to Tim and carefully took the cages from him. He tickled the noses of the mice with a blade of grass, and he pulled at them by their tails and their legs — but the little gray animals did not awaken. Rujero had previously had duty of putting the Underground Kings to sleep, and so he understood now that these mice were not sleeping an ordinary sleep, but a magical one.

This news, on which perhaps depended the very existence of Magic Land, was summed up in only four words: "The mice are asleep!"

Rujero would have wanted to send his report to the Emerald City via the usual route, along the avian network, but the birds had abandoned the forest in the area. But as luck would have it, he saw Guamoko the Great Horned Owl by the stream. Guamoko realized at once the importance of this news, and he delivered it to Kaggi-Karr without the slightest delay. When Guamoko made his appearance, Strasheela roused all the residents of the Emerald City. Faramant, Din Gior, Annie, Tim, Kaggi-Karr — all of them ran, jumped, and knocked on the people's doors (including even Guamoko, using his powerful old beak), transmitting, like a password, the phrase: "The mice are asleep!"

By that time, the populace of the City was aware of what this meant. It was a trusting little people who lived in the Emerald City, and they wished with all their hearts that the Newcomers would go back to where they came from. For that reason, they would never have told the Menvits the truth about the Soporific Water, not for anything in the world.

Their joy was beyond recounting, but there was no time to lose. The explosive mine was still attached to the spaceship. It would be up to Ilsor now to remove the mine, or at least to dismantle its mechanism. But before that could happen, they would have to relay the message "The mice are asleep!" to the leader of the Arzaks.

The journey to Ilsor was not a long one, but it was dangerous all the same. They could not send out just a single runner, for all kinds of things might happen to him along the way. The chances of accidents were studied, and in the end, the Iron Paladin, Oyho the Dragon, and seven wooden couriers (to increase the likelihood of success for the expedition) set out simultaneously from the Emerald City.

Tilly-Willy raced along the Yellow Brick Road. In his cabin sat Faramant, who groaned in pain with every leap that the Giant made. He was no Lestar, who in years of friendship with the Giant had grown accustomed to such leaps. Willy's iron steps gouged out pits of extraordinary depth. But what harm did that do? The pits could always be filled in, but the main thing now was that he gallop to his destination on time.

Tilly-Willy began to sing mischievously: "The mice are asleep, I swear by the reefs! The mice are asleep, the mice are asleep, I swear by the shoals! The mice are asle-e-e-ep!..."

Over the woods and fields flew Oyho the Dragon; the Triply Wise One himself was seated on his back. Yes, the monarch of the Emerald City had left his throne, his subjects, and his friends. He was hurrying forward to save his fabulous country, its fields and forests, but most of all, its people.

Strasheela bounced up and down where he sat, keeping time as the Dragon flapped his wings, and he sang out: "Ey-hey-hey-ho, the mice are asleep, they're asleep, they're asle-e-e-ep!"

He gazed down from time to time. Whenever Tilly-Willy lagged behind, even a little bit, Strasheela would stand up triumphantly; but when the Paladin shot ahead, he stamped his feet in wrath and urged Oyho to fly faster. There was nothing to be done; the good Strasheela was very touchy.

The wooden couriers ran along behind the Paladin, using paths that the animals had made. Their steps were not as enormous as Tilly-Willy's, but for all that, their legs flashed like the spokes of a bicycle wheel, and their wooden treetrunk-bodies seemed to be flying through the air.

They had been ordered to keep repeating the words of the message, to avoid forgetting them, and they droned ceaselessly with the words, "The mice are asleep, the mice are asleep, the mice are asleep!…"

The race that they were running with one another stimulated a feeling of excitement in the runners, and each sought to outpace the others. And whenever one of them succeeded in doing so, the current front-runner teased his competitors with names like: "Snails! Baby turtles! Crayfish without tails!"

The game reached the highest pinnacle whenever Tilly-Willy, not wanting to lag behind Strasheela, stopped for a moment to scan the skies for Oyho, and one of the couriers succeeded at that moment in pulling ahead — though admittedly not for long. The wooden runners would then let forth with a screeching that can not be imagined.

It turned out to be quite fortunate that three different messengers — Tilly-Willy, the Dragon, and the couriers — were on the road at the same time. And Strasheela's quick-witted head was everything. The words seemed to be flying down right out of the sky, and then spread along the ground throughout the entire journey as echoes repeated them: "The mice are asleep, the mice are asleep, the mice are asleep!…"

The couriers encountered no serious obstacles on the journey. But Tilly-Willy crossed the Great River by wading (he was afraid of ruining the bridge), and in its deepest parts, the water came up to his shoulders. Faramant shuddered as he listened to the waves splashing against the giant's iron breast. The Dragon had no trouble — he paid not the slightest attention to the band of blue that sparkled below him.

The wooden couriers, in crossing over the bridge, fell a little behind their competitors. However, once they were back on solid ground, they made up for it by quickening their pace again to full speed.

Night had long since fallen over Magic Land. The Yellow Brick Road ended, which meant that there were no longer any swaying lanterns illuminating the road in the dark. Tilly-Willy and the wooden runners reluctantly slackened their pace, and even Oyho began to flap his wings more softly: it was so easy to lose one's bearings at night and to fly off in the wrong direction. The singing ceased, and the seven couriers fell silent. Nevertheless, the messengers continued to head straight toward their goal, as if drawn by invisible magnets.

None of them beat the others, and they all arrived at Hurricap's pavilion simultaneously.

Chapter 38

FREEDOM

The next day, one thing was clear: the lives of the Arzaks had been saved, Mentaho and Elvina were no longer under threat of death, Hurricap's castle was still in one piece, and the ship the *Diavona* was unharmed. In the event that everything met with success, Ilsor and his companions would be able to use it to return to Rameria.

That day, magical water drawn from the well at Ranavir was used in all the Menvits' meals. No one knew how large a dose was needed to act on their robust systems, so the Arzaks poured it out generously, putting it in their soups, their sauces, and their fruit drinks.

Dinner proceeded in the customary manner. No anxiety was detectable in the Arzaks, and they served their dishes calmly, though perhaps their eyes looked a little more watchful than usual. The Arzak cooks prepared an excellent repast, the Menvits had no complaints of bad appetites, and therefore, on this occasion, they ate a great deal. The results were not long in coming. The meal was not even over before the Menvits — the pilots, headed by Mon-So, the men who guarded the spaceship (whom Ilsor had replaced for now by Arzaks), Doctor Lon-Gor, and Baan-Nu himself — were sleeping peacefully, their heads dropped down on the table.

Kau-Ruk the Navigator was the only one of them who had not been put to sleep. In recent days, it had become clear that Baan-Nu was merely tolerating him, and Kau-Ruk himself kept his distance from the General and the other Menvits.

Ilsor had it from Baan-Nu that the moment they had returned to Rameria, he was going to turn Kau-Ruk in, not to just anyone, but to the Supreme Ruler, Guan-Lo, himself: the Navigator had evidently incurred severe punishment for his unauthorized withdrawal from the battle with the Eagles. He might well be chained to a rock out in the Ramerian desert and be left there all alone. In accordance with Menvit law, survival would be his own business from then on.

"Colonel," said Ilsor, addressing the Navigator. "Would you be willing to help the Arzaks?"

385

"I'm willing," replied Kau-Ruk without even thinking. "I've had an eye on you for a long time, Ilsor, and I've come to respect you more and more. While I was wandering about here quietly, with nothing to do, I thought: you people are obviously not going to be in a servile state forever; it's obvious that you can't... And I suppose the moment for change is at hand now?"

"I propose that you join forces with us, the Arzaks," said Ilsor. "The task before us is for you and me to fly the spaceship back to Rameria. But once we're there, it'll be necessary for you to relate the events you know about, but to tell it in our way."

"I'll gladly carry out every one of your instructions," said the navigator. "But I can't promise to join your ranks, for I've somehow gotten used to being on my own." And so it was decided.

The first timid, even surprised, exclamations began to be heard now throughout the base Ranavir: "Freedom? Freedom?" Then the voices grew more and more resolute: "Freedom! Freedom!" The Arzaks, without a word, dashed toward one another to give voice to their congratulations: they hugged and kissed each other, with tears in their eyes, and some of them, like Strasheela the Wise in such moments of joy, broke out into a dance.

Special honor fell to Ilsor, the distinguished leader of the slaves, who had been risking his life for years on end, since at any moment he might have given away the fact that he *was* their leader. The Arzaks brought him a robe that had been stashed away on the *Diavona*, not even in a special hiding place, but among the other garments)for the Menvits could hardly have guessed how it would end up(.

So we have Ilsor, leader of his people, standing there in a blue robe with gold stars on it. In accordance with Arzak custom, a blue robe is worn on that especially solemn occasion when one of the people has earned himself the most exalted rank with which one can be rewarded in the land of the Arzaks: that of Friend of the People. And this time, that most exalted rank has fallen to their leader. Ilsor is extremely proud that he has lived up to his name, which means, literally, "Magnificent." His shining black eyes glow with a soft light, and are thus themselves magnificent.

The Arzaks will hearken to every one of Ilsor's words, and carry out his instructions precisely and without the slightest question.

The leader's first instruction is as follows. No one knew how long the effect of the Soporific Water would last on the Menvits. What if they should re-awaken after only a short spell? Earthlings slept for several months, and when they awoke, they were innocent as newborn infants. But the Menvits might awaken in only a few hours and go about their business as if nothing had happened. For that reason, Ilsor quickly ordered that the slumbering Chosen Ones be taken aboard the *Diavona* and loaded into the same sleeping modules in which the Extraterrestrials had made the journey to Earth.

And so it was done. By morning, all the Menvits, who were still in a state of magical sleep, had been refrigerated in pressure chambers, where their sleep would be prolonged for decades. "That's much safer," said Ilsor.

The time no doubt had come now to draft a report to Bassania, capital of Rameria. So they worked one out with Kau-Ruk the navigator, and it read as follows:

> *To the supreme Ruler of Rameria, the Worthiest of Worthies, Guan-Lo. I am hereby reporting on behalf of the Commander. No life on Earth. No possibility of continuing to endure its harsh conditions, where men can not remove their space-suits. Crew has been*

stricken with inexplicable sleep. We are heading back.

Acting Commander
Kau-Ruk, Celestial Navigator

Chapter 39

OFF TO A
DISTANT STAR

After the Soporific Water had done its work, the valves were turned off, and the guards took up their usual positions beside the magic spring.

"Yes, it's a mysterious thing, your spring," said Ilsor thoughtfully. "It clearly contains substances that have yet to be isolated, substances that put people to sleep."

"Well, you should take as much of the water as you can back to your planet with you," said Tim, his eyes flashing. "Good idea, huh? Then you could put *all* the ruling Menvits to sleep."

"Yes, do take back as much of the water as you can," added Annie.

"We couldn't possibly take all that would be needed," sighed Ilsor, smiling at the children's enthusiasm. "There's no way of transporting it. And you know yourselves that it doesn't last very long, that it loses its magical properties."

Everything was soon ready for the *Diavona* to blast off on its return journey to far-off Rameria. All that remained now was to say goodbye.

Chapter 39: OFF TO A DISTANT STAR

"I hope you haven't forgotten, Ilsor," Alfred Canning reminded him, "that Strasheela is expecting all of you at his palace."

Ilsor and his friends were for their part eager to visit the Emerald City. They wanted to make the acquaintance of the Iron Woodman and the Courageous Lion, to see with their own eyes Din Gior's fabulous beard and the equally renowned spectacles of the Guardian of the Gates. It's true what people say, that it's better to see something once than to hear about it a hundred times.

The Arzaks selected the helicopters which had sustained the least damage during the combat with the Eagles, and which their mechanics had repaired. Ilsor headed for one of these. He was already taking hold of the steering column when Kau-Ruk the Navigator, who had climbed in behind Ilsor, along with a group of Arzaks, forestalled of him. "Allow me," he said. "I know the way to the Emerald City."

"Hold it! Don't move!" someone uttered in a loud voice from the ground, right at the very boarding ladder.

The Arzak leader and the navigator, bending their heads, looked down, and Kau-Ruk froze into position and could not even straighten up again: never before had he beheld such tiny people. The ground was swarming with Gnomes wearing gray coats and multicolored pointed hoods. In their hands they held fishing rods made of thin reeds. And at their head was Castalyo, who wore a red hood.

"Is there something you want of us, friend Castalyo?" Ilsor asked the Gnome elder.

"What do you think we want?" retorted the Gnome sharply. "What a strange question! We assembled in our home, our Cave. Then Tilly-Willy the Paladin brought us here, the one over there with such long legs!"

"Ah, so *that's* all it is!" replied Ilsor, laughing. "You want to go home. Then climb into the cabin of the helicopter. My friends," he added, turning to the Arzaks, "give them a hand!"

One of the Arzaks ran down the ladder and set about carefully gathering up the gray-coated little men into a basket. Another Arzak seated them all in various places. The Gnomes filled up the helicopter. They twisted and turned about on the seats and under them, they seated themselves on the very floor, spreading their coats out beneath themselves, and they even settled in Tim's and Annie's laps.

Although the Gnomes had grown wise through experience and age, nevertheless they had remained inclined to mischievousness, and they loved to carry on, to laugh, to push one another. What shouting, shrieking, and laughter prevailed as the helicopter moved up from the ground and began to soar through the air!

The Gnomes beheld the endless blue of the sky, with the clouds hanging over it like snowballs. Below them spread the equally endless vista of fields and forests, which were all painted in green. It would surely have been uncommonly peaceful up there if the helicopter had not been whirring, and if the people themselves had not been babbling away. The Gnomes sensed that they would probably remember this flight for the rest of their lives, and they couldn't have been more delighted. Castalyo, perched on Kau-Ruk's shoulder, pointed out the way to Arachna's old domain, to the place where their grandfathers, their great-grandfathers, and their great-great-grandfathers had dwelt through the passing of centuries.

The trip was a gleeful one, and everyone was sorry when it was over — but all things must end some time. The Gnomes bade their friends good-bye, and then the helicopter set its course for the Emerald City.

A certain tradition had been started by Goodwin, and it was upheld even now: the Guardian of the Gates handed out green spectacles to his guests. Then he took everyone to the banquet hall of the Emerald Palace. The tables were already laid: the result was a real display of dishes, but the guests were more interested in another display: the display of marvels.

The Arzaks gazed with the keenest curiosity at Strasheela the straw man and at the Iron Woodman, and they were amazed at the enormous head of Tilly-Willy, with its slanting eyes and its dreadful fangs, visible through an open window. They were fascinated by the guards of honor stationed throughout the length of the hall, guards who had clearly been hewn out of wooden treetrunks and branches, but who walked and talked just like ordinary people.

"How is it possible for these extraordinary creatures of straw, wood, and iron to move about, to think, and to talk?" thought the guests. "Truly, the Earthlings have uncovered secrets that are still inaccessible to us Ramerians. Truly, Earth is a planet of wonders..."

The Arzaks did not know, and the conversation never turned to the subject, that they were in Magic Land, and that all the earthlings who lived beyond the mountains would be struck by Hurricap's land the same way as they were themselves. The guests listened with unconcealed interest to the Lion and to the equally bold Kaggi-Karr the Crow, who shared the table as equals with all the others present and who fearlessly participated in the general conversation.

"My dear Ilsor," said the Lion, "how nice it would be if your people on Rameria could be friends also with the animals, as the situation is here in our country."

"And with the birds too," Kaggi-Karr yearned. "Of course, I've been in the Outer World, but I've never yet had the occasion to fly as high up into the air as you'll be doing."

Chapter 40

IT'S BEEN TRULY
A DAY OF SURPRISES

Strasheela clapped his hands together, the main door opened, and in walked Din Gior. His golden beard, after an uninterrupted session of combing, shone like silk. In his hands the Field Marshal held a silver tray on which sparkled a medal in the form of a pattern of diamonds, completely new, just fashioned by the Winkie craftsmen.

"I consider it my duty to announce," intoned Strasheela solemnly, "that Alfred Canning and Ilsor have taken the most valuable in-i-ti-a-tive. Therefore, we simply have to reward each of them with the or-der which is henceforth to be called 'For Initiative.'" All those who were present looked at one another, in a way expressive of their delight: it had been a long time since Strasheela had last expressed himself with such learned words. Strasheela pinned on the med-als.

Then Urfin Jus — the Illustrious Gardener, as Strasheela introduced him — with the Great Horned Owl perched on his shoulder, stepped before the guests, a large silver platter in his hands. The Arzaks, of course, had seen Urfin time and again, hurrying toward the kitchen in Hurricap's castle. And they had heard about the commotion caused by the theft of the emeralds. Now, the stones that had been taken away from Baan-Nu lay sparkling on the platter. The Owl took one emerald after another from the tray and gave it to the gardener. Jus, swelling with pride, presented the iridescent green valuables to the Arzaks. "See," he said, again and again, "now you no longer need submit to the power of the Menvits."

Chapter 40: TRULY A DAY OF SURPRISES

All this was just too solemn, and the Arzaks grew flustered at such homage. At the same time, they felt uncontrollable happiness. They would be taking back to Rameria a powerful resource for their struggle, their fellow Arzaks would be emancipated from their slavery, and it would be the dawn of a great new day.

Of course, many obstacles still lay in the path toward the realization of this. Most important of all, how would they explain their return to Rameria?

The most splendid possibility would be if, after the Menvits awakened, they turned out to be still under the influence of the magic water. Then they could be fed any story during the course of the flight, and they would believe it. But if such indoctrination did not work, there was nothing that could be done, and the Arzaks would have to land the *Diavona* in the Ramerian Desert and melt away among their fellow Arzaks before the Menvit police could pick up their trail.

It was now blast-off time. Strasheela and the Woodman came to Ranavir to see Ilsor and the other Arzaks off, as did the Lion and Tilly-Willy, Field Marshal Din Gior and Faramant, Guardian of the Gates; Kaggi-Karr the Crow and Ramina, Queen of the Field Mice; Urfin Jus and his inseparable Guamoko; Mentaho and Elvina, and even Doctors Boril and Robil; Carfax the Eagle and Oyho the Dragon were likewise on hand. Alongside this singular company, whose like is hardly to be found anywhere in the whole Universe, stood the people from beyond the mountains: Annie Smith, Tim O'Kelly, and Fred Canning.

The leave-taking of the Arzaks, like all leave-takings, was a sad affair. And any promises to keep in touch by writing would seem laughable and inappropriate in the present case.

Perhaps some time the radio transmitter that Ilsor was leaving behind would come back to life and convey greetings from far-off Rameria. Perhaps... But in the meantime, all they could do was wait. The friends said farewell as if this parting were for ever.

Taking shelter in a safe spot, the entourage watched the *Diavona* shudder in shafts of flame, then rise into the air like an enormous monster, slowly at first, then faster and faster, and finally, flashing for a moment one more time, disappear completely, leaving behind it a column of yellow smoke.

Annie, Tim, and Alfred returned home safely, conveyed, as always, by Oyho the Dragon.

Time continued to march on — seconds, minutes, hours...

The guests from the Outer World dreamed frequently of Magic Land and its remarkable inhabitants. When they were awake, their eyes often turned in the direction of the World-Encompassing Mountains.

On clear winter evenings and summer nights, they often walked silently out of their houses and looked up at the dark sky, where the planet Rameria glowed with a cold, blue light near the constellation of Orion. Then they thought about the men with the heavenly faces, with whom they had grown so close...

THE END

TRANSLATOR'S AFTERWORD

With this book, I have completed at last the publication of my translations of the final two stories in Alexander Melentyevich Volkov's "Magic Land" saga. I did these translations nearly two decades ago, but for financial reasons I was unable to bring them out in book form during that time. However, technology has since advanced to the point where doing so is not only feasible, but desirable. And thus we have the present book.

It is good to see that with these two tales, Volkov is back in form. The previous book, *The Fiery God of the Marrans*, was something of a disappointment. It was clearly still a rough draft on which much work remained to be done, and it is as if Volkov had fallen behind in his schedule and, in order to meet a deadline, was compelled to submit his unfinished manuscript just as it was. (Though the book is just as popular with readers and as frequently reprinted as any of the others.) Such is not the case with *The Yellow Fog* and *The Mystery of the Deserted Castle*, each of which is worthy of being called one of Volkov's finest efforts.

The Yellow Fog (1974) is an excellent story, grim in its outlook, but with some comic relief. Arachna, the extremely wicked giantess-witch, is one of Volkov's most memorable creations. When she awakens after a sleep of five thousand years (beating Rip Van Winkle's record by a factor of 250!), she reads the chronicles kept throughout the generations by the little Gnomes who serve her (and who resemble the Smurfs more than the nomes/gnomes in the American series). Of course she wants to take over Magic Land, and her initial attempts to subjugate its people — less docile and compliant now than in the earlier books — are downright hilarious. But the situation becomes more serious when she inflicts the Yellow Fog of the title on the people. Of course, the Magiclanders call on their friends in Kansas for assistance, and with help like that, she is bound to fail! Her final fate is reminiscent of that of the wicked queen in Disney's film classic *Snow White and the Seven Dwarfs*.

With *The Mystery of the Deserted Castle* (1976), Volkov injects a science-fiction element into his saga, as a group of extraterrestrials come to Earth from a distant planet called Rameria, and where do they choose to touch down but — Magic Land! (Where else?) This story is a bit lighter in tone than its predecessor, and as Baan-Nu, the megalomaniac in charge, endeavors to conquer the land, the result is a virtual comedy of errors as effort after effort fails. Again the Kansans come to the aid of Magic Land, and again Good triumphs. Of great interest is the fact that there are two races of Ramerians — the Menvits and the Arzaks — and that the former keep the latter in total subordination, a fact which opens up numerous possibilities in thwarting the Menvits' nefarious designs.

Significant, too, is the reform of Urfin Jus, who was the supreme villain in two earlier stories. After his second failure as ruler, he thinks things over and realizes that power did not bring him happiness, and he actually becomes a good person. Thus, when Arachna approaches him and asks him to join forces with her, he declines. When the Fog is doing its worst, he comes up with a way of dealing with it and shares it with others. And in the final story, he helps the Arzaks in their efforts to throw off the domination of the Menvits.

And of course there is the environmental issue: by blocking out the rays of the sun, the Yellow Fog plays havoc with the weather in Magic Land, allowing snow to fall where there has never been any before, and making it all the more imperative that Arachna and her creation be eliminated with the utmost speed.

Readers will observe that in these two stories, Annie and Tim are no longer the main protagonists on the side of Good. Their true hour of glory came in the previous tale, *The Fiery God of the Marrans*. Now, however, when the Magiclanders appeal to them for aid in their struggle against Arachna, it is Uncle Charlie Black who steps up to the plate, and the two kids are reduced to a "Betty and Bob" team of the type that always seemed to accompany adventure heroes in old-time radio shows. And in *Deserted Castle*, it is Fred Canning (a less flamboyant character than Charlie and himself a former child hero, in *Seven Underground Kings*) who calls the shots. Thus, although they still have plenty to do in the working out of these plots, Annie and Tim are clearly no longer on center stage and must play second fiddle to grownups.

As with the earlier novels, I have kept the names and settings just as Volkov wrote them, without succumbing to the temptation of substituting the familiar American counterparts, as other translators of Volkov have done. I feel that the reading public is entitled to something that is both readable and accurate, and that is what I have endeavored to provide. However, I made one or two small additions of my own in spots where Volkov apparently slipped up.

Thus, in Chapter 14 of *Yellow Fog* (p. 105 of the present book), we read about how Urfin Jus, now a "good guy," combats the fog with a crude form of air-conditioning: he seals a small room and lights a smoky fire in it, and the particles of smoke adhere to the droplets of fog and cause them to condense out. Well and good! But if the fire should continue to burn, not only would it exhaust the oxygen in the room, but the premises would fill up with smoke — hardly an improvement over the lethal fog! So I remedied that by stipulating that the fire would be quickly extinguished at the proper moment so that one might again enjoy the clean air. In Chapter 28 of *Deserted Castle* (p. 340), I specified that Kau Ruk's belongings had been spared the general destruction of the Menvits' property, since it seemed unlikely that Volkov would want his one good Menvit to suffer. Both these additions are indicated by brackets, and I offer my sincerest apologies to purists who feel that I would have done better to keep my hands off of it.

Chapter 34 of *Deserted Castle* ("The Menvits' Last Hope") represented the greatest translation challenge in the entire series, as Ilsor's Speech Machine distorts the meanings of what the characters are saying, demonstrating in the process the risks involved when one relies too heavily on machine translation, human language being what it is. I have done my best with this chapter, but I confess that I have failed to produce anything quite so clever as the original.

As with my translations of the previous works, I have numbered the chapters, which Volkov did not do.

At the time I translated the two stories in this book, in the fall of 1989, the six Volkov novels represented virtually the entire Russian Oz-inspired corpus. Since that time, however, there has been a veritable explosion of such works, and it has reached the point where one almost needs a scorecard in order to keep track of everything.

One of the first of these was Yuri Kuznetzov's Изумрудный дождь *Izumrudniy dozhd*, or "The Emerald Rain". This book consists of four separate but interrelated stories, the best of which is clearly the first. It is a well-written sequel to the final

Volkov offering, *The Mystery of the Deserted Castle*, and relates
the adventures of Ellie's son, Chris Tall. While en route to Magic
Land on the back of Oyho the Dragon, he falls onto one of
Gingema's Black Rocks, and quickly finds himself on the planet
Rameria, through a sort of tunnel through space. He is captured by Menvit police, but he escapes from his prison cell,
thanks to the efforts of some little animals called Ranveeshes,
or Fluffies. He eventually makes contact with Kau-Ruk, the
one good Menvit, and Ilsor, the talented Arzak, and this un-
beatable team works to produce the Emerald Rain of the title,
thereby finally freeing all the Arzaks on Rameria from the
Menvits' baleful influence. In this story, Kuznetsov posits a
Ramerian origin of Hurricap, the creator of Magic Land. All in
all, this is an exciting adventure — though one wonders why
the Ramerians did not try to make use of this space tunnel in
the final Volkov book, rather than their relatively cumbersome rocket ship.

The other three sections of the book are: Жемчужина
халиотиса *Zhemchuzhina khaliotisa* ("The Pearl Abalone");
Привидения из Элминга *Privideniya iz Elminga* ("The Ghosts
from Elming"); and Пленники кораллого рифа *Plenniki
korallovogo rifa* ("Prisoners of the Coral Reef"). For all their
merits, unfortunately, they take the story quite far afield, and
are only marginally connected with Magic Land at all. Their
locales range from Elming, a sort of hyperspace venue where
people and objects exist in wave form, to an anti-matter planet
called Irena, as well as the Smoky Hill River in Kansas. The
latter part of the series brings in Charlie Black (the prime
mover in *Urfin Jus* and *The Yellow Fog*), and among other things,
his missing leg is restored. Later, Kuznetsov penned the story
Возвращение Арахны *Vozvrashchenie Arakhny* ("The Return
of Arachna"), in which the villainess of *The Yellow Fog* does not
die when she goes over the cliff, but travels down the river
and... It ends in a sort of closed circle, in which the events of
her life are repeated, presumably throughout eternity.

We must also give credit to Leonid Vladimirsky (b. 1920),
the artist whose delightful illustrations are as much a part of
the Magic Land novels as Tenniel's are with Lewis Carroll's
Alice books. In 1999, I spent a pleasant afternoon with his
daughter Aia (who is a talented artist in her own right), and
she informed me that her father was in a sense a virtual
co-author of the six Volkov books. For example, when writing
The Seven Underground Kings, Volkov originally wanted to make
it twelve kings, one for every month of the year, but it was

Vladimirsky's idea that there should be only seven, representing the colors of the rainbow. In recent years, he has shown remarkable skill as an independent storyteller, and he did a superlative job with Буратино в Изумрудном городе *Buratino v Izumrudnom gorode* ("Buratino in the Emerald City").

In order to understand this, a little digression is necessary. As it happens, L. Frank Baum was not the only foreign author whose most famous work received a Russian makeover. In the early decades of the 20th century, famed Soviet writer Alexei Tolstoy (1882 - 1945) likewise reworked Carlo Collodi's classic *The Adventures of Pinocchio*. As with Volkov, he changed the names of the main characters: the puppet hero is Buratino, Geppetto becomes Papa Carlo, Fire-Eater the Showman is now Carabas Barabas, the villainous Fox changes gender and becomes Alisa, the Blue Fairy who comes to the puppet's rescue after the two "assassins" string him up has become Malvina, a girl puppet who had escaped from Carabas's clutches and set up housekeeping in a cottage in the woods… The two stories remain essentially the same up to the point where Pinocchio/Buratino buries his gold pieces in a field, expecting a gold-bearing bush to sprout from them, and the Fox and the Cat dig them up and hightail it away from there. Then the narrative takes a totally different turn, and Buratino eventually finds a golden key (which the villains are also seeking), through whose help he opens a hidden door in the very room where he and Geppetto/Papa Carlo are living, and they find a magical little puppet theater which will assure them of success in the years to come. Purists may object to such a radical treatment of one of the world's most beloved children's classics, but one must admit that Tolstoy considerably tightened Collodi's rather loose and episodic narrative, and the villains stick around to confound the heroes in further adventures by various other writers.

With this knowledge, we can better understand Vladimirsky's achievement in *Buratino in the Emerald City*. ("Pinocchio in Oz," if you will!) After illustrating books in both series, Leonid decided to combine the two themes in a single original story, and, assuming that one can accept some serious lapses of continuity, he did it very well. In this tale, Urfin Jus, far from having reformed, is as wicked as ever, and the Ogre who tried to devour Ellie in *Wizard*, not to mention Arachna, are somehow still alive. It begins when Buratino, as a result of some intrigue on the part of Alisa the Fox, falls into a deep sleep from which he can not be awakened, and who should come along in his balloon but Goodwin, who takes them all to Magic Land so that the puppet can be treated. Meanwhile, Urfin Jus blunders into the Ogre's castle and finds the creature still alive and crunching, and in order to avoid becoming the Ogre's latest meal, he entices him to go to the Emerald City and oust Strasheela, which they proceed to do. When the travelers arrive, the Ogre decides that he wants to marry Malvina... As the story progresses, he ends up marrying Arachna instead (the villainess appearing now as more of a comic figure), Buratino is cured, and all ends happily. Urfin is borne away by Carfax the Giant Eagle, to presumably a fate worse than death!

There is also a series by an author named Nikolai Bachnow, which continues the series in another direction and, to my knowledge, is available at present only in German translation. Some of the volumes in this series are: *In den Fängen des Seemonsters* ("In the Clutches of the Sea Monster"), *Der Schatz der Smaragdenbienen* ("The Treasure of the Emerald Bees"), *Die Schlange mit den Bernsteinaugen* ("The Serpent with the Amber Eyes"), *Der Fluch des Drachenkönigs* ("The Curse of the Dragon King"), and *Die Falsche Fee* ("The False Fairy"). It is difficult at the moment to assess what impact this series has had among the reading public.

But for sheer imagination and storytelling power, the greatest honors in this field must go to writer Sergei Sukhinov (b. 1950). This is not the place to go into detail about his incredible achievement, but we can scratch the surface a little and give the reader an idea of what to expect.

Of great significance is his Гудвин, великий и ужасный *Gudvin, velikiy i uzhasniy* ("Goodwin the Great and Terrible"). Everyone who has read Baum or Volkov knows how the Wizard/Goodwin, while up in a balloon one day, was blown by a windstorm from the USA to a fabulous magical country, whose inhabitants hailed him as a great wizard; and how he later built the Emerald City and fooled the country's real sorceresses, both good and wicked, so that everyone was in awe of his supposed powers. Sukhinov's story expands the usual brief explanation into a book-length account, fleshing out the often fragmentary data that the other authors provide, and serving as a "prequel" to the major work to follow.

His supreme achievement, of course, is a series of ten novels which expand the Magic Land saga into a full-scale struggle between Good and Evil, in which the influence of Tolkien's *Lord of the Rings* is clearly evident. Here are the ten installments in this saga (for the sake of brevity, I give only their English titles): 1) *Gingema's Daughter;* 2) *The Fairy of the Emerald City;* 3) *The Sorceress Villina's Secret;* 4) *The Sorcerer's Sword;* 5) *The Eternally Youthful Stella;* 6) *Parcelius the Alchemist;* 7) *Battle Underground;* 8) *King Midgety;* 9) *The Sorcerer from Atlantis;* and 10) *The Knights of Light and Darkness.*

The saga begins as an ordinary fairy tale, with the birth of a headstrong young Munchkin girl named Corina, who takes up residence with the witch Gingema and learns magic from her, eventually going off on her own after a falling-out with her. She has grandiose ideas of becoming a queen herself, and as the first book progresses, we get our first hints of what is to come: Corina (and the reader) learns that the sorcerer who created Magic Land millennia ago (whom Sukhinov has re-named "Torn") had once vanquished an evil warlock named Pakir and banished him to caverns deep within the earth — where that villain has remained right up to the present, ever planning some day to burst back out onto the surface of the earth and take it over. In the next few installments, Pakir's threats and manifestations become ever more ominous, and by Book 6, the tale has assumed a cosmic significance. Of course, the action builds up to a climactic final battle, in which the forces of Good triumph, but just barely! For sheer imagination and storytelling power, one would have to look far to find Sergei Sukhinov's equal.

As if this were not enough, he has even written a series of shorter tales, intended for younger readers, which add to the overall conception. Each story is self-contained, and most of them are about the childhood experiences of one or another of the major characters that figure in the ten-part saga. These books are particularly valuable not only as stories, but because they give additional details about matters that are touched on more briefly in the ten-parter.[1]

Thus, we can see that Volkov's initial work has spawned a veritable cottage industry of Magic Land productions (and I haven't even mentioned the numerous tie-ins, such as dramatizations, translations into other languages, and the "Friends of the Emerald City" club which, as of this writing, is extremely popular in Russia). And Volkov's work, as we all know, goes back to that of L. Frank Baum. How likely is it that when Baum published his *Wonderful Wizard of Oz* back in 1900, he

---

[1]The interested reader may find more information on these books by checking the website www.emeraldcity.ru

had any idea whatsoever of where it would eventually lead? That one book has served as a wellspring for literally a whole library of derivative works, both American and Russian — and we are all so much the richer for it. May it continue for many ages to come!

Peter L. Blystone
October 25, 2007